TEEN
BLE

Blecher, Jennifer

Stick with me

11/03/20

Stick

with ☆

Me

JENNIFER BLECHER

Stick with Me

BEST FRIENDS

GREENWILLOW BOOKS

AN IMPRINT OF HARPERCOLLINSPUBLISHERS

Stick With Me
Text copyright © 2020 by Jennifer Blecher. Illustrations copyright © 2020 by Celia Krampien.
All rights reserved. No part of this book may be used or reproduced in any manner whatsoever without written permission except in the case of brief quotations embodied in critical articles and reviews. Printed in the United States of America. For information address HarperCollins Children's Books, a division of HarperCollins Publishers, 195 Broadway, New York, NY 10007.

www.harpercollinschildrens.com

The text of this book is set in Revival 555 BT. Book design by Sylvie Le Floc'h

Library of Congress Cataloging-in-Publication Data

Names: Blecher, Jennifer, author.
Title: Stick with me / Jennifer Blecher.
Description: First edition. | New York, NY : Greenwillow Books, an Imprint of HarperCollins Publishers, [2020] | Audience: Ages 8-12. | Audience: Grades 4-6.
Summary: When twelve-year-olds Izzy and Wren are thrown together by unusual circumstances, they find solace and solutions to nagging problems in their newly-formed friendship.
Identifiers: LCCN 2020017523 (print) | ISBN 9780062748621 (hardcover)
Subjects: CYAC: Best friends—Fiction. | Friendship—Fiction. | Theater—Fiction. | Ice skating—Fiction. | Family life—Fiction.
Classification: LCC PZ7.B61658 Sti 2020 (print) | DDC [Fic] —dc23
LC record available at https://lccn.loc.gov/2020017523

20 21 22 23 24 PC/LSCH 10 9 8 7 6 5 4 3 2 1

First Edition

Greenwillow Books

THE OPPOSITE OF IZZY

When Izzy was little, she was obsessed with opposites. Not regular opposites, like left and right. Happy and sad. Good and bad. She wasn't the kind of kid who occasionally walked down the sidewalk backward. Instead, Izzy blew milk out of a straw. She ate cereal with a fork. She wore her backpack on her stomach every single day of preschool.

It didn't make any sense.

But back then, making sense didn't matter. Izzy could color only the background of a coloring page, and her teacher would smile and say, "What a unique way to look at that picture, Izzy. You did such a nice job coloring *outside* the lines."

And it wasn't just teachers. No one in her family cared about making sense. If Izzy danced around the kitchen with underwear on her head, there was an excellent chance that her parents would laugh. Or that her older brother Nate would twirl her down the hallway.

But now Izzy was twelve. And that kind of stuff wasn't funny anymore; it was embarrassing. Izzy no longer wanted to be different from everyone else.

She wanted the opposite.

As Izzy sat at her desk watching her friend Phoebe, she got a familiar feeling, like things were the opposite of how they were supposed to be. Only the feeling didn't make Izzy smile or laugh. It made her worry about what was going to happen next.

"I'm not sure I get it," said Phoebe. Phoebe was lying on Izzy's bed. Her feet swayed in the air and her head rested in her palms. Four beaded bracelets slid halfway down Phoebe's arm. They were the same bracelets that Daphne Toll, the most popular girl in class, had started wearing a few months ago.

There were real bracelets and there were fake bracelets. The real bracelets were made of colored stones threaded on a thick elastic band. The fake bracelets looked exactly the same, but instead of stones, they were made with heavy plastic beads. The only way to tell which bracelets were real and which were fake was to listen to the sound the bracelets made when they hit one another or a hard surface.

Daphne's bracelets were real. Izzy sat next to Daphne in English and had to listen as Daphne clacked her bracelets together during silent reading time. Phoebe's bracelets were fake. Phoebe's mom had bought them in the "buy three, get one free" section at Glitz.

But Izzy had never told anyone that. And neither had Phoebe.

Real and fake. Opposites.

"Earth to Izzy," said Phoebe. She waved her hand with the bracelets back and forth. "Hel-lo."

"Sorry," said Izzy. "What'd you say?"

"I said, I don't get this sticker door. What's the point? What were we *thinking*?" Phoebe nodded toward the back of Izzy's bedroom door. It was covered with hundreds of stickers. There were heart stickers, puppy stickers, and unicorn stickers. There was a winding path of stars, fuzzy ducks wearing red rain boots, and grinning cows jumping over full moons. Around the doorknob was a swirl of whales, seahorses, and sharks. Toward the top of the door were smiling pieces of sushi, old-fashioned dolls wearing lace bonnets, and neon skulls with empty eye sockets. The bottom of the door was lined with neat rows of emoji stickers.

Izzy and Phoebe used to stare at the masterpiece that they'd created together and imagine stories about the lives of the stickers. *Green neon skull and doll in a lace bonnet had a baby named poop emoji.* That kind of thing.

Izzy shrugged. "We were thinking that it was fun?"

"I guess," said Phoebe. "But I just don't get it anymore. I don't get the point."

"There wasn't a point."

"There has to be a point, Izzy. Otherwise, what's the point?"

This was how Phoebe spoke now that she hung out with Daphne and all her popular friends. Now that she wore a stack of bracelets on her wrist and sat at Daphne's table in the cafeteria, draping her arms and legs over Daphne so that everyone could see how deeply connected they were. Now that she spun her lacrosse stick in her hand as she walked to the playing fields for practice, her ponytail held back with a navy-blue elastic headband just like every other girl on the team.

Everything had to *mean* something. And the most annoying part was, Phoebe never knew what anything meant. She just liked to wonder about it.

Like what did it *mean* that Zach bumped into her when Phoebe was putting away her iPad in science? What did it *mean* that Serena went to Dr. Forte's office on Thursday afternoon? What did it *mean* that Mr. Blair picked Phoebe last to give her presentation in English?

Here's what Izzy wanted to know: What did it *mean* that Phoebe, who'd had tons of sleepovers in Izzy's bedroom, was looking around the room like she'd never seen it before? What did it *mean* that watching Phoebe pull at the frayed knees of her jeans made Izzy wonder if her splatter-paint leggings were babyish? What did it *mean* that having Phoebe close by made Izzy feel lonelier than actually being alone?

Phoebe sat up on Izzy's bed and crossed her legs. Her bare knee popped through the hole in her jeans. "Should we find our moms?" Phoebe asked. "They're probably done talking by now."

So I can finally go home. Those were the words Phoebe didn't say. Although they both knew that the only reason Phoebe was at Izzy's house was because their moms wanted to catch up over a cup of tea.

Phoebe's mom and Izzy's mom were best friends. Sometimes Izzy imagined their moms like a drawing in a picture book: two smiling girls holding hands against a white background with the words BEST FRIENDS written underneath in thick black text. That's all the page would say, as if having a best friend was the simplest thing in the world. As if everyone had a best friend necklace from Glitz, the kind with two jagged half hearts on separate chains that fit together to make a whole.

When they were little, Phoebe and Izzy had been best friends, too. They had half-heart necklaces. They'd gone to the mall and picked them out before their first day of kindergarten. Their moms took their picture, told them how adorable they were, and bought them strawberry ice cream cones to celebrate. Because that's how things worked back then. Necklaces formed hearts. There weren't real hearts and fake hearts. There were just two halves that fit together to make a whole.

Izzy didn't know exactly when everything changed, or why. But she was certain that two simple words no longer described her and Phoebe. Their friendship wasn't just building fairy houses, or performing dance routines on summer nights while their parents ate dinner in the backyard, or making slime creations speckled with silver glitter. It was birthday parties where Izzy was no longer the one seated right next to Phoebe when Phoebe blew out the candles on her cake, school pickups where Phoebe piled into cars heading to houses that Izzy had never been invited to, and beaded bracelets and lacrosse team headbands that Phoebe wore daily and Izzy did not own.

That this change had happened slowly didn't make it any less confusing. If anything, Izzy wished that there had been something specific, like when they were little and Izzy had stuck a heart sticker on the belly of Phoebe's stuffed bunny named Carrot because she thought it would make Phoebe happy. Phoebe had been the opposite of happy, especially when she ripped the sticker off and discovered that it had left behind a sticky gray goo that matted Carrot's pink fur. As Phoebe sat on the kitchen floor with tears and snot streaming down her face, Izzy and her mom had soaked Carrot in a bucket of warm soapy water until the sticker goo came off. Then Izzy and Phoebe spent the rest of the day playing animal spa, bathing their favorite stuffed animals and laying them in the sun to dry.

By dinnertime, they were begging their moms to let them have a sleepover.

Izzy almost smiled, remembering how they brought their stuffed animals ripe blueberries stacked onto toothpicks and bowed as they presented the delicate treats. But then Izzy realized that she had no idea if Phoebe still slept with Carrot tucked under her arm. If she still chewed on Carrot's long ears when she was nervous, or threw Carrot against the wall when she was frustrated. How long had it been since Izzy had seen Carrot's large feet and black stitched grin? Months? Maybe even a whole year?

Phoebe rolled off Izzy's bed, examined her nails, and sighed. "Come on," she said. "Let's go."

"One sec," said Izzy. She swiveled her chair so that her back was to Phoebe and glanced at the drawer of her desk. Her half of their jagged heart necklace was inside. But there was something else inside, too. A stack of papers that Izzy didn't want Phoebe, or anyone else, to see.

"Come on, Iz," said Phoebe. "I'm starving."

A piece of striped washi tape was stuck across the panel of the drawer, sealing it shut. The top edge of the tape was beginning to curl away and Izzy was tempted to reach out and fix it. But there was no way to do that without Phoebe noticing. Phoebe would wonder what the tape *meant*.

And even Phoebe was smart enough to know the answer.

Izzy stood up and followed Phoebe out of her bedroom toward the back stairway. As they walked, Phoebe dragged her hand with the stack of beaded bracelets along the white hallway wall. Izzy almost told Phoebe to stop. Izzy's mom was always reminding Izzy and Nate to be careful about leaving fingerprints on the walls. But she worried that Phoebe would just roll her eyes. And Izzy had no clue what she'd do then.

Thankfully, Phoebe raised her hand to flip her hair and gather it over her shoulder. The hair flip was a classic Daphne move. Izzy had tried to draw the motion on paper. The key to getting it right was in the head tilt and upturned eyes. But the faces Izzy drew always looked deep in thought, as if they were pondering the mysteries of the universe.

The opposite of what the expression looked like in real life.

They were almost to the bottom of the stairway when Phoebe stopped and pressed one finger to her lips. Izzy nodded. Phoebe's hunched shoulders and wide grin made Izzy feel like they were still little and wearing their jagged half-heart necklaces. Izzy was relieved that she hadn't said anything about fingerprints. This moment wouldn't have happened if she had.

Leaning with their backs against the stairway wall, they heard Phoebe's mom say, "I'm so sorry. That's really tough."

"We'll figure something out," said Izzy's mom. "I'm working on a few ideas."

"How's Greg handling it?" asked Phoebe's mom.

"You can imagine," said Izzy's mom.

Silence.

What would her mom figure out? What ideas was she

working on? Izzy leaned forward to peek around the corner. But Phoebe pressed Izzy back against the wall, as if they were about to hear something interesting and she didn't want Izzy to ruin the moment.

Greg was Izzy's dad. He fixed whatever was broken in their house—rattling pipes, flickering lights, loose-hinged doors that scraped the hardwood floors. Izzy's house was super old and her parents had spent years fixing it up. They'd torn down walls, ripped up tile, and peeled off wallpaper. Izzy's mom once spent an entire week polishing the doorknobs and window locks to restore their original color. So maybe that's what her mom was talking about?

But as the silence in the kitchen continued, Izzy began to worry that her mom was talking about something way more serious than home repairs.

Suddenly Phoebe jumped from the stairway to the kitchen floor. She landed with a thump.

"Phoebe," said Phoebe's mom. "You scared me."

"What were you guys talking about?" asked Phoebe.

"Nothing," said Izzy's mom. She stood up from

her stool and pressed her fingers against the corners of her eyes. *Was she about to cry?*

"Mom," said Izzy. "What's wrong?"

"Um, I think I might be getting a cold. It's terrible timing." Izzy's mom reached for a tissue. But instead of blowing her nose, she crumpled the tissue in her hand.

Izzy's mom was starting an interior-design business. Her first potential client was coming over that afternoon to see their house and get a sense of her mom's style. All afternoon she'd been plumping pillows, refolding blankets, and straightening picture frames. Even then, Izzy's mom stuffed the tissue in her pocket and looked around the kitchen like she was searching for a spill to wipe clean.

Phoebe picked a red grape from the ceramic bowl in the center of the island. She peeled off the skin before popping the grape in her mouth.

"Are you girls hungry?" asked Izzy's mom as she scrubbed an invisible spot on the counter. "I have some frozen cookie dough in the freezer. I was going to put it in the oven later to give the house a homey smell, but I can do it now."

"Good idea," said Phoebe's mom. "What do you say, Phoebe? Want to stay for some cookies?"

Phoebe reached for another grape. "No, thanks. I'll eat at my sleepover."

"Oh," said Izzy's mom. "Okay." She glanced at Phoebe's mom.

Phoebe's mom shrugged, but just barely. As if maybe Izzy wouldn't notice.

Izzy hated how clueless they thought she was. About the cookie bribe. The shrug. The sleepover at Daphne's house that Izzy already knew about because she'd heard girls talking about it at school. The fact that Phoebe was suddenly not hungry even though she said she was starving a few minutes ago and kept reaching for grapes.

Izzy knew their moms wished that she and Phoebe were still babies so they could plop them down on a soft blanket with some squeaking toys and continue talking. But life wasn't that simple anymore. Phoebe had places to go. And Izzy was not invited.

◆◆◆

Izzy pressed her forehead against the cold glass of her bedroom window and watched as Phoebe and her mom backed down the driveway. When Izzy moved her head away, there was an oval shape where the warmth of her breath had clouded the glass. With her finger, Izzy drew a heart in the condensation. Then she slashed the heart in half with a zigzag streak.

Sitting down at her desk with a clean piece of paper, Izzy reached for the tin container where she kept her Sharpies. The tin was a deep teal color with delicate white butterflies etched on the sides. Her mom had bought it at a tea shop in London before Izzy was born. The sides were dented, and one of the butterfly's wings had worn completely off. But it was Izzy's favorite possession. She loved that the tin was the perfect size for her Sharpies, and the pinging sound each Sharpie made when she dropped it inside.

Izzy chose a violet Sharpie and drew a flower with different circles of looping petals. But her hand slipped when she tried to add detail to the stem. Izzy tore the page in half and tossed it on the floor.

She looked at the window. The condensation had evaporated, but her fingertip left smudged streaks on the glass. Great. Now she was stuck with one jagged heart in her desk and another one on her window.

Phoebe would probably love to know what that *meant*.

Izzy didn't want to think about Phoebe. That was a mistake, just like her hand slipping. Only there was no mess-up pile for bad thoughts. Bad drawings she could tear in half and throw away. Bad thoughts got trapped inside Izzy's head. It wasn't like she could just ask Phoebe why she was ditching her all the time. Phoebe would look at her like the answer was so obvious that it couldn't even be put into words. And then Izzy would feel even worse.

Izzy grabbed a fresh piece of paper and her black Sharpie from the butterfly tin. She drew a simple stick-figure girl. On top of the figure's straight-line neck, Izzy drew a round head with long hair and wide eyes.

She added eyebrows, a navy elastic headband, and rosy cheeks. Next, in alternating colors, Izzy drew a stack of bracelets around the stick figure's wrist. Picking up the black Sharpie again, Izzy added a large bubble coming from the stick figure's mouth with the words: WHY DON'T YOU GET SOME NEW FRIENDS?

Izzy almost left it like that, but there was too much blank space on the page that needed to be filled. She chose the brown Sharpie and drew a jagged mountain edge beginning at the stick figure's feet. Toward the top of the mountain Izzy added some wildflowers. But as her hand moved down the mountain, Izzy found herself turning the wildflowers into sharp-tipped spikes.

There was no denying it: the stick figure looked like Phoebe. And one gentle push would send her crashing right over the mountain's spike-filled edge.

When the drawing was done, the letters in the word bubble highlighted, and the mountain decorated with gray rocks and occasional sprouts of green grass, Izzy lifted it to eye height. The light from her bedroom window brought out the paper's texture and gave the scene depth, as if the mountain was surrounded by a wintery haze.

And finally, the thoughts in Izzy's head settled like flakes in a snow globe. They were still there, but they were quieter, as if some of the hurt and loneliness and fear that things would never get better had escaped into the crisp, saturated lines of her Sharpies.

Izzy tore off the striped washi tape and opened the drawer of her desk. She placed the drawing on top of the growing pile. Then she ripped off a new piece of washi tape from the roll and sealed the drawer shut.

WATCH WREN FLY

"Okay, Bird," said Wren's dad. "Let's see you fly."

Wren pushed off from the ice-skating rink boards. The edges of her blades carved into the frozen surface. With every stroke, Wren skated faster.

The cold, early morning air rushed over her cheeks, across her neck, and between each individual finger.

Wren inhaled. It tasted crisp, like spearmint gum.

She turned into her back crossovers, her arms wide and her legs moving in smooth inside-edged arcs.

She gathered speed. And power.

Wren waited for the click in her brain that told

her it was time. When it came, Wren balanced on her right leg, gliding backward while she prepared the rest of her body. Shoulders down. Head high. Arms back.

She stepped forward onto her bent left leg and pushed off until the toe pick on the tip of her skate blade caught in the ice.

Wren swung her body forward.

She lifted into the cold air. Where she heard nothing. Saw nothing.

Wren was flying, floating, spinning.

Two-and-a-half turns later, she landed backward on her right leg. A double axel.

The muffled sound of her dad clapping his leather-gloved hands echoed across the ice. "That's my Bird!" he shouted. "Woo-hoo!"

Wren held her landing position for the count of five. Then she turned forward and skated back to the boards.

"Amazing," said her dad. "You made that double axel look like a piece of cake."

"It's not," said Wren, her hands on her hips, catching her breath.

"Well, it sure looked that way." Wren's dad raised his fist and she bumped it with her own. Then he checked his watch. Before he could say anything, Wren skated away.

Her legs were the perfect combination of warm and strong. Her body wanted to fly again.

The feeling was like a gentle poke deep inside her brain. A combination of mental and physical. Brain and body.

It was everything working together, under her command.

She could jump. Axel, lutz, toe loop, flip, salchow.

Or spin. Layback, camel, sit, scratch.

She could stretch into a graceful spiral, or switch into a fast-paced footwork section.

On the ice, Wren was in charge.

Her dad could check his watch. Then his phone. He could cross his arms over his chest or fiddle with his wool hat.

What was he going to do? Chase her across the ice in his snow boots?

Wren's dad was the men's ice hockey coach at Dartmouth College. He knew how rare it was for her to have the entire ice rink to herself. It only happened early in the morning when the hockey teams were on a rest day. Wren's dad would use his coach's key to unlock the ice rink door and they would stand together in the dark as the overhead lights flickered on with loud buzzes and electric clicks.

At other times there were skaters who Wren needed to watch out for. Younger kids practicing waltz jumps who didn't have the speed and coordination to get out of her way. Older teenagers who left deep divots in the ice that she had to avoid.

So Wren didn't want to get off the ice until she had no choice. Until the huge rubber wheels of the Zamboni machine began their slow churn across the frozen surface, Charlie behind the wheel yelling at Wren to clear out already.

Yelling, but also smiling.

When Wren was younger, Charlie would let her sit on the bench of the Zamboni while her dad led his team through endless drills and her mom stayed home with Wren's little sister, Hannah.

"You like the view from up here?" Charlie had asked one day.

Wren had nodded. She'd gripped the cold metal Zamboni wheel with both hands, pretending to steer with exaggerated movements.

"Just you wait till you see the view of the ice from the winner's podium," Charlie continued. "That's where a skater like you should be."

Wren glanced up at him. "Me?"

"You see any other pint-size people working harder? You got fire in your belly, kid."

Then Charlie ruffled Wren's hair, which she hated, before climbing down to shovel the slushy pile of ice remains.

Wren had always been aware of it. A restless stirring. An energy that wanted her to move fast. Jump high. Spin tight.

Now the sensation had a name: fire in her belly. And Wren loved it.

She entered competitions at her rink, skating short programs to happy, chipper music. A waltz jump here. A sit spin there. Pink ribbons fluttered in her braided pigtails and wide smiles displayed missing teeth. Wren stepped onto podiums barely higher than a shoebox and bent her head as plastic medals were placed around her neck.

But then things began to change.

The competitions got farther away. They were held on ice surfaces that were harder or softer, at rinks with overhead lights that were too bright or too dim. Wren started skating against girls who wanted to stand on the podium just as much as she did.

The fire in her belly remained. But it got harder and harder to win.

Which is why no matter how many times her dad glanced at his watch, Wren wouldn't get off the ice. The only other time she had an entire ice surface to herself was during competitions. She'd been over it one hundred times and decided that was why she blew it at sectionals last year.

She let the empty ice rattle her. She lost track of her music. She lost her focus.

And on the final double lutz in her program, Wren fell.

Laney Lewis got the bronze.

Laney Lewis got to stand on the podium and compete at nationals in San Francisco against the top skaters in the country.

Wren got fourth.

There was no place on the podium for fourth. Fourth was not special. It took her nowhere.

Wren refused to let that happen again. This year she was going to place in the top three at sectionals and qualify for nationals.

Sectionals was just four weeks away. It was time to push harder than ever before.

"Seriously, Bird," yelled her dad as he pulled his cell phone from the pocket of his jeans and frowned. "We've gotta go."

"Just one run-through of my program," said Wren. "Charlie's not even here yet to warm up the Zamboni."

Wren didn't wait for her dad to respond. She skated to center ice and struck her opening pose. Gaze down. Arms overhead.

From the corner of her eye, she saw her dad shake his head and walk to the rink's sound system, cueing up her program music.

As the electric opening beats of her music played, Wren's dad yelled, "Just once. Your mom and Hannah are waiting. So after this, it's straight off the ice."

Wren nodded, but she tried to put his words out of her mind.

All she wanted to think about were her jumps, spins, and footwork sequences.

She tried to hear only the music. Feel only her body.

But Wren couldn't get in the zone. Something was off. When it came time for her double lutz, she under-rotated. The blade on her landing foot made contact at the wrong angle. Wren crashed to the ice.

She picked herself right up. She increased the pace of her forward crossovers to catch up with the music and ended her program with a strong double axel. But when Wren stepped off the ice and slid her plastic skate guards over her blades, she noticed the weight of her boots and the effort it took to move her tired legs to the locker room.

And she allowed herself to think it. Even though she hated the thought.

Thanks a lot, Hannah. This is all your fault.

Inside Lou's Restaurant and Bakery it was warm and sweet, as if the sugary icing that coated Lou's famous cinnamon buns was floating in the air. Wren unzipped her fleece skating jacket. She followed her dad to a booth in the back of the bakery where her mom and four-year-old Hannah were hunched over pieces of paper, coloring with crayons.

Wren's dad put his finger to his lips and snuck up to them, surprising Wren's mom with a kiss on the lips.

Wren expected her mom to swat him away. Or look embarrassed.

Instead, she reached her hands around his neck and gave him a long kiss.

"Eww," said Hannah.

"You're next," said their dad. He stepped toward Hannah with his arms wide, like a pretend monster. As Hannah squealed, he planted a sloppy kiss on her cheek and straightened the paper crown that was tilted on her head. Then he folded his large body into the booth beside Hannah. Wren slid in beside her mom.

"Good skate?" asked Wren's mom.

"I missed my double lutz," said Wren. "Again."

"That's okay. You'll get it."

"It's not okay. I keep under-rotating."

Wren paused, waiting for her mom to ask if her dad had caught the fall on video. Maybe she could take a look? Try to figure out what went wrong?

Twice a week Wren took skating lessons with a professional coach named Nancy. But Nancy charged by the hour and taught several students a day. She didn't have the time to sit and watch Wren's jumps in slow motion, analyzing the angle of her blade and the position of her shoulders.

But Wren's mom did. When Wren was having a tough time with a new jump, her mom would stand in the bleachers and video Wren's practices. After Wren finished her homework, they'd sit together on the couch and watch the recording.

They'd zoom in, looking for a shoulder tilted at the wrong angle. A foot lifted too high. An arm that released too late.

Sometimes, after watching Wren fall over and over, her mom would say that what they really needed was to watch puppy videos on YouTube.

And then try again tomorrow.

As Wren sat in the booth at Lou's waiting for her mom to offer to help, she realized it had been weeks since they'd watched puppy videos.

Wren understood why. She knew those videos weren't important.

But that didn't make her miss those silly puppies

getting their heads stuck in trash cans any less.

"Wren," said Hannah, tapping Wren's hand across the table. "Do you like my new crown?"

Wren nodded. "Yeah. It's really pretty. Are you going to a royal ball?"

Hannah shook her head. The paper crown slid down her forehead. "It's not a princess crown. It's for meeting unicorns."

"Unicorns?" asked Wren, looking from Hannah to her mom.

Hannah smiled. "Yep."

"Wait, what?" said Wren's dad. He tried to stand, but his thighs hit the underside of the table. Forks and knives jumped. A water glass spilled. "Did Dr. Koffer call?"

Wren's mom smiled. "Her nurse called while you were at the rink. Dr. Koffer reviewed all Hannah's tests and she thinks she can help. She had an unexpected cancellation next week. I think we should take it. Otherwise it could be months before she can see us."

Wren's dad slid out of the booth. He lifted Hannah

into his arms and began jumping in place. Hannah's crown fell over her eyes.

Wren's mom raised her phone to take a picture. "Look at me, you two. Smile."

Three college kids in the booth next to them turned and stared. But only Wren noticed. She grabbed some napkins from the dispenser and cleaned up the spilled water.

This was the news that Wren's parents had been waiting for. Hannah had epilepsy, which meant that her brain had seizures. Sometimes the seizures made Hannah's arms go stiff, or her eyes wander, or her body shake. The seizures were usually fast, but when they happened, it felt like they lasted forever.

In the year since the seizures began, Hannah had tried three different kinds of medication to make them stop. None of the medicines worked. So a few weeks ago, Hannah and her mom went to a hospital in Boston to meet with a new team of doctors.

They stayed in the hospital for an entire week. Wren stayed home with her dad.

Every night her dad's phone pinged with texts from her mom. Pictures of Hannah playing with therapy dogs, or banging on drums with a music teacher, or squeezing the red rubber nose of a clown.

Wren had leaned over her dad's shoulder as he swiped through the photos. But she barely noticed the shaggy golden retrievers. The shiny cymbals. The clown's exaggerated smile.

All she could focus on were the red, blue, and yellow wires running down Hannah's head. They were stuck to Hannah's scalp with round stickers and told the doctors what part of Hannah's brain was causing the seizures.

That's where Dr. Koffer came in. She specialized in the kind of surgery that Hannah needed. Her job was to cut out the section of Hannah's brain that was causing the seizures.

Not that Wren's family used words like *surgery* and *cut*. Words that were too hard to say out loud.

Instead, they used *unicorn* as a code name for Hannah's treatment. Their parents told Hannah that having epilepsy made her extra special, like how a unicorn would just be a horse without its magical horn. They said that if Hannah went to all her doctor's appointments and tests, maybe she'd get to do something really amazing, like meet an actual unicorn.

Wren thought the code name was stupid. It made no sense.

Special was good. Special was people cheering your name as you stood on the top of a podium.

Epilepsy was scary. Watching Hannah have a seizure reminded Wren of catching her toe pick in the ice, the moment of knowing she was about to fall but being unable to prevent it. Except Wren could handle a bruised knee. A sore hip. Hannah was so little and helpless.

But whatever, Wren's parents thought the unicorn comparison was brilliant. It stuck.

Maggie, their favorite waitress at Lou's, came up to their table. She raised one eyebrow. "What exactly are you all so happy about over here?" asked Maggie. "Did this dynamo of ours add another skating medal to her collection?"

Wren's mom shook her head, unable to answer. She put her phone down on the table, looked at Hannah, and started crying. Messy, snotty, emotional tears.

"Noooo," said Maggie, glancing from Wren's mom to Hannah. "Does this mean what I think it means?"

"It does," said Wren's dad. "It really does."

Maggie hollered. She put her hands on either side of Hannah's face. "Oh, my precious baby girl," she said. "Oh, my precious baby girl."

Hannah smiled, not seeming to mind Maggie's hands or her cooing. Their town was filled with college kids, but not a ton of families. People like Maggie knew about Hannah's epilepsy.

They prayed for Hannah. They cheered for Hannah.

They cheered for Wren, too.

But she had to earn their applause on the ice.

IZZY'S LEFT
WITH A MITTEN

Izzy followed the scent of baking cookies to the kitchen, where her mom was straightening mugs on the shelf. "Are the cookies ready?" she asked.

"Almost," said her mom. "But first can you take Row for a walk? Ms. Stallton will be here in ten minutes, and the last thing I need is Row jumping all over my client."

Izzy knelt down and wrapped her arms around Row's furry neck. "You wouldn't jump on any nice ladies would you, Row?"

Row licked Izzy's cheek. They both knew that's exactly what Row would do.

Izzy's parents got Row when Nate was six years old and just learning to play "Row, Row, Row Your Boat" on the piano. It didn't take long for Izzy's parents to realize that letting Nate name their puppy was a big mistake. It was impossible to tell the puppy "No." *No* and *Row*. Whenever Row did something bad like eat a sock, or bark at another dog, or jump on a stranger, and they tried to teach him to stop, Row thought they were calling his name. He would happily wag his tail, hoping for a treat.

Which is why Row was the worst dog in the world. But also the best. Opposites.

Izzy sighed. It was freezing out and the kitchen smelled so good. The last thing she wanted to do was take Row for a walk. But she knew how much the client meeting meant to her mom. So Izzy grabbed Row's leash from the hook in the mudroom and pulled her hat and gloves from the bin where her mom had tucked them away. As Izzy slid her hand into the sleeve of her jacket, she noticed something fluffy and bright pink under the mudroom bench: Phoebe's mitten.

Phoebe must have been in such a rush to escape Izzy's house that she'd dropped it on the way out. Izzy imagined Phoebe searching her bag and pockets, looking for the missing mitten. Phoebe got flustered easily, and it would only be a few seconds before she started turning in circles and screaming for her mom to help her find it.

Except Phoebe wasn't with her mom. She was at Daphne's house for the sleepover.

Izzy squeezed the mitten in her hand. She could toss it in her backpack to return to Phoebe at school on Monday. Or her mom could send Phoebe's mom a text. *Found P's mitten! Want to come back and grab it?* But the mitten, slightly curled from weeks of wear, felt too important to leave for a later time. It felt like an excuse.

Izzy hadn't been to Daphne's house since second grade, when Daphne invited all the girls in their class to a petting zoo birthday party. They'd sat on bales of prickly hay in Daphne's backyard as people wearing jean overalls and red bandanas placed baby ducks, bunnies, and kittens wrapped in fleece blankets into each girl's waiting arms. Izzy could still remember the warm weight of a particular baby duck, so small and soft with its coat of bright yellow fluff. Next to Izzy on her hay bale, Phoebe had held a sleeping gray kitten, its whiskers twitching as if it was having an intense dream. Izzy and Phoebe took turns brushing their foreheads against the animals in each other's laps, murmuring promises that they would love them forever.

Then Daphne, wearing a pink T-shirt with the words *Birthday Girl* spelled out in sequins and a matching ruffled chiffon skirt, had marched over to their hay bale and grabbed the gray kitten from Phoebe's arms.

"Hey," said Phoebe. "I was holding her."

Daphne shrugged. "Now it's my turn. I get to pick a kitten to keep. For my birthday. It's part of the package. So I need to test this one out."

Phoebe had turned to Izzy, her empty arms in the shape of a cradle, tears in her eyes. And Izzy just sat there, helpless, the baby duck squirming in its fleece wrap as if it sensed danger in the air. Even back then,

Daphne had a certain power. It was the baby animals in her backyard, the flounce of her skirt, the rows of goody bags each containing a stuffed animal puppy in its own carrying case. If Daphne wanted the gray kitten that Phoebe loved with her whole heart, Daphne would get it. And there was nothing anyone could do about it.

Izzy and Phoebe spent the rest of the party watching as Daphne held all the kittens, debating which one was the cutest. Every time she walked over to Phoebe's gray kitten, Phoebe's bottom lip trembled and her body curved protectively around the tiny bundle. In the end, Daphne chose a black kitten with white paws that a girl named Serena had been holding for most of the party. Serena was new that year, and quiet. She'd spent most of the party on a bale of hay near the fence talking only to her kitten. When Daphne made her final decision, plucking the kitten from Serena's arms and holding it high in the air, declaring it the cutest of all, Serena's eyes filled with tears. But not a single girl at the party moved to console her.

Daphne named the kitten Snow Stepper. And for the rest of the school year she wore a gold locket with a picture of Snow Stepper on one side and herself on the other side. The locket was long gone, apparently lost in the ocean the summer after second grade, but Izzy assumed Snow Stepper was still alive. Daphne didn't talk about her anymore, and Izzy hadn't been invited to Daphne's house since that birthday party. But now, with Phoebe's bright pink mitten in her hand, Izzy had a reason to go over. To see what it was that Phoebe and Daphne did together that made Phoebe forget the piercing look in Daphne's eyes as she evaluated the gray kitten, examining its worthiness.

"Come on," Izzy said as she led Row out of the house and into the cold. "There's something important we need to return."

Izzy was two blocks from Daphne's house when her heart started to pound. She gripped Row's leash extra tight. Up until that point, Izzy could pretend that she was simply taking Row on a regular afternoon walk. But she'd taken Row on hundreds of walks and she always did the same loop down the block, across the street, along the path to Willoway Pond, then back. She'd never walked the several blocks past the pond to Daphne's street. Until now.

There it was: Daphne's house. Izzy wished she could see inside, but the setting sun reflected off the windows, preventing any view. So Izzy had to imagine what was happening inside. Maybe Daphne and Phoebe were curled up on a fuzzy beanbag, Snow Stepper asleep beside them, painting each other's nails in matching alternating colors. Maybe Phoebe was sharing some secret as she ran a nail polish wand over Daphne's fingernails, leaving behind smooth streaks of turquoise, silver, and pink. Maybe she was telling Daphne the secret that her mom and dad sometimes screamed at each other late at night, but then acted all happy the next morning. Or that she once stole twenty dollars from her mom's wallet and used it to buy candy that she hid under her bed.

The kind of secrets that Phoebe used to tell Izzy.

Then, as Izzy walked up the stone path to Daphne's

front door, she imagined something else—that she'd ring the doorbell and Daphne and Phoebe would invite her inside to hang out.

Ding-dong.

"Oh," said Daphne, opening the door but not stepping outside. "Hey, Izzy."

Phoebe appeared next to Daphne in the doorway. "What are you doing here?"

"You left your mitten at my house," said Izzy. "I thought you'd be looking for it."

"Why?" asked Phoebe. She shook her head as if a mosquito had just flown past.

"Because," said Izzy. But she couldn't figure out what to say next. Because it's cold? Because you left it behind? Because you freak out when things are missing? Because we used to be best friends and that means maybe you'll ask me if I want to come inside, right?

But then Daphne glanced at Phoebe. She reached out to take the pink mitten from Izzy's hand. "Thanks," said Daphne. "It was super nice of you to return the mitten. And that's a super-cute dog. His name is Row, right? Like row the boat?"

Izzy looked down at Row, who for once was sitting calmly at her side. A flash of hope crossed her mind. "Yeah, how'd you know?"

Daphne shrugged. "Phoebe told me. Your brother must have been so adorable."

Phoebe looked down at her bare feet. She stepped one foot on top of the other. Her toenails were painted a deep purple, the polish shiny and new. Izzy looked at Daphne's toes. They matched perfectly.

"Anyway," said Daphne, shivering dramatically. "It's freezing. We're going to go back inside. But thanks again for dropping this off." Daphne added a cheery swing to her voice, but Izzy got the message: it was time for her to leave.

As Izzy walked away, her body hunched against the cold, she no longer wondered what secrets Phoebe was sharing about herself. She wondered what secrets Phoebe was sharing about Izzy.

Izzy hung her jacket in the mudroom and blew her nose, the warm chocolate-scented air of her house lifting her spirits a little. At least there were cookies. But when Izzy walked into the kitchen, she was surprised to see a baking sheet full of crisp overbaked cookies on the kitchen counter. There were crumbs scattered next to it, as if someone had slammed the sheet on the counter, making the cookies jump and crumble, and then walked away. Which made no sense. Izzy's mom never walked away from a mess.

Izzy almost called out, "Mom!" But then she remembered her mom's new client, Ms. Stallton. They were probably upstairs intensely debating something boring like pillow shapes. Yelling would not be appreciated. Still, Izzy was desperate to forget the embarrassment of standing on Daphne's doorstep, in the cold, with the stupid pink mitten in her hand while Daphne and Phoebe's matching purple toes gleamed in front of her. She had to do something other than sit on a red kitchen stool and search for salvageable cookie bits.

Normally when Izzy wanted to get something out

of her head, she would go straight to her butterfly tin of Sharpies. But the house was so quiet, Izzy could get away with going into her parents' office and doing a Draw Sweet on the computer instead.

Draw Sweet was Izzy's favorite YouTube channel. Dori, the teacher, had a kind voice and gave step-by-step instructions for how to draw dancing cupcakes, puppies wearing top hats, narwhals with hearts on their butts, and all kinds of happy things. The food that Dori drew was heaped with whatever made it taste good, like frosting on cakes and ice cream on cones, and her people were always smiling with large bows in their hair and eyes that sparkled.

Sometimes Izzy thought Dori was super cheesy. But that afternoon, she wanted to crawl into Dori's cheery world where bad things never happened and stay there forever. In Draw Sweet land, Izzy would be at Daphne's house picking out nail polish colors and chewing on colorful gummy candy, not standing alone, certain that Daphne and Phoebe were talking about how random it was that she had walked all the way over in the cold to drop off a single mitten. Izzy could practically hear them giggling at her expense.

But when Izzy got to the office, her mom was sitting at the computer. Ms. Stallton had cancelled minutes before she was supposed to arrive. "Something came up," said Izzy's mom. "That's all she said in her text."

"I'm sorry," said Izzy.

"Me, too," said her mom. "I really wanted it to happen."

Izzy leaned over her mom's shoulder and gave her a hug. It felt a little strange. Her mom was usually the one giving hugs while Izzy squirmed away. But her mom's hair smelled like flowers and her cheek was warm and soft. Izzy's body was still cold from the walk, so she stayed pressed against her mom for longer than she'd meant to.

On the computer screen was a picture of Nate's room. Only instead of its normal mess, the room was spotless. The bed was perfectly made and streaks of sunlight fell across an empty floor. "What are those pictures for?" asked Izzy

Her mom closed the screen. "Oh nothing," she said. "I was just fixing the photo layout on my website. How about some of those cookies you wanted?"

"No offense," said Izzy. "But they're pretty burned."

"I know," said her mom, sighing. "This whole day is a mess. Come on, it's Saturday. Let's get out of here and treat ourselves to ice cream before dinner. We need a change of scenery."

As Izzy followed her mom out of the office, some of the relief that she'd been hoping to get from Dori and Draw Sweet passed through her. Someone else was in charge of deciding what to do next. Izzy didn't have to make any decisions.

She wouldn't make everything worse, when all she wanted was to make it better.

GEEZ, WREN

When Wren woke up on Sunday morning, her parents were sitting side by side at the kitchen counter. Her dad read from his open laptop. "Sixteen Westgate Road. Forty-nine Pierce Lane." Her mom scribbled notes.

Wren opened a box of cereal. Her parents startled at the bag's crinkling noise.

"Bird," said her dad. "You okay?"

"Just getting breakfast. What're you guys doing?"

"We're looking for a place to stay," said her dad. "While Hannah's in the hospital."

"You should find a hotel with a pool," said Wren

as she poured Cheerios into a bowl. "Hannah would love that."

Neither of her parents answered. And Wren realized why. Hannah wasn't going to be swimming. She was having surgery on her brain.

Wren was such an idiot.

"We're not looking for hotels, honey," said her mom. "The doctors need to get more information before they operate. Dr. Koffer's nurse said it's usually several days of monitoring in the hospital before the actual surgery. Then Hannah's going to need to stay and recover for several days afterward. I haven't figured out the details, but I think we're going to rent a house near the hospital for at least a week. It'll be helpful to have a home base. If we need to be there longer, then we might move into a hotel."

"Oh," said Wren. "That makes sense. You can make all of Hannah's favorite foods and bring them to the hospital. And by *all*, I mean pasta with butter every single night."

Her mom smiled. But her lips were pressed tight.

"Wren, honey, you're going to need to come with us, too."

"Come with you? To the surgery?"

"To Boston. You can't stay here alone. And it's school vacation next week. You won't miss any classes."

Wren dropped her spoon into the cereal bowl. "I can't leave. I'm doing extra lessons with Nancy all week to get ready for sectionals, remember? I want to stay here. With Dad."

Wren's dad looked down at the keyboard and shook his head. "I'm going to Boston, too, Bird. It's hard timing being the middle of the season and all. But I'm going to Skype with my assistant coaches while they run practice. We all need to prioritize what matters most right now."

Wren couldn't believe it. All of them were going? With sectionals so close?

The only reason she'd slept late was because Sunday was her rest day from training. Otherwise she would have been up early stretching or working on her off-ice ballet at the barre in her bedroom.

Every day mattered. That's why she'd begged for extra sessions with Nancy during school vacation week. She was going to train extra hard and nail her double lutz.

"No," said Wren. "No way. I'm not going. I'll stay with Nora. Or somebody else."

Wren's mom shook her head. "It's too much. Asking for all that help when there's not even school. Having to worry about where you are, who you're with. Please, Wren, don't make this any harder. We'll find a rink in Boston once we know exactly where we're staying. I'll make sure you get your double lutz."

"Yeah, right," said Wren, rolling her eyes. "You're not even a real coach."

Her mom froze, the tip of her pen suspended above her notepad. Maybe she shouldn't have said that, at least not in such an accusing tone. But whatever, it was true. Her mom might memorize technique tips from *Skating Magazine* and watch YouTube videos posted by famous coaches, but she wasn't a figure skater herself.

She didn't understand. Neither of her parents did.

◆◆◆

After lunch Wren grabbed her skating bag from the mudroom and left. She needed fresh air. She needed to move.

She stomped from stepping-stone to stepping-stone as she made her way along the wooded path that led from her house to Occom Pond. Wren paused to kick a frozen pine cone with the toe of her winter boot. It didn't budge.

When she got to the pond, her friend Nora was sitting on the bench next to the pond's warming hut. Nora stared out at the skaters—the little kids bundled like marshmallows in thick snowsuits, the hockey players hurtling themselves across center ice, the college students holding hands as they flailed around the edges.

Wren considered sitting somewhere else, but the only other option was the cold ground or the crowded warming hut. So Wren sat down next to Nora.

"You missed three major make-out sessions," said Nora. "And I just got here. Like, literally, I just sat down."

Wren shrugged. She pulled off her boots. Only

the thin layer of her tights protected her toes from the cold air.

"And they were full-on make-out sessions," continued Nora. "Not just holding hands. I saw tongue. I think I even saw drool."

"Gross," said Wren.

"I know," said Nora. "Do you think drool freezes at the same temperature as water? Or do you think it's too thick to freeze? Because how majorly insane would it be if you were kissing someone and your drool froze and you got stuck together?"

Wren didn't answer.

"Wren? Did you hear me? I just asked a super-important question. About *kissing.*"

"More like a stupid one."

"Geez," said Nora. "Excuse me for trying to have fun. You don't need to be so serious all the time."

Nora was the only girl in Wren's grade who loved skating as much as Wren did. They spent a lot of time together. There were many days that Wren thought Nora was her best friend.

But there were some days that Wren wished Nora would leave her alone.

Today was one of those days.

Wren pulled her skate laces tight, double knotting the ties. She slid her hands into her gloves and zipped her fleece jacket up to her chin. Balancing on her toe picks to protect her blades, Wren walked to the edge of the frozen pond.

She stepped onto the ice.

One stroke. Two.

She inhaled the fresh outdoor air. It was different from the air inside the ice rink. It was tinged with the scent of evergreen trees and dirt.

Wren stretched her fingers in her gloves. The muscles in her legs contracted.

"Hey!" called Nora. "Wren! Wait up!"

Wren glanced over her shoulder. Her blades rocked over a bump in the ice caused by the natural freezing of the pond water. Her body wobbled and Wren slowed. She almost stopped. But then she changed her mind.

She was not in the mood to wait for anyone.

"Geez," called Nora, out of breath. "Can't you just wait up? What's your problem?"

Wren hockey-stopped. Ice shavings shot from her blades like sparks. Nora couldn't stop in time. She glided past Wren and had to turn around.

As Nora skated back, Wren was tempted to tell her everything. About the surgery. The unicorn code name. Renting a house. Even her stupid comment about the swimming pool.

Most of all, Wren wanted to tell Nora how worried she was about the skating practices she'd miss. Hannah's health was more important. Of course it was. But Wren's parents, the doctors and nurses, even the therapy dogs and clowns with rubber noses, they had Hannah covered.

No one was worried about Wren. Not in the same way. Wren had seen the distracted clicking of her mom's pen top when she'd promised to find a rink in Boston.

It was one more thing to add to the very bottom of the list.

But then Nora stepped into a mini footwork section from her program. It was a fast-paced series of three turns that ended in a lunge. Nora loved it. She practiced it all the time.

Nora was the competition. She also wanted to medal at sectionals and qualify for nationals. Nora would probably take Wren's missed lesson times with Nancy.

Part of Nora would be sympathetic. But part of her would be relieved.

And Wren couldn't bear to see it.

"My problem," called Wren when Nora skated past her, "is you."

Nora stopped. "Me?"

Wren almost took it back. But then she saw her mom and dad walking down the path. Hannah was in between them holding their hands, her body bundled in Wren's old purple snowsuit. They paused to talk to their neighbor, Mr. Morris. He bent down and gave Hannah a hug.

They looked so happy. Even as they were ruining everything.

And it made Wren furious.

She turned to Nora. "Yes, *you*," she said. "I'm tired of you following me everywhere. I just want to skate by myself."

"I'm not following you, Wren. For the record, I got to the pond first."

Nora was right. But Wren couldn't admit that. Instead, she turned and skated toward the center of the pond where a group of college students were playing hockey.

Wren stopped at the edge of the game and grabbed a hockey stick that lay in a pile.

Normally hockey players wore helmets and pads. But on Occom Pond, the hockey players barely knew how to skate. So Wren wasn't surprised when one of the players nodded at her. "Want to sub in?" he asked.

"Sure," said Wren.

He nodded at the toe picks on her blades. "Just watch those picks."

Wren had played pickup hockey before, but she had forgotten how heavy the stick was. She removed her thin gloves to get a better grip.

"Game on," said one of the hockey players.

"Bring it," said another.

It was hard to tell which players were on which team, but no one was taking the game seriously. Wren got passed the puck a few times. She was gripping the hockey stick too tight, and her return passes were sloppy.

Still, she was a better skater than anyone else in the game.

And she was determined to prove it.

Wren relaxed her grip. Out of the corner of her eye, Wren saw her dad turn away from Mr. Morris and jog down the path. Every time they came to Occom Pond, Wren's dad said that skaters who played hockey without helmets were idiots who were asking for trouble.

So she was not surprised when he yelled, "Wren! Be careful!"

Puh-lease. These players could hardly stay upright. Nothing was going to happen.

Wren got a pass. She slid the puck to a boy who fell flat on his stomach. The other team took control.

Wren skated backward, her stick on the ice, ready for defense.

Whoosh.

The puck flew past her cheek, close enough that she felt its force through the air. Wren fell back onto the ice, too startled to catch herself.

Her butt hit first.

Then her head.

Pain shot through her entire body, but Wren pushed herself back up. She ignored the offers of help and skated to the bench next to the warming hut.

Her dad was only a few feet away. She could hear the crunch of his steps on the frozen snow. Wren hung her head between her knees, pretending to retie her perfectly secure laces.

Wren fell a lot during practice, her body hitting the ice at all sorts of angles. A knee bruised. A hip banged. A palm scratched.

Wren didn't cry then, and she wouldn't cry now.

She knew how to hold back tears.

IZZY AND THE VIBE

On Sunday evening Izzy sat at her desk drawing. She was just putting the final touches on a stick-figure girl wearing one bright pink mitten who'd tripped and fallen into a puddle of wintery slush when Nate knocked on her bedroom door.

"Yo, Iz," he said. "Family dinner is in ten minutes. Put on a fake happy face."

Izzy flipped the paper over in case Nate stepped into her room. "You're the one that hates family dinner," she said. "Not me."

Nate huffed, a burst of air passing through his

nose. Nate huffed a lot. He huffed when their parents told him to pick his clothes up from the floor, to put down his phone, to wear a hat because it was snowing. The only two things that Nate did not huff about were soccer and his abs. Nate was obsessed with his abs.

"The vibe I'm picking up is that this is one of those serious family dinners," said Nate. "Mom's lighting extra candles. Chances are someone screwed something up. My money's on Dad."

"Why Dad?"

"You'll understand when you're older," said Nate as he stepped into Izzy's room and looked at her sticker door. His eyes rested on a series of smiling cows jumping over moons, as if they proved his point.

Izzy thought about the conversation that she'd overheard yesterday with Phoebe's mom. And now a serious family dinner. *What was going on?*

"Dude," said Nate. "Don't look so freaked out. It's just family dinner."

As Nate left to go into his own room, Izzy turned back to her butterfly tin of Sharpies. She thought about starting a new drawing, maybe something involving nail polish that was actually blood, or possibly poison, but she was too nervous about dinner to think of how to make that work.

Instead, she went downstairs where she found her mom decorating the dining room table with votive candles, evergreen branches, and flowers cut from her favorite hydrangea bush in the front yard. It was February, so the once silky white hydrangea petals were dry and brown. But Izzy's mom had tied the stems together with twine and placed them in a yellow ceramic vase. And suddenly the flowers looked beautiful.

Standing in the doorway out of sight, Izzy was tempted to turn around and go back to her room. Something about seeing her mom adjust the stems so that the petals rested perfectly above the rim of the vase made Izzy even more uneasy.

Izzy's mom always said that it was a gift to be creative and that someday, when Izzy was older and out of school, the world would feel full of opportunity. Izzy could be an illustrator! A painter! A fashion designer! A sculptor! Her mom made the options seem like items in a store. Just walk down the aisle and pick the one that you like best.

But decorating homes was her mom's way of being creative. It was the career that *she* wanted to pull off the shelf. As far as Izzy could tell, her mom was having a really hard time making it happen.

It made Izzy wonder what else her mom was wrong about.

Because Izzy's mom was full of promises. Not just about careers, but about friendship. She promised that someday Izzy would find a group of wonderful friends and that those friends would love her just as she is. They would all take one scoot back and invite her to sit with them on the circle rug. Okay, so her mom didn't say those exact words. But her mom did give that impression, as if she was oblivious to the fact that the circles at school were not expanding; they were getting smaller. And they showed no signs of changing.

What if nothing her mom promised was true? Suddenly Izzy wanted to escape back up to her room.

She turned to walk away, but the floor creaked and her mom looked up from the table.

"Oh, hey, Iz," said her mom. "What do you think?"

Izzy almost told the truth: that the table looked really pretty. Instead, she shrugged. Her mom hugged the napkin that she'd been folding to her chest. Izzy realized that by not answering the question, she was hurting her mom's feelings. But for some reason, it felt worth it.

Row's tail stuck out from underneath the dining table, thumping against the floor in a steady beat. Izzy crawled under to sit with him. With Row's warm body next to her and the dark underside of the wood table above her, Izzy could almost pretend that nothing worrisome was going on. No fancy family dinner, no mysterious ideas, no untrustworthy promises. No drawings hidden in drawers, no beaded bracelets, no lost mittens. She buried her nose in Row's neck, inhaling his scent of dirt and sunshine. When Izzy looked up, two pairs of feet were in front of her—her mom's black ballet flats and her dad's scuffed brown loafers.

The shoes were perfectly parallel, an unnatural

position that told Izzy her parents knew she was under the table and were deciding what to do about it. Then Nate's sneakers joined them, the laces dirty and frayed.

"I don't think we have a choice," said Izzy's mom.

"Afraid not," said her dad.

Nate said nothing, although Izzy heard him huff.

"I think we've got to go in," continued her dad. "Implement the rescue mission."

"Sounds serious," said her mom.

As her parents' feet stepped away from the table, Izzy saw her dad wrap his arm around her mom's waist. She couldn't see their faces, but there was something about the way her mom's hip pressed against her dad's body that made Izzy certain her dad was kissing her mom on the cheek. Izzy smiled into Row's neck.

The next thing Izzy knew, her parents were climbing under the dining room table, wrapping their arms around Izzy and shielding their faces from Row, who was thrilled at the unexpected excitement. Izzy tried to wiggle away, but she couldn't help laughing.

She was annoyed and relieved. Opposites.

"Okay, okay," said Izzy as her dad tried to kiss her on the cheek. "I'm coming out."

"Mission accomplished," said her dad.

"About time," said Nate. "Does nobody else smell that chicken?"

As Izzy's family carried the food from the kitchen and sat down at the table, the silliness that was in the air blew away, replaced by a calm silence. Izzy's mom smoothed the napkin in her lap. Her dad placed his elbows on either side of his plate and pressed his fingers together in a steeple grip. Nate grabbed the serving fork from the plate of chicken, but instead of digging in, he left the fork lingering in the air. Izzy didn't know where to look. Her mom? Her dad? No place felt safe.

"So now is when you finally tell us what's going on," said Nate. "We're not morons."

Izzy wanted to nod, but she was too nervous to move.

Their dad sighed. "Okay," he said. "You're right. We do have some news."

Nate huffed. "Knew it. Bring it on. What is it? Divorce?"

"What?" said their mom. "No one is getting divorced."

"Why would you even joke about that?" said their dad.

"Because we don't know what's going on!" said Izzy. There were tears clinging to the ends of her words, as if they were trying to climb over and drown them.

"Okay, here's the thing," said their mom. "We're going to be moving—"

"What!" interrupted Izzy. "Moving where?"

Every year someone at her school moved. The teachers gave the kid a gift so they'd remember all their old friends. A T-shirt that everyone signed, or a class photo with everyone's initials written on a wooden picture frame. Most kids acted all sad and promised to keep in touch forever, but as soon as the person left they would start talking about how annoying he or she was and how life was so much better without them.

Izzy could imagine all the things Daphne and

Phoebe would say about her. Yesterday's pathetic pink mitten delivery would probably be at the top of the list. A tear slid down Izzy's cheek.

"Not *moving* moving," said Izzy's mom, reaching for Izzy's hand. "We're moving into the apartment over the garage. For a week. It'll be fun. The garage apartment is so cozy."

"Exactly," said her dad. "It's got everything we need. Kitchen, bathroom, sink, shower. We'll throw inflatable mattresses on the floor and plug in some space heaters. You'll be on school break next week anyway. It'll be like camping. Or what's that word I read about . . . glamping? Glamorous camping. What could be better?"

So many things, thought Izzy.

The garage apartment was two empty rooms above the garage at the end of the driveway. There was a tiny kitchen, a bathroom that had a toilet with a chain coming down from the ceiling, and a sink that made angry gurgling noses whenever the faucets were turned on. The plan had been to rent the apartment to college students. Or something. Izzy had never given the plan much thought because the garage apartment had been empty for as long as they'd lived in the house.

"But why can't we stay here?" asked Izzy. "Is it mold?" There was mold in the school gym last year and the teachers said it could make everyone sick. After they closed the gym and removed the mold, Izzy could still sometimes feel the bad stuff entering her body. Even now, just thinking about mold made her lungs all prickly and hot. Or maybe it wasn't her lungs; maybe it was her heart.

"It's not mold, Iz," said her dad. "The house is fine. Better than fine, actually. Mom did such an awesome job decorating it that we put the house on VRBO just to see what would happen. And someone made us an offer right away."

"What's VRBO?" asked Izzy.

"Vacation rental by owner," said her mom. "It's a website where you can list your home for people to rent on their vacations."

"Someone wants to come here for vacation?" asked Izzy. "That doesn't make any sense. There's nothing special to do."

Nate huffed. "Strangers are literally moving into our house and you're worried about whether they're going to have a good time?"

"Listen, Iz," said their dad, ignoring Nate. "I don't know why these people are coming here and I don't care. I only care about us. Renting out your home is a thing that people do sometimes. To make money."

"So we're out of money?" Money confused her. Not the dollars and cents part of money, but whether her family had enough money, or not enough. Whenever Izzy asked, her parents said vague things like, "We have everything we need." Or, "We're very lucky."

But there were other times when she heard her parents talking about loans, second mortgages, and refinancing. Even if they didn't use the exact word *money*, Izzy understood the message—things were tight.

"We're not out of money," said her dad. "But we are short on cash. We have more money going out right now than we do coming in. That happens sometimes. To entrepreneurs."

Izzy's dad was an entrepreneur. Last year he quit

his job working for a big company to start ThinkText, an app that restricted users to one text per hour. No emojis, no abbreviations. Izzy's dad believed it would force people to be more thoughtful, less impulsive. In a world where everyone was bombarded with information, her dad wanted to slow things down and make texting more considerate, like writing letters used to be. The thing her dad hadn't figured out yet was how to make a lot of other people feel the same way.

Nate dropped his fork onto his plate. "This really, really stinks," he said.

Their dad nodded. "Yes. It really, really does."

After dinner Izzy asked if she could use the computer to do a Draw Sweet. She wanted to escape into Dori's pastel-colored world of joy, but there was something else she needed to do first.

Izzy opened Google and typed "vacation rental by owner" into the search bar. She clicked the link for VRBO.com. The words *destination* and *ultimate vacation* and *luxury* floated over a picture of a beach at sunset. In the middle of the screen were four white boxes to enter a destination, arrival date, departure date, and number of guests. Izzy typed "Wellesley" into the destination. She chose tomorrow for the arrival date and the day after for the departure date. In the box for number of guests, Izzy typed "4." Because that was the perfect number for her house. Four people.

A list of homes popped up and right at the top was Izzy's house. It was strange to be both sitting inside her house and looking at it on the website. Her hands trembled as she scrolled down. The first picture showed the outside of her house glowing in the sun. There was the door that her mom had painted bright red, the historical plaque with "1911," and the maple tree where they tied Row's leash to a spike in the ground.

Next were a series of interior pictures. The kitchen with the wood shelves that her dad had installed himself, the stools that her mom found at a yard sale and painted with the leftover red paint from the front door, the living room with Row's favorite napping chair. Then came her parents' room, Nate's room, and

Izzy's own room. She recognized them all. But at the same time, every room looked different than normal. There were vases of flowers in random places, and the beds were neatly made. A navy-blue lamp sat on a normally empty side table, and a cream blanket was folded across a normally bare couch. In Nate's room, the floor was spotless and the soccer trophies on his shelf were lined up like neat little toy soldiers.

Izzy remembered her mom taking these pictures. A few weeks ago, she'd come home from school to find the hallways cluttered with picture frames, patterned pillows, and stacks of books. "I'm taking pictures for my website," her mom had explained. "I need the rooms to look perfect." Izzy had been annoyed to find her desk cleaned off and the butterfly tin moved to her closet. But she'd checked her desk drawer and her drawings were just as she left them. So she hadn't given the pictures much thought.

But now she realized that the pictures weren't only for her mom's interior-design website. They were also for VRBO.

VRBO was what her mom was checking yesterday on the computer.

Renting their home was the idea she was talking about with Phoebe's mom.

And now it was actually happening.

Izzy walked away from the computer. Away from the perfect pictures of her home and Dori's make-believe world of hearts and happiness, up to her bedroom. She was lying on her bed, staring at her stickers, when her mom knocked on the door.

"Izzy, can I come in?"

"Okay," said Izzy.

Her mom stacked the pillows that Izzy had tossed on the floor into a neat pile. She rotated the shade of her lamp so that the seam faced the wall. Then she sat on the edge of Izzy's bed and put her hand on Izzy's leg. There was a blanket between her mom's hand and Izzy's leg, but Izzy felt her mom's fingers wrap around her thigh.

"You know, Iz," said her mom. "It always feels weird to knock on your door."

"Why?"

"I'm just not used to it. I don't think I'll ever be used to it."

"I'm twelve, Mom. Twelve-year-olds are allowed to close their doors."

"That doesn't mean their moms have to like it."

Izzy didn't say anything. The silence felt sad, like something had gone missing underneath Izzy's bed. A teddy bear, or maybe her stuffed lamb. Her mom ran her thumb across Izzy's forehead. Did she feel the tiny bumps that Izzy noticed when she looked in the mirror? Is that why she looked so sad?

Izzy wanted her mom to move her hand and leave it right there. Both. At the same time. Opposites.

"It's a lot to take in, huh?" said her mom.

Izzy shrugged.

"This house stuff is going to be okay, I promise. It's only one week. Then we'll be back like nothing ever happened."

"I know," lied Izzy. It wasn't the idea of moving out for a week that was horrible; it was the idea of someone else moving in. Someone else sleeping in her bed, looking at her sticker door, and sitting at her desk. What if it was a sweaty teenage boy who left his stinky socks in piles, like Nate? Or a nose picker who flicked his dried snot, like Kyle at school?

"Or if there's something else that's bothering you," continued her mom, "you can tell me. I know things aren't the way they used to be with Phoebe."

"Phoebe? Nothing's wrong with Phoebe." Izzy twisted around so that her mom's hand fell off her leg. Of course, on top of everything, her mom had to bring up Phoebe. As if something dramatic happened yesterday, instead of it being one more day in the slow leak of their best friend status shriveling to nothing.

"Okay, good," said her mom. "Because I was worried you were feeling badly about your friendship with her."

"Why would you think that?"

"I don't know, Iz. I don't know what to think about a lot of things these days."

It was an opening, a crack in the door. Izzy could kick the door open and ask her mom what she meant, or leave it closed. Izzy chose closed. She turned away from her mom and hugged a pillow in her arms.

Her mom kissed Izzy on the forehead and stood to leave. "We're coming right back, Iz," she said. "It's not permanent. You know that, right?"

Izzy nodded. But she heard Phoebe's voice in her head. What does that *mean* "not permanent"? That it doesn't matter? That it's no big deal?

Maybe it wasn't a big deal to her parents, but to Izzy moving out of their house was one more thing changing. Her friendship with Phoebe was falling apart and there was nothing to take its place. And now someone else would be living in her house and sleeping in her bed. Izzy looked at her sticker door—the chaotic swirl of animals and objects and colors. Nothing on that door made sense together, but she loved the way it looked.

Real life was the opposite. In real life, things needed to fit together. Cool girls wanted to be friends with other cool girls. Kids wanted to sleep in their own beds.

In real life, things were supposed to make sense.

IZZY IS LATE
TO THE BATTLE

On Friday morning, the last day of school before they moved into the garage apartment, Izzy stood in the kitchen and yelled, "Nate! Nate let's *go*."

"Coming," said Nate as he yawned and ran his hand through his bedhead hair.

"We're going to be late for school," said Izzy.

Izzy was tired, too. It had been five days since their parents told them about the move, and Izzy hadn't been sleeping well. As soon as she closed her eyes, she'd remember one more thing from her room that she needed to hide in the basement or put in the pile to carry over to the garage apartment. But she could still get ready for school on time. Nate, on the other hand, was standing in front of the open refrigerator staring blankly.

"Just pick something and let's go!"

Nate huffed and pulled out a slice of leftover pizza. He folded it in half and held it between his teeth as he grabbed his backpack and the car keys. "Now who's making us late?" he mumbled as he walked out the door.

Normally their mom drove them to school. Ever since starting ThinkText, their dad was rarely home during the week. He was either traveling to meet investors and computer programmers, or stuck in meetings until well after dinner. But their mom was staying home that morning to clean and pack, which meant Nate got to use the car and drop Izzy off on his way to high school. Izzy looked out the car window as Nate drove down the familiar streets of their neighborhood, coming to an abrupt stop at an intersection that had huge holes in two of the four corner lots, empty spaces where old houses had been torn down so they could be replaced with giant new ones. "Why do they knock down houses?" Izzy had asked her mom years ago when they drove past a home that was being torn in half by a bulldozer.

"There's no market for old homes anymore," her mom had said. "People around here want everything shiny and perfect."

"Like a princess castle?"

"Exactly. Everyone in this town wants to look like they live in a fairy tale."

Back then, Izzy thought that made perfect sense. She, too, wanted to live in a princess castle. Visions of sparkling ball gowns and diamond tiaras floated in her mind. Now, though, Izzy wondered about the families who had lived in the bulldozed houses. Why did they move? Where did they go? Was it their choice? Or did they have no other option?

Her parents had promised that they were only renting their house for one week, but what if ThinkText never made any money and her mom never got any clients? Was the next step selling their house? Would her yard be one of those empty holes of dirt someday?

Izzy was about to ask Nate what he thought when Nate put on his blinker and turned from the normal route to school. "Need to make a pit stop," he said. "For coffee."

"Please, Nate," said Izzy. "Not today." School started in five minutes. They did not have time for coffee.

"Today is all we've got, Iz. And today, I need caffeine."

Izzy sighed. The front window of Starbucks was decorated with evergreen trees and smiling snowmen holding hands made of twigs. Large silver snowflakes fell in a random pattern. As she walked through the door, Izzy wondered whose job it was to decorate the huge panes of glass. It was the kind of job she wanted when she was older—to take a fresh marker to an empty pane of glass and create seasonal scenes. Maybe by then she would be just like Dori, drawing only cheery pictures of suns rocking big sunglasses and bunnies hopping among tulips.

The opposite of stick figures falling down sharp-edged mountains and landing in slush puddles.

Izzy stood next to Nate in line. Nate snapped his leather wallet open and shut. Open and shut. He unzipped his coat and ran his hand through his hair.

"Are you okay?" asked Izzy.

"Shh," said Nate. "Be cool." There was only one person in line ahead of them and Nate squinted up at the menu board, like he was trying to decide what he wanted even though he always ordered the same thing.

"Can I help you?" asked the girl behind the register. She had a row of silver hoops going all the way up her left ear. Around her neck was an oval-shaped pearl on a leather string. She'd woven gray yarn around the neck strap of her green Starbucks apron and her name, Simone, was written in thick capital letters on her nametag.

"Yeah, um, hey," said Nate. "Can I get a venti iced latte with an extra shot of espresso?"

Simone took a plastic cup from the stack and began to write Nate's order.

"You forgot the vanilla," said Izzy. Nate always got a venti iced latte with three pumps of vanilla syrup.

"Shut up," said Nate, elbowing Izzy in the side. Then he rolled his eyes and smiled at Simone.

Nate was acting the way Phoebe wished Zach would act around her. The way a lot of boys acted around Daphne. Her brother had a crush.

And by the time he dropped her at school, Izzy was officially late. She had to stop at Ms. Perry's desk and sign the tardy sheet. But the tardy sheet was nothing compared to walking into class. Izzy dreaded opening the classroom door knowing that class had already started. She did not want all those eyes staring up at her, wondering what had happened.

As Izzy pushed open the door to Mr. Blair's English classroom, she wished she could project the story of her morning on her forehead, the way Mr. Blair projected his writing on his beloved SMART Board.

My brother has a crush! It's his fault we're late! Not mine!

Izzy pictured the letters in red marker. Not the crisp Sharpie kind, but something wide and flat like Simone had used on her Starbucks apron. Mr. Blair's markers were always dry and his handwriting was messy, but he never seemed to care. He called his classroom his castle and his students his academic warriors. He expected them to fight their way toward excellence. No matter the cost! No matter how fierce the battle! No matter how challenging the foe! Seriously, that was the way Mr. Blair talked.

"Ah, Izzy," said Mr. Blair as she handed him the late slip.

"Sorry I'm late."

"It happens to the best of warriors. We were just gathering around the hearth of knowledge. Take a seat."

The hearth of knowledge was a black plastic cauldron with a long cord that plugged into the wall. Izzy had seen one just like it at Party City. Mr. Blair kept the cauldron in the center of the room and, when he switched it on, orange streamers blew out like fake flames. When the year started, Izzy thought that Mr. Blair's class, with its special props and flags with inspirational quotes, would be different. Or maybe, that she would be different in it. But she'd been wrong. Mr. Blair may have thought he was teaching in a castle, but it wasn't a magical one. School was still school. And Izzy still had to do all the normal school things, like walk across the room to her normal spot near the bookshelves.

Phoebe and Daphne were on the far side of the room next to Serena and Prithi. Like Phoebe, Serena seemed to have forgotten about Daphne ripping tiny Snow Stepper from her arms and holding the kitten up high like a trophy. Serena wasn't on the lacrosse team, so she didn't wear her hair smoothed back with a navy elastic headband, and she didn't have a stack of beaded bracelets on her wrist, but she was still part of their group. She could do things like fiddle with the side zipper on Prithi's hightops or stick her tongue out at Daphne, and everyone would understand that Serena wasn't judging Prithi's style or teasing Daphne. She was just being herself.

On the other side of the circle Zach, Leo, and Eli

were staring at piece of red gum stuck to the ceiling. In between them, a row of kids sat knee to knee. The only person with space next to them was Otto. He waved Izzy over.

"You're late," said Otto.

Sometimes it was hard to know how to respond to Otto. He said things that could be mean in a confusingly nice way. Like the way he said *late* made Izzy wonder if he was worried that something bad had happened to her.

"Sorry?" she said.

"It's okay," said Otto.

Otto started to tap the floor with his feet. Otto was always moving. His feet. His head. His fingers. He was a tap dancer, and his body behaved like there was music playing in his head all day long.

"Hey, Izzy," whispered Otto. "Think fast. What's one thing that's actually two things?"

Izzy didn't answer. She was trying to look at Phoebe, but also not to look at Phoebe. Izzy was certain that Phoebe knew about her house situation.

Their moms had been texting all week, and Phoebe always stole her mom's phone to play games and take selfies. But whenever Izzy passed Phoebe in the hall, Phoebe only said vague things like, "Hey" and "See ya." Izzy kept hoping that Phoebe would pull her aside somewhere private and ask how she was feeling about having a stranger sleeping in her bed or staring at the sticker door that they'd created together.

Izzy was even up for discussing what it *meant*. But Phoebe either didn't care or didn't want to talk about it. And Izzy was left debating which of those options was worse.

Otto tapped Izzy on the shoulder. "Come on, Izzy," he said. "You've got this. What's one thing that's actually two things?" Otto held up one finger, then two. One, then two. He was wearing his favorite T-shirt. It was black and said "iTap" in large white letters. Izzy had once made the mistake of doodling the shirt in her notebook. When Otto saw it, he asked if she'd draw the same thing on the cover of his own notebook and then sign her name underneath.

Izzy had done it. But only when no one was watching.

"Come on, Izzy," said Otto. "Think!"

"I don't know," said Izzy. Her words were sharp and mean. But Otto didn't seem to notice.

"Fine," said Otto. "I'll tell you. Tap dancing. It's dance and music. Dance *and* music. Cool, right?"

"Cool," said Izzy. She just wanted Otto to stop talking. Daphne had finished whispering something to Serena and was now talking to Phoebe. If Otto would just be quiet, there was a chance that Izzy could hear what Daphne was saying.

Luckily Daphne's loud voice drifted across the classroom. "Eight more hours," said Daphne. "Then it's a whole week of freedom."

"For *you*," said Phoebe. "Theater camp is not freedom."

Daphne shook her head. "I still cannot believe that your mom is making you spend your one week of vacation at theater camp."

"I can," said Phoebe. She looked right at Izzy. Vacation week theater camp had been Izzy's mom's idea. She'd been all excited when Principal Carr had sent an e-mail announcing that Mr. Blair would be running a week-long theater camp that would end with a performance of a scene from *Little Women*. It was the perfect solution to the problem of what to do with Izzy during school vacation week. Nate was signed up for indoor soccer training, and her mom assumed she'd be busy with work. When she'd texted Phoebe's mom and convinced her to sign Phoebe up as well, it seemed that everything had fallen into place. Except for the fact that neither Izzy nor Phoebe had any interest in going.

Mr. Blair leaned over the hearth of knowledge and clicked it on. Over the whirr of the hearth's internal fan, Izzy heard Daphne say, "When is Izzy going to get her own life and leave you alone?"

Phoebe rolled her eyes. "Probably never."

The orange streamers on the hearth wiggled and danced, trapped in their plastic cage. And Izzy's body grew hot with embarrassment, her cheeks flushing. The fire was fake, but it may as well have been real.

WREN AND
THE PILE OF PEAS

Saturday morning. Wren rested her head in her hand. She stared out the car window as her family drove down the highway to Boston.

Her parents had packed the car while Wren was at the rink, and her cheeks were still warm from her intense lesson with Nancy.

Wren had landed ten perfect double lutzes. One. Two. Three. Four . . . She'd done them right in a row, with Nancy clapping her hands after each one and yelling, "Again!"

When Wren reached ten, Nancy placed her hands on

Wren's shoulders and said, "Your body will remember. I'll see you in one week, and we'll do ten in a row again."

Wren wanted to believe Nancy. But she was full of doubt.

She'd spent the past week training harder than ever, ignoring the tender bump on the back of her head from her fall on Occom Pond.

And now she was being forced to leave.

Hannah was sound asleep in her car seat, her favorite stuffed unicorn lying diagonally across her lap. Wren's parents sat in the front seats, each silent and looking straight ahead.

Wren shifted positions. She usually loved this drive. Boston meant seeing the *Nutcracker* ballet at a fancy theater with a domed ceiling accented in gold. It meant flights out of Logan Airport to fun vacations. One year it meant going with her mom to watch the Figure Skating World Championships.

Wren could still remember sitting next to her mom on the hard plastic seats way up in the highest level of the stadium. She remembered looking down at the skaters on the ice and the moment that her mom placed her hand on Wren's cheek and said, "Each skater out there was once a little girl with a big dream, just like you."

Her mom's hand was cold from the soda that she'd been holding, but to Wren it had felt like the warmest of touches.

As her dad changed lanes, Wren pressed her feet against her skating bag. The rest of her stuff was in the trunk. But she wanted to keep her skates close.

She didn't have the Dartmouth College rink. Or Occom Pond. Or Nancy.

But she still had her skates.

"Okay, team," said Wren's dad as he pulled into a driveway. "Home sweet temporary home."

The rental house had a bright red front door and a historical plaque with the numbers "1911." The bare branches of a huge maple tree spread over the front yard. At the end of the driveway was a two-story garage with a matching red door.

It was cute. Homey.

In a movie it would be where the happy family lived.

Wren hated it.

They'd barely parked the car when a woman wearing a cream sweater appeared in the driveway. She smiled and waved, matching the happy vibe of the house.

"Hello!" she said. "Welcome! You must be the family renting our house."

Wren's dad nodded and shook her hand. Wren's mom did the same.

Hannah pushed against the straps of her car seat, trying to get out. Her stuffed unicorn fell to the ground.

Wren did not lean over to pick it up. She sat frozen in the car, her feet pressing against her skating bag.

Moving made it real. Getting out of the car made it real. Even though the drive had taken over two hours, Wren could smell the ice rink on her skating jacket. The muscles in her legs were still tired from her lesson with Nancy.

Once she stepped into the fresh air and stretched her body, all of that would disappear.

"Come on, girls," said Wren's dad as he picked up Hannah's stuffed unicorn and unbuckled her car seat. "Let's go inside and get a tour."

He caught Wren's eye. There was so much fake energy in his gaze that Wren had to look away. But she unbuckled her seat belt and got out of the car.

Wren didn't take a deep breath of the cold February air. She didn't stretch her arms over her head or shake out her legs. But none of that mattered.

The scents and surroundings of her normal life were gone. Instead, there was this long narrow driveway. This cluster of dry bushes. This house that was not her house.

This place was her life for the next week.

She was stuck.

"How old are you?" asked the woman in the cream sweater as she opened the door to the house.

"Twelve," said Wren.

"Twelve! I have a daughter who's twelve! We'll be

in the apartment over the garage for the week you're here. Right at the end of the driveway. Maybe you two could play together sometime?"

Maybe not, thought Wren.

As her family followed the woman into the house and through the first floor, Wren sat on a red kitchen stool. Wren was curious about the house, but she didn't want to give the woman any babyish playdate ideas. Better to stay out of sight.

Finally, the woman and Wren's family gathered back in the kitchen. The woman placed a set of keys and an envelope in the middle of the island. "Please call if you need anything," she said. "My phone number's written on the sheet and I'm only ten seconds away!"

Her hand lingered on the island. Wren could tell by the way she looked at Hannah that she knew about the surgery. The woman had the same look as Maggie, the waitress from Lou's. And Mr. Morris, their neighbor. A thin glaze of hope covering up a deep sadness.

Then, finally, she left.

Wren's dad turned to her mom. "The house is perfect," he said. "This is all going to work out."

Wren's mom waved her hands in front of her face. "I just need a minute," she said as she turned to face the closed refrigerator.

Wren's mom needed a minute all the time.

Wren had once read Hannah a picture book that was supposed to help little kids learn about big numbers. One page showed what ten green peas looked like on a plate. Another page showed what five hundred green peas looked like in a shoebox. The last page showed what ten million green peas would look like in a house, pouring out the doors and windows onto the street.

Her mom's minutes were like those peas.

Add them together and they would fill entire days.

"Take all the time you need," said her dad, lightly squeezing her mom's shoulder. "The girls and I will go explore."

Hannah raised one arm, like she was holding a sword. "Explorers," she yelled as she charged up the stairs.

The second floor was similar to the first, with creaky hardwood floors and crisp white walls. There were colorful touches, like a patterned hallway rug and a shelf under a window stuffed with books.

Wren had wandered into a bathroom when Hannah yelled, "Wren! Come! I'm in the pretty room."

Wren followed the sound of Hannah's voice to a room at the end of the hall. It had two big windows looking over the driveway. Pink pom-poms lined the edges of white curtains. There was a desk with globs of color on its flat surface, as if someone had repeatedly colored off the edge of the page.

But there was no Hannah.

"Hannah? Where are you?"

Hannah loved to play hide-and-seek. So when Wren didn't see her, she peered behind the curtains and looked under the bed.

"Come out, come out wherever you are!" sang Wren. She tried to keep her voice soft and cheery. She didn't want to ruin Hannah's fun, but ever since the seizures began, their mom hated it when Hannah hid.

If their mom thought Hannah was hiding in this new house, she'd come sprinting up the stairs in a full-on panic.

Thankfully, Hannah giggled. The sound came from behind the open bedroom door. Hannah was sitting against the wall, her knees tucked into her chest.

"You found me!" she said. "I was hiding with my friends."

"You're not supposed to hide alone. You know that."

Hannah pointed to the door and smiled. "I'm not alone."

Wren moved the door so there was space for her to sit down. She pulled Hannah onto her lap. The back of the bedroom door was covered with stickers. Hundreds of stickers in all shapes, colors, and sizes. There were ducks wearing rain boots. Hearts in dozens of colors. Even smiling neon skulls.

It looked like someone had shot an entire sticker aisle out of a cannon and they'd all landed sticky side down on the door. Wren was mesmerized.

"Look," said Hannah, pointing toward the bottom corner of the door. "Unicorns."

"Cool," said Wren.

"Do you think they knew I was coming?"

"Maybe."

"Neigh," said Hannah as she ran her tiny finger over the unicorn stickers.

Hannah's hot pink nail polish was almost completely worn off. Wren wished she'd remembered to bring the nail polish bottle from home. But it hadn't even crossed her mind.

"Neigh," repeated Hannah. Then she nodded. "Yep, they knew I was coming. The unicorns say hi."

"Hello, unicorns," said Wren, playing along. "It's nice to meet you."

Hannah leaned against Wren and stuck her thumb in her mouth. Wren wrapped her arms around Hannah's round belly and rested her chin on the top of Hannah's head.

Hannah was so warm. Like a light bulb. Not because she had a fever, but because she was always warm. And giggling. And dreaming of unicorns.

Wren thought about what was going to happen to Hannah on Monday. The wires and the stickers stuck to her scalp. The surgery to follow.

A tear dripped down Wren's cheek. It was the size of a green pea.

There were others right behind it.

Wren pictured the ten million green peas from the book busting through the rental house's windows and doors. If she started to cry, Wren worried that she wouldn't be able to stop.

Wren wiped her cheek.

She refused to drown the house.

"Come on," she said, pushing Hannah up from her lap. "Let's check out the other rooms."

Hannah slipped her hand into Wren's and they turned left out of the bedroom. There was another bedroom of a similar size with green walls and a large collection of gold soccer trophies. Then a bathroom and a third, larger bedroom at the end of the hall with a king-size bed.

Their dad walked out of that bedroom. "What's the verdict?" he asked.

Wren shrugged. "It's okay."

"Did you find a room you like?"

"I like the one with unicorns," said Hannah.

"Unicorns?" said their dad. "This I have to see."

Hannah led their dad back to the room with the sticker door. "Wow," he said, looking at the sticker door. "It sure is pretty. But how about we let Wren have this room. The unicorns can keep her company when you're sleeping at the hospital."

Hannah paused, considering this. "Okay," she said. "Wren likes unicorns, too."

"Wren loves unicorns," said their dad. He winked at Wren and threw Hannah over his shoulder, carrying her out of the room.

Wren sat down on the bed, feeling it out.

The room reminded Wren of Nora's hand-me-down clothes from her two big sisters. "This is *new* new," Nora said whenever she got something from a store. "Not *old* new."

The room was new to Wren, but it was clearly not *new* new.

Wren thought about the girl who lived here. The one her age who was now staying over the garage. She must have pressed all those stickers onto the door and made all those marks on the desk.

Wren walked over to the window by the desk and pressed her forehead against the cold glass pane. If she tilted her head to the right, she could see the windows on the second floor of the garage.

Who was she? wondered Wren. *And what was she doing right now?*

IZZY AND THE
JUDGMENT PAINT

Izzy waited at the top of the stairs in the garage apartment, hugging her knees to her chest. Nate was out "studying" at Starbucks and her dad was at Home Depot buying tools to fix the leak in the garage sink. Her mom had left to welcome the renters.

And it was taking *forever*.

Row sat down next to Izzy and plopped his head on her lap. "Did you see them get out of the car, Row? Did you see that girl? She looked my age. Did you think she was pretty? Prettier than me?"

Izzy scratched Row behind his ear. She didn't want

to be sitting in the garage apartment worrying about who was prettier, her or this new mystery girl. She wanted to be inside her house finding out for herself. But her mom had made Izzy stay behind with Row. So all Izzy knew about the renters was what they looked like. She was relieved there were no boys staying in her house, but she'd spent so long worrying about the boy possibility that she hadn't considered what it would feel like for someone just like her to be renting her house instead.

It mattered that the girl was her age. And pretty. And that she'd kept her gaze on the ground, barely looking around as she walked into the house.

What if she was one of those popular girls who waltzed through life with tons of friends and loads of confidence? What if she thought Izzy's sticker door was babyish? What if her cool girl judgment spread over the walls of Izzy's room like paint?

What if they met, in the driveway or the backyard, and it spread to Izzy herself?

Izzy couldn't just sit there anymore. She stood to find Row's leash. If she took Row for a walk, she'd have to walk down the driveway, past their car. Maybe she'd run into the girl unloading more bags. She'd be able to see if the girl had braces, if her skin was clear, if her ears were pierced. She could look for elastic headbands and beaded bracelets. Not the exact ones that Daphne and Phoebe wore, but something that gave off the same vibe of belonging.

And maybe, if she seemed friendly, Izzy would ask the girl her name.

But as Izzy was about to clip the leash on Row's collar, her mom opened the door at the bottom of the garage stairs.

"So who are they?" asked Izzy.

Her mom paused, and leaned against the wall of the stairway. "They're a really nice family."

"That's all? A nice family? What about that older girl? Is she twelve? Did you ask?"

Izzy's mom nodded but didn't say anything. She walked up the stairs to the apartment and sat down at the folding table that was covered with blue-and-white checkered fabric. Her mom didn't pick up Row's leash or straighten the pages of paper that Izzy had left in a messy pile.

"What?" whispered Izzy.

"That poor family," said her mom.

"They didn't look poor," said Izzy. The older girl had been rolling some kind of fancy bag and the younger girl had been carrying a clean white unicorn with a glittering pink mane.

Izzy's mom shook her head, as if Izzy had disappointed her somehow. "The little girl has epilepsy."

"What's epilepsy?" asked Izzy.

"It's a condition where kids have seizures," said her mom. "It's very scary."

Before Izzy could respond, her dad walked in carrying a plastic bag from Home Depot. "What's scary?" he asked. "What'd I miss? Please tell me I don't need to go back for mouse traps."

"The little girl staying in our house has epilepsy," said Izzy.

Her dad exhaled a long breath. He placed the

plastic bag on the folding table, the hard objects inside hitting against each other with a metallic clang. "Man, I'm sorry to hear that."

"They're checking her into Children's Hospital on Monday," said Izzy's mom. "Apparently there's a surgeon there who's the best in the field. She's going to be admitted for at least a week."

"That stinks," said Izzy.

"It more than stinks, Iz," said her mom.

Izzy's dad walked over and wrapped his arm around Izzy's shoulder. He gave her a gentle squeeze. "Anything we can do?" he asked.

"I told them about theater camp," said her mom. "I'm going to forward them Principal Carr's e-mail in case there's room for Wren to sign up."

"Wren?" asked Izzy. "That's the girl my age?"

Her mom nodded. She smoothed a wrinkle in the checkered fabric covering the table.

"But she's not even from here," said Izzy, shifting out from her dad's grip. "It's makes no sense for her to go to theater camp."

"Come on, Iz," said her mom. "How about a little empathy, huh? That family is dealing with a lot right now. You're old enough to start thinking about other people."

Her mom stood up and pulled her phone from her pocket. She turned to face the window over the sink. Izzy stared at her mom's back, feeling as empty as a blank page. Izzy thought about other people all the time. Sometimes it felt like all she did was think about other people. About Phoebe and how she ditched her. About Daphne, Serena, and Prithi, and how they sucked Phoebe into their friendship like a vacuum. About her dad and how stressed he sometimes looked at the end of the day. About her mom and the client who cancelled at the last minute.

How was Izzy also supposed to think about a girl she'd never met? A girl who looked like the kind of person that Phoebe would love to hang out with at theater camp? The kind of girl who would slide into her very own bedroom and old friendship?

Her mom put down her phone. "I'm going to lie

down for a bit," she said. "Then how about we go to the library."

"Great," said Izzy, under her breath.

Phoebe and Daphne were going ice skating that afternoon before Daphne left for a week-long ski trip. And Izzy was going to the library with her mom. Opposites.

"I could use some help with the sink," said her dad.

He said it kindly. Hopefully. But Izzy shook her head and walked into her sleeping space. She slid the curtain shut.

So much had changed in just an hour. Earlier in the day, when she'd walked into the apartment for the first time, Izzy had been relieved to see that her dad had installed a large piece of plywood to separate her space from Nate's space. Her mom had hung fabric in the place of doors, striped for Nate and polka dots for Izzy. The air mattresses on the floor were made up with comforters and pillows in colorful pillowcases. There was a wood crate in the corner of Izzy's area where her mom had placed her butterfly tin of Sharpies.

Izzy had thought the space was cool, in a glamping kind of way.

But now she looked at the pile of her clothes stacked in the corner and wanted to kick them over. The space wasn't cool; it was small and dark. It smelled like sawdust and wet towels. Izzy imagined that girl, Wren, unpacking her clothes in Izzy's real room, laying out the perfect first-day outfit. She'd probably float into theater camp on a thick, fluffy cloud of popularity.

And Izzy would be stuck watching from the ground, gazing up at what she could never seem to reach.

9

WREN MINUS TWO

"All right, Bird," said her dad as he stood up in his hockey skates. "It's you and me and the ice. Nothing else matters."

"And about one hundred other people," said Wren. Her dad had found a rink near the rental house with Saturday afternoon public skating. They'd rushed to get there. But so had tons of other people. The ice was crowded.

"Forget about them," said her dad. "Block them out. What do I always tell my players?"

"Grind and grit," said Wren.

"That's right. The two magic G's. You have to work through the daily grind to find your inner grit. That's how the magic happens."

Wren nodded. Her dad's sayings played in her head like a catchy radio song.

Grind and grit.

Head and heart.

Train your brain and your body will follow.

But as Wren took her first strokes, she wanted to tell her dad to wake up and look around. There was no space here for any magic.

The ice was choppy with tracks and dense with people. Some skaters pushed milk crates; others hung on to the boards. Loud music played from a staticky overhead sound system.

"Time to represent," said her dad. He had a proud look on his face, like he was patting himself on the back for sounding young and cool.

Wren didn't want to ruin his mood.

She dodged a dad holding a little kid between his legs.

She veered to the left as two boys pushed off the boards without looking.

She stopped abruptly when a small girl lost her balance and fell right in front of her.

Then she heard a loud voice behind her. "Yikes."

"Wipeout," sang another voice.

"Big-time," said the first voice.

Two girls her age skated by wearing black leggings and tight athletic shirts, stacks of colorful beaded bracelets on their wrists. One of them noticed Wren staring.

"Who's that girl?" Wren heard her ask.

"No idea," answered the other. "And who cares?"

Who cares? thought Wren. *Watch this.*

Wren skated past the bracelet girls. They wobbled as they turned to watch.

Their eyes both fed Wren and made her hungry. She pushed even faster toward center ice.

"Bird," called her dad. "Be careful. This is public skating ice."

Wren nodded. She turned backward into a deep

inside edge. Then she stepped into a layback spin, arms overhead in an open circle, her back deeply arched.

The ceilings lights spun into tight circles.

Wren knew those girls were watching. She exited the spin and smiled right at them.

"Whatever," said one of the girls. "I can do that."

"Really?" asked her friend.

"Of course. It's not that hard. She's just showing off."

The bracelet girl turned backward and tried to find her balance. Her arms wiggled. Her body tilted. But her lips were pressed tight in concentration. She stepped forward on an inside edge and tried to spin.

Wren almost called out for her to stop. Spinning on an inside edge was difficult under the best of circumstances. It was physically impossible the way the girl's body was tilted.

The girl went down. Hard.

"Daphne!" screamed her friend.

Wren stood back as several adults surrounded

Daphne, the fallen girl. She was crying and clutching her wrist.

A man wearing a red skate patrol uniform helped her off the ice. Daphne's friend followed behind. Wren's dad came up next to Wren and put his hands on his waist.

"Poor girl," he said.

"She was showing off," said Wren.

"*She* was the one showing off?"

"Yeah. Didn't you see? That girl had no idea what she was doing."

"Wren," said her dad, "you can tell yourself whatever story you want. But we both know what happened out there."

A tickle of guilt crept into her mind. Maybe it was a little bit her fault.

Or maybe not.

Wren remembered what her dad had said last weekend when she'd landed a double axel. *You make it look like a piece of cake.*

It only looked easy because Wren worked so hard.

Because she trained every day, even when her head throbbed from a hard fall or her legs were exhausted from an earlier workout. It wasn't her fault if people didn't understand that.

Wren skated away and pushed into another layback spin.

Two fewer people on the ice meant more room for her.

That night Wren's family drove into town for dinner. The main street was lined with brightly lit stores and restaurants.

"There it is," said Wren's mom, pointing to a restaurant with funky light fixtures hanging from the ceiling. "That's the place Julie recommended."

"Who's Julie?" asked Wren.

"The woman whose house we're renting. She left us a list of all her favorite places in town."

"That was thoughtful," said Wren's dad.

Wren rolled her eyes.

"Can I get a picture of you girls?" asked Wren's

mom once they were seated at a table. "Just a quick one."

Wren sighed and put her arm around Hannah, posing for the stupid picture. But the flash from the phone reflected off the window behind them and they had to shift over so their mom could try again.

This time Hannah grabbed a breadstick and stuck it up her nose.

"That will not be going on next year's holiday card," said their mom, looking at the image on her phone and laughing. Then she cleared her throat. Put the phone down.

Wren expected her mom to leave the table. To take a minute. Instead, she reached for Wren's hand. "Wren," she said. "We want to talk to you about something."

"It's something good, Bird," said her dad. "Don't look so worried."

"The schools here are closed this week for February break, just like at home," said her mom. "Julie mentioned that there's a theater camp being held at the middle school. It's open to all sixth and seventh graders."

"Yeah," said Wren. "So?"

"Julie's daughter is attending the camp," said Wren's mom. "I thought it might be fun for you. It'll give you something to do during the day. You'll meet some kids your age."

"I don't want to meet kids my age," said Wren. "I don't want to meet anyone here. I just want to skate as much as I can and leave as soon as possible."

Hannah looked down at the breadstick crumbs scattered across the table. Wren didn't want to make Hannah feel bad, but theater camp?

Wren's mom reached for her hand. "I already e-mailed the principal and explained our situation. She responded right away. There's plenty of room in the camp and they'd love to have you."

"No way," said Wren. She wanted to throw something. Or hit someone. But she wasn't little like Hannah. No one would joke about a holiday card picture if Wren poured her glass of water on her mom's head.

Wren looked at her dad. He had to help her.

Instead, he frowned. "I checked online," he said. "That rink we were at is running a hockey camp all week. There's no daytime ice."

"I knew this would happen," said Wren.

Her mom and dad locked eyes. There was an entire silent conversation in their gaze. But it wasn't a conversation about solutions or alternate plans.

Theater camp was the plan. Just like renting the house was the plan.

And there was nothing Wren could do about any of it.

WREN CONTEMPLATES A CRUNCH

Monday morning. Wren woke to the sound of footsteps on the creaky rental house floors. The sky was still dark, and it took her a moment to remember that Hannah had to be at the hospital early that morning.

But as soon as she remembered, Wren sprang out of bed. She needed to give Hannah one last hug before she left.

Hannah was in the kitchen holding her stuffed unicorn by its pink glittery mane. Their dad sat on a red stool drinking coffee. Their mom stared out the front window, her arms wrapped tight around her body.

"Neigh," said Wren.

"Neigh," said Hannah.

"I'm going to come visit you at the hospital this afternoon," said Wren. "I want to meet all your new unicorn friends."

"Okay," said Hannah. "You can."

Wren's mom came over and kissed Wren on the head. "Thank you," she whispered. "I love you."

"I love you, too," said Wren.

Wren was furious at her parents. For dragging her here. For signing her up for theater camp. For messing up her training.

But on top of her anger, covering it like a thin pair of skating tights, was something else: a desire to lean into her mom's arms and stay there forever.

Instead, Wren hugged Hannah, only letting go when headlights shone through the kitchen window.

"The car's here," said her mom. "Time to go, Hannah."

Wren nodded. She gave Hannah one last squeeze. She petted Hannah's unicorn and kissed it good-bye.

Then she walked upstairs to her new old room and got back into bed.

She couldn't stand to watch Hannah leave.

Traffic. Wren's dad didn't think there'd be this much traffic getting to theater camp.

"I should have taken Julie up on her offer to give you a ride," he said.

"Thanks a lot," said Wren.

"Sorry, Bird. Of course I want to take you on your first day. It's just . . ." He dropped his head to the steering wheel. "I kind of want to body check someone. Just slam someone or something, nice and hard."

"So do it," said Wren.

"I'm too old."

"I can do it for you. Will that help?"

Her dad laughed. "I know you're kidding, Bird. But just so we're clear, the last phone call Mom needs right now is that you got kicked out of theater camp. Or that I got arrested."

"I know," said Wren.

Then her dad winked and said, "But thanks for offering."

They didn't speak for the rest of the ride. Wren looked out the window as they drove past large houses with long paved driveways. She missed the rink, of course. But also the wooded path that led to Occom Pond. Lou's and its cinnamon bun scent. The college kids who threw Frisbees on the main green.

The roads here were crowded, but the sidewalks were empty.

There were too many houses and not enough trees.

And then it got even worse.

They arrived at theater camp.

The middle school was a low brick building, separated from the road by a huge empty parking lot. It was all straight lines and hard surfaces. Wren gave it one last try. "Please, Dad. Please let me come to the hospital with you. I'll sit in a corner and read all day. I won't eat. I won't talk. I won't ask to use your phone. Not even once."

"Bird," said her dad. "I need you to be a team

player this week. And we both know . . ."

"There's no *I* in team," muttered Wren.

"Exactly."

The front door was locked. For a second Wren thought she might be saved. But then her dad pushed a silver button on an intercom and the lock released. A small woman wearing gray sweatpants and a baseball cap popped out of a nearby office.

"Hello there," she said. "You must be Wren and company."

"In the flesh," said her dad.

"Wonderful!" said the woman. "I'm Principal Carr. And like I always tell my students, please don't judge a book by its cover. If you've got to work while everyone else is on vacation, you might as well be comfortable doing it."

Wren's dad laughed, like it was some great joke.

In addition to the sweatpants and baseball hat, Principal Carr was not wearing shoes. Her toes pressed through her thin white cotton socks.

What would happen if I accidentally stepped on them?

wondered Wren. *Would there be a crunching sound? Or would they just squish under my boots?*

Then Principal Carr extended her hand. "It's such a pleasure to have you here for the week, Wren," she said.

Principal Carr's fingers were long and frail, like the lead in refillable pencils. The kind that breaks when you push down too hard.

Crunch, decided Wren. Not squish.

"How about I show Wren to the auditorium?" said Principal Carr, looking at Wren's dad. "And allow you to get on with your day."

There it was. The head tilt. The tight smile. The sympathetic eyes. Of course her mom told Principal Carr all about Hannah. Her mom told everyone about Hannah.

Wren's dad nodded and pulled Wren close. "Love you, Bird," he whispered. "You've got this, right?"

"Yeah," said Wren. "I've got this."

She didn't want him to let go.

Being alone on the ice felt like power and

freedom. Being alone in this unknown school felt like punishment.

Wren pulled away.

"Okay," said her dad. "See you this afternoon."

Wren followed Principal Carr. The hallways were lined with metal lockers and the linoleum floors were gray with a million tiny specks. Lights buzzed in their plastic covers.

"Now, Wren," said Principal Carr. "I hear you're staying at Izzy's house. What a nice girl Izzy is. You two must be good friends already."

Or not, thought Wren.

Yesterday Wren had seen Izzy leave the garage apartment and walk her dog down the driveway. Izzy had paused at the end of the driveway and looked up at the window where Wren was standing.

Instead of waving, Wren ducked.

She had no idea if Izzy saw her.

She wasn't even sure why she ducked. It was a split-second decision. Her body reacted before her brain had time to think the action through.

"Here we are," said Principal Carr, pausing in front of a set of doors. "You're in for a treat, Wren. Mr. Blair is one of our finest teachers, and he's got a real passion for drama. It's going to be a great week."

As Principal Carr pushed open one of the doors, its handle releasing a metal-on-metal click, Wren was tempted to run. Down the hall. Into the parking lot.

And then what? Where would she go next? She had no way to get to the hospital and she didn't even know the rental house address.

Wren was trapped.

IZZY AND
THE SUPER-TRAGIC TRAGEDY

From the corner of her eye, Izzy noticed a rectangle of light as the auditorium doors opened. She sank down in her seat and glanced at Phoebe, who had chosen a spot at the far end of Izzy's row. Phoebe's eyes would tell Izzy who was walking in the door: Wren or Daphne. They were the only two people who hadn't been checked off Mr. Blair's attendance list.

If it was Daphne walking through the doors, Phoebe's eyes would flicker with joy. Daphne had broken her wrist ice skating on Saturday and her parents cancelled their ski trip.

"Daphne's super bummed," Phoebe explained that morning when Izzy's mom drove them to theater camp. "But honestly, I'm kind of glad. This week will be so much more fun now. But don't tell Daphne I said that. 'Kay? Promise?"

Izzy promised. And then she'd looked out the car window and thought that having Daphne at theater camp was going to be the opposite of more fun. It was going to be miserable.

If it was Wren walking through the doors, Phoebe's eyes would squint in examination mode. Phoebe had asked Izzy tons of questions about Wren. What did she look like? What was she into? Did she even do theater? But Izzy had no answers. Just yesterday Izzy had seen Wren in the window and waved. And Wren had ducked out of sight.

Izzy's mom had described Wren as quiet and slow to warm up. But Izzy disagreed. A quiet, slow-to-warm-up girl would at least wave back.

The auditorium doors closed. Phoebe turned and squinted. It was Wren.

Izzy sank lower in her seat. She worried that Wren was actually more mean than quiet.

Mr. Blair jumped off the stage where he'd been sitting flipping through pages on his clipboard. "Ah," he said. "A new warrior. Welcome, welcome. You must be Wren. Please join us on the theatrical battlefield."

Wren chose a spot in the back of the auditorium. Izzy glanced at her over the seats. Wren was looking at her lap, her hair hanging loose on either side of her face. When the doors opened again a minute later, Wren didn't move one bit. But Phoebe squealed and clapped her hands. It was Daphne, a blue cast on her left wrist, a stack of beaded bracelets on her right wrist. Next to her was Serena.

"Serena," said Mr. Blair. "To what do we owe the pleasure of your company? I don't see you on my list."

Serena froze. She looked behind her at the closed auditorium doors, as if they might provide an answer. Serena's expression reminded Izzy of Snow Stepper being ripped from Serena's cradled arms, confusion mixed with anger. "My mom signed me up," said

Serena. "She said she signed me up?"

Mr. Blair stuck his pen behind his ear. He flipped a page on his clipboard. "Hmm. Well, fear not. Take a seat and you and I will get this all sorted at break time."

Serena sat next to Daphne and Phoebe. But instead of joining in their conversation, she stared straight ahead, her body stiff, her eyes fixed on the black curtain backdrop.

"Okay then," said Mr. Blair as he walked to the exact center of the stage. "All warriors are now present and accounted for, which means that we can commence with the grand theatrical tradition of the first day icebreaker. And for this morning's festivities, we will be playing two truths and a lie."

Someone behind Izzy groaned, probably Eli or Zach. They groaned about most things. In a row toward the front, Otto bounced happily in his seat. Wren was still way in the back by herself. Other kids were scattered throughout the auditorium in groups of twos and threes, some with their feet pressed against the seat backs in front of them, others with their legs tucked into their chests.

"What was that?" asked Mr. Blair. "Battle cries of excitement? Excellent! Now, the way this works is that I will assign everyone a partner. Please tell your partner two truths and one lie, then your partner will present what they heard to the rest of the group, who will then have to determine what is fact and what is fiction. Are we ready?"

"Ready!" said Otto.

"Wonderful," said Mr. Blair. "Now, for partners may I please have . . ." Mr. Blair paused and drummed on his thighs. Then he started walking up the center aisle, assigning partners from different sections of the auditorium.

Please not Wren, thought Izzy as Mr. Blair stepped closer, calling out name pairs. *Please not Wren*.

"Next I would like Otto and Daphne. Phoebe and Eli. Serena and Zach. And last but not least, Izzy and Wren."

Daphne sighed and threw her head against the back of her seat. Phoebe patted Daphne's shoulder in consolation. Serena leaned over in the opposite direction, as if she was retrieving something from the next seat, but Izzy didn't watch long enough to see what it was. She was too distracted by her pounding heart. *Wren.* She was partners with Wren.

Should she walk to Wren? Or let Wren walk to her? Or maybe they should meet somewhere neutral, like the stage?

Yes, thought Izzy. Neutral would be best. Izzy waited for Otto to tap dance up the aisle toward Daphne, his jazz hands waving. Then she slid between the seats and began to walk, not looking back until she reached the three wide risers that led to the stage.

Wren was a few feet behind, her eyes looking at the floor. Izzy continued up, choosing a spot at the edge of the stage where she could dangle her legs over the side. Wren sat next to her.

"Hi," said Izzy.

"Hey," said Wren.

Izzy was glad she'd chosen that spot. It was better than having to sit facing each other. The decision gave her a boost of confidence. But still, they sat in silence, Wren's feet beating a steady rhythm against the base of the stage.

"I like your leggings," said Izzy.

Wren's leggings were a blue camo pattern, and Izzy really did like them. But mostly she was just looking for something to say. All the other pairs were already talking, sharing their two truths and one lie. When Wren didn't respond, Izzy wished she could take the words back. There were a million more important things she could have said. Like, *Sorry about your little sister.* Or, *Does this feel super weird to you, too?*

But then Wren smiled. "Is that a truth or a lie?"

"A truth," said Izzy.

Wren nodded. "I like your door of stickers."

"Is that a truth or a lie?"

"A truth."

"This is super weird," said Izzy.

"Truth or lie?" asked Wren.

"Do you even need to ask?" said Izzy.

"Not really," said Wren.

They both laughed. It was a laugh that was filled

with so many awkward things—the stage lights shining in their eyes, that they were totally messing up the icebreaker game, that Wren had slept in Izzy's bed the last two nights—so that the laughter grew from a quiet giggle to a full-on explosion.

Mr. Blair looked at them. And so did everyone else.

As Izzy tried to stop laughing, she noticed that Daphne was staring at Wren with a particularly angry look in her eyes. Daphne was usually fake sweet on the outside, especially in front of teachers. But she was glaring right at Wren.

Wren must have noticed, too. "It's sort of my fault that girl broke her wrist," whispered Wren.

"Truth or lie?" asked Izzy, confused.

"Truth," said Wren.

Wren told Izzy about the skating rink and Daphne's fall. Izzy didn't want the story to end. She wasn't happy that Daphne broke her wrist, but she loved being wrapped up in Wren's tale, sitting there on the edge of the stage as part of a pair.

Last year Dr. Forte, the school counselor, had

friendship lunches with the girls in Izzy's class. Every Thursday, Dr. Forte picked ten girls to eat lunch together in her office. They sat in a circle on Dr. Forte's pale green carpet and talked about what it meant to be a good friend, how words can have different meanings depending on how they're said, and how actions that might not seem like a big deal to one person could be hurtful to someone else.

As Dr. Forte chewed on the ends of her tortoiseshell reading glasses and the girls slurped from juice boxes and crunched on chips, they shared stories about times they hadn't been invited to birthday parties or had heard their names whispered from deep inside tight huddles on the playground at recess.

Izzy had been chosen for friendship lunch five times over the school year, and she loved every one of them. Sitting there, kneading a paper napkin between her fingers, the world outside Dr. Forte's office disappeared. Phrases that often swirled in Izzy's own mind—*What did I do wrong? Why don't they like me? Why does it have to be so hard?*—were spoken by other girls.

When the bell rang, signaling the end of lunch period, Izzy often felt dizzy, as if the air inside Dr. Forte's office, with its inspirational posters and potted plants on top of tall metal filing cabinets, was more dense than the rest of the school building. She'd be slow to stand and end up at the back of the line to throw away her trash. But then she'd look up and someone—one time it was Grace, another time it was Serena—would be holding the door open, waiting for her.

As the friendship lunch girls walked back to class, laughing about how if anybody told a fart joke about any one of them the others would totally have her back, Izzy wondered if maybe this was the beginning. Maybe she didn't have to worry so much about Phoebe drifting toward Daphne and leaving her behind. Maybe some girl in friendship lunch would fill the void.

But that hopeful feeling had never lasted very long. Eventually there would be a Monday morning when Izzy learned that she hadn't been invited to a movie or a sleepover. She'd walk through school seeing all the groups that she didn't belong to: the lacrosse team wearing their navy elastic headbands, the orchestra kids practicing to perform at morning assembly, the ballet dancers who'd leave early dismissal slips at Ms. Perry's front desk every Friday in December so they could get to Boston in time to perform in the *Nutcracker*.

At the end of friendship lunch, Dr. Forte loved to say: "Friendships are complicated, girls. Think of them like an ocean wave. They're always changing, rising and falling, but the movement can be beautiful."

One whispered conversation on the edge of the stage didn't count as a friendship. And anyway, if Wren were a wave, Izzy suspected she'd be the really strong kind that can knock you right over.

But as Izzy sat on the auditorium stage scrambling to make up two truths and one lie about Wren, a hard task because they'd been so busy laughing that they'd forgotten the point of the game, she felt a flicker of hope.

Maybe she wouldn't have to spend this week all alone.

WREN'S FIRE

Wren's dad was waiting outside of the school, just like he'd promised. They drove straight to see Hannah.

The hospital was enormous. A maze of hallways and elevators and lobbies. Wren couldn't believe that Hannah was somewhere deep inside.

How would the unicorns possibly find her?

Wren shook her head. Tightened her ponytail. There were no unicorns.

But she desperately wished that there were.

"Almost there," said her dad. He was looking at

the hallway signs and muttering directions to himself. "Just one more elevator and then a left past the cafeteria sign."

"Okay," said Wren, more to herself than to her dad.

"Just remember, Hannah's had a long day. They implanted the wires and she's off her medicine so she's already had a few seizures. Which is good, right? It's all part of the process."

Wren's dad spoke in his coaching voice. With a we-can-do-this pep to his words.

The seizures helped the doctors learn about Hannah's brain. That increased the chances of the surgery being successful. But her dad never looked this tired when he spoke to his hockey team. And when Wren stepped inside Hannah's hospital room, she understood why.

Hannah was asleep. Her head wrapped in white gauze. The same colorful wires that Wren had seen in photos months ago ran down Hannah's cheek. Next to her bed, machines blinked with charts and numbers.

Wren's mom looked up from her chair, her right hand gripping her phone. She stood up and wrapped Wren in a hug.

None of them said a word. But there was an electric hum in the air that made the space feel noisy.

Wren walked over to Hannah and squeezed Hannah's hand. She smelled glue. And a chemical scent. She kissed Hannah's cheek.

When Wren looked back, both her parents were crying.

Wren's mom dabbed her eyes. She wiped her nose with a tissue. "How was theater camp today?" she asked with a forced smile. "Are you hungry? I know I could use some food."

Theater camp felt like a different country, one that Wren could barely remember visiting. And she was not hungry. But she nodded, wanting to get away from the smells and the wires.

As they walked down the hallway, Wren let her mom hold her hand and her dad throw his arm over her shoulder. They moved like a lurching multi-legged creature. Awkward and ambling. But Wren didn't try to wiggle away.

For once, she didn't mind slowing down.

Over dinner in the hospital cafeteria, her parents told Wren that Hannah would be okay.

The doctors were the best in the world.

Someday their stay here would feel like a blip, a hiccup, a long-ago, really tough time.

And Wren tried to believe them.

But something grew inside her.

It started as worry, but it spun into a more familiar feeling.

A restlessness. An ember. A flame.

She needed to skate. Not just to practice her double lutz, but to feel like herself again. Because here, in this cafeteria, in this hospital, in this city, Wren was twitchy and jammed.

Her fire needed air.

By the time Wren and her dad got back to the rental house, it was late. Her dad had to jump on a call with his assistant coaches. Her mom was spending the night with Hannah at the hospital.

Wren went upstairs to Izzy's room. She did three sets of crunches and push-ups. Then she ran through the choreography of her program, the strong electric beats of her music playing in her head.

But Izzy's room was too small. When Wren tried to do even a waltz jump, she crashed into the bed.

So she moved out to the hallway, but it was too narrow. And the rug on the floor provided too much friction.

After spending all day inside the windowless school auditorium and all evening in the car and the hospital, Wren was ready to explode.

She looked out the window, down to the driveway.

It was flat and empty and hard.

Perfect.

Wren zipped up her coat and walked out the back door. She had just landed her third single axel when a dog raced down the driveway and jumped on her, almost knocking Wren over.

Next came Izzy, a leash dangling from her hand. "No, Row!" yelled Izzy.

The dog dropped to the ground and rolled onto his back, his paws scrambling at nothing but the cold night air.

"No, Row!" repeated Izzy. "Bad dog!"

Wren laughed. She scratched the dog's belly. "Is that his name? Noro?"

Izzy smiled. "Just Row. It's a long story. I was taking him out to use the bathroom and he saw you jumping out here. He bolted before I could put on his leash."

"Sorry," said Wren.

"What are you doing anyway?" asked Izzy. "It's freezing. And dark. And . . . freezing."

"Off-ice training," said Wren. "Once I get moving I hardly notice the cold. I've got a really important skating competition in three weeks. So I need to practice however I can. If I were home I'd be skating every day, but here . . ."

Wren looked toward Izzy's house and hoped that

her glance was explanation enough. She was not in the mood to talk about everything the house implied. Hannah's hospital stay. The upcoming surgery. Her parents' worry. Wren's own worry.

Thankfully, Izzy nodded. She knelt down and grabbed Row's collar. "Can you do it again?" she asked. "That jumping thing?"

"Yeah," said Wren.

Nothing compared to being on the ice. But doing jumps on land was better than not practicing at all.

Wren still got to spring and twist. She could give her body that moment of weightlessness that it craved.

Wren took a few mini jumps, then pressed off her bent left leg into a single axel. One-and-a-half turns later, she landed on her right leg, bouncing in place to absorb the impact of her landing.

Izzy let go of Row's collar and clapped.

It was only one clap. Because as soon as Izzy let go, Row bolted.

One second Row was sitting next to Izzy, his tongue hanging lazily out of the side of his mouth, and the next second he was a blur of brown fur running down the driveway toward the street.

"No, Row!" yelled Izzy.

"Come back!" yelled Wren.

Izzy stretched the leash across her forehead, panic in her eyes. She looked back at the garage, then down the driveway to the street, then back at Wren.

Wren made the decision that Izzy could not. "Come on," she said, pulling Izzy's arm. "Let's go."

Together, they ran. Past houses lit from within and underneath streetlights.

They were fast, but Row was faster.

"He's going to the pond," said Izzy, her breath creating tiny puffs of clouds. "It's his favorite place."

"How far?" asked Wren.

"One more block. There's a wood sign that marks a path. He'll turn there."

"Then he'll stop?"

"He better."

Panting, they reached a wooden post. Wren followed Izzy down a path into the woods. The ground was uneven and soft with pine needles. Occasional stones slowed their pace.

It reminded Wren of Occom Pond.

Row sat at the end of the path, lit by moonlight.

He thumped his tail against the dirt as Izzy threw her arms around his neck. "No, Row," said Izzy as she clipped his leash onto his collar and kissed the top of his head. "You're the worst dog in the whole world and I'm never, ever going to forgive you."

Row licked Wren's hand, but Wren barely noticed.

She reached her foot onto the surface of the pond.

It was frozen.

"Does anyone skate here?" asked Wren.

"I'm not sure," said Izzy. "I think I might have gone once, a long time ago."

Once. A long time ago.

So it was possible.

"We should go back," said Izzy.

Wren looked across the pond. Its oval shape. The dense trees beyond. There was an occasional stick frozen into the ice surface, a pebble or two, but it was certainly big enough to skate on. If she planned it right, she might even be able to fit in a double lutz.

Beside her, Izzy began to bounce. She was not wearing a coat.

"Okay," said Wren. "Let's go."

When they got back to Izzy's house, their parents were waiting at the end of the driveway. "Bird," said Wren's dad, wrapping her in his arms. "Thank God."

"I was one second away from calling the police," said Izzy's mom, raising her phone and shaking it side to side.

"What were you thinking?" asked a man who had to be Izzy's dad. He gave Izzy an long kiss on the head.

"Row ran away," explained Izzy. "All the way to Willoway Pond. We had to chase him. It happened so fast."

Wren nodded, her head pressed into her dad's chest. He was wearing his favorite Dartmouth hockey sweatshirt. It was worn and soft. It smelled like home.

But that's not why Wren left her head there. She was thinking about the ice.

And she wanted to stay wrapped in that thought for as long as possible.

"I'm so sorry," said Izzy's mom. "This was the last thing you needed to worry about."

"They're back now," said Wren's dad, hugging her tight. "It's all good."

"So we're still on for tomorrow morning?" asked Izzy's mom.

"Sure thing," said Wren's dad.

After Wren said good-bye to Izzy and walked with her dad into the house, she asked, "On for what?"

"Izzy's older brother is going to drive you guys to theater camp tomorrow morning," said her dad. "That okay?"

Wren nodded. She didn't care about theater camp or how she got there. "There's a pond two blocks away," she blurted out. "It was frozen."

"Was it cleared for skating? Like Occom Pond?"

"I don't know," said Wren. She did know. Occom

Pond had all kinds of signs warning people not to skate unless the ice was marked safe with green flags.

This pond had no signs. No flags. But the ice felt just as solid as Occom Pond. And Izzy seemed to remember skating there.

"Well then," said her dad as he woke his sleeping laptop. "End of discussion."

For now, thought Wren.

She walked upstairs to Izzy's room and threw her jacket on the floor. Her muscles were warm and she placed her foot on Izzy's desk to stretch the back of her legs. But as she brought her chest to her shin, her foot slipped and caught on the handle of a drawer.

The drawer skidded open just a crack.

Wren lowered her foot. She meant to close the drawer, but inside she saw a single piece of paper. It was facedown, but the imprint of colorful marker shone through.

Wren couldn't resist looking.

It was a drawing of two stick figure girls. Each girl had a colorful stack of beaded bracelets on her wrist.

One stick figure girl was holding a bright pink mitten with a word bubble that said: WHAT IF I CATCH HER GROSSNESS? The other stick figure girl said: THEN I'LL DITCH YOU IN A HEARTBEAT.

Wren smiled. She'd never seen stick figures with such attitude.

She almost slid the drawing back in the drawer. But it was odd that there was just one sheet of paper, all alone.

Maybe this page was part of a story and Izzy had left it behind by mistake?

She would give it to Izzy at theater camp tomorrow and find out what those stick figures were talking about.

Wren placed the piece of paper on top of her jacket so she wouldn't forget. As the sassy stick figures came to rest, Wren tingled with something other than dread when she imagined the rest of the week.

A touch of excitement.

IZZY IN PARENTHESIS

"Quick pit stop," said Nate on Tuesday morning as they turned down the street toward Starbucks.

Izzy glanced at Wren, who was sitting next to her in the backseat. "He wants to see a girl," she said.

"What was that?" asked Nate. He turned down the music that was blaring a never-ending guitar medley. "You're in awe of my superior driving skills and my refined taste in caffeine?"

"Not exactly," said Izzy.

Nate turned the music back up. "Sorry," he said, shrugging. "Can't hear you."

Izzy smiled. Izzy was glad that Phoebe was driving separately for the rest of the week. Apparently Phoebe convinced her mom that she deserved every last minute of sleep since it was technically vacation week. And she glad that Nate was driving to theater camp instead of Izzy's mom. Even though Nate was making them stop at Starbucks and they'd probably be late, things were easier with Nate around. If Izzy's mom were driving, she'd be glancing at Izzy and Wren through the rearview mirror, her eyes searching for clues. Were Izzy and Wren talking? Were they becoming friends? Was that a laugh she heard?

When Nate looked in the rearview mirror, it was to yell at a car that was driving too close. And he played the music so loudly that Izzy and Wren could barely talk. After all her recent carpools with Phoebe, feeling like she was always on the verge of saying the wrong thing or not knowing the answer to an impossible question, it was a relief just to sit next to Wren, their bags on the seat between them, and look out the window.

"Arrived," said Nate as he parked in front of

Starbucks. "You guys wait in the car."

"No way," said Izzy. "That's not fair."

Nate huffed. "Fine. Come in. But be cool, okay?"

Izzy and Wren waited by the door while Nate walked up to the counter. He snapped his wallet, open and shut. Open and shut.

"He's got a crush on that girl, Simone," said Izzy. "The one with the gray yarn on her apron and all the earrings. I think she's in college."

"Is he going to talk to her?" asked Wren.

Izzy shook her head. "He just orders, does this smile thing, and leaves."

"Then how do you know he has a crush?"

Because it's obvious, thought Izzy. It's in the way his cheeks flush and he fiddles with his hair. The snapping of his wallet. How he saves all the money he makes from refereeing youth soccer except for the twenty dollars a week that he calls his "crucial coffee fund."

Izzy had done doodles of Nate holding a Starbucks coffee cup with two big red hearts in the place of eyes. But she'd never shown the drawings to him.

Nate's crush wasn't like the crushes at school, where the whole point was to get the other person to know you like them and then deny the crush as soon as that other person found out.

Nate's crush was something that he wanted to keep secret, even from his friends. A few weeks ago, Izzy and Nate had been out for pizza with Nate's friend Tom when Izzy spotted Simone walking with three other girls, all of them carrying bags with the Wellesley College logo. The bags were tan with blue straps and the Wellesley College girls always carried them around town. The bags weren't all that pretty, but the way the girls carried them over their shoulders, stuffed full of laptops and notebooks, made Izzy jealous, and a little worried. Bracelets, headbands, bags. Maybe it never ended?

Nate and Tom had been debating whether the referee from last week's indoor soccer game had it in for them when Izzy elbowed Nate in the side, nodding toward Simone. Nate froze.

"Dude, you good?" asked Tom.

Nate nodded. He began walking again, at a faster

pace. "Totally. Thought I had something in my shoe. My bad."

Izzy was tempted to tell Tom about Simone. To point Simone out with an ooh-la-la tone to her voice. When she didn't, the look of relief in Nate's eyes was worth her silence. Nate was normally the one who looked out for her, especially in public. He let Izzy tag along to get pizza with his friends and sit in the front seat of the car when he picked her up from school.

Even now, telling Wren about Nate's crush, Izzy worried that she was betraying Nate. But Wren was not Tom. Wren was not Phoebe. Wren had popped into Izzy's life and would pop right back out in four more days.

Surprisingly, the thought made Izzy a little sad. But also grateful. Wren was safe.

Mr. Blair made a trumpeting noise with his hands circling his mouth. "Warriors, gather with me on the stage. The time is drawing near for today's theatrical battle. We know the players, we know the location, but do we know how it will all unfold? No! We do not!"

"Do we care?" whispered Wren. "No! We do not!"

Izzy laughed and followed Wren up the risers to the stage. Daphne and Phoebe walked up the opposite risers, with Serena behind them. Daphne held her blue cast and glared at Wren.

Once again, the look made Izzy nervous, but Wren didn't seem to care. They reached the stage and sat down. Wren spread her legs wide and stretched her chest to the floor. Izzy picked at some dirt that was wedged between the wood planks. When Izzy looked up, Phoebe was fiddling with the stack of bracelets on her wrist and staring at her. There was a hint of warning in Phoebe's dark brown eyes.

Izzy wanted to shrug it off, like Wren would. Instead, the opposite happened.

Phoebe's gaze seeped deep into Izzy's body.

"Now, warriors," said Mr. Blair. "Sadly, one week does not give us enough time to perform an entire production. My deepest apologies to the theater gods. What I am handing out now is a scene from the classic novel *Little Women*, which I have taken the liberty of altering to fit the needs of our esteemed group. We will be working on this scene for the remainder of the week. I would like everyone to read it through, then write down on an index card the part that you would most like to play. I can't promise you'll get your first choice. But I will do my best."

Mr. Blair passed out stacks of stapled pages and blank index cards. The first page listed the cast, along with a description of the characters in parenthesis:

Amy March (artistic)
Jo March (spirited)
Meg March (gentle)
Beth March (shy)
Jenny Snow (meddling)
Laurie (friendly)
Mrs. March (nurturing)
Mr. Davis (strict)
Student 1, 2, 3
Townsperson 1, 2, 3

As Izzy looked at the list of names, she wondered what someone would write in parenthesis about her? Creative? Nice? Or would they describe her differently? Loner? Quiet? A part that no one would choose to play.

Izzy began to read. The scene started at the house of the four March sisters. Amy (artistic) is complaining because she doesn't have money to buy pickled limes like all the other girls at school. Her sister Meg (gentle) takes pity on Amy and lends Amy money to buy the limes. When Amy gets to school, Jenny Snow (meddling) tells the teacher Mr. Davis (strict) that Amy is hiding forbidden limes in her desk. Mr. Davis punishes Amy by making Amy throw her precious limes out the window. Then he smacks Amy's hands and tells her to stand in front of the class until recess. When Amy gets home, Mrs. March (nurturing) and Amy's sisters provide comfort and Mrs. March tells Amy that she never has to go back to that school. Jo (spirited) goes to collect Amy's things from Mr. Davis. The scene concludes with Laurie (friendly) and the March sisters gathered together singing and laughing.

Izzy was almost done reading when Otto tapped her on the shoulder. "You should go for Amy," he whispered.

"Why?" asked Izzy.

"Because the script says she's artistic and you're the best artist in our grade. Everyone knows that. You'd be good at playing her."

"Thanks," said Izzy.

Otto nodded. "You're welcome." He drummed his hands against the stage and went back to reading.

The best artist in our grade. There was no art award at the end of year assembly or art team to try out for. They didn't even get letter grades in art, just a simple pass or fail. But Otto wasn't mocking her or trying to make it seem like kids were talking about Izzy behind her back. It was one of his Otto statements that passed from his mind to his lips in one straight line, not the swirls and zigzags that Izzy sometimes felt.

Izzy read the last few sentences and flipped back to the list of characters. She looked down at her blank index card. Pickled limes sounded tangy and gross.

Just thinking about eating one made Izzy shiver. But Amy's lines about wanting to keep up with the girls who brought pickled limes to school made Izzy think of beaded bracelets and lacrosse team headbands, even the matching Wellesley College bags. All the objects that separated those who were part of the group, from those who weren't.

It wasn't just Amy's love of art that Izzy recognized; it was her longing to belong. After a moment of hesitation, Izzy wrote *Amy* in Dori's favorite bubble letters. She added a heart off to the side for good luck.

Halfway through the morning, as Mr. Blair struggled in the dark to get his laptop to play the pickled lime scene from the movie version of *Little Women*, Izzy left the auditorium to use the bathroom. The lights in the hallway were bright, so at first Izzy didn't notice that Daphne and Phoebe were standing next to the pile of bags, Daphne shaking her head, Phoebe with her hands stacked on one popped hip. By the time Izzy saw them, it was too late to turn around. She'd been spotted.

"OMG, Izzy," said Phoebe. "What. Is. This?" Phoebe held a white piece of paper in her hand, her stack of bracelets on her wrist. The paper was worn, not crisp, so it bent in half.

Izzy shook her head, confused.

Phoebe straightened the page, pinching the top and bottom, and shoved it close to Izzy's face. It was one of Izzy's stick figure drawings. She'd drawn it after walking to Daphne's to return Phoebe's pink mitten, but she'd never finished it. She got distracted with a better drawing of a girl with one mitten falling into winter slush.

The last thing Izzy remembered was putting that drawing in her desk drawer. Except she'd moved all her drawings into the garage apartment. Had she left this one by accident? Still, how did Phoebe have it?

Izzy reached for the drawing, but Phoebe moved it away. "How could you do this to me?" said Phoebe.

"I didn't do anything," said Izzy.

"Oh, really?" said Daphne. "So those two girls with the bracelets aren't supposed to be me and Phoebe?

Because I know that's Phoebe's pink mitten and I know you're the one who drew this. And just for the record, I would never ditch Phoebe even if she did catch your grossness. She's one of my best friends ever."

"God, Izzy," said Phoebe, shaking her head. "When did you become such a bully?"

Izzy stepped back, leaning her back against a locker. *A bully?* It was just a drawing. It was her thoughts and feelings on a page. No one was supposed to see them, not ever.

"Where did you find that?" asked Izzy.

Phoebe shrugged. "Wren gave it to us."

"I don't believe you," said Izzy.

"Why wouldn't she?" asked Daphne. "Wren obviously knew it was a drawing of us and she thought we might want it."

"No," said Izzy. Wren barely looked at Phoebe and Daphne, and she certainly never spoke to them. Why would she give them the drawing?

"We could go talk to Mr. Blair about it," said Phoebe. "If you want to. He'd probably love to see this."

Daphne smiled. Then she shook her head. "Don't worry, Izzy. We won't tell anyone. Unlike you, we don't enjoy being mean to other people. But I think I'll keep this. Just in case we need it later." With one wrist in a cast and the other wrist loaded with bracelets, Daphne folded the paper in quarters and slid the drawing into her back pocket.

Together, Daphne and Phoebe returned to the auditorium. Gentle music played through the open doors. Izzy sank down to the hallway floor and dropped her head to her knees. With that piece of paper in her back pocket, Daphne could easily make her into a mean girl.

Izzy (mean).

In her heart, Izzy knew she was the opposite of that. Her drawings were everything she felt but didn't know how to explain, or even who to tell. Was she supposed to keep it all inside? Or be like Dori, drawing cute, cuddly things that only exist in some pretend, pastel world of joy?

A world totally different from the one Izzy actually lived in.

WELCOME TO PLANET WREN

The *Little Women* scene had been playing for a few minutes before Wren couldn't take it anymore. All those sisters in their bonnets and capes trudging through the snow. She needed to get out of there.

The school hallways were wide and flat, like Izzy's driveway, but better. Less friction. Wren wanted to take off her shoes and do axels in her socks. Or scratch spins. Or anything.

She glanced at Mr. Blair. He was sitting in the front row, flipping through the stack of index cards and writing notes on his clipboard. Izzy and some other kids had already snuck out. He'd never know Wren was gone.

Wren stepped into the hallway and saw Izzy slouched against the lockers. "That movie is so boring," said Wren. "Never go back."

"Did you find one of my drawings?" asked Izzy.

Wren slapped her forehead. She walked toward the pile where everyone threw their bags. "I forgot to give it to you this morning. It's right here."

"No, it's not."

"What?"

"Daphne and Phoebe have it," said Izzy. "They said you gave it to them."

Wren froze. "No way," she said. "I would never give them anything."

Wren picked up her bag. The zipper was open. The drawing that she'd tucked inside the main pocket was missing.

Those girls had gone into her bag and stolen Izzy's drawing.

Wren wanted to pull Izzy from the floor and go find them. But Izzy's bottom lip was trembling.

Her head shaking back and forth.

"They're so mad at me," said Izzy. "They're never going to forget this."

"Why?" asked Wren. "It's just a drawing."

Izzy looked up, her eyes wet with tears. "It's not just a drawing. It's a drawing of them. And now they think I'm a bully and they're going to show the drawing to everyone and use it against me. I know it. It's bad enough that I have no friends; now everyone's actually going to hate me."

"That's not true," said Wren. But even as she said it, she knew that Izzy had a point. Girls like Daphne and Phoebe didn't let insults go forgotten.

"I'm really sorry," said Wren. "I didn't realize. I found the drawing in your desk last night and thought you might be looking for it. I was going to give it to you this morning, but I guess the Nate crush thing distracted me."

Wren smiled, and she really hoped Izzy would, too.

Instead, Izzy stood up. Tears ran down her cheeks.

"This is my life," said Izzy. "You can't steal my room, steal my drawings, and ruin everything. I wish you would just leave me alone forever."

"*I'm* ruining everything?" said Wren. "They're the ones who went into my bag. You're the one who drew the picture. How is it my fault?"

Izzy wiped her cheeks. "Because you're the one who brought the drawing to school." She turned to walk away, down the hallway toward who knows where.

Wren couldn't just let her go. "Hey, Izzy," she called. "Truth or lie?"

Izzy stopped walking, but she didn't answer.

"Okay, truth," said Wren. "Maybe there's a reason you don't have any friends."

The words left Wren's mouth sharp and glistening, like the toe pick of her skate blade aiming for the ice before a jump, its sole purpose to dig deep and lift Wren up.

But it only took an instant for Wren to know what was coming next: a crash landing. A painful thud.

Izzy's shoulders shook. She took a few slow steps, then began to run.

And Wren wished she could take the words back.

Wren sat in the hallway for ten minutes. Twenty

minutes. The red numbers on the clock above the lockers flipped in a steady pace.

And still, no Izzy.

After half an hour, the doors to the auditorium opened and everyone spilled out, heading to their bags for food. Daphne and Phoebe wore triumphant grins. Serena walked a few steps behind them. Zach and Eli tried to trip each other. Then came Otto, the one who was always moving.

That is, until Otto changed course and sat down next to Wren.

"You're new," said Otto.

Wren did not answer. Otto did not take the hint.

He raised one finger to the corner of his mouth. "Not to this planet," he said. "Unless, maybe you are new to this planet." He tilted his head to the side and formed pretend binoculars with his hands, focusing them in a rotating movement. "Interesting. She does not talk. She does not eat. Has she come to take over our realm?"

Wren smiled. She couldn't help it. If anyone was from another planet, it was Otto. It would be an odd planet. But not a mean one. There was too much joy in Otto's voice for meanness.

Otto pushed himself up, his body as rigid as possible. "Snack," he said. "Must get snack. Human beings need food. Will return soon." With his legs swinging in a side-to-side motion, Otto robot-walked to the pile of bags.

Wren's stomach growled. But there was no way she was walking over to get her snack. What if Izzy suddenly returned and saw her standing near Daphne and Phoebe? It was too risky.

Snack in hand, Otto robot-walked back. He sat down in one smooth motion. "Pretzels," he said. "Crunchy human food, good human food. Space invader want to try one?"

Wren smelled salt and yeast. She couldn't resist. "Thanks," she said as she reached her hand into Otto's pretzel bag.

"She speaks our language! It's a galactic miracle!" Otto threw both hands into the air. As his pretzels spilled, Wren laughed, the worry and anger and tension in her body escaping through her mouth.

Otto, no longer a robot, tossed a fresh handful of pretzels into the air like they were confetti. As they fell onto Wren's head and body, she laughed even harder.

Wren wiped the pretzels from her leg. When she looked up, she saw Izzy peering around the corner.

Wren swallowed a pretzel.

She swallowed her laughter.

But it was too late; Izzy disappeared again.

Otto put his pretzel bag down. He pulled on the ends of his lips making an exaggerated clown frown. "Space alien sad?"

A simple question. But in real life, as an actual human being, the answer was complicated. Wren was sad, but with a ton of other emotions as well. Anger, regret, confusion, sadness: they all floated in the hallway like the confetti pretzels.

And Wren didn't want to stick around for them to fall on her head.

"Get a life," she said.

She walked back into the auditorium. All alone.

Just how she wanted to stay for the rest of the week.

IZZY REACHES FOR RED

Nate picked Izzy up from theater camp. Luckily he was in one of his guitar music blaring moods and Izzy didn't have to say anything other than "Hey" and "Okay" for the entire ride home. Nate dropped her at the garage apartment, then reversed down the driveway, off to see Tom, or stare at Simone, or whatever. Nate had tons of options. Izzy had a narrow staircase to climb all by herself.

As she walked up the creaky wooden stairs, Izzy heard Row's paws scrambling across the floor and her mom yell, "No, Row!"

They were sounds Izzy had heard her entire life, as familiar as the dents in her butterfly tin. Izzy climbed a little faster. There was a good chance that she would get to the top of the stairs and find chocolate chip cookies baking in the toaster oven. Maybe her mom would sit with her at the folding table and Izzy would recount everything that had happened that day. And, just like when Izzy was little, her mom would know exactly what to do.

But when Izzy opened the door at the top of the staircase, there were no cookies. The folding table was pushed to the corner and her mom was standing on a chair with her fancy camera in her hands.

"Thank goodness you're home," she said. "Can you grab Row? He keeps ruining my shots and the lighting's perfect right now. I only have a few minutes to get this."

Izzy put her bag on the folding table and told Row to sit. Her mom's camera lens was trained on Izzy's sleeping space, which had been transformed. The polka dot curtain was tied back with a wide navy ribbon, and the air mattress was styled with funky patterned pillows that Izzy recognized from Phoebe's basement. Her butterfly tin was in the center of the overturned wooden crate and a string of twinkle lights looped across the wall right below the ceiling. Below the lights, a dozen Polaroid-style photos of Izzy and Phoebe were taped to the wall with floral washi tape.

"I hope you don't mind that I reprinted some old pictures," said Izzy's mom from behind the camera. "It hit me this morning that I could photograph the garage apartment for my website. I'm going to make a 'glamping chic' section as a way to show my range of styles. Here, look."

Izzy looked into the camera's square screen and a different world emerged. The sunlight pouring across the floor and the pictures on the wall made it look like some cool girl was about to belly flop onto the mattress to text her friends. She'd roll onto her back as she smiled about all the different group chats she had to juggle.

This cool space that her mom had created and the girl who belonged there were the opposite of Izzy. And suddenly, Izzy did not want to tell her mom what had happened at theater camp that afternoon. It was too embarrassing even to share with her mom.

"Looks awesome," said Izzy.

Her mom smiled. "Thanks. It really does. Next up is Nate's space. Wish me luck."

But her mom didn't need luck. She knew exactly how to fix problems. Money troubles? Rent your house. Stuck in an ugly situation? Some new throw pillows might help. Want to attract clients? Win them over with your wide range of cool styles.

And then there was Izzy, who was left peeling pictures of an ex-best friend off the wall, with nothing to put in their place.

That evening Row scratched at the garage apartment door. "No, Row," said Izzy. "We're not doing that again." She stood up from the folding table where she'd been drawing and pulled Row's collar until he collapsed on the floor next to her chair.

Her dad was still at work and her mom was at book

club. Nate hung from a wooden beam doing pull-ups and grunting out numbers. "Five, four, three, two, one. Done." Nate dropped to the floor.

"Do you want a medal?" asked Izzy. "Or a trophy?"

"Dude," said Nate. "Cheer up. And also, respect the biceps." Nate flexed his arm, showing off his muscles.

Izzy rolled her eyes and went back to her Draw Sweet tutorial of a dancing cupcake with a pink hair bow. After the day she'd had, Dori and her smiling objects were all it felt safe to draw. Following along, Izzy wrote, "Hope You Had a Yummy Day" in bubble letters underneath the cupcake.

The drawing was safe, but it was also babyish and stupid. Cupcakes didn't do kick lines or wear hair bows. They didn't have huge eyes with thick eyelashes. Izzy grabbed a black Sharpie from her butterfly tin. She crossed out "Yummy" and wrote "Horrible" instead.

And she felt a tiny bit better. Maybe Daphne and Phoebe had a point? Maybe Izzy was mean?

She was about to start a new drawing when Nate peered over her shoulder. He made a gross *glug glug* sound as he downed a glass of milk. "Interesting," said Nate, wiping his mouth with his forearm. "You've got a dark side, Iz. Never would have guessed it."

"Why? Because you think I'm little and stupid?"

"Hell, no," said Nate. "I think you're little and awesome. At least some of the time. But you're not usually so bummed out. Spill it."

Nate sat down at the folding table with a bowl of Raisin Bran and spooned overflowing loads of cereal into his mouth. Izzy stared at the metal spoon diving in and out of the milk. Did she want to tell Nate what had happened? Not really. But Nate was right; she was so bummed. More than bummed. She was terrified about what was going to happen next.

All afternoon Izzy had been replaying the image of Daphne folding the drawing into quarters and sliding it into her back pocket. Izzy's name wasn't on the drawing. She could always deny making it if she got in trouble with a teacher. But it wasn't only the teachers Izzy was worried about. She was worried about the other kids. Girls like Serena who were totally on Team

Daphne. Boys like Eli and Zach who loved to catch a whisper of someone else's mistake and spread it around school. Even Otto, who was suddenly all friendly with Wren, would probably think she was a bully.

And then there was Wren herself. She would be leaving soon, of course. But Izzy cared what Wren thought about her. Last night, racing to Willoway Pond to catch Row, they'd laughed so hard, a kind of laugh where nothing else mattered in the world. And when they got back to the house and their parents were waiting for them in the driveway, Izzy had felt the same thing as when they'd sat with their legs dangling over the edge of the stage after two truths and a lie: hope that she'd made a new friend.

Izzy hadn't meant to be so mean to Wren. But when Phoebe shoved that drawing in her face, the gray metal of the lockers and the linoleum floors closed in on her, and the only way Izzy could breathe again was to blame someone else for what had happened. Even if it wasn't entirely Wren's fault.

"Come on, Iz," said Nate. "You can tell me."

Izzy hesitated. Nate was in high school, and popular, but he was also her brother. Izzy remembered the chart on his wall where he would get a sticker for every night that he didn't wet the bed, the speech therapist that he had to see for years because he couldn't say his *l*'s, the time he knocked over an entire gallon of milk when he didn't make the sixth-grade travel soccer team. So Izzy spilled it. Then she slid her stack of stick figure drawings out from under her air mattress and spread them on the folding table for Nate to see.

Nate looked through the first few with the spoon gripped between his lips, a serious look in his eyes. Then he dropped the spoon and started to laugh.

"What?" asked Izzy. "What's so funny?"

She almost gathered the drawings back up. But Nate stopped her. "All of it is funny. The hair flips, the attitude. If I saw these stick figures in a dark alley, I'd probably run the other way and start crying for Mom."

Nate turned his chair so that his arms leaned over the back. "Listen, Iz," he continued. "Everything you just said about Phoebe and Wren and whoever else was all about what *they* did to *you*. *They* ditched you. *They* wear matching stuff. *They* didn't invite you inside. You don't have to just take it. If you can send stick figures hurtling down a spiked mountainside, you must have some fight in you. At least these drawings say something."

"They do?"

Nate nodded. "More than a cupcake wearing a hair bow. Keep going. But add in some kind of superhero. He could be devastatingly handsome with ripped abs. You might want to call him Nate. Just a suggestion."

Izzy flipped through her drawings. The turned backs, the eye rolls, all the judgment. Izzy drew those stick figures saying mean things because she didn't want what they represented stuck inside her head.

But what if Nate had a point? What if she reworked the drawings? Added a superhero? Someone to fight back? Would she feel even better?

Izzy picked a red Sharpie from the butterfly tin. Izzy didn't draw with red very often. She used it mostly for flower petals and eyes in the shape of hearts, but it felt like the right color for a superhero cape. The point was crisp, the color strong. But as Izzy brought the Sharpie to a clean piece of paper, she couldn't decide what the superhero should look like.

Not Nate. She was sure about that. But should it be a person? Or maybe an animal? Row could make a great superhero. Izzy could turn his floppy ears into wings and send him flying through the land. Or maybe she should create some kind of masked girl wearing all black with a flowing red cape?

Izzy tapped the Sharpie against the folding table. Row perked up at the noise, thumping his tail as if he might get to go out for a walk. It was around this time last night that Row took off for Willoway Pond. Izzy remembered hesitating, unsure of what to do. Yell for her mom? Chase after Row? But then Wren had pulled her arm with a we've-got-this sparkle in her eye.

Izzy put down the red Sharpie. She picked up a pencil that her mom had left behind. With a light grip, Izzy began to sketch the rectangular shapes of her driveway and house, a few round hydrangea bushes and the large maple tree with its bare branches. She drew Row, his tail wagging, and Wren right behind him, her arms pumping. She placed Row and Wren close to the street, so they were more outlines than detailed people. Then she began to draw herself. But how? From what angle?

Izzy was never great at drawing bodies; that's why she liked the stick figures. But even if Izzy made herself a stick figure, how would she draw her own face? Would she make herself super pretty with long, Draw Sweet lashes and perfectly round eyes? Or would she add the bumps on her forehead and her way-too-thick eyebrows? The last time she'd drawn her own face was for a self-portrait assignment in second grade. Everyone loved her drawing, oohing and aahing over her oval face when most kids drew circles, and the slope of her nose when most drew harsh triangles.

Izzy wanted the oohs and aahs. But she wanted something else: to be proud of what she drew. Not because it looked realistic, but because it reflected the girl she wanted to be.

Someone with friends, who knew what to do next.

WREN'S LONG LIST

The good thing about Wednesday morning was Wren didn't have to get a ride with Izzy. Her dad dropped her off at theater camp on his way to the hospital.

The bad thing was she still had to go to theater camp. She had to see Izzy. And Daphne and Phoebe. And Otto.

The list of people who Wren did not want to spend time with was long.

But as she opened the auditorium doors, her eyes searched for one of them in particular: Izzy. She sat a few rows back from the stage, drawing on the sole of her shoe with a pen. What was she drawing? Hearts? Stars? Arrows dripping blood?

Before Wren could get close enough to tell, the lights in the auditorium switched off and on. Off and on. Mr Blair's voice boomed over the sound system. "Theatrical warriors, please gather on the stage to receive your parts and scripts. We will then embark on a full cast read-through of our very own, very special *Little Women* scene. I don't expect you to memorize your lines, but I do expect you to absorb them. To embody them. To make each and every word count."

Wren had written "Townsperson 3" on her blank index card. She'd figured a character unworthy of a unique name probably had the least amount of lines. She hoped Mr. Blair wasn't going to punish her by giving her an actual part. With an actual name.

The auditorium now fully illuminated, Wren hung back as the other kids walked up the risers and settled across the stage.

Daphne, Phoebe, and Serena wandered off to the left side. Daphne sat slowly, holding her blue cast in the air as she sank down. Phoebe and Serena sat on either side of her.

Zach and Eli walked to center stage. They laid on their backs like dead snow angels.

Izzy sat crisscross on the right side of the stage. Otto crossed one leg over the other, did a full spin, and then plopped down next to her.

Wren let everyone else fill in the gaps while she tried to decide on the right place to sit. She ended up near Izzy. Not close enough that it seemed like she wanted to sit next to Izzy, but not far enough that it seemed like she wanted to sit next to Daphne and Phoebe.

It turned out there was no right place to sit. There was only a least-wrong place.

Mr. Blair stood in the middle of the stage holding a pile of scripts. He cleared his throat and handed the top script to Izzy. "Congratulations to our Amy," he said. "May your love of pickled limes flourish forever."

Izzy smiled and blushed. She put the script in her lap and immediately began to flip through the pages.

Wren smiled, too. But Izzy didn't look in her direction to notice.

Phoebe recrossed her legs. "Pickled limes," she said, puckering her lips and shuddering. "Disgusting."

"Amy just wants the popular girls to like her," said Daphne, loud enough for everyone to hear. "It's the perfect role for Izzy."

Izzy stopped flipping. Her cheeks reddened.

Mr. Blair flicked his head toward Daphne. Daphne dropped her gaze, but she bit her lower lip to hide a smile.

Wren's hands clenched into a fist. She thought of her dad's hockey players and how they sometimes had to be held back from throwing punches during intense games. Wren wasn't going to punch Daphne. But she understood the urge.

Mr. Blair walked over to Daphne, planting his feet firmly in front of her. He held out Daphne's script. "And here we have our shy, humble, sweet Beth. Someone who thinks of others first and herself last. I trust that you will be able to do the part justice, Daphne?" Daphne reached up for the script, but Mr. Blair did not release his grip on the pages until Daphne nodded and whispered, "Yes."

Wren was cast as Townsperson 3. She flipped through her script, pretending to focus on her irrelevant lines about the recent cold spell and the town's supply of fresh bread.

She was actually scanning Izzy's and Daphne's lines. Wren hadn't read the scene when Mr. Blair handed it out yesterday, and she'd snuck out of the movie. She kept hoping that Beth would have to get down on her hands and knees and beg Amy for help. Or advice. Or, best of all, forgiveness.

But the scene ended with all four March sisters sitting around the kitchen table, happy as Laurie sang and a gentle snow fell outside the window.

Daphne begging for anything was as unlikely as craving pickled limes.

Wren wanted to tear the script in half.

Instead, she spent the rest of the day listening to lines about "tender hearts" and "grave countenances."

She rolled her eyes as Mr. Blair encouraged her to "Breathe some life into Townsperson Three's words. Make them soar."

Wren wanted to soar. Just not with words.

By the time her dad pulled into the parking lot at the end of the day, Wren was bursting with energy. She'd been so careful all day. Careful to avoid eye contact with Izzy, to keep her distance from Daphne, to not smile when Otto begged Mr. Blair to end the scene with a tap dance number.

Her body was stiff from the effort. It craved movement.

Wren flung the car door open, buckled her seat belt, and asked, "Can we skip the hospital today? Please. Can you check your phone for a rink?"

"Whoa, Bird," said her dad. "How about a hello?"

"Hello," said Wren in the same flat tone she'd used for Townsperson 3.

"Hello to you, too," said her dad. "How was your day?"

"Dad, quit it. Just answer my question."

He sighed. There was defeat in his exhale and the slow way he shook his head. "Not today, Bird."

"Is Hannah okay?" Wren shifted nervously in

her seat, the seat belt tightening against her chest. She hadn't thought about Hannah all day. What if something happened?

"Hannah's okay," said her dad. "The therapy dogs came today, which was fun. And they're getting some good reads on her brain activity. Looks like they might operate soon. Maybe even tomorrow."

These were all positive things—therapy dogs, seizures that sent signals, even scheduling the brain surgery. Wren shifted to face her dad. "So why can't we try to find a rink?"

"Oh man, Bird. I wish we could. But Mom wants to sleep at the house tonight. She's desperate for a full night's rest and a decent shower. We were planning to have dinner in the cafeteria. Then you and Mom would go back to the house."

Wren looked out the window. She pressed her palms against her thighs.

"Let's just get through today," continued her dad. "Then we'll see if we can find someplace to skate. Maybe on Friday."

He lifted one hand off the steering wheel and held out his pinky finger, expecting Wren to link her pinky in his. Wren kept her hands on her thighs. If Hannah had her surgery tomorrow, there was no way they'd find a rink the day after. And they both knew it.

Pinky promises were weak, just like the fingers they were named after.

After dinner in the hospital cafeteria, as Wren's mom was kissing Hannah good-bye, Hannah had a seizure. Her arms flailed, her legs went rigid. The machines in the corner of her room lit up with electric numbers. A nurse stepped into the room. She gave Wren's family a tight-lipped smile of sympathy.

There was nothing to do but wait it out.

Wren held Hannah's hand. Her mom knelt at the edge of the bed. Her dad stroked Hannah's leg.

Then, almost as quickly as the seizure came, it ended.

And Wren's mom needed a minute.

The result? She just couldn't leave Hannah.

So Wren and her dad walked back to the car, carrying a pile of her mom's dirty laundry. On the ride back to Izzy's house, Wren thought about sectionals. The podium. Her double lutz.

As soon as they got to the house, Wren's dad went into the living room to Skype with his assistant coaches. And Wren saw her chance.

She grabbed her skating bag. It was still right where she'd left it days ago at the mudroom door.

She didn't ask permission to leave. Wren knew what her dad would say, and she did not want to hear the answer.

Slowly, quietly, she opened the back door. After days of following everyone else's plan, Wren was making her own plan.

The air wasn't as cold as the night before, but it felt just as biting.

The first steps were the hardest. The plastic wheels of her skating bag ground against the driveway and Wren worried that Row might hear and come sprinting out again.

That was the last thing Wren needed.

She kept her head down, her shoulders hunched.

When Wren made it to the end of the driveway, she looked back. The lights were on over the garage. Maybe Izzy was somewhere inside practicing her lines? Maybe she was thinking about the drawing? Or Daphne's mean comment that day about her play part?

But there was nothing Wren could do about that.

She turned left at the sidewalk. Through a window she saw her dad talking at his computer screen, his hands clamped behind his head. He would be like that for hours. Wren was free.

As she walked, Wren looked into the windows of other houses. They were full of families doing regular family things.

No one noticed her. No one even *knew* her.

She paused. Maybe she should turn back? But turn back to what? Izzy's room with her door of stickers? Her dad focused only on his computer? Her script crumpled at the bottom of her bag?

No. Wren had to keep going.

Finally Wren saw the wooden post and sign for Willoway Pond. The path. As she stepped from pavement to ground, Wren's confidence returned.

The cold air. The dirt path. The skates in her bag. The fire in her belly. *This* was who Wren was.

Down she walked until the frozen ice spread before her, lit by moonlight. Wren was ready.

With her feet still in her boots, Wren tested the ice. It had been a particularly cold winter and Occom Pond had been frozen since the end of December. But it was a few degrees warmer here, and Wren knew to be extra careful.

She listened for shifting. She felt for any give in the surface.

She heard and felt nothing.

Wren slid off her boots and put on her skates.

The surface was rough, probably not great for her blades.

But once she got moving, none of that mattered.

Wren was finally skating again.

IZZY SEES SWIRLS

Izzy was eating breakfast on Thursday morning when her mom got a text.

"Wren's not going to theater camp today," said Izzy's mom, reading from her phone. "They just scheduled her sister's surgery for this afternoon, and Wren wants to be there." She exhaled. "I hope everything goes okay. Maybe there's something we can do to help. Load up the fridge or leave a lasagna."

Izzy looked down at her bowl of cereal.

"Let me text Phoebe's mom," continued her mom. "I bet she can swing by and pick you up today so I have time to hit the grocery store."

Phoebe. Ugh. Izzy was relieved that Wren wouldn't be at theater camp, but that still left Phoebe and Daphne.

"If Wren's not going, can I skip camp, too?" asked Izzy. "Please."

"No, Iz. You made a commitment."

"You're the one who signed me up," said Izzy. "I didn't even want to do theater camp."

"Come on, Iz. It's the second-to-last day. Aren't you getting costumes today and blocking the scene? Mr. Blair needs his Amy."

"What about his Townsperson Three?"

Her mom didn't respond. They'd read through the script last night. Her mom knew Wren only had a few lines, and it was obvious that Mr. Blair had added them just so there would be enough parts for everyone.

Someone else might have been disappointed. But yesterday Wren had read her lines as if she couldn't have cared less. And even though Izzy had initially been excited to get the part of Amy, it didn't last long. Daphne's comment about Izzy just wanting to be popular had cut through Izzy like a knife, slicing away her pride at being cast as both an artist and the lead role. Then Wren had read her lines like a monotone zombie, reminding everyone of just how pointless theater camp was in the first place.

When they did a second read-through, a lot of kids followed Wren's lead, their performances getting worse and worse. Daphne and Phoebe seemed to mess up their lines on purpose, laughing like it was a hilarious coincidence. Eli, who was playing Mr. Davis, spoke with such fake exaggerated anger that his spit globs landed on Izzy's cheek. Only Otto seemed to be trying hard, mostly because he'd convinced Mr. Blair to let him do a tap routine for the grand finale instead of singing.

"Please, Mom," said Izzy. "It's just theater camp. It's so stupid."

"That attitude is going to get you nowhere, Iz. And please stop whining. You're way too old for it."

Izzy dumped her bowl of cereal into the sink even though it was half full and the soggy Cheerios would clog the drain. "I'm old enough to decide that I'm. Not. Going."

As soon as the words left her mouth, Izzy realized that she didn't stand a chance of getting her way. Sometimes it felt like twelve wasn't even a real age, but more of a joke.

Too old to stomp your feet and whine. Too young to actually decide anything important.

Mr. Blair had raided the costume closet and found a cardboard box full of bonnets and cloaks. Izzy stood in the hallway with Phoebe, Daphne, and Serena sorting through the pile. The wrinkled costumes smelled like mothballs.

"Here," said Phoebe, pinching a white bonnet patterned with tiny rosebuds between her fingers and passing it to Daphne. "This would be great for you, Beth."

"Ugh," said Daphne. "I hate being Beth. She's such a loser scaredy-cat."

"Not really," said Serena, who was playing Mrs. March.

Daphne froze, her hand with the stack of bracelets

gripping the bonnet. "Yes, she is. She doesn't even go to regular school."

Serena looked down at her shoes. "Beth is scared of things. But it's because she cares about everyone and really watches over them, you know? She doesn't want anything bad to happen to her family."

Yes, thought Izzy. *You're right*. Even though Daphne was doing a terrible job playing Beth, it was obvious from the written lines how much Beth loved her family. But Izzy didn't say anything. As far as Izzy knew, neither Daphne nor Phoebe had mentioned the drawing to Serena, or anyone else. Maybe they'd forgotten about it, or maybe they were waiting for the right moment. Either way, it was safest to stay quiet and not risk finding out.

"She also doesn't want anything bad to happen to Laurie!" said Otto. He jumped out from behind a row of lockers, wearing a top hat and a velvet coat with brass buttons. He bowed, unfurled his arms in tight circles, and did a fast tap dance move with his feet. "At your service."

"Whatever," said Daphne. She tried to tie the

bonnet under her chin and accidentally hit herself in the face with her cast. She threw the bonnet to the ground. "This is so annoying. Let's talk about something way more important."

"Like the epic sleepover Saturday night?" said Phoebe.

"Yep," said Daphne. "I went to the mall and made these."

Daphne walked over to her bag and pulled out four blue envelopes, almost the exact color of Izzy's techno blue Sharpie. The envelopes were sealed shut, but there was something bulky inside that made them wrinkle. Daphne handed one to Phoebe and, after hesitating for a second, one to Serena. There was a third envelope in her hand.

Izzy knew the envelope wasn't for her, but she couldn't help hoping that it was.

"Can I open it now?" asked Phoebe. She held the envelope in her palms, like it was a delicate robin's egg.

"Sure," said Daphne. "Go for it."

Phoebe carefully slid her finger under the seal. It

was not how Phoebe normally did things. She wasn't the person who made a careful slit in a pack of Skittles and gently poured the candy into her open palm. Phoebe was the person who tore the pack open so fast that Skittles exploded into the air. But with this envelope, Phoebe was slow. And gentle. She reached her hand inside and pulled out a beaded bracelet.

Another matching bracelet. Izzy would have turned away, but the bracelet was different from any other beaded bracelet that Izzy had ever seen. The beads looked tie-dyed in bright colors—fuchsia, tangerine, violet—all swirled together on each individual bead.

"OMG," said Phoebe, sliding it onto her wrist. "It's an ultra rare. With real stones."

"Of course," said Daphne. She held out her wrist, where the exact same bracelet rested on top of her stack.

"So this is my ticket?" asked Phoebe. She pulled out a techno blue piece of paper from the envelope and held it far enough away that Izzy could easily read every word.

Congrats!

You've been invited to Daphne's Epic Sleepover on Saturday night!

Only people with this exact bracelet will be allowed to enter!

Absolutely Positively No Exceptions!

See you then!

XOXO Daphne

"Yep," said Daphne. "No one can get into the sleepover without one."

Serena examined her identical tie-dye bracelet, then slid it on. Daphne walked toward Izzy, the third envelope in her hand.

And Izzy couldn't help it. Her heart beat faster. It made no sense that Daphne would give her a bracelet.

It was the opposite of what should happen. But that didn't stop Izzy from desperately wishing it would.

Daphne held out the techno blue envelope to Izzy. "Hey, Izzy," said Daphne. "Since Wren's not here would you mind giving this to her? Tell her to open it ASAP."

As Izzy held the envelope in her hand, she noticed Wren's name written in capital letters.

The envelope was never meant for her.

That afternoon, Izzy did a horrible job in the dress rehearsal of their scene. She was supposed to be heartbroken to throw away her pickled limes, but she could barely remember how many limes she was supposed to throw, or where she was supposed to throw them.

Why? Why would Daphne invite Wren to the sleepover?

It was all Izzy could think about. Finally the rehearsal ended. Izzy was stuffing her cloak back into the cardboard box when Otto appeared. "She's trying to make you upset."

"Who?" asked Izzy.

"Daphne. She's trying to make you angry."

"How do you know?"

"Because," said Otto. "It's her specialty. Everybody has one thing they're really good at. Mine is tap dancing; yours is drawing. And Daphne's is making other people feel bad. She's the queen of mean." Otto crossed one foot in front of the other, did a full turn, and shook his hands as if to say, Ta-da!

"It's not the same thing," said Izzy. She agreed with the general idea, but being mean wasn't a specialty. It was just who Daphne was.

"Why not?" asked Otto. "She practices all the time and she's really good at it. I don't see the difference."

Otto had obviously been thinking about this. Kids at school mimicked Otto behind his back. They followed him down the hallway doing exaggerated tap dance moves. But Otto always ignored them. He tacked flyers about his tap dancing recitals on the bulletin board next to the library and handed out personal invitations to his favorite teachers with a big smile and a firm handshake. So Izzy assumed that he didn't care. But maybe he did, more than he let on.

"If you let her bother you, she'll win," said Otto. "Then you'll be just like everyone else. Congratulations. Victory to Daphne!"

Otto walked off, shaking an imaginary trophy in his hands, Daphne's name echoing in Izzy's ears.

MAKE THEM PROUD,
WREN

Hannah's surgery was a success.

Wren's mom was so relieved that she agreed to switch places with Wren's dad. He would spend the night in the hospital, and she would go back to the house with Wren to sleep in a real bed.

They would order pizza and watch a movie. Or at least some puppy videos on YouTube.

But as soon as they got back to rental house, Wren's mom laid down on the couch. Within seconds, she fell asleep.

Wren placed a blanket over her mom, folding it

under her chin. Then Wren did something she hadn't done in a long time: she kissed her mom's cheek.

For years, kissing her mom made Wren feel babyish. Immature.

But that evening, when her lips pressed against her mom's cheek, Wren felt older. And responsible.

She checked the time. Six o'clock. She could skate for an hour and still be back in time to warm the lasagna that Izzy's mom had left by the back door with cooking instructions taped to the top.

Wren would wake her mom to a fully prepared dinner. Her mom would be so happy. And proud.

Over dinner Wren could tell her mom about Daphne and the debacle with Izzy's drawing. Or they could talk about next week. What Wren needed to focus on in preparation for sectionals.

But first, she was going out to skate.

Wren closed the back door behind her. She rolled her skating bag down the sidewalk. There were more cars on the street than last night and headlights shone in her eyes.

Maybe one of the kids from theater camp would drive by and see her walking in the dark. Maybe they'd wonder where she was going.

But no one would pull over to ask.

Well, Otto might. Even after Wren told him to get a life, he still smiled and clapped silently after she spoke her pathetic play lines.

But no one else would. Not even Izzy. She'd barely looked at Wren since the horrible thing Wren said in the hallway.

Wren reached the Willoway Pond sign. She turned down the path. The moon was not as bright as the night before and Wren stumbled on a tree root. Her skating bag slammed against her leg.

But she made it to the end of the path. The low moon cleared the treetops and shone on the pond. And the entire world lightened.

Wren laced her skates and balanced on her toe picks as she stepped onto the frozen surface.

She took a few slow strokes, her legs adjusting from the forward motion of walking to the sideways sliding of her pushes against the ice.

When she'd skated last night, Wren didn't try to jump. The surface was too uneven, and she wasn't sure how thick the ice was. It had been enough just to stroke and spin.

But now, Wren couldn't resist. Hannah's surgery was over. She'd be going home with her dad in two days.

Home to the ice rink. To Nancy. To Nora. And all the other girls she'd be competing against at sectionals in just over two weeks.

Wren turned backward.

She would start with a toe loop. A simple half turn rotation that was part of her warm-up routine. If that went well, she'd move on.

To salchows and axels and maybe, just maybe, a double lutz.

Wren reached her left toe pick into the ice.

It dug deeper than she'd expected.

Wren hockey-stopped. Looked down.

The crack ran from the entry point of her toe pick to a few feet away.

She froze.

Groan. Groooaaan.

More cracks. The lines were delicate. Alive. They spread like branches on a tree, growing outward from a central base.

Wren's heart beat was so strong in her chest that she wondered if its vibration was making the ice shift. Because otherwise, her body was as still as it could possibly be.

She was terrified to move.

Wren thought about the Polar Bear Plunge at the Dartmouth Winter Carnival. The college kids carved a circular hole in the ice at Occom Pond and stripped down to their bathing suits to jump in. They wrapped ropes around their waists before jumping, and someone on firm land held on to the other end. When Wren had asked her dad why the jumpers needed the ropes, he explained that falling into water that cold can shock the system and cause someone's heart to stop beating. The rope was to pull people up in case that happens.

"It's the definition of youthful stupidity," her dad

had continued as a girl in a bikini jumped into the hole. "Flirting with death for fun. She must be from California."

"Why California?" Wren had asked.

"Because no one from New Hampshire would ever be that stupid."

That was the worst part.

Wren had known skating on an unmarked pond was stupid.

But she'd done it anyway. With no rope. No one waiting on firm land.

19

IZZY LEAPS

Izzy lay on her air mattress, the techno blue envelope with Wren's name resting on her stomach. She ran one corner of the envelope under her fingernail. Then she flicked the envelope toward the ceiling, hoping it would float through the air like a feather. Instead, it landed smack on Izzy's face. If she threw the envelope in the trash underneath the kitchen sink, it would probably still find its way back to her.

There was only one way to get rid of this thing: Izzy had to give it to Wren.

If you let her bother you, she'll win. That's what Otto had said.

Wren would be gone in two days, but Daphne wasn't going anywhere. Izzy did not want to let her win.

Izzy walked into the kitchen area where her mom was making a salad. "Can I go see if Wren's back from the hospital?" she asked. "To check how she's doing?"

Her mom smiled. "That's a wonderful idea, Iz. Want me to come with you? I want to make sure they saw the instructions for the lasagna."

"It's okay," said Izzy. "I'll ask."

"Just come back soon. Dinner's in ten minutes."

The driveway stretched before her, as if it had somehow gotten longer. Izzy hoped Wren's dad would answer the door. Izzy wanted to hand off the envelope and run back to the garage apartment. She did not want to talk to Wren.

Ding-dong.

It was strange to ring the back doorbell to her own house knowing that her family wasn't inside, that

Row's scampering feet would not be charging across the hardwood floors.

Ding-dong. Ding-dong.

Izzy was about to walk to the front door and slide the envelope through the brass mail slot when Wren's mom appeared. Izzy hadn't seen her since the day Wren's family arrived, and was surprised by how tired she looked.

"Can I help you?" asked Wren's mom. She kept the door half closed, as if Izzy was a kid selling cookies for a school fundraiser.

"Is Wren home? I have something for her."

"Something for Wren?"

"From theater camp today."

Wren's mom raised her hand to her forehead. "Oh, you must be Izzy. Of course. Come in, please. Wren's inside."

Izzy stepped into the house. *Her house.* So many things were different. The teakettle was on the wrong half of the stove, the red stools were covered with crumbs, and wrinkled hand towels were shoved in a corner of the counter.

"I know it's a mess," said Wren's mom. "The whole week has been a whirlwind. I promise we'll clean everything up before we leave. Let me just get Wren." She walked toward the stairs to the second floor. "Wren! Wren! Izzy's here to see you!"

They waited ten seconds. Thirty seconds. Wren was obviously ignoring them.

"It's okay," said Izzy. "I just wanted to give this to Wren. I don't need to talk to her." Izzy tried to hand the envelope to Wren's mom, but she had started walking up the stairs.

"It's just . . . I know she's here somewhere," said Wren's mom. "Where else would she be? Come on, let's check her room."

You mean my room, thought Izzy as she followed, the wooden stairway railing so familiar in her hand. They walked down the hallway with the clean white walls, past Nate's room with its row of soccer trophies, and into her own room. The bed was made and the desk clean. A pile of Wren's clothes was folded on top of the dresser.

Deep inside, under all the hurt and confusion, Izzy

was grateful that at least Wren had taken good care of her room.

Wren's mom turned in a circle. She opened the closet door. She patted the pockets of her jeans, as if she was feeling for her phone. "Oh my God, Wren! Wren! Where is she? Did she go out? She doesn't know anyone here. Does she?"

Izzy gripped the envelope in her hand. Had Wren actually had become friends with Daphne and Phoebe? Had Wren actually given them the drawing? Had they bonded in the school bathroom, or hung out after theater camp yesterday without Izzy knowing? It was highly unlikely, but possible. And it would explain the invitation with Wren's name on it. Daphne and Phoebe knew Wren was renting Izzy's house. Maybe they'd stopped by and told Wren about the epic sleepover in person? Maybe Wren had gone to one of their houses to hang out?

"I'll go get my mom," said Izzy. "She has a school directory. Maybe she can call around."

Wren's mom sat down on Izzy's bed, nodded, and started to sob.

Izzy barely noticed the pounding of her legs or the cold against her cheeks as she ran through her house, down the driveway, and up to the garage apartment. It was only when Row jumped on her, his paws digging into her thighs, that Izzy realized how fast she'd sprinted up the stairs. "Mom, Wren's missing!"

"Missing?"

"Her mom doesn't know where she is. She's not at the house. Maybe she went to Daphne's house. Or Phoebe's. Can you help?"

"Of course. I'll come right over."

Izzy waited by the door as her mom put on a sweater and grabbed her phone. She almost left the techno blue envelope in the garage apartment, but at the last minute she shoved it in the front pocket of her coat. Then she ran back to the house with her mom, standing at the kitchen island as her mom texted Phoebe's mom and tried to remember the password for the school directory to find Daphne's information.

Wren's mom paced from the kitchen to the mudroom and back. She froze. "Wren's skating bag.

Where is it? I could've sworn I saw it here."

Izzy looked out the window to the driveway where she'd found Wren jumping in place in the freezing night air. She remembered Wren's question about Willoway Pond—*Does anyone skate here?*

"Mom," said Izzy.

"Hold on, Iz. I need to concentrate."

But Izzy couldn't wait. She zipped her coat all the way up and went for the back door. "Wren might have gone to Willoway Pond. I can go check."

"The pond at night? No way."

"Please, Mom," said Izzy. "I'll be right back."

Izzy's mom brought the top of her phone to her lips. She looked at Wren's mom, who stood with her hands interlaced at her chin.

"Okay," said Izzy's mom. "Go check. But come right back."

WREN AND
THE ANGRY ICE

Exhausted from standing, Wren lowered her body to the ice.

She reached for the slippery surface with tented fingers, an attempt to ease the transition and distribute her weight. To keep the ice happy.

The ice was not happy. Its cracks splintered and grew.

But it held. For now.

Wren wasn't wearing a watch and didn't have a phone. Based on the stiffness in her fingers and the numbness of her toes, she'd probably been stuck for at least an hour. Her mom might wake up soon. Maybe she'd call Wren's name and realize she wasn't home.

Or maybe not.

And that was only half the problem.

The other half was that no one knew where she was.

Wren tried to scream. "*Help!*" But her tired voice refused to cooperate.

She could see houses through the tree branches, but they were faraway. Their windows shut. Their doors closed. Keeping out the cold.

"*Help!*"

Wren wiggled her toes in her skates. Slowly she brought her knees to her chest and wrapped her arms tight.

She didn't dare move anything else.

Wren thought about the shiny, dense ice of the Dartmouth College rink. Sitting next to Charlie on the hard bench of his Zamboni machine. Back then, she'd been so certain that one day she'd stand on a podium. And everyone would be so proud.

But now, stuck on this fragile ice in the dark, Wren thought about something else that happened at the rink that year. Nancy had tried to start a synchronized skating team. She'd gathered her students and shown them a video of a team from Connecticut that did back crossovers with their arms linked and deep lunges in between one another's outstretched arms. Nancy had lined them up by height to try to repeat what the Connecticut girls had done.

And Wren had hated it. She didn't want to count in unison as she did back crossovers or be responsible for steadying someone else's balance in a spiral.

The other girls' hands pressing on her shoulders just slowed her down.

Wren wanted space to build her crossovers. To launch into her jumps. To twist into her layback spins.

Unlike the rest of her life, when Wren was skating, no one could drag her down. There was no Hannah to worry about. To talk about. To plan around. No Nora to offend. No Izzy to scare away.

When Wren was on the ice, she could accomplish amazing things all by herself.

And now look what she'd done.

All by herself.

The shore wasn't far, but she didn't have the courage to move toward it. What if the ice cracked completely and she fell through? Would the cold water instantly stop her heart?

The thought made her chest tight. Her breath short.

Wren could only sit and wait.

And wonder if she was going to die.

Then she heard a rustling through the trees. A familiar voice. "Wren! Wren! Are you there?"

It was Izzy. She was running to the edge of the ice, waving her arms.

Yes, thought Wren. *I'm here.* But when she opened her mouth to speak, the words scratched against her throat and faded to nothing.

"Hold on," said Izzy. "I'm coming to get you."

Izzy tested the ice with her foot. She frowned,

walked a few steps away, and tested another spot.

"I don't know," yelled Izzy. "Maybe I should go get our moms. They're home. I told them I'd be right back."

"No!" It took every bit of strength for Wren to yell the word. Izzy couldn't leave her. *Please don't go.*

"Okay," said Izzy. "Okay, I'll stay. But can you try to come in? Do you think you can do it?"

Izzy crouched at the edge of the ice and stretched her arms toward Wren. She wasn't close to reaching, but she was there. Izzy had found her. Wren had to try.

Wren shifted onto all fours. She pressed her palms flat on the ice, her fingers spread wide, covering the cracks like Band-Aids.

Band-Aids that Wren wasn't sure would stick.

"You can do it," said Izzy. "Go slow."

Go slow. The words echoed in Wren's mind as she began to move.

Right hand, left hand. Right knee, left knee. Wren was careful to keep her toe picks clear of the ice. To slide, not thump.

"You're doing it," said Izzy. "Keep going."

The splintered surface with its cracks and grooves was terrifying. But Izzy kept her going.

"You're almost there," said Izzy. "Come on, Wren. You've got this."

Right hand, left hand. Slide.

Wren was close. But as she shifted forward, the ice underneath her hands gave way.

Frigid water seeped over her knuckles. Her wrists.

Wren gasped.

Her palms hit the hard-packed mud bottom of the pond.

The water was cold and sharp as it rushed up to her elbows. Wren's body clenched tight.

But when she looked up, Izzy was on her hands and knees. Coming to get her.

IZZY'S IMPOSSIBLY
BIG THING

Izzy crawled a few inches before the ice at the edge of the pond cracked. But she knew from Row splashing in during the summer that the water was shallow this close to shore. Izzy braced herself for the cold and stepped in, wading toward Wren. As she approached, Wren reached up and Izzy slid her arms beneath Wren's shoulders. Together they made their way out of the pond and collapsed on the sandy dirt.

Wren's feet splayed open and the wet blades of her skates shone in the moonlight. The wavy glow of white moon on steel was beautiful, except that Izzy was panting too hard to appreciate it. She dropped her chin to her chest, taking comfort in the rise and fall of her body. They were both all right. At least, she hoped so.

"Are you okay?" Izzy asked Wren.

Wren nodded, her lips a deep purple.

Izzy's breath began to slow and she leaned forward to lift the clinging wet denim material from her lower calves. She wiggled her toes inside her soaked boots. When Izzy sat back up, Wren made a noise, as if clearing her throat to speak.

"Thanks for saving my life," whispered Wren.

Izzy didn't know how to answer. *You're welcome? No problem?* Had she really saved Wren's life? It seemed an impossibly big thing to do. But before Izzy had found her, Wren was trapped in the center of the ice. And now here they were. Together and safe.

But before Izzy could answer, voices called from the direction of the path. "Izzy! Wren! Girls!"

"Mom," said Wren in a raspy voice.

"Down here!" yelled Izzy. "We're down here!"

In a flurry of rustling leaves and pounding steps, their moms appeared at the opening to the path and wrapped them both in hugs. Izzy's mom kissed her cheek, her forehead, her cheek again. Then she pulled away, noticing Izzy's wet legs and jacket sleeves. "Did you fall in?"

"Wren's soaked," said Wren's mom. "That water must be freezing. I should take her to a doctor—Izzy, too."

Izzy's mom reached her hand over to Wren's cheek. "You're right. Better to be safe. There's an emergency room in the next town over. Come on."

Izzy stood, her arms wrapped tight around her body, as her mom and Wren's mom helped Wren up. Wren grimaced, releasing a small wheezing sound.

"Your skates," said Izzy. "Do you want to take them off?"

"No," said Wren. "Please . . ."

"It's okay," said Wren's mom. "I've got her." With one smooth motion, she wrapped Wren's arm around her neck and slid her hands underneath Wren's body, lifting Wren as if she weighed nothing at all.

Izzy reached for her mom's hand and followed them up the path. With each step, moisture squished between her toes and under the soles of her feet. Her jeans clung to her legs and the sleeves of her jacket twisted around her arms. Outside, Izzy was shivering with cold. But inside, her mom's fingers squeezing her palm, she was warm. Opposites.

WREN SEES THE LIGHT

A knock on the sticker door.

Wren opened her eyes. The bed was so cozy, so familiar, that for a second she forgot what had happened last night.

But then Wren moved her arm. The bandage where the IV needle had been inserted brushed against the sheets. And it all came rushing back.

The icy cold. The heated blanket. The oxygen monitor tight over her finger.

"Come in," she said.

The sticker door swung open. Izzy flopped down

at the end of the bed. "Were you still sleeping?" she asked.

Wren looked to the window. A bright midday winter sun shone around the curtain edges. "What time is it?"

"Almost noon," said Izzy. "Isn't that great!"

"Great?" Wren's head ached. The doctor had warned her about that. She remembered something about staying hydrated.

"We missed theater camp," continued Izzy. "Even my mom didn't have the energy to get up this morning. I mean, I know you almost died. But at least something good came out of it."

Izzy smiled. But then the corners of her mouth dropped. "Sorry," said Izzy. "I didn't mean . . ."

"Anytime," said Wren. She did a pretend bow, like Otto might, one arm at her waist and the other outstretched as if holding a tray.

Izzy laughed. And so did Wren. The shaking made her head hurt. But it was so worth it.

Except then Wren remembered there was

something else she needed to say and she stopped laughing. She should have said it in the hospital last night. But she and Izzy had been taken to different exam rooms. And when they were released, at almost two in the morning, Izzy fell asleep as soon as they got in the car.

But now, Wren had no excuse. "I'm sorry for what I said about you not having any friends."

Izzy bit her lower lip. She hesitated. "The thing is, it's kind of the truth."

"No," said Wren. "Not anymore."

Izzy shifted on the bed. Crossed her legs underneath her. She spun the hospital ID bracelet, the same kind that Wren had, around her wrist. Then Izzy stood up and reached into the back pocket of her jeans.

"Here," she said. "This is for you. It's from Daphne."

"Daphne?" asked Wren, feeling bumps in the envelope. "Is there poison inside? Because almost dying once is enough for me."

Izzy shook her head. "It's an invitation. Open it."

Wren pulled out a piece of paper the same color as

the envelope. She held the paper so Izzy could see, but Izzy barely glanced at the words before turning away.

It was an invitation to an epic sleepover at Daphne's house. But why would Daphne ever invite her?

Confused, Wren pulled out the other item in the envelope: a red beaded bracelet.

Izzy gasped. She leaned over and touched the bracelet with one finger.

"What's wrong?" asked Wren.

"I think it's a setup," said Izzy. Izzy explained how Phoebe's and Serena's envelopes had bracelets with tie-dye beads. "Daphne probably wants you to come so she can turn you away at the door. She probably didn't think I would see you open the envelope. She really is the queen of mean."

"But there's no way I would ever go to her sleepover," said Wren. "Never ever."

"That's not the way Daphne thinks. She thinks everyone wants to hang out with her, no matter what."

Wren nodded in agreement.

The question was: What to do about it?

IZZY'S IDEA

The next afternoon, Saturday, Izzy went back to hang out with Wren. She sat at her desk, doodling on a piece of paper. Wren was stretched out on Izzy's bed, her bag of clothes packed and waiting by the closet. Wren's mom and dad were at the hospital with Hannah. Wren and her dad were going to drive back to New Hampshire right after dinner. Wren's mom would sleep at the hospital and bring Hannah home in a few days.

"We can't let them get away with this," said Wren. She picked up the techno blue envelope next to her on the bed.

"She's Daphne," said Izzy. "She gets away with everything. It's the way life works."

Wren slid the red beaded bracelet over her hand so that it stacked on top of her hospital ID bracelet. "Do you have any scissors?" she asked. "This hospital bracelet is so annoying. I need to cut it off."

Izzy looked at her own hospital ID bracelet. It was embarrassing, too embarrassing to admit to Wren, but Izzy wished Wren would keep hers on just a little while longer. She liked the way they matched.

Still, Izzy got the scissors from her desk and brought them to Wren on the bed. She was about to hand the scissors to Wren when she froze. Their matching hospital bracelets, the red beaded bracelet, the invitation to the epic sleepover, her butterfly tin of Sharpies on the desk.

They were dots that connected to form a plan.

"Wait a second," said Izzy. "I have an idea."

Two hours later, Nate backed down the driveway with Wren and Izzy in the backseat. "We need some music," said Nate. "Something doomed, because you two are up to no good."

"Just drive, Nate," said Izzy.

She and Wren had thought about walking. But the sun had already set and there was no way their parents were going to let them wander out in the dark anytime soon. So they'd convinced Nate to take them out for pizza before Wren left for New Hampshire with her dad. With just one quick stop first.

"Over there," said Izzy, pointing to Daphne's house. "The house with the lights."

"Be fast," said Nate. "I've got a date."

"A date?" asked Izzy.

"A date with destiny. If my little sister can save someone's life, I can ask a girl out. At least if I make it before closing time." Izzy smiled. She wanted to say something cheesy like "Way to go," or "I know she's going to say yes." But she was too nervous about what she and Wren were about to do. She'd have plenty of time to talk to Nate. Her time with Wren was almost up.

Lights glowed through the windows of Daphne's

house. Izzy couldn't see Daphne, Phoebe, and Serena inside, but she felt a buzz in the air knowing they were there. Nate pulled to the curb and turned off the engine.

"Okay," said Wren. "Let's do this."

Wren got out of the car and walked up the stone path that led to Daphne's front door. Izzy followed, stepping off the path and into the shadows by some bushes. Her body shook with nerves as Wren continued up to the front door and reached for the doorbell.

Ding-dong.

Daphne appeared right away, as if she'd been standing in the front hall waiting for this very moment. "Oh, hey, Wren," she said with a big smile. "Are you here for the sleepover?"

"Awesome," said Phoebe, who appeared next to Wren.

Waiting in the dark, Izzy's legs felt soft, like she might collapse. She was tempted to hobble out, tap Wren on the shoulder, and drag her away before they went any further. But then Wren said the exact line that they'd rehearsed in Izzy's bedroom that afternoon, both of them laughing as they tried different voices, joking that Mr. Blair would finally be proud of them for adding emotion to their words.

"Thanks so much for inviting me to your epic sleepover," said Wren in the happy tone they'd settled on. "I have my bracelet."

"Perfect," said Daphne. "Can I see it? Obviously it's your ticket to come inside."

"Sure," said Wren.

Izzy took a few cautious steps onto the grass. She watched as Wren pushed up the sleeve to her jacket. On Wren's wrist was her hospital ID bracelet with four letters written in crisp black Sharpie: *N I C E*.

Phoebe shook her head. She crossed her arms over her chest. "That's not the right bracelet, Wren. You have to have the right bracelet."

Daphne stepped closer to Wren, ignoring Phoebe and squinting at Wren's wrist. "'Nice'? Like you want to tell me how nice I am? I mean, thanks, Wren. That's super sweet. But that's not the bracelet that came with your envelope. Do you have that bracelet? Maybe then you can come in."

Wren shook her head, pretending to be confused. "Oh, right," she said, slapping her forehead. "Silly me, I do have another bracelet."

That was Izzy's cue. There was no turning back. Izzy stepped out of the darkness and onto the stone path. She moved slowly at first, but as she got closer, Izzy saw the confusion in Phoebe's and Daphne's eyes. She saw Serena standing on the stairs holding a fat black cat with white paws. Izzy stepped next to Wren and pushed up her own jacket sleeve. Written on her hospital ID bracelet in black Sharpie were the letters *T R Y*.

Daphne looked from Wren's bracelet to Izzy's bracelet. "Nice? Try?"

Serena put the cat down and stepped forward. She read both bracelets out loud and laughed.

"What does that even *mean*?" asked Phoebe.

"Come on, Phoebe," said Izzy. "I know you can figure it out."

Phoebe stuck out her lower lip. She looked from the bracelets to Daphne.

Daphne hesitated. She flipped her hair. Then she opened her mouth to speak. "It means that . . ."

But Izzy didn't let Daphne finish. "It means that you can do whatever you want with my drawing. I know who you are and so does everyone else. Come on, Wren. Let's go."

Izzy grabbed Wren's hand and they ran to Nate's waiting car. It was just like the night they chased after Row, how they'd sprinted together through the dark, laughing at nothing except the thrilling combination of excitement and fear and hope.

Maybe Nate had been right when he said that her drawings were missing something.

Maybe what they were missing was not one superhero, but two.

TWO

WEEKS

LATER

24

WREN'S KEY CHAIN

Wren shook out her legs. She stretched her hands over her head.

There was one skater left. Then it would be her turn to take the ice at sectionals.

Wren glanced up several rows to where Hannah, her dad, and her mom sat in small plastic seats. Hannah waved her stuffed unicorn in the air. She wore a pink fuzzy hat that protected the stitches on her head. She looked just like any other healthy, unicorn-loving four-year-old. Which, thanks to the successful surgery, she was.

Wren's dad mouthed, "You've got this, Bird."

Her mom pulled her arms in tight, reminding Wren about what she'd been practicing that week with her double lutz.

Wren nodded. She wiggled her toes in her new skates. Her old ones, which were perfectly broken in, had been lost somewhere in the hospital. Probably stuffed in a trash can with all kinds of needles and bandages. Wren was bummed that she never got a chance to say good-bye.

It had taken a few days to get used to her new skates. She'd worn them around the house, even eating dinner with them on, and now they felt just right.

"Almost time," said Nancy.

Wren got her water bottle from her skating bag and took a sip. Before Wren left, she and Izzy exchanged hospital bracelets. Wren had attached Izzy's bracelet with the word *TRY* to the handle of her skating bag, like a key chain.

A reminder of a week that she never expected to want to remember.

The skater on the ice finished her program.

Wren's name echoed across the empty stretch of ice.

Nancy lifted Wren's chin. She looked Wren in the eyes. "Go out there and show them what you've got."

Wren skated to center ice and got into her opening position. As she waited for her music to start, Wren glanced at the seats next to her family.

Izzy and her mom were sitting very straight, their arms linked. Izzy smiled and gave Wren a thumbs-up.

Wren would do this next part on her own.

But knowing they were all there watching gave Wren strength.

And when she landed her double lutz, she could hear them cheer.

IZZY MAKES ROOM

Two days after Wren's skating competition, Izzy stood in the front yard of her house. The blue car was still parked in the driveway. "No, Row," said Izzy. "We can't go inside yet."

Her mom was meeting with the potential client who'd cancelled three weeks before, and Izzy was supposed to keep Row out of the house until she left. But then Row noticed a squirrel climbing up the maple tree in the front yard. Row lunged, and his leash slipped out of Izzy's grip.

"Row!" yelled Izzy. She ran to the tree and grabbed

the end of Row's leash. "No, Row. Bad dog."

Izzy led Row, his tail wagging with pride, to the back door. She sat down on the step. The sun was strong and Izzy closed her eyes. Flashes of tangerine orange and bright yellow appeared behind her eyelids. As soon as she got back inside, she'd practice mixing the different yellows of her new oil pastels. She liked how oil pastels blended on paper to create shadows, texture, and depth.

Her life was more complicated now than Sharpie stick figures shouting words trapped inside speech bubbles. It was opposites—good and bad, easy and hard, best friends and sworn enemies—and also everything in between.

"Hey, Izzy," said a voice.

Izzy opened her eyes, surprised to see Serena standing in front of her.

"What are you doing here?"

"My mom's meeting with your mom," said Serena. "Your mom invited me in, but I told her I'd just wait in the car."

"Your mom is Ms. Stallton?" asked Izzy. Serena's last name was Tallis.

"She goes by her maiden name now," said Serena. "My parents are getting divorced and my mom wants a totally clean start. With everything. And just so you know, I wasn't avoiding you. I just didn't feel like coming inside and listening to our moms talk about bathroom tiles and window curtains, like they're going to magically fix everything."

Izzy smiled. "Do not get my mom started on curtains."

Serena laughed and kicked a pebble with her sneaker. "Hey, Izzy?"

"Yeah?"

"I'm sorry. About everything with Daphne. I didn't know about the red bracelet trick until the day of the sleepover when you and Wren didn't show up to theater camp. Daphne spent the entire day worrying that her plan would fall apart. So I thought there was a good chance that Wren wouldn't even come to the sleepover. I probably shouldn't have gone anyways, but my mom was home packing boxes and anything was better than doing that. And also, I just didn't want to be left out."

Izzy nodded. She remembered walking with Phoebe's pink mitten in her hand, ringing the doorbell at Daphne's house, and hoping that Daphne would invite her inside.

"I always knew Daphne was mean," continued Serena. "But I didn't know how much she liked being mean until that night."

"It's her specialty," said Izzy. "She's the queen of mean. That's what Otto says."

"Otto makes me laugh," said Serena.

"Me, too," said Izzy.

"Maybe we could all sit together at lunch or something?"

Izzy smiled. "Yeah."

Serena's mom opened the back door, bags of colorful fabric samples in her hand. Izzy brought Row inside and went up to her room. She pressed her forehead against the window, watching as Serena and her mom backed down the driveway. Her breath did not cloud the glass. There was no condensation heart to slice in half with her finger.

Izzy sat down at her desk and opened the drawer. Her jagged half-heart necklace was shoved in the back, the chain a tangled mess. Over the past two weeks, Izzy had been tempted to throw it out, but she never did. Instead, she put Wren's hospital ID bracelet with the word *NICE* in the necklace's old place.

The bracelet had wrinkled at the edges and curled in on itself. The opposite of the flat, shiny heart.

But Izzy didn't care how the bracelet looked. She knew what the bracelet *meant*. And she also knew there was plenty of empty space beside it for whatever might come next.

ACKNOWLEDGMENTS

Thank you to my editor, Martha Mihalick, for being a true partner in shaping this story. It is a joy and an honor to write with you.

Thank you to my agent, Alex Slater, for believing in me every step of the way. I'm so grateful to be on your team.

Thank you to the incredible people at Greenwillow Books. To Virginia Duncan for the caring and insightful comments, Tim Smith for indulging my debates over comma placement, Sylvie Le Floc'h for the gorgeous pages, and the entire marketing, publicity, and sales teams for working so hard to get this book and so many others into the hands of readers. And to artist Celia Krampien for the beautiful cover and interior art.

There are so many wonderful pediatric doctors and nurses who have brightened my toughest days. For specific medical advice on this book, I was fortunate to rely on Dr. Ann McCarthy and Dr. Vishnu Cuddapah. Any mistakes are mine alone.

Thank you to the librarians who hand my books to readers, the teachers who recommend them to students, the booksellers who present them to customers, and the young readers who write to me. Hearing from you makes me smile for days.

To my brothers, Alex and Ben Ende, all the sibling love in these pages goes out to you.

Endless hugs and kisses to my daughters: Ella, Liv, and Aven. You girls are the heart of everything I write. And to Winnie, the real-life Row who we love so very much.

This book is dedicated to my husband, Jeff. As everything I write should be.

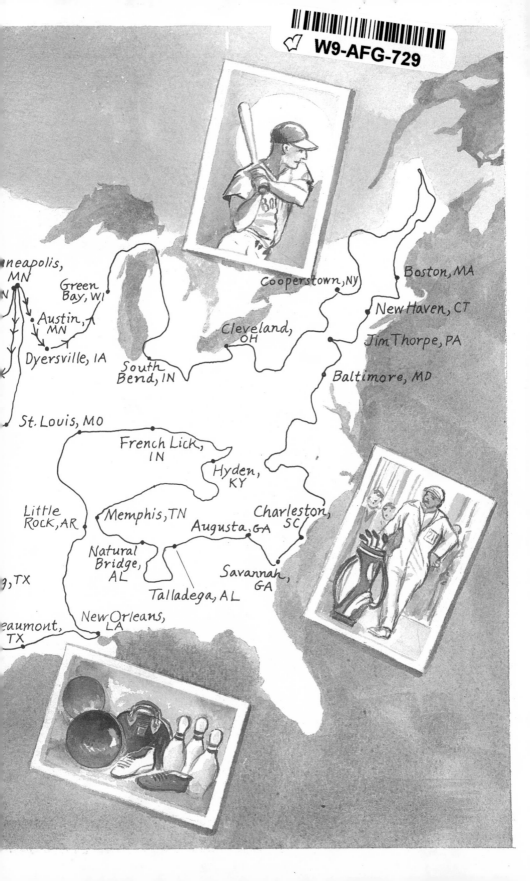

Minneapolis, MN

Green Bay, WI

Austin, MN

Dyersville, IA

South Bend, IN

Cooperstown, NY

Boston, MA

New Haven, CT

Jim Thorpe, PA

Cleveland, OH

Baltimore, MD

St. Louis, MO

French Lick, IN

Hyden, KY

Little Rock, AR

Memphis, TN

Charleston, SC

Augusta, GA

Natural Bridge, AL

Savannah, GA

Talladega, AL

, TX

New Orleans, LA

Beaumont, TX

Road Swing

Steve Rushin

Road Swing

Doubleday

New York • London • Toronto • Sydney • Auckland

PUBLISHED BY DOUBLEDAY
a division of Bantam Doubleday Dell Publishing Group, Inc.
1540 Broadway, New York, New York 10036

DOUBLEDAY and the portrayal of an anchor with a dolphin are trademarks
of Doubleday, a division of Bantam Doubleday Dell Publishing Group, Inc.

Book design by Maria Carella
Map and road illustration by Martie Holmer

Library of Congress Cataloging-in-Publication Data
Rushin, Steve.
  Road swing / by Steve Rushin. — 1st ed.
    p.   cm.
  1. Rushin, Steve.   2. Sportswriters—United States—Biography.
3. Sportswriters—Travel—United States.   I. Title.
GV742.42.R87A3   1998
070.4′49′796092—dc21
[B]   98-17852
                                                        CIP

For my dad,
who wants to be a sportswriter in his next life.

Acknowledgments

During the course of this project, many kind people gave me guidance, encouragement, time off, toll money, directions out of New Jersey, and other indispensable assistance. I owe all of them a great debt—literally so, in most cases. I should implicate by name David Bauer, Peter Carry, Bill Colson, Debbie Cowell, Richard Demak, Richard Deutsch, Rob Fleder, Michael Jaffe, Jay Jennings, Greg Kelly, Tim Kurkjian, Rick Lipsey, Mike McCollow, Mark Mulvoy, Esther Newberg, Rich O'Brien, Rob Robertson, Bill Thomas, and Alex Wolff. I am especially grateful to my brothers and sister—Jim, Tom, John, and Amy—who unaccountably waived their respective rights to sue.

Road Swing

1

" 'Working press'?" a Pittsburgh Pirate once said to me with a sneer. "That's sorta like 'jumbo shrimp.' "

"My favorite oxymoron is 'guest host,' " I replied chummily. "You know, like they used to have on *The Tonight Show?*" But he didn't know. And he didn't care. In fact, he thought I was calling *him* a moron, so he calmly alit from his clubhouse stool and chloroformed me with his game socks.

But I see his point. My life's work is not work. Indiana University basketball coach Bobby Knight likes to say of sportswriters: "Most of us learn to write by the second grade, then move on to bigger things." Most of us stop throwing chairs and calling ourselves Bobby by the second grade, too—but I see *his* point.

As a writer on the staff of *Sports Illustrated*, my day job hasn't changed since I was eight. I was raised in a house with mint-green aluminum siding and spent my days watching ballgames in our wood-paneled den. My father loved wood paneling and even had it installed on the exterior of his station wagon. He'd have preferred mint-green aluminum siding, but it wasn't available on the '74 Ford Country Squire.

Pity, because the Country Squire looked like the crate it was shipped in. It was not so much a motor vehicle as an oak coffin with a luggage rack, proof that you really *can* take it with you. Every summer vacation our family of seven vacuum-packed ourselves into it, then raced across the country as if through one continuous yellow light, pausing only long enough to attend some big-league baseball game—in Houston or Anaheim or Cincinnati—before hauling ass back home. The destination didn't matter. The important thing was that for nine innings once every August, Dad forgot the Kafkaesque problems of his suburban existence. Namely, that his house was rusting. And his car had termites.

It all seems so long ago. My brothers and sister grew up and got jobs. I grew up and became a sportswriter, though it hardly seems like a grown-up pursuit. The naked manager of the California Angels once threw his double-knit uniform pants at me in anger, something that happens all the time to baseball writers, which may explain why we're so comfortable wearing polyester. Whereas a similar burst of pantsfire across a conference table at IBM would no doubt be considered inappropriate, especially when the trousers in question were mottled with moist tobacco stains. (Please, God, tell me they were tobacco stains.)

It is hard to believe now, but the heroes of my youth were all as smooth and wholesome as Skippy peanut butter. This surely owes something to the fact that I never saw them naked, that I knew almost nothing whatsoever about them. I loved a Minnesota Twins catcher named George Mitterwald, but only because I loved the name George Mitterwald. Beyond that, I was faintly aware that his middle name was Eugene and he lived in Orlando. Or that his middle name was Orlando and he lived in Eugene. And that the Fun Fact on the back of his 1974 Topps baseball card said: "George likes to take home movies." If George liked to take anything else—fistfuls of amphetamines, long walks in women's clothing—I was blissfully unaware of it.

For some years now, I have wanted to return to that state of blissful oblivion, preferably without a prescription. Which brings us to the book that you now hold in your hands. It is an effort to revisit the twin pursuits of my youth: epic car trips and an unhealthy obsession with sports, usually combined. I wanted to get into my fully alarmed Japanese car and drive to American sports shrines for a year, or until I became fully alarmed myself. The idea was to write a kind of sports-addled *Blue Highways*. Only bluer, locker rooms being what they are.

The root of this road trip, the genesis of my exodus, lay in Norway. Two weeks into the '94 Winter Olympics, I found myself in a frigid Lillehammer parking lot with a mob of other unlaundered scribes, violently clamoring for complimentary underpants being thrown from the back of a Hanes truck. We lunged desperately at each promotional three-pack like bridesmaids at a bouquet. There wasn't time to indulge size or style preferences: If a packet went skittering across the icy pavement, we tore after it and then into it, hyenas on the veldt.

It was all very sad. I retired to my dimly lit dorm room that evening, dined on reindeer jerky, and passed the balance of the night quietly chafing in mesh briefs three sizes too abbreviated. In hours such as this, a man is given to sober self-reflection. My life, it occurred to me, lacked a certain *gravitas*.

The very next evening came the women's figure-skating final. I attended the event simply as a spectator, and my ticket seated me, serendipitously, next to an elfin gentleman who introduced himself as Al Harding. He was a kindly and gregarious factory worker from Portland, Oregon, and none of us sitting near Al seemed to mind that his Olympian daughter, Tonya, had been accused very recently of the contract kneecapping of a rival skater. On the contrary, Al became fast friends

with all of us, including a ten-year-old boy from Atlanta who gave Mr.
Harding a pin bearing the likeness of Whatizit, a.k.a. Izzy, the cartoon
mascot of the '96 Summer Olympics.

"What is it?" Al asked, examining the pin.

"Whatizit," replied the boy,

"*What* is it?"

"Whatizit!"

"Howzat?"

"*Izzy.*"

"Who's he?"

"Izzy!"

"Izzy, is he?" Al finally responded in a moment of relative clarity.
"Well, I'll have to wear Izzy when I go to Izzy's: That's the name of my
favorite restaurant in Portland." Al pinned Izzy to his parka like a prom
night boutonniere, then leaned in toward the boy as if to share a confidence. "You know," Al stage-whispered, "Izzy's has fifty-seven different
compartments in its salad bar."

Well. Where to begin? It struck me at once that I had never heard a
more eloquent statement of American culutral values (compartments in
a salad bar being my homeland's equivalent of stars in a Michelin guide);
that I had never been to Portland or indeed to an Izzy's (a chain of
pizzerias in the Pacific Northwest); that it had been years since I had
attended an athletic event as a spectator (and I genuinely missed the cut-
and-thrust of cheap-seat conversation; the trough-style urinal is our
modern-day town hall); and that I had never, until that very moment,
witnessed a figure-skating . . . match? Meet? Pageant?

It was a revelation. Entering the arena that night, fans were con-
fronted by a sign filled with pictograms depicting the myriad items pro-
hibited inside. Among these were the standard knives and bottles and
cartoon bombs, to be sure, each one circled with a slash through it. But
there was something else, too, circled and slashed: the silhouette of a toy
poodle. This was the first sporting event I had ever attended, in a lifetime
of attending sporting events, whose organizers felt it necessary to tell
fans: No poodles.

Once inside I saw why, of course. The crowd was liver-spotted with ladies wearing floor-length furs and G-force facelifts. No doubt each had checked a dog at the door, dogs that looked like fright-wigged wood-chucks, if woodchucks wore cable-knit sweaters.

All of which is to say that, in a hockey arena five thousand miles from home, I'd had a series of small epiphanies. The red lamp was lit above my own goal. After a decade devoted to sports and travel—every-thing I have ever covered has been an away game; my entire adult life has been what announcers call "an extended road swing"—I hadn't seen as much of the world, or of the world of sports, as I had smugly assumed.

Shortly after returning from Norway, I resolved to look again at my country by grazing at the endless salad bar of American sports: from the garbanzo beans of celebrity softball to the leafy lettuce of NBA basket-ball.

I had a sudden desire to visit the boyhood home of Larry Bird in French Lick, Indiana, and to buy Topps bubble-gum cards and to attend a high school football game and to hang out with pool hustlers and to watch Louisville Sluggers being "Powerized"—whatever on Earth that means. I wanted to put my finger to the pulse of American sport, and I wanted that finger to be one of those giant foam rubber index fingers worn by pinheaded fans across the land.

In short, I resolved to hit the road and to cover it all—cover it like . . . well, like the capacious salad bar sneeze guard at Izzy's pizza res-taurant in Portland, Oregon.

Fear not. I had no interest in "rediscovering America," which trav-elers and travel writers have been doing at least since the time of Colum-bus, who rediscovered the New World half a millennium after the Vi-kings arrived. At the same time, I have no doubt that one *can*, through the keyhole of sports, see into an entire culture, even one as far-flung and diverse as American culture. (" 'American culture,' " you say. "That's sorta like 'jumbo shrimp.' ")

In the same year that I was preparing this book, I would have occasion to pass a twelve-hour flight delay in Air India's perhaps-too-grandiosely-named Maharajah Room at Indira Gandhi Airport in Delhi. I spent much of the night in front of the crackling hearth of an ancient television with horizontal-hold problems, a Zenith at its nadir. It was broadcasting a World Cup cricket semifinal between India and Sri Lanka from a sold-out stadium in Calcutta. Prone next to me on the sectional sofa, a slumbering old Indian lady with horizontal-hold problems of her own farted mournfully, her sari billowing out each time like lace curtains in a breeze.

When India looked to be hopelessly out of the match, despondent fans set fire to the stadium. The match was called on account of arson. An announcer wailed about the shame of a nation. And the old woman on the sectional sofa sprang bolt upright from her sleep—all at once, like a police academy firing range target—and dolefully shook her head at the TV. I was on assignment at the time for *Sports Illustrated*, and what occurred to me that evening, not for the first time, was that . . . sports illustrate.

If not exactly a looking glass, it seemed to me, sports can at least serve as a funhouse mirror, reflecting back an unmistakable caricature of a nation. Here now was my opportunity to go through the looking glass: twenty-thousand-mile American road swing.

And so I consigned my few worldly possessions to a six-by-twelve steel box at one of those U-Lock-It ministorage facilities patronized primarily by serial killers and consigned myself to another six-by-twelve steel box, a leased Nissan Pathfinder that I laded with nothing but the barest of necessities: thirty-six compact discs, a set of golf clubs, a dozen foul cigars that might double as long-burning road flares in the event of an emergency.

Which is how it was that I arose one stormy July morning in Minneapolis, in the year before my thirtieth birthday, and abruptly embarked on a busman's holiday. I had no fixed itinerary, except to travel the nation in two grand loops, like the grand loops of the lowercase *l*'s that punctuate the $995 card-show signature of Bill Russell. My sister-in-law once approached the ex-Celtic legend on an airplane and said excitedly, "Mr. Russell, your name is an answer in today's USA Today crossword puzzle." To which Russell replied testily that he didn't give a fig. Or words to that effect. I have often since wondered what the clue must have been: "Cantankerous cager"? "Peevish pivotman"?

But I digress, which is half the fun of any journey. Agape on the shotgun seat lay a Rand McNally Road Atlas with all of its varicose-veined possibilities. I am one of those people who cannot look at a map without feeling a child's sense of wonder at all that awaits me out there: Boos (Illinois) and What Cheer (Iowa), Baskett (Kentucky) and Ball (Louisiana), Sliders (Virginia) and Heaters (West Virginia). Who knew what I might see?

For now, I could say only this: I wanted all of my lunches to be racing-striped in ballpark mustard, noisily dispensed from a flatulent squeeze bottle. I wanted to eat all of my dinners from a Styrofoam fast-food clambox that yawned in my lap while I drove seventy miles an hour and steered with my knees. I wanted all of my afternoons to dwindle down in the backward-marching time of a scoreboard—:10, :09, :08 . . . —that physics-defying device that allows a person lucky enough to mark his or her time by it to grow younger.

I wanted to stave off adulthood. I wanted to see America. I wanted to have fun. Over the next several months, my only calendar would be the multicolored mosaic of one team pocket schedule or another. Shakespeare asserted in Henry IV that "If all the year were playing holidays, to sport would be as tedious as to work." Surely Shakespeare was full of shit, and I intended now to prove it. Leisure City (Florida), here I come.

So I joined Interstate 35 and traveled south out of Minneapolis in a cold gray mist. It was like driving into a sneeze. The radio reported ninety-four-mile-an-hour winds in southern Minnesota, as well as golf-ball-, baseball-, and softball-sized hail. Wonderful. It was raining sporting goods, and I was following the perforated yellow line of the highway, like a trail of dripping nacho "cheez" that would lead me to the lost soul of American sports. Or whatever it was I was looking for.

A sign said that this ribbon of road had been adopted by the WOMEN OF
TOMORROW. How oddly uplifting, I thought, that a group of preopera-
tive transsexuals should find time to clean up the interstate highway
system. The notion left me feeling strangely proud to be an American as
I pulled off the highway for a late lunch in Austin, Minnesota, which
exports to the world a uniquely American product of its own. HORMEL
FOODS hollered a large billboard in town. WHERE GOOD FRIENDS MAKE
GOOD FOOD. Never mind that this "good food" consists principally of
Spam, the processed porklike substance whose name is an apparent con-
traction of "Spoiled ham." The locals were proud nonetheless.

The streets of SPAM TOWN USA—another billboard—were littered
with a dyslexia of large plastic letters blown free from movie-theater and

fast-food marquees. It looked as if God had barfed Alpha-Bits on Austin. I had come here hoping to catch the city's celebrated Spam Jam. Held over three days each July, the Spam Jam is what the Olympics would be if Olympians used Hormel products instead of sporting goods. It is a capital idea and one that works remarkably well. A can of Dinty Moore beef stew, for instance, is roughly the same size and weight as a shotput shot, if not nearly as flavorful.

But it wasn't meant to be. A poster in a bank window informed me that the extravaganza came and went just last week, climaxing with a three-mile SPAM WALK FOR HEALTH. But I could still catch the Chimilewski Polka Band at the street fair on Thursday night. Marvelous. I could feel time receding already—to a simpler, more delusional era when Spam was synonymous with good health and polka music was not yet an oxymoron.

Buoyed by the thought, I left Austin after lunch, hope and Spamburger lodged in my heart. I steered south, toward Iowa and a landscape as flat as ballpark beer. Every twenty miles I passed through some tiny town, each one time-warped and almost too picturesque. The businesses all had names like Koster's Kar Korner, Kountry Kinfolk, Kum 'N' Go, and Kopper Kettle Kafe. With each mile, my pulse quickened. And is it any wonder? I was making for a cornfield near tiny Dyersville, Iowa. I was on my way to the Field of Dreams.

It was clearly a place with curative powers, a Medjugorge of the Middle West. Six years after the film *Field of Dreams* was released, the movie's principal shooting location—a ballfield cut into a cornfield—continued to draw five hundred visitors every summer day. The figure is astonishing, because Dyersville is centrally located in the middle of nowhere. Townsfolk have to drive 175 miles just to get to Des Moines. This is the municipal equivalent of the man who is so sick that he'd have to rally just to die.

And still they came, twenty thousand tourists annually, tripling the town's population daily. What's more, they arrived from all over the world, bursting through the front door of the Dyersville tourism office and asking, *"Wo ist die Fieldofdreamz?"* Really. In any language, "it's the number-one question we get," confirmed the town's tourism director, Julie K. Frye, whose name was carved magnificently from a single piece of driftwood on her desk. "Right after 'Do you have a bathroom?'"

Frankly, I was worried that Dyersville would *be* a bathroom, a tourist-choked toilet. But its streets were still storm-slick when I arrived in early evening—the town was gleaming in the gloaming—and the people were all so solicitous that I instantly felt like a heel for having doubted them. "Did you know," Frye had asked me, "that ghosts walk out of the corn every Sunday to play ball with fans at the field?"

"Real ghosts?"

"No," she said. "Just locals with regular jobs and stuff. But I was talking to one of them last week, and he said that he's never met a rude person out there. Everyone at the Field of Dreams is so *nice*." Indeed, the last entry in the guest book on her desk was signed. "The Fravert Family of Loyal, Wisconsin," and I couldn't help but think—the Fraverts of Loyal, they sounded so . . . *nice*.

Having secured the last vacant room at the Colonial Inn, I strolled across the street to the Country Junction restaurant. I was seated beneath wagon wheels and farm implements while an aproned matron served a rack of ribs unrivaled in size since the opening credits of *The Flintstones*. Unbidden, the waitress then brought tottering side dishes of green beans, coleslaw, macaroni salad, hash browns embalmed in melted American cheese, a basket of fresh-baked bread, and so many Millstream lagers that I thought I was manning a conveyor belt in a bottling plant. My server hovered like a specter until I shoveled it all in.

Understand, I am a skinny man, and Iowans treat skinny strangers as Mormons treat agnostics. Which is to say, with a missionary's zeal to convert. Only when I looked like a snake that had swallowed a hamster was I allowed to hoist myself from the table, retrieve my car, and repair to a gas station next door. "You're in luck!" the woman behind the counter said when I had filled my tank. "I have one bag left!" She hooked a thumb ominously toward a sign outside: FREE POPCORN WITH GAS!

"Back off!" I snapped, trying not to sound ungrateful. "I was just taxidermied at the Country Junction." Suddenly I regretted not having a souvenir T-shirt emblazoned with those very words.

"My husband and I built that place," she volleyed back cheerily. "Just sold it last year."

Her name was Jeanine Koch, and I asked her for directions to the field. She tore a printed map from a tablet full of them, then catapulted into a story about the heady summer of 1988, when Kevin Costner and the Universal film crew descended on Dyersville.

"They were here for two months," Jeanine said. "Only they didn't live here. They lived in Dubuque." She made the second syllable sound like "puke." "I'm not much for TV people, but my daughter, she saw the red-haired guy from *thirtysomething* one night at dinner and just about fell over. It shook her all up."

I didn't know how to respond to this. "Well," I said dumbly. "I can't wait to see the field in the morning." It was almost nine o'clock, and I was ready to collapse in a blubbering blackout-curtained coma back at the motel.

"Why don't you go now?" she suggested.

"My guidebook said it closes at six."

Jeanine looked at me sideways. "It's just a *farm*," she said. "Like anybody else's. The man who owns it, he doesn't care. There were people out there in the storm today. I'm sure there's people out there right now. Go on. Go *on*." She made a little whisk-broom motion with the back of her hands, like an umpire sweeping home plate, and off I went, almost involuntarily, like flotsam: north out of town and across a rickety one-lane bridge, where a strolling old farmer and his wife waved to me giddily in unison. I found myself grinning inanely and waving back. Seconds later, I passed a Jeep whose Iowa plates read GHOST 1. The driver waved giddily, grinning inanely. Then I was plunging down a private road and up a long dirt drive, feeling at once dopey and like a trespasser, when it abruptly appeared around a bend: the familiar white farmhouse and wraparound porch, its wooden swing creaking softly in the evening breeze.

Four cars were parked on the drive—two from Illinois, one from Georgia, another from Missouri. I added my Minnesota plates to the mosaic, turned toward the field, and—*clang!*—fairly heard my jaw drop like a cartoon anvil.

The grass was the brilliant green of highway signage. From home plate, the field fanned out to a wall of rustling corn that stretched to the horizon. The sun was sinking into the stalks in left field like an enormous beach ball alighting in the bleachers. And silhouetted against that circle as if spotlit, a father and son played catch.

The father was in a catcher's crouch, butt cleavage peering from the décolletage of his Wranglers, and as he shouted, "Chuck it in there, Tucker" or "Tuck it in there, Chucker"—honestly, it was difficult to tell which—the beatific smile on his face left no mistake about it: His were the Georgia plates.

Still, the scene was captivating, and I didn't care if it was corny in every conceivable sense. I couldn't wait to return first thing in the morning. And yes, it really was the field that I dreamed about as I slipped into unconsciousness at the Colonial Inn.

I awoke to a TV news report that baseball-sized hail had dimpled much of the area yesterday. A beaming plump woman in a floral-print housefrock produced one such hailstone from her freezer and proudly displayed it like a pie for the camera. The reporter then announced gravely that "bowling-ball-sized hail" had fallen "elsewhere" in northeastern Iowa. There were no pictures. But it's my duty to warn you: One can be killed in Iowa by a bowling ball that has dropped from the sky. And try keeping a straight face while delivering *that* eulogy.

My father once very nearly killed himself at a driving range when he drove a golf ball sideways, directly away from his body, on a line perpendicular to his stance. The bullet pinged off a steel post that divided the driving stalls and rocketed right back at him, raising a cartoon lump on his left knee before careening harmlessly toward a cluster of luxury sedans in the parking lot. But had the ball struck him in the temple, say, or in the nuts, he would have died instantly, or wished he had anyway. And the coroner likely would have ruled the tragedy a suicide-by-banana-slice. As dignified deaths go, this would have ranked somewhere below a Buddhist monk setting himself alight to protest man's inhumanity to man and just above being conked on the noggin by God's bowling ball while standing in the middle of a vast Iowa plain.

Which is where I found myself after breakfast, back at the Field of Dreams. A man named Don Lansing owned the farm and farmhouse. He owned the ballfield, too, with the exception of left and center field and the corn behind it, which belonged to Al and Rita Ameskamp, who billed their property, somewhat desperately, as LEFT AND CENTER FIELD OF DREAMS. Both Lansing and the Ameskamps had trailers parked at the field, from which they sold T-shirts, refreshments, and souvenirs so inexpressibly useless—decorative spoons, pewter corncobs—that one could only be listed as ORNAMENT: $2.50. Needless to say, I bought three of them. A gray-haired lady at the Lansing stand tended to a dozen clamoring souvenir seekers. It looked like the floor of the New York Stock Exchange. I asked her if it was always like this. "No," she said. "It gets busy in the afternoon."

Still, there was no admission charge. Commercial shoots and corporate shindigs were forbidden on the property. Lansing and the Ameskamps maintained the field at their own expense, and Lansing even provided four Porta Potties for the tourists. I wondered how this could be and went to ask the great man himself. I found him reposing on his grand front porch, lemonade and tinkling ice cubes sweating through a tall glass. It was not yet noon and ninety-four degrees. Lansing had foregone the wooden porch swing for an aluminum-framed lawn chair, the kind whose nylon latticework leaves your ass looking like a flame-broiled hamburger when you rise.

An affable man of fifty-three, the farmer told me how movie producers selected his property for its obvious beauty, then became baffled that corn didn't immediately spring from the ground, literally on cue, like obedient extras. " 'Eighty-eight was the drought year," Lansing explained with the certainty of a sommelier. "And the corn—well, the corn wasn't for shit." His face fissured into a shy smile at the swearword. "The movie people kept asking, "What's going on here?" But we irrigated it and irrigated it and, finally, up it come."

Lansing dragged contemplatively on a cigarette. "Now," he exhaled, "I gotta keep it up every year, because everyone who comes here wants to walk out of the corn." Indeed, as the farmer spoke, all along the perimeter of the outfield, tourists photographed each other popping out grandly from between cornstalks, like Johnny Carson from behind a curtain.

There must have been fifty people on the field—playing catch, running the bases, shagging flies. A biker in a black leather jacket, black jeans, black boots, and grimy Oakland A's cap roared up on a black Honda, dismounted, took a few snapshots, and roared back down the drive in a melancholy dustball, an American flag fluttering from his seat. Just beyond the porch, a feed-capped man with two crooked rows of nubby yellow teeth, like corn on the cob, videotaped Lansing's upstairs bedroom window with the dementia common to all people who Camcord inanimate objects. "That's it," the hayseed said, elbowing his unmoved wife. "That's where he had his dream."

"He," of course, was Kevin Costner's movie character, and his dream was a disembodied voice that came in the night and whispered, "If you build it, he will come." So he built a ballfield, and the ghost of Shoeless Joe Jackson emerged from the corn to play ball with other decedents, among them James Earl Jones. Ultimately, Costner is reunited with his estranged father. *If you build it, he will come.*

Dave and Patty Emrick came from Pittsburgh with sons Tyler, Trevor, and Trenton, stopping on their way to Yellowstone via Mount Rushmore. They packed gloves, balls, and a bat expressly for the field. "It appealed to me, mostly," said Dad when asked why he abandoned the interstate for this. "It was real sentimental to walk onto that field. I did what everyone does, I suppose, and stepped out of the corn."

Becky DuBuisson, a widow from Boulder, Colorado, arrived in 1994 on a cross-country drive with her aunt. Ms. DuBuisson had been having a recurring dream, in which she was told to be at the field at midnight on New Year's Eve with a hot dog and a root beer. When DuBuisson arrived in D-ville, the field lay silent beneath a down comforter of snow. She ran the bases in the muffled night. She came back several times in the next year, and just yesterday she became engaged—to Don Lansing, who had already given her the world's biggest diamond.

I asked Lansing why these tourists came, and he didn't respond for a moment. Then it occurred to me, alarmingly, that he hadn't heard a word I'd said today. I had just noticed that he wore small rubber earplugs. He had been taking a break from mowing the lawn when I found him. He appeared always on the verge of answering, but I couldn't tell for sure. It was like anxiously waiting for a car engine to turn over on a winter's day. But finally he spoke, to my visible relief.

"I think they come for as many reasons as there are stars in the heavens," he said. "Some think that Kevin Costner lives here. A lot of people don't understand that Universal built this field—they think my family built it before there was a movie. And then a lot of people don't know that the *house* is real. They think it's just a movie set."

Wasn't he bothered that some people still treated his house as a movie set, taking photos through windows and so forth? "Naw," he said. "For the most part, they respect my little area here. Sometimes at night they'll ask me to turn on the lights"—there were six stancheons surrounding the field—"but I only do that for special occasions." Lansing pointed to a stancheon 280 feet down the right field line. "Joe Pepitone hit the top of that one," he said, mentioning the ex-Yankee with a toupee like a shag toilet-seat cover. "No one else has done it."

Indeed, every September a host of ex-big leaguers descends on Dyersville to play a Celebrity Game. This year Rollie Fingers, Lou Brock, Brooks Robinson, and Maury Wills were among those confirmed. It always draws a big crowd. "It's neat to see all the people and where they come from and their reactions to the field," said Lansing. "We've had 'em from Australia, Japan, all over Europe. Places without baseball."

What could possibly be the appeal to someone who doesn't know baseball? Lansing chewed on that question as if it were a cud. The farm had been in the family for ninety-five years. Lansing played ball on the property with his father, LaVern, and LaVern played ball there with his father before that.

"I think," Lansing said at last, "it has a lot to do with fathers and sons."

Now we were getting somewhere.

3

On, Wisconsin is the state university's fight song and—if you say it fast enough—the answer to the question: "Where did God drop His most ridiculous creatures?"

Really. A friend of mine once spent the day with Milwaukee Brewer owner (and Commissioner of Baseball) Bud Selig, who chose for lunch his favorite drive-in custard stand near County Stadium. Selig procured two hot dogs for himself and, seated on the leather upholstery of his Lexus, immediately licked the ketchup lengthwise off his wieners. "Mmmmm!" he said, turning to his lunch companion. "I love ketchup!" As custodian of our national pastime, Selig may be the most powerful man in the sport. What this bodes for baseball is perhaps better left unpondered.

Still, this was my kind of state. When I was going to college in Milwaukee, an anonymous caller claimed to have poisoned the Usinger's sausage factory downtown. To reassure the panicked populace, the mayor appeared on newscasts and the front pages of newspapers biting lustily into a Usinger's bratwurst. It was an unforgettable tableau, and the point has remained with me: This is how you paralyze Milwaukee— taint the city's sausage supply.

Just being in America's Dairyland now got me longing for nacho "cheez" the lurid color of a school bus, with the viscosity and thermal breakdown of forty-weight Pennzoil. I became energized by the thought of eating brats at a Brewers game while watching the grounds crew groom the infield wearing polyester *lederhosen* as the crowd sings the obscure *second* verse to *Beer Barrel Polka*. (Instead of "Roll out the barrel," it begins "Zing! Boom! Tarrarel!"—surely the world's cheapest rhyme.)

I had entered Wisconsin from its southwest corner, near Fairplay, a name on the map that evokes what sport ought to be about, but a notion that now seems long forgotten. Perhaps it never really existed at all. "Serious sport has nothing to do with fair play," George Orwell wrote sixty years ago. "It is bound up with hatred, jealousy, boastfulness, disregard of all rules, and sadistic pleasure in witnessing violence," all of which aptly describes a Dallas Cowboys' game of today.

In any event, if fair play is now scarcely in evidence, the same goes for Fairplay. The town turned out to be but a single road with twenty ranch-style houses right next to each other. Fairplay appeared to combine all the banality of suburbia with all the shortcomings of small-town life. I saw only one commercial entity, a Shaklee–Avon facility, but even I'm not stupid enough to pay a house call on Shaklee salespeople, which is something like stopping a Hare Krishna in an airport and saying, "I have a six-hour layover. Could I trouble you to tell me about your organization?" So I drove on.

NEED A LIFT? asked a hand-painted billboard when I returned to the highway. CALL ON JESUS! I occupied the next hour slowing for hitchhikers, asking if they needed a lift, telling them to "call on Jesus," then lurching off with but a patch of rubber to remember me by. Which is how I arrived, happily, at the House on the Rock.

In the early 1940s, a man named Alex Jordan built a weekend retreat on a sixty-foot-high chimney of sandstone in Spring Green, Wisconsin. Soon the house sprouted one addition, then another, until it began wandering like Don King's syntax this way and that over forty acres of land. The interior is decorated in the same swank-fifties-lounge style that I imagine Dean Martin's place must have been and is kept ridiculously dark, the better to obscure the escape routes when you learn that the entrance fee is an astounding $14.50.

It is worth every penny, for the House on the Rock is now a museum housing Jordan's astonishing collection of random junk, most of it really, *really* cool. Inside, for instance, is the world's largest merry-go-round, a thirty-five-ton carousel with twenty thousand lights and 269 creatures, none of them horses. There are entire self-playing orchestras, such as the Hupfeld Phonolizst Concertina Model A from 1907 Leipzig, Germany, with its 1,350 horsehair strings, three violins, and a single rotating bow that plays a heartbreaking rendition of *Blue Danube*.

Turn a corner and the menu from the last day of the *Titanic* is displayed with—this being Wisconsin—inordinate attention paid to the ill-fated ocean liner's many on-board cheeses: Cheshire, Stilton, Gorgonzola, Edam, Camembert, Roquefort, St. Ive's, Cheddar—the list reads like the Monty Python cheese sketch. Strolling the halls, I was particularly alarmed by a collection of authentic Burma-Shave signs with horrific thoughts for anyone just embarked on a drive across the country:

A MAN, A MISS

A CAR, A CURVE

HE KISSED THE MISS

AND MISSED THE CURVE

BURMA-SHAVE.

Or:

HER CHARIOT
RACED 80 PER
THEY HAULED AWAY
WHAT HAD BEN-HUR
BURMA-SHAVE.

Or:

HE LIT A MATCH
TO CHECK GAS TANK
THAT'S WHY THEY CALL HIM
SKINLESS FRANK
BURMA-SHAVE.

Spectacular. But the best display by far, and the reason I had come, was the modest assembly of ancient sepia newspapers flaking on the walls. Pasted in various corridors were sports pages from the 1930s and 1940s with headlines like BLAME CUB SLUMP ON SLIM SLAB CORPS. (Say it aloud. It's poetry.) The stories themselves were filled with pitchers who "hurled cypher jobs," batters who "collected clutch bingles," baserunners who "expired at the cash register," and visiting pitchers who—I swear to God—"toed the alien humpback." There was a scribe in Pennsylvania who, describing the turning point of any contest, would invariably write: "That's when Mr. Mo Mentum changed uniforms." This language is ridiculous and entirely incomprehensible, of course, and I must say I love each and every word of it. It seems to me a shame that it's now as dead as Latin.

To me growing up, the front section of the newspaper was the wrapper that kept the sports section dry on my doorstep. I loved the tortured, ludicrous names given to sports columnists. Max Nichols in Minneapolis wrote "The Nichols' Worth." I recall a columnist in Vermont, first name Donald, who wrote—who may still write—a daily dispatch called "By Don's Early Light." I dreamed of one day seeing my own mug shot above a column of type headed "Something Up My Steve" or "Ali Baba and the Forty Steves" or something equally zippy.

The stories may be clearer nowadays, but the sports sections are all full of ads for gambling hotlines and alcohol rehab clinics and penile-implant surgeons and strip joints out by the airport. As a sportswriter, I have often wondered who my readers are, and I like to think better of you than advertisers do. To judge by the papers, you are a desperately lonesome, possibly impotent, alcoholic bettor, and I don't believe that for a minute. Now, if you'll stop inflating that doll with a keg tapper, we'll move on.

Because of the state's singular lack of diversions for young millionaire athletes, Wisconsin is the home of four NFL training camps, and I was determined to see at least one of them. So I drove to Platteville, summer home of the Chicago Bears, and joined two thousand people staring at an empty practice field from a small hillside. For sixty minutes, nothing happened. After ninety minutes, a flunky emerged and set up orange cones and upside-down Rubbermaid trash cans. For fifteen more minutes, we literally watched grass grow. Finally Bears rookie Rashaan Salaam materialized in a doorway, and grown men were now drawn to him like metal shavings to a magnet.

"He ain't even legal yet," a fan who looked like Mike Ditka told his buddy, in reference to Salaam. "Just think, you were enterin' Prospect High School when his mother was pinchin' him out."

"Dat," replied the buddy, "is a scary thought."

The buddy also looked like Ditka. Just as old spouses grow to resemble each other, or some pet owners look like their pooches, Bears fans dress and chew gum and grow mustaches like "Da Coach." Indeed, when Chicago fired Ditka, they replaced him with near-doppelgänger Dave Wannstedt, who looks like a sketch of Iron Mike done by a police artist with Parkinson's.

Following the appearance of Salaam, a gauntlet of autograph jackals appeared at the doorway that led from the locker room to the practice field. Bear backup quarterback Steve Walsh emerged and a boy of no more than ten yelled, "Steve, you promised me an autograph this morning!" Walsh nodded without making eye contact as he signed for others. "If he doesn't give me one, I'll kill him!" the kid said to his little brother. Both wore Bulls T-shirts signed by virtually every professional athlete in Chicago. "I'll tell him he sucks," the kid went on. Walsh soon signed for the little twit, signed for everyone, signed for a half hour straight, and the ten-year-old said to him, "Thanks, Steve! Good luck this year!"

On my way to the car, I heard the clashing of shoulder pads, and as I caught a whiff of the Porta Potties that sat atop the hillside, I was overcome by a tidal wave of nostalgia. Just as smelling the crumb of a French pastry set Proust off for several volumes, I suddenly recalled how it was fashionable at high school football games in suburban Minneapolis to tip over Porta Potties with people inside them—an impulse I now resisted.

I once mentioned this curious custom to Jack Armstrong, who at the time was a member of the soon-to-be World Series champion Cincinnati Reds and the starting pitcher for the National League in the 1990 All-Star Game. I cannot for the life of me remember how the subject came up, but these things do in locker rooms, trust me. Armstrong, the athlete with the All-American name, drew me aside and told me a story, which I will share with you now as we make the long drive from Platteville to Green Bay, a real football town.

Armstrong was raised in Neptune, New Jersey—Jack Nicholson's hometown—and from 4 A.M. to 6 A.M. every day each summer for seven years, he worked on a boat called *The Lenny* that ferried vacationers twenty miles into the Atlantic Ocean to go fishing. "We'd have sixty lines all cast in different directions," Armstrong said. "I'm supposed to keep 'em all straight, plus sell jigs, hooks, and Cokes, help pull in fish and unhook 'em—all of it at the same time. All these tourists become Indiana Jones out there, cutting sandwiches with the same knives they're using to cut bait. Pretty soon everyone's sick. You're helping one guy pull in a bluefish while another guy's throwing up on your back. There are pieces of bologna dribbling down your shirt, but it doesn't faze you. People paid their good money and you have to be polite. After a while nothing, and I mean *nothing*, affects you. A guy gets a hook stuck in his eye, you cut off the line, tape the loose end to his head, call the Coast Guard, and help pull in another bluefish."

The Lenny had a fifty-gallon septic tank on board. In theory, a mate would pull a lever and the boat would evacuate its payload, as it were, into the ocean. (Remember this on your next visit to the Jersey Shore.) But the sewage tended to solidify, and it was often left to Armstrong to dive overboard with a broomstick, hold his breath, swim beneath the boat, poke at the trapdoor, and dart away before the cargo dropped. Alas, the contents weren't always so easily dislodged. He remembered spending an eternity underwater, summoning the last of his breath, giving a mighty poke, and looking up. Before he could dart, a tidal wave of waste washed over him.

"I'm in nothing but cutoffs," Armstrong said. "I'm swallowing this stuff. I'm wondering, 'Was that a piece of *corn?*' The guys on deck think I've drowned. But I'd always eventually resurface, looking like the Creature from the Black Lagoon."

Well, what can I tell you. Just recalling the story in the car made me hungry, so I stopped for a snack at the Schultz Cheese Haus, a faux Bavarian chalet with signs shouting WE SHIP CHEESE ANYWHERE IN THE U.S. YEAR-ROUND and WE CUT TO WITHIN ¼ LB. ON YOUR BULK CHEESE ORDERS. Surveying all this cheese, I was suddenly seized by a powerful melancholia for the victims of the *Titanic*.

I bought a lunch of cheddar curds—little coronary rubber bullets— and beef jerky. Near Oakfield, a sign said YOU JUST PASSED MARY ANN'S REAL GOOD FOOD. Whether this message was intended for people who hadn't been to Mary Ann's, or people who had just eaten there, I couldn't say. My radio was tuned to "the hits of yesteryear, 1280 WNAM." That's W-'Nam. I thought northern Wisconsinites were perhaps nostalgic for the Vietnam War, but then I passed through Oshkosh, in the middle of its annual aviators' convention, and realized they pined for an earlier war era altogether: The sky was choked with Fokkers and

Piper Cubs. Farther up Highway 41 at DePere, a billboard said BUYING A CASKET? CALL YOUR FUNERAL DIRECTOR FIRST! And I felt my brain slowly leaking out my ears.

It was moments later that I saw the exit for Lombardi Avenue. "I go home down Lombardi," Packer coach Mike Holmgren has noted. "I pass the Lombardi Plaza and Lombardi Middle School. The name—you can't escape it in Green Bay." Indeed, Lombardi Avenue is four lanes flanked by the Lombardi Plaza strip mall, the Lombardi Theaters cineplex, the—there it was!—Lombardi Middle School. (Motto: "Learning Isn't Everything . . .") I fell in behind a green Dodge Intrepid with Illinois plates GO PAKRS. A backyard fence facing Lombardi had been painted, green letters on a yellow background, BRETT ON THE PACK TO GO FAVRE, a pun so contorted I thought surely the homeowner must have his own sports column.

I made a left at Lambeau Field and headed for the Packer Hall of Fame, opened by President Gerald Ford in 1976. A photograph inside shows Ford having inordinate difficulty removing a green sheet from a commemorative plaque, but otherwise the hall is a shrine to two men. Earl (Curly) Lambeau founded the Pack in 1919 after playing for Knute Rockne at Notre Dame. Lambeau's nickname with the Fightin' Irish was "The Bellicose Belgian"—an oxymoron at least on par with "working press" and the kind of moniker we have happily done away with in sports. Fighter Primo Carnera, after all, was "The Tall Tower of Gorgonzola," meaning . . . what, exactly? That he literally stunk to high heaven?

Anyway, the Packers were nicknamed the Packers because their first uniforms were donated by the Acme Meat-Packing Company, the same outfit that still supplies arms to Wile E. Coyote. I spent a happy hour losing myself in Lombardiana. The Hall of Fame displays hundreds of gifts that were given to St. Vince—silver steak knives, inscribed paperweights, a janitor's ring of various keys to various cities—and each item reposes under glass, like the Hope Diamond, each marked by a tasteful donor's card.

Just before dusk, I exited the hall, passing beneath the sign Lom-

bardi had hung in the locker room: HOW WAS YOUR ATTITUDE TODAY?
Just fine and improving rapidly, I thought as I tuned the car radio to the
day's big sports news: Chili con carnage was narrowly averted at the
Brewers game in Milwaukee when Chili Davis of the California Angels
went bat-in-hand after a fan in the stands who had heckled him—apparently for Chili's failure, earlier in the game, to collect a "clutch bingle."

Fairplay, Wisconsin, indeed.

Just beyond Deadmans Point on the Upper Peninsula of Michigan, I passed into the EASTERN TIME ZONE, suppressing mild disappointment that there was only a small sign and no actual dotted line across the highway, as on my map. Now I couldn't dance a jig on either side of the border, shouting at my fellow vacationers, "Look, I'm going back in time! Now I'm stepping into the future! Now I'm going back in time! Now I'm stepping into the future . . ." And so forth until somebody shot me.

I had entered Michigan—with its orgasmic YES! M!CH!GAN! WELCOME! sign—via Peshtigo, Wisconsin, which declared itself FOOT-BALL STATE CHAMPIONS WIAA-5, 1983. These sad signs, I would discover, were all over the Upper Peninsula, and each had the gone-to-seed air of a middle-aged ex-quarterback, bullshitting in a bar about some long-ago glory. There ought to be a statute of limitations on such city-limit boasts. Really, the signs only advertise that the town you are about to enter has seen better days. They might as well be expiration dates: PESHTIGO— BEST BEFORE 11/15/83.

If sports occupy too prominent a place in American life, nowhere is this more evident than in small towns. In Menominee, where the highway swerved to greet the Lake Michigan shoreline, I passed a house with a basketball hoop in its driveway and an electronic, arena-caliber scoreboard bolted to the garage. The marquee at the Taco Bell in town said GOOD LUCK AT STATE, MEN ALL-STARS! On the radio, the Delta County Big-League Girls were hammering East Jordan–Alpena in Michigan's state softball semifinals. When the score became 10–0, the "mercy rule" was invoked and East Jordan was put out of its misery, an apposite gesture in the home state of Dr. Jack Kevorkian.

It was a Saturday night in late summer on the U.P., and every motel was booked with wedding parties. Highway 2 was clogged with the automotive cholesterol of August—station wagons with steamer trunks gaffer-taped to their roofs; minivans stuffed with the annual inventory of an average Toys "R" Us; Winnebagos towing cars towing trailers bearing speedboats.

Sometime after eight o'clock, I despaired of finding lodging for the night and began to curse aloud a phenomenon I had never before noticed: that moteliers—the word, I fear, flatters them—have largely done away with NO VACANCY signs, presumably because they were too useful.

As a result, I had to pull off the highway at five-minute intervals, park, and approach a front-desk clerk who would tell me cheerily, "Why, we sure *do* have . . . a full house tonight." Or "We have *one* room available . . . next Thursday." Soon I was simply lurching into the fire lane in front of each motel, storming through the front door, and shouting, "I *know* you don't have any rooms for tonight! Am I right?!" And then charging back to my still-running car as the stunned desk clerk nodded confirmation. And so the evening passed.

Downtown Escanaba—HOME OF '81 STATE CLASS A FOOTBALL

CHAMPIONS—was predictably forlorn with two once-grand theaters, the Michigan and the Delft, now apparently derelict on Ludington Street. Passing the Wells Sports Complex on the way out of town, I was again unaccountably saddened by its sign: HOME OF '91 STATE PEEWEE B CHAMPIONS. I mean, *honestly*.

I spun the radio dial hopefully, as if playing the slots. A sports-radio jock-jockey out of Detroit said of some Tiger or another, "He couldn't hit sand if he fell off a camel." I flailed at the seek button and got another station on the U.P. As I drove through the gathering darkness, winding through tall pines on a licorice whip of road, past knotty-pine lodges, ANDEKER BEER signs winking in their windows, a stentorian voice filled the Pathfinder.

"Chances are, sports are at the center of your memories," the voice began. "Whether you were playing football on Friday nights or going to the dance after the Big Game. Playing catch with Dad or watching your own children play. We at First Bank of Escanaba salute the athletes of today—making the memories of tomorrow on the Upper Peninsula."

And, not for the first time, I felt chastened, exposed as a cynical dipshit. Those signs, those towns—they were beginning to make sense to me.

After crossing the five-mile span of the Mackinac Toll Bridge, I arrived on the oven-mitt mainland of Michigan and abruptly abandoned the interstate. At once, I was plunging blindly through pitch blackness, a paste of insects on my windshield and headlights, ominous animal noises issuing from the void. I was lost in a forest, on a serpentine road laid out like Lombard Street in San Francisco. Near Lewiston, I at last approached a large blue sign of the sort that promises hot food and warm accommodations, the welcome icons of crossed-knife-and-fork and man-asleep-in-bed. I slowed and flashed my high beams. Alas, it was not as I had hoped. PRISON AREA the sign read. DO NOT PICK UP HITCHHIKERS.

Sigh.

I drove for several more hours, navigating with my head thrust out the window like a dog's. At 3 A.M., having long before sent my road atlas windmilling into the backseat, I fell in behind a banana-colored lowrider, its dragging muffler throwing up sparks, leading me like a lighthouse beacon into a friendly port, rich with five-star resort hotels. Or so I hoped. The car's bumper beckoned with a sticker that said SAVE THE PLANET: KILL YOURSELF. My unwitting guide took me past Steve's Workingman's Pub, then by a series of similarly named joints. Evidently, this anonymous town was where the prison escapees of Lewiston settled comfortably into exile.

The smell of the burg was overwhelming, though not unpleasant. And oh so familiar, though I could not immediately identify it. And then it hit me. The air—it was fragrant with . . . Froot Loops. I had stumbled, unmistakably, into Battle Creek.

You may know Battle Creek as the home of Tony the Tiger. But to me, it will always be the home of Roger Gibson. He was a buildingsupply salesman who labored through two decades in his basement to build a miniature Montreal Forum—a kind of "Three-um"—replete with functioning 400-bulb scoreboard, TV cameras, remote-controlled Zamboni (with cigar-smoking driver), press box, concession stands, and players fashioned from the pliable skeletons of Pink Panther dolls. Gibson was the sort of sports obsessive I could understand, a man who told me five years ago, "I can't seem to remember my wife's birthday, but I can still remember when I started all this—on January 9, 1974, at 1 P.M."

What amazed me was, Gibson had never been to the real Montreal Forum. He had constructed his from a mental photograph filtered through television. He was fifty-nine years old when I interviewed him, and when my small item appeared in *SI*, Montreal's *Sunday Gazette* flew him into town for a Stanley Cup finals game. The Canadiens allowed him to skate on the ice before the tilt, which the Habs came from behind to win in double overtime. Gibson called the evening "the highlight of my life," and who can blame him? The Canadiens and *Gazette* have ever since occupied a warm place in my heart.

And now, so, too, did Cereal City. For Battle Creek clutched me to its breast. I found a room, having clocked more than 800 miles on the

day and night. My body felt incomplete without a car strapped to it, in
the way you feel like a midget after removing a pair of skates. I slept for
four uneasy hours—still feeling the infernal car on me, like the phantom
leg of a new amputee—until housekeeping flushed me from my room
and back onto the road.

I skipped breakfast, content with the contact high of the Kellogg's
plant, and, once on the highway, felt the gravitational pull of Chicago.
Chicago was bearing the worst of the Midwest's unspeakable heatwave,
which had already claimed 550 lives in the city, mostly elderly without
air-conditioning. Even now—at midmorning with the air-conditioning
on—it was like living in a trouser press.

"A grisly discovery on the South Side," enthused a voice on a
station out of Chicago. "Police say they've found a human skeleton encased in cement or concrete in a bathtub in an abandoned building."
Suddenly it seemed best to steer clear of Chicago.

And so I joined the Indiana Toll Road near LaPorte and turned east.
WATCH YOUR SPEED! WE ARE! warned a sign.

"Watch your syntax! I is," I replied and stepped down hard on the
accelerator, suddenly happy to be young and free, on a long stretch of
road that was neither.

The Chicago Cubs were evidently enduring a slump—something to
do with their "slim slab corps"—but this didn't seem to matter to Eddie
Vedder, lead singer of the band Pearl Jam, who was saying on all-sports
radio WMVP, "I don't have to tell the people of Chicago about Wrigley
Field. This is the coolest *bleep*in' place. I hate baseball. I just like the
Cubs." I knew Mr. Vedder to be a knowledgeable sports fan, for Pearl
Jam's original name was Mookie Blaylock, an homage to the point guard
of the same name. And I tended to share his dim view of baseball. Or, I
should say, of *major-league* baseball, which is why I was now making for
Fort Wayne, Indiana, America's prototypical minor-league sports town.

Just beyond the Knute Rockne Rest Stop, I succumbed to something like narcolepsy and managed to drive in a deep and dream-filled

haze to a Holiday Inn in South Bend. There, I secured a room and repaired to Gipper's Lounge in the lobby, where the beer taps rise out of deflated footballs and the iconography of Notre Dame football fills the walls.

I nursed a beer—making a mental note to never again order a drink decanted from a deflated football—and buttonholed the one catatonic customer at the bar. A ballgame was being previewed on ESPN.

"Who's playing?" I asked earnestly, eager for human contact.

The man looked at me as if I had just taken a leak on his loafers. "Twinkies," he slurred at last. "And Stinkees."

This turned out to be the Twins and the Yankees, playing in Minneapolis. Seeing my hometown appear on the bar's battered television, my only companion a comatose auto-parts salesman from St. Louis, I felt a fleeting stab of longing for home. The drunk continued talking long after I left the bar—left him there like a selection on the jukebox that I now regretted making. I retired very early to my room, to pass the evening as I might.

I wrote these lines on my PowerBook. The computer has a built-in Spell-Check program that seeks out any words on its screen that are not in the dictionary, then impetuously "corrects" these "misspellings." Spell-Check, for instance, changed the first sentence of this paragraph to read: I WROTE THESE LINES ON MY POWERBOAT—an image that I rather enjoy.

Inevitably, I invented a solitary game to pass the time in motel rooms. I began running the names of famous athletes through Spell-Check. It began while I was watching the Simpson trial on CNN. Dr. Henry Lee was disparaging Dennis Fung in front of Judge Lance Ito when I idly typed in ORENTHAL SIMPSON. As God is my witness, the computer came up with ORIENTAL SYMPOSIUM instead.

Soon I was serving up BJORN BORG, and the computer was returning BORN BORE. When I wrote the name of born boor Ilie Nastase, Spell-Check spat back ILL NAUSEATES. Clearly, I was onto something.

Spell-Check could crystallize the essential character of an athlete, offering a new name that fit that person better than his or her own.

In Spell-Check, for instance, Hall of Fame pitcher and recovered cocaine addict Fergie Jenkins was rechristened FORGO JUNKIES. Gary Moeller, fired as football coach at Michigan for drunken debauchery in a Detroit restaurant, become one GAMY MAULER. Anyone who has seen Anfernee Hardaway play basketball knows he is INFERNO HARDWARE.

Conversely, some long-held illusions were shattered like glass backboards. When I wrote the name of a six-foot-nine-inch basketball great from cosmopolitan Houston, Spell-Check exposed Elvin Hayes as an ELFIN HAYSEED. Likewise, wholesome hurler Orel Hershiser became the hedonistic ORAL HASHISH. Who knew that Dodger ace Hideo Nomo was in fact a HIDEOUS GNOME? With the deft dropping of a letter here, the apt addition of a letter there, Spell-Check saw into the human soul.

And if you happened to be seven feet, seven inches tall, the software kicked in a *couple* of corrections to your name—neither of them flattering, but both summing up your basketball skills quite tidily. I wondered which Spell-Check suggestion would be preferred by Manute Bol: MANURE BOWL? or MANURE BOY?

Thirty miles west of Fort Wayne, I came upon the Lite-Breeze Mobile Home Park, which triggered two powerful associations: (1) if I ever develop a tornado-magnet trailer park, I won't put a reference to wind in its name, and (2) as a child, my father lived in a trailer in Fort Wayne.

It is one of the few non-sports-related details I knew about his boyhood. I had only heard him speak of his own father once, in the summer after my mother died, when he and I took a parody of a vacation—to the Middle East, in July, after the Gulf War. Flying into Tel Aviv on El Al, he became exasperated by the questions on the exhaustive Israeli customs card: "Favorite Beatle?" "Vertical leap in inches?" "Paper or plastic?"—that sort of thing. "Why do they need to know my father's name?" my father asked at one point. "*I* don't even know that."

This wasn't strictly true, because my dad presently revealed that his father's name was Jack and that sometime during the Depression, Jack abandoned his infant son and made for Oakland, where he eventually opened an eponymous saloon. Karmically, the neon sign he ordered for the joint—JACK'S—arrived having been somehow misspelled FACK'S. Which is how there came to be a spectacularly unsuccessful Bay Area bar by that name.

Arriving for the first time in my father's hometown, I found my way to the Allen County War Memorial Coliseum, a wonderful old rust hulk of an arena, abutting the park in which John (Johnny Appleseed) Chapman is buried. The coliseum was once home to the great Fort Wayne Zollner Pistons, who in 1941 succeeded the Fort Wayne General Electrics as the city's professional basketball team. I loved these old industrial names. Far from smacking of the sinister corporate sponsorship of today, they evoked in me something like the opposite: the unmonied working-class roots of professional sports, and those who played them, and those who paid to watch them *be* played.

After the war, Fort Wayne also supported the G.E. Voltmen of semipro baseball, the Fort Wayne Daisies of the All-American Girls Professional Baseball League, the Fabulous Fastball Pistons of professional softball, and the Fort Wayne Komets of the International Hockey League. My old man himself claimed to have been a spit-bucket boy at professional wrestling events; a star of the city's (no, the state's) most formidable ever football team; an acolyte of Fort Wayne's Emil (Red) (Six-Yard) Sitko, a man so legendary he needed two nicknames, who was something like twenty-six when he was still starring for Frank Leahy at Notre Dame; and the personal valet of one Bobby McDermott, the simply supernatural Zollner Piston who—my father has always obstinately insisted—was a frequent and deadly accurate shooter from . . . half-court. (Sure, Dad. Have another martini.)

Before every Piston home game of the 1949–50 season, my dad met McDermott in the the arena parking lot and carried his bag to the locker room door. It was a way to get in for free, and every other Piston had a similar arrangement with a neighborhood kid. Before the season finale, McDermott told my father to see him outside after the game, and when they met, the future Hall of Famer gave the future Father of Me his entire uniform. My father never forgot it, and I have always considered this a bond as strong as blood: Both of us, my dad and I, have caught the soiled uniform pants of a professional athlete.

I was now in the parking lot of the former home of the Pistons (and current home of the Fort Wayne Fury of the Continental Basketball Association), because it adjoined the lot for Municipal Stadium, home of the Class A baseball Fort Wayne Wizards, whose game I had come to see tonight. With two hours to kill, I decided to take a stroll downtown, where, to my astonishment, I stumbled upon a slim book called *Fort Wayne Sports, Yesterday and Today* by a history professor named Michael C. Hawfield.

I took the book into the ballpark, settled into a seat along the first base line, and opened the intriguing volume. In its 96 pages, to my profound surprise, was a section on my father's (apparently legendary) 1950 Central Catholic High School team, which outscored its opponents 368–37 on its way to winning the state football championship. There was, likewise, a tribute to Emil (Red) (Six-Yard) Sitko, who was indeed a twenty-six-year-old fullback for the Fighting Irish around the time Leahy recruited my father, who would play at Purdue instead. And, finally, on page 91, I found an extraordinary fanfare for Bobby McDermott.

"He typically would take no more than one or two steps past the center line, take a second to set his feet together, and fire a high arching shot, usually into the basket," Hawfield wrote. Rochester Royal Al Cervi recalled in the book a pregame warm-up in which "Bobby was putting on an exhibition. He made ten for ten and then fifteen for fifteen, all from midcourt. The crowd was cheering and I was, too! You couldn't let him get to the ball. I remember a game in the Chicago Amphitheater, which had the longest court in the United States—112 feet. He scored three times on me from the midcourt line. That's 56 feet, and twice his shot brushed my fingers!"

It is a disquieting discovery: to learn that my own father had, for all these years, been telling me tales that were apparently . . . *true.* How

dare he not lie to me. I had always smugly dismissed his stories out of
hand, but now—now I would never know *what* to disbelieve. Or so I was
soberly reflecting when a lady in this otherwise empty stadium said I was
sitting in her seat. Her hairdo had the same shape and colors as a Soft-
Serve vanilla-chocolate swirl cone.

I reexamined my ticket. She took notice of my notebook. I confessed I was a writer. She said she was upset with *Sports Illustrated*, a
declarative statement that she nonetheless ended with a question mark.

"*Sports Illustrated* done an article on John Daly?" she elaborated
after introducing herself as Darlene. "And they were crackin' on him?
And it kinda pissed me off, 'cause they said if he won"—I gathered she
was referring to that summer's British Open—"he could go into that R &
H for drinks with the members?"

"The R & A," I interjected, a tad pompously, as if I were a member. "The clubhouse of the Royal & Ancient golf club."

"Yeah, anyway," she said. "The members didn't want him to? And
Sports Illustrated was askin' him if he would go in anyway, and he said he
wouldn't if he had to use, you know, *etiquette?*" At this magic word—
"etiquette"—the woman's young son yelled, "Who *farted?!*" Darlene
roared at the witticism, but cuffed the kid all the same.

"Anyhoo," she went on, "I was readin' the article on my way home
from work? I always read in the car, 'cause it's one hour up and one hour
back every day? I knock off six books a week? Course, now that 69 is
down to one lane, I can't read as *much*, gets kinda dangerous . . ."

I thanked Darlene and moved as far away from her as the stadium
architecture would allow.

The Wizards were getting their asses handed to them on this
night, 7–0, courtesy of the Wisconsin Timber Rattlers. Wizard manager
Dan Rohn appeared admirably well adjusted to this fate. He wore the
look of a man who had the immeasurable misfortune to spend his youth
as a capable second baseman in the Cubs' farm system during the years
that Ryne Sandberg was the Cubs' second baseman.

No matter. The game was a mere vehicle for the Wizards' delirium of promotions: For every action on the field, there was an equal and opposite overreaction by a host of sponsors working the stands. It was all somehow irresistible.

"If the Wizards come from behind to win in the ninth, they're *'getting away with a win'!"* intoned the PA announcer. "And one lucky fan will *'get away for a night'*—to COURTYARD BY MARRIOTT!"

"GTE's Long Call for Long Ball," he announced a little later. "Any Wizard home run means a free five-minute long-distance call from the seat of one lucky fan!" For some reason, I saw Darlene's son dialing Dubai and asking the uncomprehending Arab who answered, "Is Hugh Jass there?"

Likewise, if any Wizard were to hit the bull's-eye in the BEN DAVIS CHEVROLET sign in left center field, he *and* "one lucky fan" would each win $50. This appeared unlikely at best, as the spot was the size of a compact disc and 350 feet from home plate. (The single cheapest sports promotion I have ever seen took place at a minor-league basketball game in St. Paul. A contestant had once chance to chip a tennis ball with a golf club through a basketball hoop 100 feet away. Had anyone achieved this geometric impossibility, he or she would have received, if memory serves, a certificate for one free Big Mac with the purchase of another.) But what the hell? Given the sheer number of giveaways and side-shows—sumo wrestling at the seventh-inning stretch; the venerable nameless game in which two fans spin until they vomit, then sprint to third base—it was almost true that everyone was a winner on this night, and there was a happy buzz as we filed out afterward. No one cared that the game was a four-hit debacle: Each of us was one lucky fan.

Gorged on entertainment and making for the turnstile, I saw the home team's Merlinesque mascot, Wayne the Wizard, accosted by a little boy. "You're cuckoo!" the child said, poking Wayne in the belly.

"Cuckoo for Cocoa Puffs!" came a voice from deep within the costume. The kid shrieked, elated, and giggled all the way to the parking lot.

In my room at a nearby Super 8, I turned the TV up loud, so as to outshout the phlegmatic air conditioner, and an ad came on for an epic, five-volume videocassette library of sports bloopers: pitchers getting hit in the nuts by line drives, gymnasts racking their balls on the pommel horse, pole vaulters vasectomizing themselves with their poles, wide receivers getting gelded by goalposts—every classic clip was there, a hilarious litany of debilitating injuries, all set to circus music.

I laughed and laughed and drifted into a deeply satisfying slumber.

I awoke to subzero temperatures and what sounded like a straining locomotive and slowly came to the unwelcome conclusion that I had spent
the night in a refrigerated boxcar.

But it was only the emphysematic air conditioner. I arose, turned
off the demonic appliance, and opened a window on Fort Wayne. A
rolling ball of heat hit me in the face, as if I'd opened a bag of microwave
popcorn. It was already ungodly at 8 A.M.—too hot to do anything. Indeed, experts at the University of Michigan's Population Studies Center
were forecasting a decline in births nine months hence.

This was bad news for football manufacturers, for I'd been told that
every male child born in Massillon, Ohio, received, before he even left
the hospital, a complimentary pigskin from the Massillon High School

football booster club. Is this a great country or what? And so I was on my way to the cradle of American football, the sixty-mile corridor from Massillon to Canton to Cleveland.

Ohioans like to pose a riddle: "What's round on both ends and 'hi' in the middle?" The answer is, of course, "Ohio," though technically speaking, the state isn't "hi" in its middle at all, but rather flat, devoid of life, and breathtakingly boring. I drove through it now, at the speed of refrigerator fungus.

There are more than 2 million farmers in America, working 972 million acres of farmland, and I got stuck behind every last one of them on Highway 30, their tractor bumpers bearing the dispiriting orange triangle of the slow-moving vehicle. Time itself was a slow-moving vehicle in these parts. Barns bore the fading ad slogans of another epoch: CHEW MAIL POUCH TOBACCO—TREAT YOURSELF TO THE BEST! Amish quiltmakers stood cheek-by-jowl with the keepers of hillbilly porno shops. Sometimes literally, to judge by the photos in the magazines sold by the latter. A man sold TRAIL BOLOGNA from the back of a truck, and I numbly wondered: What the hell is *that* a euphemism for?

My plan was to plumb the football ethos of northern Ohio, and I at last made my way to Massillon (22 TIMES STATE FOOTBALL CHAMPIONS). A horse-drawn buggy plied the main drag into downtown, leaving a path of what I feared was "trail bologna" in its wake. I followed that path directly to a sports bar whose electronic score ticker was flashing the fall schedule of the Massillon High School football Tigers. That schedule was also painted on a billboard downtown and included one game at the Orange Bowl in Miami, to be televised on ESPN.

Massillon was the first high school to land an athlete on a Wheaties box (Chris Spielman in 1983). Its stadium, named for former Tiger (and Hall of Fame) coach Paul Brown, seats eighteen thousand. The school's current coach was doing ads for a local copier service on TV. It isn't a high school, it's an NFL franchise, I reflected while nursing another beer ten miles to the east in a Canton bar called the Hall of Foam.

Canton is also home to the Pro Football Hall of *Fame*, which is housed in a building that looks, inexplicably, like a giant Airwick air freshener. Inside, O. J. Simpson's bronze bust was lighter than the other likenesses, for his noggin had just spent several days out of doors, having been stolen from the hall and later abandoned along the interstate by a panicky headknapper. It was now secured to its pedestal, I think, by a pair of Frankenstein bolts in the neck.

A few heads down, Vince Lombardi's nose was eroding, rubbed to a high shine by hall visitors, who believe his schnozz has the same mystical qualities as the Blarney Stone. Yes, sir: If I wanted to know why football was now America's game, northern Ohio would do just fine.

So I spent two days in the region, marinating myself in Massillon, learning to speak Cantonese, and then setting fire to my notes. Because scant weeks after I left the state, the Cleveland Browns announced that they were moving to Baltimore, and all of northern Ohio abruptly became a very different place. So I returned and spent an enlightening week.

Upon arrival in Cleveland, I checked the phone book in my room, idly wondering if the city had any residents *named* Cleveland Brown. Lord knows, it had enough people with the surname. Indeed, the two most famous Browns were Browns: team founder Paul Brown and fullback Jim Brown. And, sure enough, the White Pages listed a Cleveland Brown III. I dialed the number and, after several rings, an older woman answered. Delighted with myself, I asked to speak to Cleveland Brown.

After a pause, the woman said, "He's deceased."

I stammered apologies. With some embarrassment, I babbled that I was a writer, curious to know what Cleveland Brown thought of the imminent departure of the Cleveland Browns, and, honestly, if I had known . . .

The woman began to laugh. "Cleveland Brown III was my husband," she said, giving her own name as Carrie. "And he was born in

1929, before there was a football team. But you should call my son. He's Cleveland Brown IV. And *his* son is Cleveland Brown V. They live in Middletown." She gave me their number. "I'd like to see the Browns stay in town. But you tell people that *all* the Cleveland Browns aren't leaving. And if you talk to my son," she said in parting, "tell him I wish that *my* Cleveland Browns would come home sometime." I assured her that I would do so.

"We're *trying* to move back to Cleveland," Cleveland Brown IV told me when I finally reached him by phone. "And no," sighed the thirty-eight-year-old nuclear medicine technologist. "My son and I are not changing our names to Baltimore Brown, though I get asked that fourteen times a day. Happened just this afternoon at the auto-emissions inspector."

Of course, at the time of my visit, the other Cleveland Browns *were* planning a move to Baltimore. And when that football team was set to leave, what the Cleveland Brown family asked of the Cleveland Brown franchise was this: Leave your once-noble name in Ohio.

"I'm not much of a football fan," confessed Cleveland Brown, who spent eleven years, nine months, and eighteen days traveling the world in the Air Force and another five abroad as a nondenominational mission-ary. "But when the Browns said they were moving, it really affected me. Not because of my name. But because for fifty years, support for that team by the people of Cleveland has been phenomenal." And that, of course, is what made this particular move so extraordinary. And so ex-traordinarily sad.

When Browns owner Art Modell announced his intention to move the team to Maryland, well . . . "I have to believe he didn't anticipate what the response would be," WHK radio host Ron Brienes told me over beers at a downtown Cleveland sports bar called Coach's.

That was a howling understatement, for Cleveland Stadium was immediately stripped of all of its advertising; the coaches' and players' TV and radio programs were summarily cancelled; and twenty-four hours a day throughout the metropolis—in the airport, outside the convention center, above the city's most prominent intersection—electronic message boards flashed STOP ART MODELL, exactly like those public-service ad campaigns to STOP TEEN PREGNANCY or STOP V.D.

But the people of northern Ohio had only begun their collective impersonation of Glenn Close in *Fatal Attraction*. From this day forward, Modell is unlikely to publicly appear again in Cleveland, except as an effigy. At the time of my visit, he was living in exile in Florida. "In one stroke, he has torn down everything he ever did," wrote Bill Livingston in the Cleveland *Plain Dealer*. "He has wasted thirty-five years, exactly half his life." And that would be sadness enough for one chapter.

But more melancholy still were the many thousands of others who had involuntarily lost something forever. And make no mistake: Though Cleveland was promised another franchise for 1999, things would never be the same again. "What I have now are eighteen years of memories in my basement," thirty-four-year-old John (Big Dawg) Thompson, leader of the Browns' famous Dawg Pound cheering section told me one evening. "At least there's no way Modell can touch them. Screw him."

To understand why Cleveland was a single exposed nerve over a football team, you must understand two things, neither of which is necessarily obvious. "Football is America's sport," explained seventy-two-year-old Dante Lavelli, impeccable in a blue blazer, rep tie, and scalpful of silver hair. "And northern Ohio is the cradle of football: Massillon High School, Ohio State, the Hall of Fame, and the Cleveland Browns.

"When I was in high school," this dapper gentleman continued, "before the steel industry went bad, the main thing was to get a ticket to Massillon's game on Saturday, even though I played for Hudson High School myself. Around '39 or '40, Massillon played Alliance at the Rubber Bowl in Akron in front of forty thousand people. They never lost. They won about eighty in a row and beat three colleges—Mount Union,

Kent State, and Akron U.—and none of 'em scored a touchdown. *That's* how good Massillon was."

From Hudson High, Lavelli went to Ohio State ("Twenty-five guys out of thirty-three are still living from our 1942 team!" he said proudly) and from Ohio State to the Browns, where he won the NFL championship in 1950. ("We were like a family, those teams.") In 1975, Dante (Gluefingers) Lavelli was inducted as a receiver into the Pro Football Hall of Fame, just down the road in Canton, and as he spoke, these memories of a lifetime washed over him like a warm bath.

Until, that is, Modell was mentioned. Lavelli had been chatting pleasantly in the furniture store he owns in suburban Rocky River. A big Browns helmet hung from the showroom's façade. He had held season tickets since his retirement thirty-five years ago. But now he went ballistic and began loudly defaming the Browns' owner in a way that no publisher's attorneys would allow me to hint at, much less print. Nor, on reflection, did Lavelli want me to. "I'm at the end of my rope," he explained, semiapologetically, after he had calmed down. "It's just that everywhere you go, waitresses, salespeople, truck drivers, eighth-grade kids—everyone mentions the guy, and after a while, you get tired of listening to it." He sighed. "It's hard to accept."

Lavelli stepped outside the store to grab some air, and his right-hand man approached. John DePolo was a sunny sixty-nine-year-old who spoke in the soothing tones of an Irish priest, good cop to Lavelli's bad. "You have to understand his emotions," DePolo said softly, with simple concern for his friend. "This isn't just football that's being taken away. It's a part of people's lives."

It's a part of people's lives. Every autumn Sunday thirteen-year-old Jenny Sheeler watched the Browns with her sister Katie and their parents, Pat and Russ. They hung Browns signs in their house in Twinsburg, Ohio, and rooted in their Browns warm-up suits. "To know that when I have my own kids, I can't bring them to Browns games, that hurts me," said Jenny, standing outside Cleveland Stadium before a Browns game. "It's sad that we can't come to games as a family anymore."

"The Browns are the only real team I've known," said thirteen-year-old Angela Woody, flanked by her little brother, Michael, and her father, James. "They're a part of the history of our family."

And so it went, across every age, gender, and racial demographic in the city. Ron Brienes invited me to sit in on his radio show, and I was struck by two consecutive callers, both men. It wasn't static that made their voices crack on the air.

"I have a four-year-old who I wanted to raise a Browns fan, like I was," said a man who identified himself as Brainchild. "And this sucker Modell has snatched that away from me. When you have grown men crying about a football team, you can't say it's only about sports. It goes way deeper than that. . . . It's who we are. Football is in our blood. The Cleveland Browns are in our blood."

"As I view it," said the next caller, who didn't give his name, "Art Modell has murdered my memories. He's murdered a friend. I'm going to the [final Browns'] game, even though I know my money goes straight into Modell's pocket. But I'm not going for him. I'm going for my father, who raised me on the Cleveland Browns. I'm going for Bernie Kosar, who cried when he had to leave the Cleveland Browns. I'm going to see a friend. And to pay my last respects."

I was beginning to notice that every fan I listened to grieved more for family than for football. I couldn't help but think of Don Lansing, saying "fathers and sons" when asked why people still visit his Field of Dreams. I thought of my own old man and how sports were always a Fixadent bond anchoring the temperamental dental plate of our relationship. *That* is what the game means in northern Ohio. That is why grown men cried.

And cry they did, every last one of them. For eighteen years, John Thompson had been a Browns season ticketholder. For the last ten, he had also been Big Dawg, the most visible Browns fan in a world full of Browns fans.

How full? The official Browns Backers club purported to be the largest for any professional team on the planet, with 120,000 dues-paying members in 310 chapters from the United States to the United Kingdom to Japan. When the move was announced, Browns Backer president Bob Grace took a call from the Australian chapter president, who asked, "Should we disband?" (They should not, he was told.)

Indeed, while living abroad for sixteen years, Cleveland Brown IV heard knowing comments about his name wherever he traveled, from the Philippines to Naples, Italy. "Browns fans are everywhere," he confirmed. And none is better known than Big Dawg.

So I let the Big Dawg eat. He had agreed to join me for dinner at Coach's, the Cleveland sports bar and grill from which he and Brienes broadcast their radio show. I half-expected him to order a Gaines Burger and to snuffle it up with his mouth. But, in fact, this 300-pound computer parts salesman didn't order food at all. His familiar dog mask was at home, unlikely to be worn again. But his own face looked hangdog enough.

On another evening not long before this one, Big Dawg had been honored before a Cleveland Crunch indoor soccer match. His wife and twin daughters accompanied him. "In the third quarter," he said, his eyes suddenly reddening at the rims, "they announced that it was my daughters' ninth birthday. Their names are Megan and Michelle. We didn't know they were going to do that." Clearly it moved him, for his eyes misted when he mentioned the gesture.

In the wake of the Crunch festivities, a fan approached Big Dawg and said, "Man, the Browns must have *really* been good to you over the years."

And the Big Dawg replied, "The Crunch have done more for me tonight than the Browns did in eighteen years."

The irony had already occurred to him earlier in that evening as he kicked out the first ball to start an . . . *indoor soccer match?* It was the

Crunch who were thanking him for two decades of devotion to the
Browns. And so that night, as applause rolled down the arena aisles and
reached this giant man, he couldn't help himself.

Beneath a rubber hound-dog mask, he wept.

I would have preferred to have filed a happier report, to have given
Cleveland a cleaner bill of health. Lord knows, no other American city
has endured as many journalistic proctological procedures as this one. I
myself once made the mildest of Cleveland jokes in the pages of *Sports
Illustrated*. In response, Clevelanders mailed me dozens of newspaper
and magazine articles, each describing the city as a twentieth-century
Camelot.

And while that may be pushing it, Cleveland really *was* better than
it had ever been. This had much to do with professional sports. The
pennant-winning Indians played in sold-out Jacobs Field, across from the
Cavaliers' glittering Gund Arena. "They've taken a Rust Belt city from
the outhouse to the penthouse," Lavelli had told me. "And the Browns
in a renovated Cleveland Stadium would have added to that glory."

In fact, the squalid stadium looked even more abject now that it
slouched next to the Rock & Roll Hall of Fame. I toured the latter,
pausing at the poster for Pearl Jam's first gig, when they were still
Mookie Blaylock. The building is a grand glass pyramid, designed by
I. M. Pei, that hosts three thousand visitors a day, seven days a week, all
year long. As buildings go, these two—the stadium and the Rock & Roll
Hall of Fame—were DeVito and Schwarzenegger in *Twins*. And yet, "I'd
rather have the Browns than the Rock & Roll Hall of Fame," said Ken
Johnston of Toledo while visiting the latter.

And who in northern Ohio would have disagreed? Jim Brown versus James Brown? It was no contest. The war in Bosnia had been ceremonially resolved that same week in Ohio—the Dayton Accord; it sounded
like an agreement to regulate the mayonnaise industry—but still all talk
circled back to the Browns.

I consulted the telephone directory again. In Cleveland, the gods are in the book. I found a listing for one of the toughest sons of bitches to ever play pro football, in its cartoon-violent, Cold War incarnation, no less. If anyone could give me a sober assessment of football in northern Ohio, it was Lou (The Toe) Groza. This was one grown man without tear ducts.

We met for lunch near his home in Berea, five minutes from the Browns headquarters and practice facility. Groza was raised above his father's saloon, across the street from a steel mill in Martins Ferry, Ohio. The Toe was on Okinawa, steeling himself to storm the Japanese mainland and end World War II, when he read in his Army division's newsletter of a new professional football league being formed. In the next day's mail packet, he found a contract from Paul Brown. Again, this was *on* Okinawa, *during* the war. And though he was not yet twenty-one—the deal wouldn't be legally binding—Groza signed to become an Original Cleveland Brown. On one condition: that he return to the States alive.

It was an absurd story, no less so for being true, but Groza made it back all right and became a Hall of Fame offensive tackle and defensive tackle and placekicker whose field goal won the 1950 NFL championship game. Now, at my request, he stared down the broad avenue of this century and placed the team's move in perspective.

"You look back on your life," said the Toe, "and where you came from and all that has happened since, and I suppose that something like this . . . well, it becomes just another incident in a lifetime." He was reflecting over a Reuben in an otherwise Italian restaurant, trying to make sense of it all.

But an hour later he had taken me to his home, where he was surrounded by mementos of his remarkable existence, and there it emerged that the demise of the Browns was more than just another incident in Lou Groza's lifetime. Of course it was.

"Our first home game was against the Miami Seahawks," the Toe recalled, gazing out on his backyard. "It was an exciting time, right after the war. I had last played in a freshman game at Ohio State in front of maybe five hundred people. I never played in a varsity football game. So to come down that tunnel at the stadium and to run out of the dugout and have eighty-two thousand people cheering. . . ." He smiled at the memory. "God, it made you feel about this small." Two kielbasa-thick fingers were held an inch apart. "It was thrilling," said the Toe. "And the crowds have been like that for fifty years."

He had long been a part of those crowds, a Browns season ticketholder for the three decades since his retirement. He, too, must have been bewildered when Modell announced the move, no? The Toe didn't answer. But Jackie, his wife of forty-six years, did.

"We could have cried," she said.

Turns out they did. The Toe was asked to speak at a rally outside Cleveland Stadium, but once there, he felt the tears quicken and he could not continue for the lump in his throat. It was an epochal moment—almost literally the melting of a polar ice cap—and as stark a sign as any that an era had passed sadly in Cleveland.

I made motions to leave. An Ohio State flag flew above the Groza garage. A gray gloom gathered outside the window. But the Toe remained silent, lost in his thoughts of pro football in Cleveland. His eyes went slick as freshly Zambonied ice.

"It's like a fire has just burned out," he said at last. "And all you're left with is ashes."

I'm not one for political labels. If I've ever used the phrase "right wing" in a sentence, that sentence was "The 'right wing' for the Blackhawks had his nose bitten off" or "Miss, please tell the pilot the 'right wing' is on fire." So it is with some dismay that I use those words—or, rather, word: "right-wing"—to describe the sporting attractions of the Keystone State. But I must. For they were.

WELCOME TO PENNSYLVANIA bubbled a sign at the border. AMERICA STARTS HERE! It was about time. Following my captivity in what is, evidently, communist Ohio—Cincinnati Reds, indeed—I longed for the decadent pleasures of a round of golf. I cleared customs and exchanged currency near Hermitage and learned from a rest-stop leaflet that an estimable public course was but a mile away. I hastened to it and secured a tee time for the following dawn.

On August 22, 1936, Alf Landon opened the eastern portion of his doomed presidential campaign at Tam o' Shanter Golf Club, at the center of a "rock-ribbed Republican" stronghold, according to the caption on a photograph that hangs in the clubhouse. In the picture, 110,000 Alfophiles stood huddled on a lush fairway, yearning to vote Republican at the height of the Depression. It looked like a Woodstock for the well-bred—it looked like Goodstock—and the photograph only deepened the unease I was feeling about my newfound fondness for the game.

For a few years now, golf has been a guilty pleasure of mine. Except that it seldom gives me pleasure. No, golf is not a guilty "pleasure" at all, come to think of it. What is it then? Just plain . . . guilty? Yes, I'm afraid it is. And on any number of charges.

According to a kindly woman who fielded my call at the National Golf Foundation, there were 15,390 golf courses in America at the end of 1995. The average parcel of land devoted to each course—*excluding* clubhouses and parking lots and the like—was 120 acres. In other words, actual golf holes cover 1,846,800 acres of American real estate. That's an area 61 percent the size of Rhode Island, a state which exists expressly to be demeaned in comparisons such as this one.

When you throw in clubhouses, parking lots, golf-supply stores, the National Golf Foundation, and touring pro Craig Stadler, golf surely consumes *more* space than the Ocean State. As America turns away aspiring immigrants who wash up at her shores half-dead on rafts, I wonder: Is this a defensible use of such landmass? The answer, I fear, depends on your handicap.

Comedian George Carlin has seriously proposed constructing housing for the homeless on all of the world's golf courses. And while I stop short of endorsing that plan—apart from anything else, it would displace hundreds of workers in the funny-slacks industry—I do fear that a nation in relentless pursuit of leisure may have thrown its priorities out of plumb.

Or so I was reflecting as I arose before daylight at the Hermitage

Holiday Inn, retrieved a complimentary *USA Today*, and turned by force
of habit to the Minnesota section of the "Across the USA" page. I now
reproduce verbatim, and without further comment, the news nugget
that I saw there:

MINNEAPOLIS—A bonfire set by transients living under a bridge melted
fiber-optic cables Friday, depriving thousands of Minnesotans weekend
access to the Internet.

Tam o' Shanter was laid out among the rolling hills of western
Pennsylvania, like a green silk tie across a rumpled bedspread. The course
was all poker-table fairways and bent-grass greens, trimmed with hard-
wood pines that drew open, here and there, to Technicolor views of the
Shenango Valley. Or so suggested the lyrical leaflet from the rest stop.
And the leaflet didn't lie.

I had hoped to be sent off with a quotable trio of "Tam-Oh" regu-
lars. Golf, unlike any other pursuit I can think of, allows you to chat up
strangers on the road without being taken for a sexual deviant or religious zealot. In the week before I embarked on this trip, I played a
valedictory round at a Minneapolis muni with my brother Tom and another friend. We were sent off with a stray out of towner who wore a
drooping shirt sleeve where his right arm should have been. As we
walked uneasily to the first tee, Tom summoned the compassion for
which he is renowned and told me with a deep sense of foreboding:
"We're about to get our asses kicked by a guy with one arm." Truer
words were never spoken.

The guy—I'll withhold his name and hometown to spare him the
ignominy of having golfed with the Rushin brothers—swung right-
handed clubs with his left (or front) arm, as if hitting a backhand in
tennis. He had only been playing three years, yet his tee shots were a
marvel, as long and true as the movie *Gandhi*. He chipped and putted
capably enough and was on his way to a 90 when darkness overtook us.
Tom and I, meanwhile, posted scores that would be record daytime high

temperatures in Death Valley and generally just tried to get around without blurting something inappropriate, like "What's your handicap?"

He would have forgiven the blunder, for he was self-deprecating throughout the round, often over our protests. "Every year there's a golf tournament for gimps," he said when we had finished and were parting in the parking lot. "The next one's in Las Vegas. People come in from everywhere. I'm not good enough to play in it yet—these guys are *really* good. But maybe you could write about it some time." I agreed, threw my clubs in the back of my truck, and there they remained until I pulled up to Tam o' Shanter, divining rods that would lead me to local characters.

Alas, the course was empty but for groundskeepers at daybreak on this weekday, and I was sent off—in that festive phrase so familiar to the single traveler—as a "party of one."

As I walked toward the first tee, from which Landon made his unhistoric address, an old guy in overalls approached me with a gardening implement spot-welded to the shaft of a three-wood. He thrust the steel-clawed business end of the thing in my face, in the manner of Felix Unger showing Oscar Madison the cigar impaled on his umbrella in the opening credits of *The Odd Couple*. He said, "Think I could get a patent for that?" I nodded vigorously and slowly backpedaled toward the tee box, where I got away without further incident.

Now, I play golf like I play the piano. Which is to say, I don't, though every time I see a piano, I have a fleeting delusional notion that I can sit down at it and play Bach's *Goldberg Variations* flawlessly, or at least a reasonable facsimile of *The Entertainer*. And every time I get to the first tee of a golf course, I have an equally psychotic impulse that I will shoot 80 that day. It has never happened, and almost certainly never will, but so what. Some people keep in their living room an expensive grand piano that they cannot play. I keep a costly upright set of golf clubs.

As it turns out, there is much to be said for a solitary round of golf. For starters, all of the footprints on the dew-soaked greens were mine;

they looked like an Arthur Murray dance chart for something called "The Four-Putt." Whenever I drove the ball to an obscure and heavily foliated corner of the course, which was often, a guy on a riding lawn mower would tear off in pursuit of it and invariably return with a ball that was not even the color of the one I hit, but which I graciously accepted as my own. Better yet, I rained golf-ball-sized hail on the many homes surrounding the course and felt utterly bereft of self-consciousness in doing so. In this way, golf is legalized vandalism for adults. "Serves 'em right for living on a golf course," said in Latin, is a legal defense against breaking windows in forty-seven states. With a cymbal crash of glass, I once smother-hooked a tee shot through the window of a fairway condominium in Palm Springs. "What should I do?" I asked my partner, who happened to be my father.

"Take a drop," he shrugged.

But the best thing by far about my round at Tam-Oh was not having to wait for anybody. I played as if chased by rangers with Rottweilers. At sixteen, I caught up to a couple of kids who must have snuck onto the back nine or had teed off the night before, but they insisted I play through. I failed to break Sam Snead's course record of 65, but I may very well have set a course speed record, clocking in in under a couple of hours.

A friend of mine has long insisted that Steve Scott, the great American miler, once played a full round of golf in twenty-eight minutes—putting out on every green, lugging a variety of clubs, stopping for cigars and a cold beer at the turn—a feat that supposedly put him in *The Guinness Book of Records*. I have no idea if this is true—I've never read beyond those two fat twins on motorcycles—but it seems to me a skill worth possessing.

(In the interests of setting the record straight, it just so happens that a man named James Carvil played a full round in twenty-seven minutes and nine seconds at the Warrenpoint Golf Course in County Down, Northern Ireland, on June 18, 1987.)

If America really did consolidate all of her courses into a single state called Golf and those links were all linked in one epic layout, this supercourse would have 226,287 holes and measure roughly 68 million yards. At a brisk three-and-a-half-hour pace per eighteen holes, you could finish a round in almost exactly five years. Steve Scott and James Carvil would require a mere nineteen months. Neither timetable is realistic, of course: You would need time to eat and sleep and to phone the office every fifty thousand holes. But a man's reach should exceed his grasp, right, or what's a heaven for?

The instant I left Tam o' Shanter, rain fell in great sheets, as if rigged to a bucket above my car door. I was driving south toward Pittsburgh, where the Pirates were to host the Houston Astros that evening in a rare "Twi-Nite" doubleheader, one of many useful contributions sports have made to contemporary American illiterature.

I wanted to enjoy a "Lite" beer and nacho "cheez" at a "Twi-Nite" twin bill and maybe buy a "Fotoball" emblazoned with a team picture of the White "Sox." But the longer I drove, the harder it rained. The doubleheader looked to be gravely endangered. A radio report said Barry Manilow was scheduled to perform an outdoor concert that same evening in Pittsburgh, and suddenly it made sense, this biblical deluge.

The world outside my windshield was a wavy liquid blur. It was like driving into a movie flashback. And still a defiant dollop of birdshit clung to the bottom center of my windshield in the cuticle that the wipers couldn't reach. I couldn't take my eyes off it. Which was a shame, because everywhere in Pennsylvania were signs saying WATCH FOR FALLING ROCK, as if you could avoid a boulder falling from a high eminence and pancaking your car.

In Pittsburgh, I decided to forge on eastward, through Latrobe (hometown of Arnold Palmer and Rolling Rock beer) and past the biblically flooded city of Johnstown (once again under flood alert). I corkscrewed my way up the Appalachian Mountains, the terrain gradually becoming hillier, the town names hillbillier: Boltz, Munster, Mingoville. Somewhere to my left was a municipality called Glen Campbell. No doubt this sounded like a good idea when *Rhinestone Cowboy* was a hit, but I had to think the name was now a source of mild morning-after embarrassment to its citizens, as sure if they had named the place Peter Frampton, Pennsylvania. I drove on until I reached a city that saved the world through baseball, a city with "sport" in its very name.

On July 16, 1964, at the evocative Cow Palace in San Francisco, Barry Goldwater accepted the Republican nomination for the presidency of the United States, vowing to make communism "give way to the forces of freedom." That same day President Lyndon Johnson did him one better, signing a federal charter of incorporation that granted tax-exempt status to Little League, Inc., of Williamsport, Pennsylvania—provided that the organization "promote Americanism" in thirty countries outside the United States.

Little League had been doing just that since shortly after Carl E. Stotz organized a three-team baseball league for nine- to twelve-year-old boys in Williamsport in the summer of 1939. His Little League Baseball flourished following World War II, when GIs came home desirous of having children of their own at whom they could yell things like "Get your bat off your shoulder!" and "This pitcher's got nothin'!" It was not only great fun. It was "good Americanism."

A 1950 letter from J. Edgar Hoover hangs in the Little League Museum in South Williamsport. In it, the FBI director reminds kids that "a clean, healthy body begets a clean, healthy mind, and the two are absolute essentials to good Americanism." That Hoover may have drafted the letter while wearing pink pumps and a feather boa is not relevant here. The point is that Little League so successfully promoted "good Americanism"—which my dictionary describes as "Allegiance to the United States and its customs and institutions"—that its brand of baseball is now played by 2.5 million children in eighty-three countries of "the free world." (The free world still doesn't include Cuba and North Korea, two hotbeds of the game, but *was* expanded to include girls in 1974, thanks to a court order.)

There is a Little League Pledge posted in the museum, which be-gins, "I trust in God, I love my country. . . ." But every summer Bud-dha-fearing Big Mac aficionados from the Far East win the Little League World Series in quaint Lamade Stadium next door. Its dimensions are two-thirds that of a big-league ballpark, so that a visiting adult sports-writer feels one-third larger than actual size when he enters.

Eight feet tall, I stomped Godzilla-like into Little League's Hall of Excellence. Promotional literature states that enshrinement in the hall is "the highest honor afforded a Little League graduate and recognizes role models for today's Little Leaguers." These role models for nine-year-olds include conservative columnist George Will, conservative spelling whiz Dan Quayle, and "1988 Distinguished Little League Graduate" Steve Garvey, the ex-Dodger conservative and alleged serial philanderer who always calls to mind an item from David Letterman's Top Ten Least Popular Exhibits at the Baseball Hall of Fame: "Number 8—Steve Gar-vey's bed and on-deck circle."

Wandering Little League headquarters, I saw America from the outside. The majority of visitors on this day were Asian tourists, and I could hear them marvel in their native tongues at a display of twenty silver dollars encased in a polyurethane cube. These were "the first $20 donated to start the Little League Foundation," whose first disburse-ment, apparently, was to buy a clear polyurethane cube in which to display those twenty silver dollars. Amazing.

I spent several minutes fogging the glass on a display case of base-balls autographed by Little League graduates who went on to minor celebrity in the game. Each athlete simply scribbled his signature on the horsehide: Ed Ott, Bo Diaz, Lee Mazzilli—these names needed no fur-ther embellishment. Ah, but insecure sports nerd Richard Nixon scrawled an anxious little afterthought to *his* signature. "Richard Nixon," he wrote, before deeming this insufficient and adding: "37th President of the U.S.A."

Roone Arledge once told me a story: When he was the president of ABC Sports in 1971, he hired the anvil-headed Frank Gifford away from

CBS. Gifford's first assignment at ABC was to announce the Hall of Fame exhibition football game in Canton. But when Nixon decided to drop in on the game, suddenly—horrifically—Gifford's first assignment was to interview the President.

Minutes before the broadcast, Nixon told Arledge what a fan he was of the New York Giants in those days when Gifford embodied that team. In fact, when Nixon practiced law in New York, he often attended postgame parties at Giff's place. And then the President of the United States said a most curious thing to the president of ABC Sports. R.N. told R.A.: "I'm sure Frank would remember me."

When the Leader of the Free World boasts fretfully of his friendship with Frank Freaking Gifford, you know sports matter—a bit too much, perhaps. I was reflecting on this notion when I saw near the Nixon baseball the tribute to Arnold S. White, a onetime Southern Region director of Little League who collected the business cards of famous Americans, a collection his family later unloaded in Williamsport. We are richer for it: There was a blank appointment card from Dr. Jonas Salk, which read 24 HOURS NOTICE IS REQUIRED FOR CANCELLATION, a deadpan calling card for Dr. Albert Einstein, PROFESSOR OF PHYSICS and the simple but powerful business card of John D. Rockefeller, CHAIRMAN, STANDARD OIL. I looked for a card for Richard M. Nixon, 37TH PRESIDENT OF THE UNITED STATES, but couldn't find one.

Still, I truly enjoyed the fact that Rockefeller had a business card and could just see the old coot dropping one into a goldfish bowl at T.G.I. Friday's, in the hope of winning the August free lunch raffle.

The very idea made me peckish as I hit the road and heard on the radio about the "new Choco Taco at Taco Bell!" *A chocolate taco*. There was now, officially, nothing left to titillate the taste buds of Americans.

I drove and drove through the drizzle. Mist hung in the hills like cigar smoke beneath a low ceiling. The ubiquitous WATCH FOR FALLING ROCK signs were at last borne out by a Dodge that sat empty on the shoulder of I-81. An orange distress flag fluttered from a fender, and a boulder-sized hole gobbled most of the rear windshield. I drove on, toward the gray-flannel skies above Cooperstown, New York, waiting for the sky to fall, contemplating my own mortality, and composing cautionary roadside verse to remember me by:

> HE DIDN'T WATCH
> FOR FALLING ROCK
> HE'LL NEVER SNIFF
> ANOTHER JOCK
> BURMA-SHAVE.

Baseball was first described as the "national pastime" in 1857, according to *The Dickson Baseball Dictionary*, but *The New York Times* was already reporting in 1881 that the sport had been displaced as the "national game"—by, of all things, cricket. And while I have an excellent true story about cricket, involving a West Indian bowler named Michael Holding, an English batsman named Peter Willey, and a BBC announcer who actually said, "The bowler's Holding, the batsman's Willey," that is not the point I want to make here.

My point is that baseball may never have been the consensus American obsession that we now think it used to be. But I must tell you: The game *does* exert a strange patriotic hold, especially if you happen to be driving in Upstate New York in a Japanese Pathfinder, named for the

fourth installment of *The Leatherstocking Tales*, a series of American frontier novels by James Fenimore Cooper, whose father founded Cooperstown, twenty-five miles south of Dolgeville, where lumbermen harvested the Adirondack white ash that became the bat that hit the ball
over the fence to win the pennant for the '51 New York Giants.

That bat is now enshrined *in* Cooperstown—at the Baseball Hall of
Fame—as the instrument that fired "the shot heard round the world."
That phrase was orignally penned by Emerson to commemorate the Rev-
olutionary War battles at Lexington and Concord, but I daresay is now
more often associated (by cretins like you and me, anyway) with Bobby
Thomson's dinger at the Polo Grounds. There's nothing wrong with
that—the United States has a long tradition of recalling its history in this
backhanded way. De Soto discovered the Mississippi River, but is better
remembered as a boxy automobile. Ethan Allen is no longer a soldier,
but remains a furniture store. If I said, "I just devoured an O. Henry,"
you would think I had been eating, not reading. And you would be right.

I shared the road into Cooperstown with cyclists and horseback
riders. The highway followed a river on which canoes idled under trees
hung with rope swings. I was finally out of range of Binghamton's diabol-
ical 103.3 FM, which dedicated itself, unaccountably, to "keeping the
seventies alive!" In short, things were uncommonly pleasant until I drew
into Cooperstown proper and the radio reported that Mickey Mantle was
not going home from a Dallas hospital today, as scheduled. He had been
hospitalized for a liver transplant, after which he was diagnosed with
lung cancer, and was now enduring blood transfusions, all of which put
him, I inferred, on his deathbed.

The news colored my tour of Cooperstown. In any other circum-
stance, the place would be ludicrously charming. I strolled leafy Leatherstocking Street, its white homes visible behind black wrought-iron gates,
American flags flapping heavily from the grand front porches, and what
looked like gas lamps burning in all the front yards. And yet . . .

And yet, the streets surrounding the redbrick Baseball Hall of Fame
and Museum were a white man's *soukh* of souvenir emporia, selling

speculative Mantle memorabilia to a hungry throng in khakis and madras shirts and "vintage" Brooklyn Dodger caps. I can't say that Mantle was being exploited: The man had scrawled his name on more crap than Jackie Collins at a crowded book signing. But the sales-pitch implications of his impending death—"Buy now, for he'll never sign again!"—lent an even tackier aspect to the countless commemorative plates and Mantle baseballs that would soon be crowding a thousand Mickey mantelpieces in American living rooms. There was even brief public speculation that souvenir hounds sought Mantle's original *liver*, a notion too dizzyingly depressing to dwell on.

As I escaped the lunacy of the Cooperstown streets and sought refuge inside the Hall of Fame, I remembered that Mantle came from Commerce, Oklahoma. I repeated the address over and over, trying to persuade myself that it was a kind of cosmic blessing on the goings-on outside: "Commerce, OK. Commerce, OK. Commerce, OK. . . ." But, I must tell you, it didn't help.

Well, the Baseball Hall of Fame is just unbelievably captivating, and if you've never been there, then you really ought to drop this book this instant and fly to Cooperstown immediately. Really, I'll wait. Go on. Go *on*.

The place had all the elbow room of the Tokyo subway and the lines moved at the pace of plate tectonics, but so what? Save for a bullet-proof display case, I could have touched Lou Gehrig's shabby address book, which was open to a casual notation, in Lou's hand, on the "R" page: "Babe Ruth, 345 W. 88th St." It was somehow humanizing and awesome at the same time, like a WHILE YOU WERE OUT message slip to Zeus, reminding him to call Ares. And similar knee-buckling items were everywhere.

Sportswriters had their own (out-of-the-way and much-ignored) corner of the hall, I am proud to say. It housed an exhibit called "Scribes and Mikemen," two coinages of that inane and archaic sportswriterese

that I so adore. "By 1900, most sportswriters covered the game from
press boxes protected by chicken wire," said a caption beneath an actual
length of chicken wire. Indeed, pecking away at typewriters in a chicken-
wire cage, sportswriters could scarcely be distinguished from actual
chickens. And an examination of the resulting prose wouldn't clarify
matters much, I'm afraid.

A *Sporting News* column called "Clouting 'Em with Joe King" was
on display and bore the unutterably euphonious headline, SHALLOW
HURLING BALKS BUCS 'N' BIRDS. I couldn't get it out of my head and
strutted around repeating it softly: " 'Shallow Hurling Balks Bucs 'n'
Birds.' 'Shallow Hurling Balks Bucs 'n' Birds.' " I looked and sounded a
bit like a clucking chicken myself when at last I left the Hall of Fame and
went blinking back out into the Cooperstown sunlight in a brand-new
"vintage" Minnesota Twins cap.

On the way to the Pathfinder, I passed a storefront that identified
itself as THE OFFICIAL AUTHORIZED RICHIE ASHBURN SOUVENIR MEMORA-
BILIA HEADQUARTERS. Thank goodness, was all I could say. Never again
will I have to buy knockoff Richie Ashburn trinkets from a West African
with an open briefcase in Times Square. I was a happy man.

If this book were a movie, time's passage would be signaled by
pages peeling rapid-fire from a wall calendar. The screen would dissolve
to a map of New England, and a tiny sedan would race across it, leaving
in its wake a mazy line through upstate New York, Vermont, Maine, and
New Hampshire. Jaunty music would swell on the soundtrack as we
quick-cut to a montage of memorable moments in . . .

Saratoga County, New York. The marquee outside a fire department
lamented: RACE TRACK—WHERE WINDOWS CLEAN THE PEOPLE. I fell in
behind a Toyota Camry with New York license plates reading FISHGOLF.
Increasingly sports-addled, I asked myself: "They *do?*"

Ethan Allen Highway, Vermont. Was it me, or was this state too
artsy and precious for its own good? I actually saw a speed-limit sign on

an *easel.* All the buildings were called The Inn at Blood Hill or Collins Antiques at Beaver Pond, exactly the kind of yuppified names—alas—we now give our stadiums. Oriole Park at Camden Yards. The Ballpark at Arlington. The Palace of Auburn Hills. I passed The Danville School and thought of former Princeton basketball coach Pete Carril, who said he would never recruit a player from a school whose name contained the words "The," "Friends," or "Ecole." He surely never signed a kid from Vermont.

St. Johnsbury, Vermont. I drove into a Norman Rockwell painting. Beneath a canopy of stars in a cloudless navy sky, thirty men and women in crisp white shirts—the St. Johnsbury Band—played Sousa marches and polkas and *Yankee Doodle Dandy* in a lighted gazebo on the town square. Old couples drew up lawn chairs and children played hide-and-seek among the shrubs and the statues and a Civil War cannon from the U.S.S. *Magnolia.* The band closed this last concert of the season with *The Star-Spangled Banner.* Sixty people removed their Red Sox caps and placed them over their hearts. At the firehouse across Main Street, firemen pulled down Old Glory and folded it, military-style, into a tight triangle, so it looked like one of those finger footballs of thick folded paper that you'd flick through finger uprights during idle moments in junior high.

Lancaster, New Hampshire. I strolled past the Rialto Theater and the Sportsman's Lounge Bowling Alley to S. N. Evan's drugstore, with its five-stool lunch counter of white Formica and its old aproned guy in the back selling licorice at a candy counter, and I began to wonder: Was New England for real, or an elaborate put-on constructed for my benefit? The answer became clear—it was the latter—after I looked in the window of the Lancaster Diner and a feed-capped patron named Pete said, "C'mon in, it's good." I did and it was, though what "it" was was beyond me: I ate a "frappe" and a . . . *"hamburg sandwich"?* You're kidding me, right? You mean to say there are places in the world, much less America, where the word "hamburger" has yet to gain currency?

Portsmouth, New Hampshire. I was sucked into the city's infamous traffic circle and spent several days trying to escape before I was finally flung out, like a ball from a speeding roulette wheel, toward Boston and some truly treacherous traffic.

At its creation in 1956, the federal interstate highway system was pitched as a speedy way to flee urban centers in the event of an atomic attack. Bostonians still drive as if they are doing just that.

Cars passed me on both shoulders and on the grassy median strip. Abandoning the freeway only made matters worse. The Boston street "system" was evidently drawn up by a six-year-old with a Spirograph. I know the city is old, but Boston has had—what?—a century now to prepare for the Automotive Age? I was heading to Fenway Park for the Red Sox sold-out night game against the Orioles and wanted to stop on the way to venerate a life-sized statue of my all-time sports hero. But I became hopelessly lost. I pulled into a gas station and called a Massachusetts tourism 800-number and asked for directions to the Sports Museum of New England. A woman responded, "It's near the Museum of Science."

"Where's that?" I asked and inferred from the brief but accusatory silence that ensued that the woman considered anyone who would visit the Sports Museum before the Museum of Science to be an imbecile of the first order.

But I had my reasons. The Sports Museum of New England, in a mall in East Cambridge as it turned out, was home to a 300-pound statue of Celtic superstar Larry Bird, carved from a single block of bass wood. 'Nuff said, right? A cigar-smoking statue of Celtic overlord Red Auerbach sat on an outdoor park bench in Fanueil Hall, but it was bronze and could survive the elements. The bass-wood Bird would presumably erode out of doors, so that we'll never know—alas—if birds would refrain from shitting on a statue of one of their own.

That statue—of Bird poised to shoot a free throw—was done by a sculptor named Armand LaMontagne, who labored sixty hours a week for six months to liberate Larry from the 1,800-pound woodblock. It

ain't exactly Michelangelo's *David*, and I'm sure the sculpting community regards the work as the statuary equivalent of a *Dogs Playing Poker*
painting, but I frankly don't care. It was a measure of the artist's devotion that LaMontagne carved fifty thousand pebbles on the basketball in
Bird's hand. The least I could do was pay homage.

So I did. The trouble was, Fenway Park was a good two miles across
the Charles River from the bass-wood Bird, an epic distance to cover in a
Boston rush hour. The trip took an hour. By the time I was on Beacon
Street (and the stadium was in sight), so were twenty-thousand other
hot, irate, game-going motorists. The avenue was a clot of idling cars. A
fire truck materialized from around a corner, sirens wailing, and blew its
apocalyptic horn. A traffic chopper swooped overhead. We were now
one jackhammer short of an Excedrin commercial.

At the appearance of the fire truck, a stump-necked man with a
face like a stewed tomato leaped from his car and began menacing the
driver of the van in front of him. "GET OVER GODDAMMIT A
BUILDING'S BURNING ASSHOLE WHAT THE HELL IS THE MAT-
TER WITH YOU YOU STUPID FUCKIN' JERK. . . ." This madman,
in a soiled sleeveless undershirt, was banging on the window and yanking
on the door, evidently trying to extract the bewildered driver through
the keyhole.

The van had Ontario plates. The poor driver was a bearded man in
wire-rimmed glasses. His wife and son cowered next to him. He had
nowhere to drive but up on the sidewalk, an option that was perfectly
obvious to all the Bostonians on Beacon Street, but wouldn't occur to a
law-abiding Ontarian. When at last he pulled onto the sidewalk, destroy-
ing his side mirror and clipping a parking meter, the fire truck screamed
through the intersection and I and a dozen other cars followed it, a lead
blocker on the punt-return team.

As for the Canadian family we left behind, I am sure they never
forgot their first Red Sox game and went home secure in their stereo-
types of Americans—as a hurried, violent, baseball-loving people with
no dress sense whatsoever.

Otherwise, it was a beautiful evening. I paid a small ransom to park near Fenway and fairly sprinted to an aromatic walk-up window on Yaw-key Way that sells FRIED CLAMS, FRIED DOUGH, FRENCH FRIES, AND DEEP-FRIED ONION RINGS. I bought a dozen Deep-Fried Fat Bombs—or something that turned the takeout bag diaphonous with grease—and tried my best to fathom how anyone could want to tear down Fenway Park. There was, unbelievably, a plan afoot to do so. Sure, Fenway was built when Wilbur Wright was still alive and is only accessible by airlift, but isn't that the point? Someday soon the Sox will play in a place with plentiful parking and a name like The Greensward at Walden Pond, and you can bet there will be no cholest-o-plex of fried fooderies across the street to provide sustenance for visiting sportswriters. What a shame.

On the bright side, the notion that any visit to Fenway might be one's last only intensifies the experience. A full moon hung like a foul ball behind the grandstand along the first base line. The infield was mown in concentric circles rippling out from the pitcher's mound; and the outfield was mown in diagonal stripes, like a club tie.

Only a few years earlier, I had walked onto that field before a game and tried to get California manager Doug Rader to declare Angel south-paw Chuck Finley "the best left-handed pitcher in baseball!" I did this for no other reason than my editors at *SI* wanted to put Finley on the cover, beneath the billing: THE BEST LEFT-HANDED PITCHER IN BASEBALL! I asked Rader a thousand different ways—"Would you call Finley the best left-hander in baseball?" and "Would you *please* call Finley the best left-hander in baseball?" and "Surely Finley is the best left-hander in baseball!"—but he wouldn't bite. So I glumly retreated to the press box and watched Finley last exactly one-third of an inning in his start that afternoon. The Angels lost 16-to-something in ninety-five-degree heat, and afterward, in the visitor's clubhouse, Rader hurled his uniform pants at me. He later said he was aiming for the laundry trolley, but the poly-ester trou hit me in the chest and—cloaked in static cling—crawled down my body like a Slinky down stairs. Memories.

Tonight's game was a sellout of 33,588, so I again took a seat in the press box, this time behind Hall of Famer (and Oriole executive) Frank

Robinson. In the third inning, Red Sox designated hitter Jose Canseco hit the longest ball I have ever seen—indeed, the longest Fenway has ever seen—over the Green Monster in left and over the netting above it and somewhere into the distant night. Canseco posed for several seconds at home plate—he looked like an Armand LaMontagne statue—and, as an afterthought, ran the bases.

Or didn't "run" them exactly. He made a tentative tour, as if the umpire had just ordered him to rise up and walk after a lifetime spent in a wheelchair. It took him ages to cross the plate. It was extremely amusing. Someone asked Frank Robinson what would have happened in his next at-bat if *he*, in his day, had taken a home run constitutional like Canseco's. "There wouldn't have been a next at-bat," Frank said: "I wouldn't have made it around the bases." He would have been sacked by the pitcher, in other words, before he got to second base.

It went like that all night, the Red Sox banging balls off light stancheons and outfield walls on their way to eleven runs and seventeen hits, and afterward I went to the home clubhouse to marvel at Canseco. He was entirely devoid of self-consciousness—he could have happily talked about his home run for the remainder of the homestand. Far from offensive, he was almost endearing, the picture of the elite athlete in his pampered prime.

"When it's hit, it's hit," Canseco told a rapt press corps that must have numbered thirty people. "It stays hit. You know, the fans like it when—as soon as you hit the ball—the outfielders don't even move." As soon as Canseco hit the ball, *Canseco* didn't move, either. But I kept that to myself, and some other provocateur reported—simply to pull Canseco's string—that the shot was officially measured at a mere 420 feet. No way, said Jose: "That ball went a *long* way. You can't really tell by where it lands. But I know when I hit it close to five hundred feet. I know."

He was right. It was later discovered that the ball landed across Lansdowne Street, in front of Mama Kins, the club in which the band Aerosmith got it start. Imagine if Canseco had hit the ball a quarter-century earlier, just as members of Aerosmith were exiting an early gig, smiting them down before they ever recorded such indispensable LPs as . . . *Big Ones*. The world would be a poorer place, indeed.

I spent the night in a stucco-intensive, Tudor-style motel in suburban Foxboro. In the morning, I inserted a quarter into the soda machine that was thrumming outside my room. But, bleary-eyed, I missed the coin slot and connected instead with a tangle of exposed wiring sprouting from a USE CORRECT CHANGE light that had been broken out by vandals. An unholy jolt shot through my right hand and shuddered up my arm to my shoulder blade. Lights dimmed throughout Foxboro until I prized my fingers free. This is what it must feel like, I thought, to be executed by lethal joy buzzer. Smelling like fried bologna and the right side of my body numb, I managed to drive, like a stroke victim, into Newport, Rhode Island.

At one point in his blessed existence, Cornelius Vanderbilt's personal fortune was more than in the whole of the U.S. Treasury. While $200 million doesn't sound like much today, it went a fair ways in the late 1800s, when any number of mirthless American industrialists were building increasingly obscene summer homes alongside each other in Newport. The ground floor of Vanderbilt's seasonal retreat, The Breakers, occupied a full acre. Not to be outdone, the Astor family equipped their nearby Beechwood estate with a *gold ballroom.* It is easy to see why the American sociologist Thorstein Veblen coined the phrase "conspicuous consumption" in 1899 after a visit to Newport.

I came to Newport to see how the other half plays and, sure enough, a spirit of extravagant one-upsmanship was evident in the island's sporting pursuits. I walked along America's Cup Avenue past the crowded marina and yacht club, where every couple looked like the Captain and Tennille. I made a left on Memorial and peered into St. Mary's, the church in which John and Jackie Kennedy were married in 1953. How they heard their vows over the unmufflered motorcycle racket that was now rattling the stained-glass windows, I do not for the

life of me know. This evening was the opening night of the Newport Jazz
Festival, and the streets were awash with unwashed day trippers.

I rejoined their number and traced the notes of a tinkling piano up
the street to the Newport Casino, which is not now and never has been a
casino. It is, rather, where tournament tennis was launched in America,
and tournament tennis in turn gave us excesses like Andre Agassi, giant
novelty checks, and the sponsored prize. This is typically (in the words
of author Martin Amis) something tasteful, like "a solid-gold helicopter."

The casino is an enormous, gabled, horseshoe-shaped Victorian edifice that wraps around a central grass tennis court. There are a dozen
other grass courts on the grounds, the oldest grass courts in continuous
use in the world. A grand piano was being tuned at center court, where
Ray Charles would open the jazz festival tonight, but ordinarily the
court is used for competition. In 1881, the casino began hosting the U.S.
Lawn Tennis Championships, a tournament that moved to Forest Hills,
New York, in 1915—and changed its name to the U.S. Open. (They
would also change the surface.) The courts at the casino are advertised as
available for public use, though I'm certain that privilege would require a
small loan to fulfill.

People with posh accents and parasols milled about the casino
grounds. The building itself now houses the International Tennis Hall of
Fame, but was built as a men's club by *New York Herald* publisher James
Gordon Bennett, Jr., in 1880.

Bennett is described in casino literature as a "somewhat eccentric
man-about-town, tennis buff, and wag" who belonged to the Newport
Reading Room, the most exclusive and tight-assed men's club of its day.
He was also fabulously wealthy. One day for laughs, he persuaded a
friend named Captain Candy—who sounds like an effeminate superhero,
but was in fact a British cavalryman and polo player—to ride his steed
into the Reading Room. When the good Captain did so, monocles could
be heard falling into soup tureens throughout the club.

Predictably, Bennett had his guest privileges revoked. And so he
built the $64,000 Newport Casino with the professed desire that it be, in

the grand tradition of this profligate island, "far larger and more elaborate" than the Reading Room. It was certainly that and remains so to this day, a National Historic Landmark. I could have happily passed the day and night smoking cigars in the enormous library, with its overstuffed leather chairs and baize gaming tables. I would read the world's great newspapers, which hung like bathtowels from wooden gripper rods, until Ray Charles's *Georgia* filtered in from the lawn.

Except that Ray was long-ago sold-out, and I had no more business in Newport. There *is* no business in Newport. So I crossed back over the toll bridge out of town, deposited the remainder of my money with a booth attendant, and thought: The rich really *are* different from you and me. They don't have nearly as much fun.

I entered Hartford, Connecticut, via the Dexter R. Coffin Bridge. Now there's an appropriate name. In the previous ten years, an astounding forty-six construction workers had been killed on Connecticut highways. And construction workers in Day-Glo vests were everywhere, leaning on shovels the length of the state. Viewed from above, I-91 must have looked as if traced by an orange highlighter.

I came to Connecticut from the north because I'd zipped back to Massachusetts after Newport to do a flyby of the Basketball Hall of Fame in Springfield. I was frankly getting my fill of Halls of Fame, though this one was invigorated by artifacts of a forgotten time in America when professional basketball was the Jewish game. So the Cleveland Rosenblums could visit the Philadelphia Hebrews, whose Gil Fitch would change into a tuxedo after games and lead his big band for dancing on the Hebrew home court, which happened to be the ballroom of the Broadwood Hotel. Henry Kissinger's Harlem Globetrotter jersey was enshrined, as well as a brick relief sculpture of former Celtic announcer Johnny Most—"made possible by the International Masonry Institute." A poster advertised the HOUSE OF DAVID COLLEGIANS—WORLD'S GREATEST BEARDED STARS—WHISKERS, WHISKERS, WHISKERS—TOURING

COAST TO COAST—35,000 MILES BY AUTO. I was "whiskered, whiskered, whiskered" myself, and in dire need of doing laundry. It now occurred to me that it was no accident that I walked entire wings of the hall alone. Stink was coming off me in squiggly cartoon vapors.

So I crawled south into Connecticut on I-91, my progress slowed by construction and then halted altogether when a nineteen-year-old worker was "mowed down," as the tragedy would later be described on the *Action 8 TV News*, and airlifted to a local hospital. At one point, I covered a single mile in forty minutes. Finally I gave up, exiting the freeway in New Haven and going in search of a Laundromat.

When at last I located one, a squat old Italian woman with an ass you could set a Scrabble board on enlisted my help in unloading her dainties from a second-story dryer. How she got them in there in the first place—hook shot, stilts, catapult—I cannot say. I only know that I found myself in a Laundromat behind the Happy Panda Restaurant in Orange, Connecticut, handling the delicates of a strange old woman who gazed up at me with great affection. And if that doesn't prompt you to take inventory of your life, well, you haven't been paying attention.

Freshly laundered, I took in a Celebrity Softball Blowout at Yale Field, where George Bush once played first base for the Elis. I parked with due reverence on the Yale Polo & Equestrian Ground—we didn't have college polo in Milwaukee—and watched ridiculous singer Michael Bolton enter the park in his own sausage casing of a uniform. He was the only celebrity to bring his own equipment, too. Bolton has his own touring softball team and a softball instructional video. He hit a home run in every at-bat, and his frizzy mudflap flounced as he ran the bases. And still Bolton was upstaged by bearish singer Meat Loaf and seven-foot Knick center Patrick Ewing.

Loaf's imprudent first-inning decision to stretch a single into a double nearly resulted in a Celebrity Blowout of Both Knees, while the sight of Ewing taking his cuts was simply surreal. He looked irreversibly entangled at the end of each swing, like a man in an invisible straitjacket. It was all good fun for a great cause. The game was a benefit for the

Special Olympics. The stands were filled with the mentally challenged and members of the Michael Bolton Fan Club, and everyone went home happy.

New Haven is neither New nor a Haven. It is, rather, Old and a Hazard. I was staying in a New Haven hotel whose front desk was full of mean little reminders: LOCK YOUR CAR, WE'RE NOT RESPONSIBLE FOR DAMAGE TO YOUR VEHICLE, GUESTS MAY BE SHOT IN THEIR SLEEP, and so forth.

On the closed-circuit hotel channel in my room, a video instructed me over and over to *always* use the main entrance when coming in after dark, to lock *all* available door locks (and these locks were manifold, believe me), to check my window locks *every* time I entered the room, and to feel free to call the front desk for confirmation should someone knock at my door "claiming" to be hotel staff.

"Claiming"? What kind of hotel *was* this? Evidently, the kind in which killers lurk outside your eighth-floor window and icepick murderers masquerade as chambermaids.

I kept the TV on for company. Alas, the remote was bolted down, so that I had to lift and point the entire nightstand to change the channel. It was exhausting and before long I was asleep—albeit uneasily, with one eye open.

I awoke to somber music issuing from the television and fumbled for my glasses. It was past noon, and flags hung at half-staff in Yankee Stadium. Over the picture, Scooter Rizzuto ad-libbed an oddly eloquent elegy: for a teammate and era just passed this morning. Mantle was dead.

"I get to thinking about how many fathers named their *daughters* Mickey because of Mickey Mantle," said the Scooter. "And it's not a bad name: *Mickey*. . . ." I did a quick lap with the flipper: Footage of the Mick flickered in slow-motion on channels 2, 4, 7, 9, and 11 in New York. I imagined this was how state television in Iran marked the passing of the Ayatollah.

I checked out of the Paranoia Plaza and returned to the road, enraptured by the radio. "The Mick," said a disbelieving caller to all-sports station WFAN, "he ran down fly balls like a *deer.*"

I drove south, around New York City. I tried to imagine a deer running down a fly ball. I briefly pined for the love of a good woman named Mickey. But these happy reveries didn't last.

Instead, my multiple layers of cynicism were stripped away like house paint with each successive caller—most of whom had outer-borough voices that *could* strip house paint, but were so sincere and obviously bereaved that I began to feel uneasy and slightly ashamed, a stranger at a wake.

Callers in their forties and fifties ascribed Messianic qualities to Mantle. A host noted that "Number Seven passed away on the Seventh Day" and paused to let the myriad theological implications sink in. Mantle had, undeniably, worked medical miracles of a sort. A week before his transplant there were 12 requests for organ donor cards in Dallas. The week after there were 700. An outraged caller said, "It's time we got to the bottom of cancer!"

Mantle's abrupt decline as a player was cited as a cause of the nation's descent into the violence and chaos of the late 1960s. "Mickey's first year as a total physical wreck was 1965," said Phil from Riverdale. "And that was also the start of the counterculture."

"In many ways," said Bill from Long Beach, "Mickey took the place of my father, who died in 1956."

A gentleman named Wally phoned to tell a story of "two bruddahs," one of whom rooted for Maris and one of whom rooted for Mantle to break Ruth's single-season home run record in the summer of '61. "Near the end of the season," said Wally, "the one rootin' for the Mick had heart surgery and was dyin' and said after the operation, 'I heard the record was broken. Who did it?' " Here the caller struggled to continue. "And the bruddah . . . the bruddah lied . . . the bruddah told him, 'Da Mick did it!' " At this, the caller burst into sobs. I was left to infer that the bruddah died happy. So, too, Mantle. He was reported to have told doctors in his final weeks that he didn't want to know how long he had to live. In fact, what he said was "I'll take it day to day." As I followed the Palisades Parkway into New Jersey, Yankee Stadium not three miles east across the Hudson, I thought: How else should a dying ballplayer be listed, if not "day to day"? How else should he play those days, if not "one at a time"?

It is often written that "sports are a microcosm of life." And it is almost as often written—by people who think they're being clever—that "life is a microcosm of sports." But it took Mickey Mantle to write a true corollary to both of these clichés: In him, for the first time, death was a microcosm of sports.

8

What becomes of a myth-riddled athlete from rural Oklahoma when he's dead? I decided to visit the grave of Jim Thorpe and find out. By the kind of cosmic coincidence that placed, say, the boyhood home of Neil Armstrong on Neil Armstrong Drive, Jim Thorpe was interred in Jim Thorpe, Pennsylvania. Thorpe, it seemed to me, was at the center of an extraordinary T-junction in American life—where Americana, American history, and American sports meet up.

Here was an American Indian robbed of his Olympic medals, because he once took $60 a month to play semipro baseball, in violation of the Olympics amateur code, and later "relocated"—if not against his will, then certainly without his volition, as that relocation took place several months after his death when a dying town sought new life by buying the remains of the "world's greatest athlete."

Prior to that death, Thorpe spent some years as a "casting director for American Indians" in Hollywood and is said to have given Jay Silverheels his first role. Silverheels went on to pop-cultural immortality as Tonto in the TV show *The Lone Ranger*. And yet, when Hollywood made the movie *Jim Thorpe—All American*, the title role went to . . . Burt Lancaster. I don't want to hang the history of the Republic on all of this, but Thorpe *does* seem to speak to certain relevant themes: our general sports delirium, the shameful treatment of Native Americans by Whitey, and the desperate compulsion for every grease spot on the map to attract a "tourist attraction" that might float its economy.

Before I entered Jim Thorpe—may I rephrase that? Before I arrived in Jim Thorpe—not much better, I know—I made a tactical decision to steer clear of Manhattan. (Speaking of American Indians getting robbed.) For one thing, parking in New York City would have cost me my right arm, which was just now tingling back to usefulness after the Foxboro soda machine fiasco.

For another, New York would probably have sucked me in for several days. I lived in New York for three years and moved out the instant my bosses allowed me to, but I still go back voluntarily every few months and stay for as long as I can bear it. New York is like TV. I profess to dislike it, and much of it really *is* terrible, but even the terrible stuff is entertaining, and I find myself unable to turn away. As an example, I point to the city's indigenous street sports. In the middle of the intersection outside my apartment one noon, a warrior from the elite Gurkha military tribe of central Nepal was menacing pedestrians with a broadsword. While New Yorkers nimbly evaded the Nepalese madman (while simultaneously pretending not to notice him), police dropped him with enough tranquilizer darts to "fell an elephant," as subsequent news reports took great delight in noting. In New York, walking to work was *American Gladiators* or *Wild Kingdom* or both.

And yet it is also the feel-good capital of the world. Only in New York can a young man slip while scrambling over a high wrought-iron fence; impale himself on a spike that passes through the soft flesh under his chin and protrudes through his open mouth; be left to dangle, several feet off the sidewalk, like a speared smelt as a murmuring crowd gathers 'round; be photographed in said position by a passing paparazzo; be cut out of the fence by the Fire Department with the spike still in his chin like a toothpick through a cherry tomato; be rushed to the hospital; be told by a dozen wise guys that he looks like Steve Martin with the rubber arrow circa 1978; and be painfully disimpaled by a team of doctors. . . .

Only in New York can a young man endure all of this and *still* be described in the next day's tabloids as MISTER LUCKY!—singled out, in a city of 7.5 million, as Gotham's most Fortune-kissed citizen.

In the years since I left New York, I have occasionally felt like a released prisoner unable to adjust to life on the n outside, one who keeps committing petty crimes in the hope of being sent back. It's irrational, I know, but that's the strange push-pull of the place. Driving on the tattered outskirts of the city now, it took great willpower for me to forge on, away from the Manhattan skyline, and toward the postapocalyptic landscape along the New Jersey Turnpike.

I was traveling with a British-authored guidebook to the U.S.A. In it, the turnpike was called "stupendously ugly," a description that does a disservice to the thoroughfare and only hints at its epic unsightliness. Outside my windows was a smoking miasma of industrial wasteland. Greater Newark was a never-emptied ashtray, smokestacks like crushed-out cigarette butts, stained by rust-colored lipstick, shrouded by ashen skies that literally smoldered. If Simon and Garfunkel were still in business, they would be counting the EPA violations on the New Jersey Turnpike. I hung a right near Perth Amboy and slashed west across New Jersey on I-78, reentering Pennsylvania near Easton.

I'd driven through Easton many times (don't ask) and knew it to be the hometown of former heavyweight champion of the world Larry Holmes. For years, he was the owner of Easton's Larry Holmes Motor Hotel. Except that the façade was always missing multiple letters and usually read along the lines of:

LA   HO   MO   HO

Alas, the LA HO MO HO was no mo'. Since my last visit, Holmes apparently sold the joint, and it now looked even more derelict, if that were possible. I had hoped to grab a bite in Flossie's coffee shop, named for Larry's mother, but as this was no longer an option, I drove on the forty or so miles to Jim Thorpe, climbing ever higher into the mountains northwest of Allentown.

Jim Thorpe died on March 28, 1953, in his trailer home in Lomita, California. He was sixty-four. He was to be buried in Shawnee, in his native Oklahoma, but the city had only enough money to ship his body in from the coast and could not afford to erect a memorial suitable to Thorpe's greatness. Only three years earlier, the Associated Press had named Thorpe the greatest athlete of the first half of the twentieth century, for obvious reasons. The man won gold medals in the decathlon and pentathlon at the 1912 Olympics, played major-league baseball from 1913 to 1919, then pro football from 1919 to 1926.

So, spurned by Oklahoma, Thorpe's widow (and third wife) took a fairly extraordinary step, burial-wise: She declared Thorpe's corpse a free agent.

Patricia Thorpe thought a natural alternative burial site might be Carlisle, Pennsylvania, where Jim had been an All-American running back for the Carlisle Indian School. So she traveled to Pennsylvania to make an inquiry. The widow Thorpe was in her room at the Bellevue–Stratford in Philadelphia when she heard a news report about Mauch Chunk and East Mauch Chunk, rival Pennsylvania towns now twinned in a postwar depression. Their coal mine closed, their railroad depot in disuse, the two Chunks started a Nickel-a-Week citizen development fund that had raised $17,000 to purchase *something* that might render the towns upright again. All of this is a long story short, but Mrs. Thorpe and the towns struck a deal: The Chunks would build a "suitable memorial" to Thorpe and rename their newly combined town for him, and she would in turn deliver the body.

I learned all of this at the wonderful Victorian public library in Jim Thorpe, where a kind librarian named John, who had spent thirty-five years as an English teacher in Jim Thorpe, gave me fat folders of yellow news clippings that turned to fairy dust in my hands and skillfully evaded my pointed queries about what he thought of the whole Jim Thorpe business.

I read that Thorpe was disinterred in Tulsa, where he had apparently rested in temporary repose, arrived in Allentown via the Reading Railroad, and was transferred by hearse to the former Mauch Chunk. It was his first-ever visit to Carbon County and not the ideal way to go. Children were let out of school to watch the procession, and the peripatetic Thorpe remains were temporarily entombed at Evergreen Cemetery.

A permanent mausoleum—costing $12,500 in nickels—was finally dedicated on May 30, 1957, before five thousand spectators. The "ground from several world-famous stadiums" was strewn about the tomb. There were plans to attract the Pro Football Hall of Fame to Jim Thorpe, perhaps a cancer hospital in his name, and even a tasteful Jim Thorpe Teepees motel. But none of it materialized, and by 1966, the citizens of Jim Thorpe (Jim Thorpers? Jim Thorpeans?) nearly passed a referendum that would have re-renamed the town Mauch Chunk (Mauch Chunkers? Mauch Chunkies?).

By the mid-1980s, a flurry of stories had accumulated in the local library about Thorpe's heirs, who wanted his remains returned to Oklahoma. "He's going to stay here," Jim Thorpe's mayor told Jim Thorpe's son, Jack, during a 1983 summit meeting. Replied Jack, "He belongs to the world." Members of Thorpe's Sac and Fox tribe evidently believed that his spirit would continue to roam unless the great man was returned for a proper tribal burial.

I drove to the outskirts of town to see the mausoleum for myself. There was a small turnoff on Route 903, like a circular driveway. In the center of that "U" was a twenty-ton crypt enlivened by twelve relief sculptures of Thorpe: on horseback, playing baseball, high jumping, and so forth. Carved into the russet Minnesota granite were the words:

FINAL RESTING PLACE

JIM THORPE

ALL-AMERICAN

The tomb was all alone here, wedged between a woods and a neighborhood of mixed zoning. An Olympic flag, fringed and faded, flew above the crypt, as did a tattered and very Old Glory—bleached pink, white, and sky-blue by the elements. Scattered about the ground was a sandwich bag, a circle of beer cans, a Doritos packet, a . . . *discarded mailbox?* I got the overwhelming impression that this was the spot—every town has one—where high school sophomores get together to drink illicitly and talk about blowing this pop stand when they turn eighteen.

It is shatteringly sad to see garbage at a grave. For some reason, I couldn't stop thinking of the seventies public-service commercial in which the old Indian sheds a single tear at the sight of litter.

The grass lot was overgrown with weeds and scabbed with dirt patches. There were four sickly saplings tied to a life support of ropes and stakes. I counted six shrubs. The only tribute to Thorpe were two stalks sprouting pink and yellow blossoms placed at the base of the memorial. I picked them up. They were plastic. Traffic whooshed by not twenty yards away. In twenty minutes, two cars used the turnoff to make U-turns. Just before I left, another car pulled in and the driver got out, his engine still running. He looked toward his muffler, then looked at me and said, "Thought somethin' was fallin' off." Then he drove away, coughing out a cloud of exhaust.

Well, what can I say? The shittiest thing about Jim Thorpe's drive-up tomb is that the rest of the town seemed to be in a state of renaissance, with antique shops and a fifties diner and other amenities that an indigent place could not indulge. And overlooking the downtown historic district was the lovingly restored Asa Packer mansion, a monument to one man's greed, now owned and maintained by the Borough of Jim Thorpe.

Packer sounds like a real hoot, a railroad baron who would sit in the cupola atop his four-story Victorian castle and make sure his trains rolled into the Mauch Chunk depot on time. At his death in 1860, he was the third-richest man in America, worth $54 million. That's about $3.2 billion in today's economy, and yet he paid the vastly talented artisans who carved one thousand rosettes into his English post-oak paneling and the heads of the Gospel writers into his mantelpieces all of fifty cents a day. I could see their magnificent handiwork because the house was open for tours. As I say, it was all meticulously maintained.

But this wasn't Asa Packer, Pennsylvania, was it? You mean to tell me that the Borough of Jim Thorpe can't raise a new American flag above the Grave of Jim Thorpe? A man involuntarily riding out eternity in a strange land a thousand miles from his place of birth—a man brought to town to do, in death, what he did in life: make money for others? They can't pick up the trash at his tomb? I left Jim Thorpe, half-hoping that Thorpe's soul *had* wandered from its lonely mausoleum.

I sped south on the northeast extension of the Pennsylvania Turnpike, trying to resist unhappy conclusions about who we choose to remember as American heroes and why. One thing is certain: If you want your memory preserved, die in a mansion full of Honduran mahogany, not in an L.A. trailer. Or so the lesson seemed to me.

9

Here's a happy ending. Babe Ruth is buried in the Gates of Heaven Cemetery in Mount Pleasant, New York. Now, doesn't that sound like a . . . *pleasant* place, at least under the circumstances? What's more, the priest who was with Ruth in his final hours told the press, "The Babe died a beautiful death." I mention these things: (1) because I was heading to Ruth's hometown of Baltimore, and (2) lest you get the idea that I hold some kind of grudge against the Grim Reaper.

On the contrary: As a traveling sportswriter, Death has been my constant companion on the road. This can be vexing, especially when Death gets the aisle seat on airplanes. But I've learned to accept his grim presence and have even grown grateful for the extra pair of eyes when scanning stadium parking lots for my rental car.

A few years ago, Death came knocking at the door of my Omaha hotel room. That was more than I could say for housekeeping, which earlier had burst in unannounced while I was watching Spectravision in my underwear. But I digress. I was in Omaha to cover the college baseball World Series. One morning I sat bolt upright in bed, awakened by a tornado siren, which startled me, as I hadn't requested a wake-up siren. Still, it wasn't the first time a hotel had awakened me indiscriminately, oblivious to time and the sign on my doorknob. I reflexively returned to sleep.

Seconds later, like the seat backs and tray tables that equip my subconscious, I returned to an upright position. In a sweat, I recalled that a twister had devastated parts of Colorado earlier in the week. A member of the Georgia Bulldogs, who were staying across town at the Sheraton, would later tell me that he turned to his roommate at this very moment and said, "We have five or ten minutes before we die."

I was hustled by hotel security from my fifth-floor room into the lobby restaurant, where guests ducked under tables, stood in doorways, and crouched beneath countertops. Having eaten there the night before, I immediately sought protection beneath a basket of dinner rolls. And though a tornado never did touch down, I knew that I hadn't cheated Death, but had merely put him off for another month or so. In that way, Death isn't so different from the woman in charge of my American Express bill, who haunts me monthly from her Phoenix office.

What I'm trying to say is, the road has never really risen up to meet me. In my rookie year as a scribe, baseball lifer Don Baylor counseled me in the Milwaukee Brewer clubhouse: "I tell young players and young writers the same thing. Travel isn't easy. You better learn to pace yourself."

And indeed, I have learned many things while living in hotels in the years since. I am now a biblical scholar. I know the life story of J. Willard Marriott as if it were my own. Inspired by the intricately folded end squares of toilet paper that invariably hang in my bathrooms, I have taken a keen interest in the Japanese art of origami.

I have learned the Indonesian words for "Do not disturb" *("Di-*

larang mengganggu") and the Czech phrase for "Please make up room now" (*"Prosim, uklidte pokoj"*). But I never did learn to pace myself. My twenties were one long road trip, though the first half of that phrase— "road"—seldom entered into it. Air travel dominates my life. All of my bookmarks are boarding-pass stubs. I look forward to having "small children" someday, if only to make me eligible for preboarding.

I know the three-letter luggage-tag abbreviations for airports— ORD, LGA, DFW—as I once knew my state capitals. Indeed, before I embarked on this trip, I had begun to notice that all of my conversations with colleagues were degenerating into a dispiriting game of one-downsmanship.

"I flew into Java standing up, in 'straphanger class,'" I once casually mentioned to my fellow *SI* writer Franz Lidz, a man so road-ravaged and bonus-point-padded that he has the free use of a National rental car in perpetuity. "The air was rough and . . ."

"They didn't have pressurized cabins?" Franz interjected.

"Of course they did."

"Oh," Franz said casually, as if it were hardly worth mentioning. "It's just that the cabin wasn't pressurized on my Air Zambia flight. The beverage service was a single bottle of Coke passed around the cabin and . . ."

"Unappetizing," I interrupted. *"Almost* as unappetizing as the meal service on Bulgaria Air, which distributed Wet-Naps in packets bearing an instructional three-panel cartoon of a woman (1) tearing open the packet, (2) unfolding the Wet-Nap, and (3) using the Wet-Nap to vigorously scrub her deep-pile armpits. . . ."

"Last week," Franz trumped me, fresh from a trip to China, "the captain came out of the cockpit to greet passengers, and a minute later *another* pilot came out to take a leak. And the cockpit door swung shut behind him. And locked." As the plane flew inexorably onward, Franz swore, two Chinese pilots spent a harrowing interval trying to break into the cockpit with a dinner fork.

The lessons of this and other conversations were manifold. Suffice to say that I was happy to be driving. That I was happy to be driving in

America. And that I didn't miss the company of frequent-flying Bulgarian women with the body hair and table manners of Ed Asner.

If you've ever run through the rain forest swaddled in Saran Wrap, you have some small notion of what it is like to be outdoors in Baltimore in August. It's a tad humid. My T-shirt was pitted out even before my arrival, as I went by white-knuckle way of Philadelphia's Schuylkill Expressway, which is somehow pronounced "Skookle," but is known to locals as the "Sure-Kill."

The Sure-Kill shot me, hair raised and pulse racing, into Delaware, which had an immediate and counterbalancing sedative effect. Delaware is the Major Major of states—distinguished by its lack of distinction, impressive for its unimpressiveness, noteworthy for a general unnoteworthiness. The state government reluctantly concedes this fact and even contributes to it. A sign at the border says: WELCOME TO DELAWARE: HOME OF TAX-FREE SHOPPING. About three seconds later—or exactly the length of time it takes to say, *"That* was the best they could do?"—they take another desperate stab at it: FIRST TO RATIFY THE CONSTITUTION. I checked my road atlas for further dope.

> *Capital:* Dover
> *Nickname:* Diamond State
> *Highest Point:* There really isn't one to speak of.

I left Delaware only twenty minutes after arriving, as the state is just twenty miles wide at its northern tip. The landscape had the agreeable, forgettable suburban look you might expect—Delaware even sounds like Tupperware—then abruptly merged into Maryland, which was celebrating the 100th anniversary of Babe Ruth's birth.

To my delight, the first city across the Maryland border was Elkton. Ruth once did a radio show in which he had a single scripted line. For reasons that I cannot begin to imagine, he was supposed to say: "As the Duke of Wellington once said, 'The Battle of Waterloo was won on the playing fields of Eton.' " But when he went on the air, the Bambino, bless him, got slightly mixed up and said: "As Duke Ellington once said, 'The Battle of Waterloo was won on the playing fields of Elkton.' "

As the playing fields of Elkton retreated in my rearview, darkness fell like a wet wool blanket on eastern Maryland. I drove for another hour into Baltimore, where I had no trouble finding a room, which was a bad sign. It meant that the Orioles were out of town, for they are always sold out at home and have a corresponding effect on city hotels.

I would not, alas, get to see my role model in life: the proprietor of Boog's Barbecue Stand, just beyond the right field bleachers in Camden Yards. Babe Ruth may have famously eaten a dozen hot dogs between games of a doubleheader, but ex-Oriole slugger Boog Powell never bothered waiting for a game to end. When the O's played in Milwaukee, he used to dispatch a clubhouse attendant to the stands to procure a pair of bratwurst slathered in red sauce. Standing in the tunnel behind the dugout, Boog would swallow the sausages in a violent trice, as if feeding timber to a wood chipper. "I'd walk to the plate with red sauce all down the front of my uniform," he once told me. "I'd tell the manager, 'I'm bleedin' like a stuck pig!' "

A giant man who bleeds condiments and could hit a baseball a fair distance, Powell was the rightful heir to Ruth in Baltimore throughout the sixties and early seventies. Babe begat Boog. Powell now split his time between Baltimore and Key West, where he practiced what he called the full-barbecue lifestyle, which included copious amounts of fishing, competitive beef eating, and professional beer drinking (as a pitchman for the Miller Brewing Company). He was, in short, everything I aspired to be. At home I kept a copy of his barbecue manifesto, *Mesquite Cookery*, signed "To Steve, Keep Cookin'! John 'Boog' Powell." The great man is on the cover, standing at a grill beneath palm fronds. With his right hand, he skewers a hunk of beef the size of a bedroll. From the tongs on his left hand dangle five lascivious sausage links, each of which must be sixteen inches long. He looks not just enormous, but enormously contented. "Barbecue," Powell likes to say, "is an attitude."

I knew what he meant. It had been weeks now since I'd paid a bill, answered a phone, made a bed, burned a calorie, or eaten a vegetable that wasn't ketchup. I was completely without a care or responsibility. I was feeling very barbecue indeed as I tucked into my bed *du nuit*—they were magically clean-sheeted every night—and ignored the lurid alarm clock on the nightstand. My only deadline was the Boogian checkout time of noon. In the days when the Orioles played at Memorial Stadium, Powell lived in a rowhouse behind the ballpark. "Hell, I'd grill after night games," he once told me. "Fire it up at eleven o'clock, smoke is pouring in the neighbors' windows, their heads are popping out, and they're yelling, 'We know *you* don't have to work in the morning, but the rest of us do.' 'Hell,' I'd reply, 'if I had to work in the morning, I wouldn't be out here.' "

As I say, I was similarly unencumbered as I lay down to sleep in Baltimore. In fact, that was my only anxiety on the road—not knowing where I'd sleep each night. And even then I took comfort in the Tao of Boog, which stated that a man can happily lay his head anywhere, so long as he is near baseball, beer, and beef. This particular Holiday Inn had a view of Camden Yards. At various times in my life, I have lived in apartments with vistas of Wrigley Field in Chicago and the Metrodome in Minneapolis. I was raised in Bloomington, Minnesota, when that suburb was the home of Metropolitan Stadium, which was in turn the home of the Twins and the Vikings. So when Minnesotans went to the Met, it was not to take in *Aïda*.

"I used to leave that park after a weekend day game and never make it to the hotel," Boog once told me. "Those people could *tailgate*. You'd sit down, have a couple of beers, their grill is going, and the next thing you know, they're saying, 'Hey, it's late, you might as well stay here.' " And Boog would crash in his newfound friends' Winnebago, a mobile home away from home.

Over the years, I've developed that same facility for sleeping soundly anywhere. Because most big-time sporting events are played at night and everything that I cover requires me to be on the road, I have spent many wee hours of my adult life staggering from a stadium to a nearby hotel, groggy and gorged on ballpark food. I suffer from insomnia, but only at home. What this says about my life, and my prospects for leading a more normal one in the future, I would rather not dwell on.

In the morning, I walked to Babe Ruth's birthplace, two blocks northwest of Camden Yards. The air was warm and heavy and foul, like God's halitosis. Mercifully, the narrow row house at 216 Emory Street had central air-conditioning. Aside from that anachronism, the tiny room in which Babe was born had been faithfully restored to exacting historical detail. If you ignored the red velvet rope across the doorway, and the humidity-control device (or was it a smoke alarm?) jutting from the ceiling above the bed, and the low whisper of the AC, and the car alarm shrieking outside, the room was exactly as it was when Ruth came into the world on February 6, 1895. Or February 7, 1894. Nobody can say for certain when he was born, which made me wonder how they knew *where* he was born and on what kind of sheets. In the end, like millions of others, I simply took it on faith that this was the spot.

In that way, Ruth's birthplace reminded me of the very spot— marked by a star—in the Church of the Nativity in Bethlehem where Jesus is believed to have been born. So much of the Ruth mythology is Christlike: being sent away by his father to live among others (at the St. Mary's Industrial School), going out into the world to heal the sick (by hitting home runs for hospitalized children), foretelling his own future (with his famous "called shot"), and so forth. In the museum that adjoins the Ruth house, there is a collection of sheet music and records for the countless popular songs about the Babe: *Batterin' Babe (Look at Him Now); Oh! You Babe Ruth; Along Came Ruth; Babe Ruth (He's a Home Run Guy); Babe Ruth! Babe Ruth! (We Know What He Can Do); Our Bambino; Babe; Joosta Like Babe-a-Da-Ruth* and, released immediately after his death, *Safe at Home*, which played over and over in the museum on what sounded like a Victrola. "Safe at home, safe at home, yes tonight the mighty Babe is safe at home. . . ." I tried to think of a man who was the subject of as many hymns and again could only come up with one name: Jesus.

Japanese soldiers said (or were said to have said) to GIs in World War II, "To hell with Babe Ruth"—or, as seems more likely, "Fuck Babe Ruth." The insult was intended as the ultimate sacrilege to Americans— taking the Babe's name in vain. To which Ruth replied, according to his obituary in *The New York Times*, "I hope every Jap that mentions my name gets shot—and to hell with all the Japs anyway." I can tell you that a century after his birth and a half-century after his death, Ruth was still Ruthian, a potent totem of America. A friend of mine is proud to own Ruth's old bathtub, which surely says *something* about the Babe's endur- ing hold (and something far more disturbing about the kind of friends I have).

I left the teeming Ruth museum and turned my car toward Wash- ington, D.C., stopping ten minutes out of town to buy toiletries at the Westview Mall in Catonsville, Maryland. To my surprise, a Babe Ruth look-alike in full vintage Yankee uniform was strolling the mall, greeting shoppers. He was uncanny—he looked Joosta Like Babe-a-Da-Ruth— and a great many of the mall's predominantly black patrons eagerly shook his hand. Amazing, given that African American attendance at major-league baseball games has historically been so infrequent as to be almost statistically unmeasurable. Mall security had assigned this neo- Ruth his own personal rent-a-cop, and I later learned (from the guy's voluminous news clippings) that his name was Buster Gardner. And though Buster drove a tow truck in Oberlin, Ohio, he also had a heavy schedule of appearances at parties and such the year 'round. How many other long-dead historical figures can one make a living looking like? I contemplated that question back in my car and again came up with but one deific contender: Elvis.

Elvis and the Babe died on the same day—August 16—twenty- nine years apart, prompting the minor-league St. Paul Saints to honor both men with a promotion called "Two Dead Fat Guys Night." Only one other man could be said to possess the charismatic DNA of the Babe and the King. According to *Pop Culture Landmarks*, a book I cannibal-

ized in the Smithsonian gift shop in Washington, D.C., retired NASCAR
driver Richard Petty was "Elvis behind the wheel of a race car."

"His race-car number, 43," the book went on, "is as well known as
Babe Ruth's number 3."

Thirty-six hours after reading those words, I was in Petty's hometown of Level Cross, North Carolina, thrilled to be in the South at last.
To be sure, I had long before crossed the Mason–Dixon line, the border
between Pennsylvania and Maryland, as surveyed by Charles Mason and
Jeremiah Dixon between 1763 and 1767. (I just looked that up.) Before
the Civil War, the line was also the boundary between the "free states"
of the North and the "states that enjoy stock-car racing" of the South.

But it wasn't until I passed from Virginia into North Carolina that I
felt fully immersed in Southern culture. That's when an AM radio station reported that President Clinton was this very week on vacation in
Jackson Hole, Wyoming, with one Mort Engelberg, identified as "the
producer of *Smokey and the Bandit.*" The reporter said this reverentially,
making *Smokey and the Bandit* sound as important as *Citizen Kane.* But
the fact that our Southern President was vacationing with the man behind *Smokey and the Bandit* said more about our Southern President, I
fear, than it did about *Smokey and the Bandit.*

That film, cineasts will recall, followed Burt Reynolds in a black
Trans-Am as he eluded a Southern redneck sheriff in a patrol car. The
film was, in short, stock-car racing. *Smokey* was successful enough to
spawn a sequel precisely because the premise appealed to that primal
urge of human beings to haul ass, preferably through the South, preferably in a sports car of American provenance.

When I crossed into Randolph County, south of Greensboro, a sign
stated: THIS SECTION OF HIGHWAY 220 DEDICATED IN HONOR OF RICH-
ARD PETTY. And while 220 was the main tributary into Level Cross,
Petty ought to have been honored along a different stretch of Tobacco
Roadway. Months after my visit, I would read in *The New York Times*
that "Mr. Petty, driving a Dodge pickup, bumped the car ahead of him
on Interstate 85 because he felt it was moving too slowly at sixty miles an

hour." No wonder Senator Jesse Helms once signed a photograph to Petty with the words: "I'm so proud of you—you're a *great* American." Some North Carolinians thought Petty was destined for the presidency— FROM THE OVAL TRACK TO THE OVAL OFFICE, according to a bumper sticker in the Richard Petty Museum in Level Cross.

The museum and Petty's office were in a complex of low white buildings that collectively resembled an Army barracks. Petty's circular logo was everywhere: a drawing of his face—or, rather, a drawing of his wraparound shades, cowboy hat, and trademark leer, all suspended in air like the Cheshire cat's grin. It resembled the Presidential Seal of some demented nation—a nation of rusting trailer homes and cars up on blocks, to judge by the landscape I passed on approach to the Petty compound. I was reminded of Jeff Foxworthy's line: "You might be a redneck if . . . your house is on wheels and your car isn't."

I parked next to a red Ford pickup identified by its Virginia plates as HIGS RIG. On the wood-paneled walls of the museum were incendiary photographs from the King's last ride at the Hooters 500 in Atlanta. There was a degree of some sort from Pfeiffer College in Misenheimer, North Carolina. There was a key to "the City of Alabama." Trophies shaped like spark plugs propped open doors, through which thirty-five thousand visitors passed every year.

I had the half-cocked notion that I might gain an audience with Petty, but I was disabused of the idea immediately. A dozen other members of the Petty bourgeoisie had come seeking same. "Can I see Richard just for a minute?" a sensationally overweight man asked a woman who served as a kind of jill-of-all-trades, selling tickets and souvenirs in the museum and parrying requests to see Richard. "I'm a friend of his from way back. I grew up with him. I saw him here a few years ago. Just tell him it's Bucky Dawson. Dickie Dawson's cousin. I'm takin' my son to college and I'm only in town for one day and I was there when he started on the dirt tracks and . . ."

The woman's brow was pleated with worry. "I'm afraid it's changed since you were here last," she told Bucky. "The calls don't go straight through anymore. He's back there in his office, swamped. He's just swamped. He's a very famous person, you know. He has no time. Now, everyone must have an appointment *days* in advance."

Bucky looked at the woman hopefully, hearing nothing that she said. "I'll call his secretary," the woman finally sighed, revealing herself to be but an outer-ring suburb of secretarial service to the King. "Maybe *she* can come over and see you." The woman punched up an extension. "There's a gentleman here who wants to see Richard," she said with the man standing a foot away. "Says he grew up with him. [Pause.] I know. That's what I *told* him."

"Tell her Bucky Dawson," said Bucky Dawson.

"His name's Bucky Dawson. [Pause.] I know, I tried to tell him that."

"Tell her Dickie Dawson's cousin," said the unsinkable Bucky Dawson.

"He's Dickie Dawson's cousin."

Finally the woman hung up. "She's gonna try to come over and talk to you. See, it ain't like it used to be. Have you been to a NASCAR race recently? It's all about the sponsors and the money. Everyone's uptight. It's no fun. And everyone's *drunk*. I work here, and I don't even go anymore."

Considering that Appalachian moonshiners helped to pioneer and popularize stock-car racing, the allegation of mass drunkenness made sense. But the thought that stock-car racing had become too *corporate*, well, that was hard to conceive. She might as well have said that corporations had become too . . . stock-car-racing-like.

But it's true. Turns out Richard Petty was back in his office contemplating a campaign to become the Republican lieutenant governor of North Carolina. In the end, he did not run. In a museum photograph, one of Petty's stock cars was parked in the White House driveway, where the King posed with Helms and President Reagan. Did he really aspire to go from oval track to Oval Office? He could leave his car on blocks in the driveway, and put the White House on wheels, and make his logo the Presidential Seal.

From Level Cross I drove five miles east to the town of Climax, where I stopped to call all my friends and say, "I've reached Climax." And then I drove and drove and drove, through crepuscular light, admiring at length the alliterative attractions of North Carolina—pines, piedmont, palmetto. Poverty, too. I saw entire Main Streets anchored by businesses with names like Hi-Fashion Wigs and The Bent Can discount grocer. There was greater deprivation in the mountains to the northwest, but as I fell in behind a car whose bumper sticker read KISS OUR APPS, I felt fortunate to have skipped any region which chose that as its ad slogan.

It grew late and I grew tired. I rode in the wake of a Ford pickup—BOWHUNT on its North Carolina plates—and began to despair of ever finding a motel. A series of shrill billboards advertised SOUTH OF THE BORDER (78 MILES), a tourist complex with OVER 10,000 MEXICAN ITEMS (46 MILES) and 20 HONEYMOON SUITES—THEY'RE *HEIR* CONDITIONED! (38 MILES). The billboards brilliantly exploited this unspeakably boring drive, but by the time I reached KEEP YELLIN', KID, THEY'LL STOP! (31 MILES), I was more or less sleepdriving. The U.S. Department of Transportation estimates that fifty-six thousand accidents are caused each year by drivers nodding off at the wheel, and I believe it. At the next exit, I had to pull over for the night, even if it meant sleeping in a parking lot.

To my profound relief, the next exit—Lumberton—was a small oasis of cheap motels and greasy spoons. Lumberton, Lumberton . . . why was the name so familiar? It hit me as I was drifting to sleep in the Super 8: Michael Jordan's father, James, was napping roadside near here in the small hours of the night when he was murdered for his Lexus sedan. In the morning, I walked to the Denny's in Lumberton and made the mistake of saying "Non" when asked for my smoking preference. I was ushered to a four-table holding pen near the kitchen. In North Carolina, evidently, the smoking section *is* the restaurant. It was a wonder that there were any smokers left to go to Denny's, as the habit kills four hundred thousand people a year . . . smoking, not going to Denny's.

I wanted to order the "Moon Over My Hammy" sandwich, but couldn't bring myself to say the words. Not only does it sound imbecilic, but "hammy" is sport slang for "hamstring," and the moon over my hamstring is something I would rather not eat, or even think about over brunch. So I ordered the club.

And then I drove to the coast. Hurricanes were vaguely forecast for the lower half of the Eastern seaboard, and by the time I reached Jordan's hometown of Wilmington—James Jordan's unrealized destination on the night of his murder—it was raining in the manner of a horse pissing on a flat rock. I soldiered on, southward.

10

I clung to the coastline along Highway 17, traveling south into monsoon-sodden Myrtle Beach as if through one unceasing car wash. The town billed itself as THE MINIATURE GOLF CAPITAL OF THE WORLD—City of Light was already taken—and, sure enough, some two dozen Lilliput courses lined the Grand Strand, a magnificently garish main drag.

Franz Lidz once played every one of those courses in a single weekend and had given me some useful background on the game. "Tom Thumb golf," as it was originally called, was first played in 1926 at a Tennessee resort called the Fairyland Inn. The game had become so popular by the end of the Roaring Twenties that it spawned a hit song, *I've Gone Goofy Over Miniature Golf.* Some folks did just that: A course was laid out on the grounds of a state hospital for the insane.

Of course, no one in Myrtle Beach was certifiably demented—
Vanna White grew up here, but she had long since moved away—and
the citizenry knew better than to brandish long metal sticks in a storm.
Even the tourists remained indoors. The courses were deserted and I
kept driving, on and on through the endless sprawl.

Where there weren't minigolf courses, there were cavernous gift
shops, whose names—The Curious Mermaid, The Gay Dolphin—
sounded like the titles of nautically themed porno films. So did Three-
Ball Charlie, come to think of it; he was an oddity on display at the
Ripley's Believe It or Not Museum. Three-Ball could insert a tennis ball,
billiard ball, and golf ball side by side in his mouth, according to museum
propaganda, "and whistle at the same time!" (They always add these
dubious flourishes, don't they? The Ripley's people cannot help themselves.) The point is, Myrtle Beach had every manner of diversion and
was precisely the sort of place my dad would never let us stop on family
vacations. I finally understood why. It was awful.

The traffic had become treacherous. Ahead of me, truck tires threw
off a massive spray, like giant dogs shaking themselves dry. I kept a death
grip on the steering wheel, releasing it only long enough to dry my
sweaty palms on the air-conditioning vents, in the manner of a professional bowler.

For the next ninety miles, I more or less hydroplaned in the wake of
a dilapidated pickup that was apparently held together by its bumper
stickers: VIETNAM VET AND PROUD OF IT; DON'T BLAME US, WE VOTED
FOR JEFF DAVIS; HAVE A DIXIE DAY—the x in "Dixie" formed by the
Confederate flag. I felt like Boss Hogg pursuing the Dukes of Hazzard
until at last we parted company in Charleston, where the first shot was
fired to begin a terrible war—the one that turned brothers against brothers and wives against husbands and all that.

I am talking, of course, about golf. Charleston claims to have
America's first course, Harleston Green, and America's first club, the
South Carolina Golf Club, both established by Scotsmen in 1786. The
Scots still had a Hibernian Society in town, for I passed its grand head-
quarters on my drive in. The Hibs sponsored an annual Highland Games

in which kilted Southern Scotsmen performed traditional feats of Scottish athletic skills—tossing cabers, dead-lifting boulders, sprinting with greased boars under each arm. Scotsmen are a lot like Southerners, when you think about it, though the former have more penetrable accents.

But back to golf. Harleston's Green was little more than a large public gathering ground on the southwestern edge of Charles Towne, as the city was then known. But members of the South Carolina Golf Club contributed funds to maintain that green and thus gave birth to the phrase "greens fee." Or so the story goes.

Likewise, a gunmetal-gray mist often enveloped the course—as indeed was happening throughout the entire South Carolina low country today—prompting players at Harleston Green to wear highly visible red jackets. To this day, golfers still favor red blazers, canary slacks, white loafers, and the like, and we have Charleston to thank for *that*.

Charleston launched other national crazes, as you know. When not playing miniature golf in the 1920s, Americans were doing the dance inspired by the city. I must say, Charleston damn near moved me to dance when I arrived, in early evening, to row after row of antebellum homes and a skyline silhouette of church steeples.

I ditched my bags in a motel room and set out, adrenalized, to see the city on foot. For a happy hour, I strolled the cobbled streets in the rain—umbrella in hand, spotlit by streetlamps—and felt myself coming down with a serious case of Gene Kelly. But the weather worsened as I went until, eventually, I was leaning hard into a gale. Pedestrians walking toward me mistook me for a street mime. I feared I might be beaten.

After a struggle, I managed to make it to Waterfront Park at the city's southeastern edge. Standing at the end of a pier, I strained to see the man-made island of Fort Sumter, somewhere out there in Charleston Harbor. But it was invisible in the gloom. The olive-green water was leaping and frothing, churning like a Maytag washer. Flags snapped violently in the wind. It was just the kind of backdrop that asshole TV reporters loved to have in their hurricane dispatches, the kind that said, "Look at me! I'm standing in a hurricane!"

I had begun to second-guess the life decisions that brought me to these circumstances—in wet socks at the very end of the continent, my entire estate in ministorage—when I heard Irish music. It was filtering out of an ancient stone tavern steps from the pier, and I hurried toward the golden light spilling from the front windows.

It was called the Griffon. A fireplace blazed inside. Guinness taps bowed like Japanese businessmen. A barkeep washed out pint glasses with a white rag. In the warm glow of the fire, I shook out my soggy baseball cap and tucked into a plate of fish and chips. It was battered cod, what the bartender called "low-country lobster."

"Been a long time since I've seen a Twins hat like that," said another guy at the bar. He smoked a stogie the size of a closet rod.

"They haven't worn these since '86," I said of the navy cap with an interlocking TC on the crown. "I got this one in Cooperstown." Unsure if this dateline was sufficient, I added, "Cooperstown, New York."

"Cooperstown," replied the guy, a forty-five-year-old named Rob. "On my dad's seventieth birthday, my brother and I flew him into New York. Huge baseball fan his whole life, but he'd never been to Yankee Stadium. We went there first, then we went to Cooperstown. Jim Palmer was going in that year. It was the first time in something like fifteen years that the ceremony was rained out. But we had a great time. At the end of the trip, we went to Hyde Park. My brother and I said, 'We'll wait outside, but you take as long as you like.' 'Cause Roosevelt doesn't mean anything to us, but to my dad's generation, he's God."

Of course, all three of them had toured Monument Park at Yankee Stadium and the Baseball Hall of Fame and Museum, because some gods speak to every generation, even to those as different as Rob's and his father's.

The pub's owner, Michael Calder, was pleased with the crowd coming in from the rain and expressed cautious hope for the Griffon's long-term prospects. "There's no cable TV east of Bay Street," Calder said of the avenue that runs roughly north and south, one block west of the waterfront. "But we got ABC and Fox, so we'll have football on Sundays and Monday nights."

Televised football was indeed more critical than beer nuts if he wanted to attract beer nuts like myself. But there was something still more compelling on TV as we spoke. A newscaster said something I had never heard before. It brought me up off my barstool. The weekend forecast for my next destination—Savannah, Georgia—called for "a 100 percent chance of rain."

The newscaster introduced this menacing weather system as "Tropical Depression Jerry." It has always struck me as a distinctly American need—to know the first name of the force of nature that might kill you or destroy your home. "Hi, my name's Jerry and I'll be your Tropical Depression."

Passing through Bluffton, South Carolina, in a horizontal rain, I considered stopping at the Squat 'N' Gobble, but feared its name might be more accurate the other way around. I drove on to another diner, where this was certainly the case. Five minutes after eating, I was forced to pull over.

Why are the keys to American gas station rest rooms, like the keys to swish European hotel rooms, always attached to ungainly objects? The theory is that a patron will think twice about making off with a key that is dangling from a pepper mill or spot-welded to a bowling trophy. This particular key was lashed to what appeared to be a railroad tie, which I urgently dragged behind me like a wooden leg.

The bathroom looked as if someone had just exploded in it. A condom dispenser leered from the wall; I considered buying several, if only to protect myself against the syphilitic toilet seat. What other purpose could the machine possibly serve? Were truckers really trysting in this abatoir? The entire room was a petri dish of disease. A sign above the sink should have warned: EMPLOYEES MUST AMPUTATE HANDS BEFORE LEAVING. I got in and out like a cat burglar—flushing with my knee, working the faucet with my elbows, turning the doorknob with my shoe sole.

I drove another twenty miles to the northern outskirts of Savannah, where the weather obliged me to pull over and park on the shoulder. I have never seen such rain. It fell with an Old Testament fury. It made a sound like God's fingers drumming on my rooftop.

I despaired that Jerry would wash out the weekend's high school football openers, which were my reason for being in Savannah. The rain abated slightly, to mere water-cannon-caliber ferocity, and I drove as if on a water-park flume ride to the Marriott high-rise hotel on the swollen Savannah River.

Rain lapped into my seventh-floor room through the bottom of a door that opened onto a deck. The carpet became darker and darker as this minitide approached my bed. I snapped on the TV and learned that the Atlantic tide would reach eight feet tonight. I switched to a sitcom and heard a sentence that seized me by the lapels: "We interrupt this program to ACTIVATE the Emergency Broadcast System." This was not a test. Savannah was flash flooding. I was trapped, indefinitely, in Atlantis, Georgia.

Mercifully, the Marriott was hosting a national convention of "Primitive Baptist Ministers." The lobby was filled with regal black men wearing double-breasted ice cream suits and silly gold medallions and women balancing enormous festive hats shaped like Bundt pans. Tables were set up in a conference room, at which men and women sold silly gold medallions and enormous festive hats. It was infectious. The football games were indeed washed away along with much of Savannah, but my own Tropical Depression was lifting.

By morning, Jerry had done likewise, and I went for a walk through Savannah, a city of absurd beauty and squalor. I concentrated on the beauty—historic mansions, trees dripping Spanish moss, cemeteries full of men killed in duels—and thought how General James Oglethorpe got it right when he laid out Savannah in 1733.

We will not see its like again. Savannah has twenty-one public squares; Hilton Head Island has twenty public golf courses. The cities are separated by thirty miles, yet one is the past and one is the future. With that in mind, I made an immediate decision to drive directly to America's most sacred golf town and see the Augusta National Golf Club.

I walked back to my car along sidewalks of seashells bleached white in the sunshine and thought: Try saying *that* five times fast.

Because of the foul weather emanating from the Tropics, I had to perform an emergency appendectomy on the United States and cut off the unnecessary appendage that is Florida. Now, with every mile I drove inland, the weather improved perceptibly.

I had forgotten that Augusta is closed during the month that takes up most of its name. When I found the famous club, I drove alongside its wall of high hedges, glimpsing an occasional and tantalizing sliver of fairway. It was actually titillating in a way, like an inch of a woman's ankle left exposed in Victorian times. Of course, after several solo weeks on the road, I was getting turned on by crossing the rumble strips before toll booths. But you get my point.

The green wall was broken only by a forbidding white gate that bore a stately sign: AUGUSTA NATIONAL GOLF CLUB—MEMBERS ONLY. I had to view the course through the half-inch of space where the gate was hinged to the wall; from there, the course looked otherworldly, to be sure, but somewhat less magnificent than it does in those helicopter shots we see every April on TV. So I sought a better vantage point.

A little farther along from the MEMBERS ONLY gate was another break in the wall, filled by another impenetrable gate, bearing another elegant sign: POSITIVELY NO ADMITTANCE. I drove still farther along the perimeter of the club, and still another gate bore still another sign: MEMBERS ONLY. Another hundred yards, another gate, another sign: WHY DON'T YOU FUCK OFF BACK TO MINNESOTA?

Well, it might as well have said as much. Augusta's august officials were not reticent about expressing their distaste for the mildest of media interlopers. Jack Whitaker of CBS was once famously barred from broadcasting the Masters after calling the Augusta gallery a "mob." Likewise, Gary McCord had been removed from the CBS crew for saying the greens had been "bikini-waxed." Reeking, unshaven, living out of my car—I calculated my odds of getting in as poor at best. But I really wanted to be inside, if only to escape Augusta proper.

The one thing those helicopter shots never do is pull back to reveal the world outside the walls of the golf club. Now I knew why. Perhaps I had been spoiled by Charleston and Savannah, but I found Augusta singularly lacking in character. I can't say it surprised me that James Brown had come out of the city, only that anyone still came *into* it.

Particularly black people. To say that Augusta was racially polarized would be inadequate. No black man was allowed to join Augusta National until 1991, and the tournament's founder, Clifford Roberts, once said: "As long as I'm alive, golfers will be white and caddies will be black."

Two miles south of Augusta National is an all-black neighborhood called The Hill. On the weekend that Tiger Woods won the 1997 Masters by 12 strokes—a black golfer with a white caddy—I would return to Augusta and visit The Hill. On Saturday night, hours after Woods had effectively seized the green jacket by its lapels, twelve black men stood outside a bar beneath a sign that said NO WETTING ON BUILDING. The bar's façade bore a mural of Tommy (Burnt Biscuit) Bennett, who two years earlier caddied for Woods at the Masters. All of the men outside the bar were golf caddies, and each had waited for this moment for decades.

"Am I excited?" said a forty-seven-year-old called Jap, nursing a Bud tallboy and marveling at the stupidity of such a question. "If golf was all-black and one white guy was doing this, wouldn't *you* be? Hell yes, I'm excited."

"Tomorrow will be special," said forty-two-year-old Barry Barnes, an Augusta caddy since 1971. "I'll be home tomorrow to watch Tiger get the green coat. Everyone you see out here tonight, they'll be inside watching tomorrow."

"It's the same way everyone used to go inside and listen to Joe Louis on the radio," added a man with a salt-and-pepper beard.

My guide to The Hill was a garrulous thirty-seven-year-old named Derrick Dent, a onetime Augusta National caddy and nephew of Senior

PGA star Jim Dent. On Sunday, as Woods was making his way around the front nine, Derrick met me at noon in front of the O.K. Pantry convenience store, nursing a bottle of Molson Golden that his wife, he said, had filched from the fridge of one of the rented homes she cleaned for corporate bigwigs on their annual Masters boondoggles.

Dent took me to the *other* Augusta—Augusta Golf Course. A muni abutting an airfield, the hardscrabble course was known to locals as the "Cabbage Patch." It was a place where blacks could play. "The Augusta, *Chronicle* ran a column last week saying it was ludicrous for Nike to say that Tiger can't play some courses because of the color of his skin," said Dent. "Well, let me tell you, there's a course in Augusta called Green Meadows—maybe Tiger Woods can play it, but Derrick Dent can't. And it *is* because of the color of my skin. There's no actual rule. It's just unwritten: You don't go there."

"I don't think they'll ever accept us regular black folks in the country clubs," said Scoby Bentley, fifty-two, once a caddy at Augusta National, now a caddy on the Nike Tour. "Maybe Michael Jordan and Tiger Woods. I would encourage them to form black country clubs."

As Woods was going to 18 under in the Masters, a dapper fifty-six-year-old black gentleman with the glorious name of J. B. Tutt sat at a Formica table in the Cabbage Patch clubhouse, wearily answering the telephone. "You want to join Augusta National?" Tutt chortled to a caller from Montreal. "This is Augusta Golf Course. But I hope you got a million-dollar entrance fee if you want to join Augusta National." A man called on his car phone from Detroit, asking for souvenir scorecards. "You want Augusta National," said Tutt, giving the man the phone number he had long ago committed to memory.

A year earlier Costantino Rocca called the Cabbage Patch, asking what his Masters tee time was for the first Thursday. "I think you want Augusta National," Tutt told the Italian star.

I asked Tutt how old he was and he said: "Old enough to be dead and not have anybody know the difference." But then he conceded he was fifty-six and that he grew up sneaking onto golf courses in Augusta. "When I was younger," he said, "I'd stand at the tee and say I was Jack

Nicklaus. I never cared what color Lee Trevino was. I loved Doug Sanders because I loved the way he dressed. I think golf people look at Tiger
as a great talent who happens to have a dark complexion.''

Derrick Dent agreed. He took me to a tidy white house on The Hill
where some friends and relatives had gathered to watch the end of the
Masters on a small black-and-white TV set propped up on a metal folding chair on the front porch. "This is history," said James Reid, fifty-
nine, inviting me to draw up a chair. "So we might as well watch it on a
black-and-white Philco."

Black and white. The words came up again and again that day on
The Hill. "With Tiger, I'm not motivated by the color of his skin, but by
the magnitude of his talent," said Dent.

The statement echoed Martin Luther King, Jr., a fact that wasn't
lost on Reid. "Dr. King said you don't judge a man by the color of his
skin, but by the content of his character," Reid said as Woods worked his
way around Amen Corner on TV. "We all got to go in that hole someday. I don't know if you've heard, but nobody gets out of this life alive.
And when that time comes, do you really think God cares what color
you are?''

No, but the trouble with eternal rewards is, you have to wait an
eternity to get them. On that Sunday in Augusta, some residents of The
Hill were given a modest down payment on theirs—one that can never
be taken away. "That's destiny," Dent said softly, watching Woods swing
away on the Philco. "That is God's work. Ain't nothing you can do about
that."

Dent was an impossible man to dislike, with a facility for language
that I had rarely encountered, even hanging around writers. When an
enormous woman in stretch pants walked by us and said hello, he said
hello back, then nudged me as she receded out of sight. "You ever seen a
booty like that, Steve?" he asked me out of genuine curiosity. *"Hoooo!*
She got some *junk* in the *trunk.''*

I missed him on this visit, for white Augusta was about as static a place as you can imagine. I drove in the rain past the Masters Bowling Lanes, the Green Jacket steakhouse, the Augusta Greenjackets minor-league baseball stadium, the Masters Corner stop 'n' shop—WE'RE MASTERS AT CONVENIENCE. There was a Hooters in the Fairway Square strip mall. David Owen reported in his golf book *My Usual Game* that Red Lobster had been voted the city's best seafood restaurant.

Golf-centric communities are by their very nature unexciting. It is their lack of stimuli that understandably attracts retirees to them. And the retirement lifestyle has always appealed to me. So it wasn't that I had any prejudice against Augusta on those grounds. On the contrary.

I have spent two vacations in Palm Springs, California, which has some seventy-five golf courses; where a putting green greets visitors at the airport, like a lily pad on a tarmac pond; where golf-cart dealerships outnumber car dealerships three to one; indeed, where high-speed eight-lane thoroughfares incorporate perilous Golf Cart Lanes; and where every January ex-Presidents like Gerald Ford and ex-celebrities like Tom Smothers drive balls off of mottled octogenerians in the gallery at the Bob Hope Desert Classic. The city's median age is something like eighty-nine, and its congressional representative was Sonny Bono, and yet, for about three days every other year, it is paradise.

No, sir, I have nothing against golf-dominated communities. Just this one. I jumped on the Bobby Jones Expressway and drove toward Atlanta. As soon as I did, things began to brighten, metaphorically and meteorologically. Broad shafts of light bored through the clouds, and as dusk drew nearer, the sky took on the colors of a bruise. It was like driving into the front of a Hallmark card—the maudlin kind inscribed YOU MEAN MORE TO ME THAN WORDS CAN SAY or MY DEEPEST SYMPATHIES ON YOUR HERNIA SURGERY. But still: It *was* beautiful. Even I had to admit as much.

11

The South was an alien land. At an International House of Pancakes outside Atlanta, I mutely pointed to pictures on the menu by way of ordering. The waitress produced a pencil from her hairdo and said: " 'Rooty-Tooty-Fresh-'N'-Fruity'? Okeydokey, Sugarbooger." For all I knew, she had just addressed me in Flemish.

For some reason, every Southern waitress called me "Sugarbooger." And every Southern man was called something still more ridiculous. Such as his given name. The athletic director at the University of Alabama was one Hootie Ingram. The president of the Charlotte Motor Speedway was called Humpy Wheeler. The football coach at Lumberton High School in North Carolina was named Knocky Thorndyke. These were grown men in positions of authority. And yet, if they were to meet, a mutual friend would have to introduce them to each other by say-ing: "Humpy, Knocky. Knocky, Humpy. Humpy, Hootie. Hootie, Humpy . . ."

Over breakfast, I was reminded why I no longer cared to cover major-league baseball. The "Local News" section of the Atlanta *Journal-Constitution* reported that "Atlanta Braves pitcher John Smoltz is com-plaining to Fulton County officials that a neighbor's house"—which the story later described as "mammoth"—"has cast a shadow over his swim-ming pool." Pity, isn't it, when your neighbor's castle throws your pool in the shade?

I had an intense and not entirely rational desire to leave Georgia, a state governed by a man named Zell, for Alabama, a state governed by a man named Fob. But before doing so, I toured downtown Atlanta, where a grand new civic edifice was going up alongside the state capitol. A sign said: FUTURE SITE OF JAMES H. "SLOPPY" FLOYD VETERANS ADMINISTRA-TION BUILDING. I paused, passing a moment in grudging admiration for the people of the Peach State, and marveled to myself . . .

They build monuments to men named Sloppy.

In Alabama at last—four words I never anticipated writing—my route roughly followed the Robert Trent Jones Golf Trail, eighteen championship courses laid like a charm bracelet from the Talladega Na-tional Forest to the Redneck Riviera. Of course, I hadn't driven to Dixie to golf. I had driven to Dixie to see souped-up purple pickup trucks inscripted with jocular Deep South nicknames, like STATUTORY GRAPE. That very vehicle was on display at the Talladega National Raceway, the world's foremost repository of redneck racing relics. I drove straight there in a fever of anticipation.

Visitors to Talladega are greeted by a stately sculpture garden crea-tured with Chromosaurs. These are painstakingly rendered replicas of the great dinosaurs—some as tall as twenty feet, weighing eight thousand pounds—made entirely from the chrome bumpers of American automo-biles manufactured between 1949 and 1976. Clearly, this was sacred ground for Southern gearheads, and when I arrived, the raceway was awash with the kind of folks who put the "hick" in "motor VEE-hickle."

The South is full of these people, easily identified by their automotive accoutrements: Yosemite Sam mudflaps, horns that play *Dixie*, bumper stickers bearing Churchillian epigrams—MY OTHER CAR'S A PIECE OF SHIT, TOO; MY SON BEAT THE SHIT OUT OF YOUR HONOR STUDENT; SHIT HAPPENS. Shit like that. And, of course, car stereos that make a man's pickup throb like a human heart. Somewhere in North Carolina I heard a car-stereo installer's commercial warn, "Remember: If your mirrors ain't shakin', you've been taken."

I pulled into the Talladega lot and parked next to a Thunderbird whose Tennessee vanity plates—FORDFRK—identified its owner as either (1) a Ford freak, or (2) as former Baseball Commissioner Ford Frick. And then I bounded eagerly into the Talladega showroom.

I venerated the "first successful overhead camshaft ever produced," its beauty undiminished by my lack of any earthly idea as to what it might *be.* I stood atremble before the needle-nosed Budweiser rocket car. It has forty-eight thousand horses, goes from zero to 400 in three seconds, and is, I am told, endlessly impressive when pulling away at intersections. On the Great Salt Flats of Utah in 1979, driver Stan Barrett got the thing up to 739 miles an hour—and might have exceeded 800, but for the wind drag on the gunrack.

Men and women stood in genuine grief before an enormous checkered flag that served as a kind of wailing wall for fans of the late Davey Allison, a NASCAR driver recently killed in a crash. A *helicopter* crash, I should say, for race-car drivers are almost never killed in car crashes. Nor even seriously injured. For reasons that have not been satisfactorily explained by science, Southern race-car drivers are essentially indestructible.

Sure enough, the visitors' center at Talladega was littered with the twisted metal of memorable crashes. Over here was what looked like a crushed aluminum beer can: It was driven in the Winston 500 by Phil Parsons, who—a caption assured me—"survived this crash with only a minor fracture of his left shoulder blade." Over there was an abstraction of steel driven at Daytona by Andy Farr, who "sustained only a cracked sternum." ("It's only a cracked sternum"—the kind of thing I imagine Knocky Thorndyke might tell his Lumberton High football players.) Finally I examined the scraps of Reynolds Wrap that were all that remained of the "worst crash in racing history," on April 7, 1990, at Bristol Racecourse. The mess looked the way a car might after being dropped from a cargo plane at thirty-five thousand feet. The only parts still recognizable were the engine, seat, and hood—this last painted with the leering face of Mr. Kool-Aid, whose glee is grotesque, given the circumstances.

The driver was Michael Waltrip, and I prepared myself for the inevitable caption. "Miraculously," it read, "he sustained no serious injuries."

My own car was holding together remarkably well, though the engine had begun to make a disquieting sound, along the lines of "Knocky–Humpy, Knocky–Humpy, Knocky–Humpy . . ." So I stopped for a simple oil change outside of Birmingham. I won't say the name of the place (it was Jiffy Lube), but they charged me—the agitator with the Yankee plates—$105. Is that a lot? I thanked them for the privilege, and wondered if I hadn't made a terrible mistake in coming here.

The Birmingham phone book lists a James Crow, but I resisted the temptation to dial him up, determined to give the city a clean slate. I was immediately happy that I did so. Downtown Birmingham was tidy and handsome, its spotless sidewalks a residual effect of Bull Connor firehosing pedestrians throughout the 1950s and 1960s.

I fetched a sandwich at Sophie's Deli. A signed photo of Alabama football coach Gene Stallings hung, in apparent exile, with the health-inspection certificates behind the counter. A bank's time-and-temperature display said it was ninety-eight degrees at noon. I sat beneath an enormous shade tree in a verdant public square filled with the integrated working men and women of Birmingham and unwrapped my sandwich. I wasn't sure what it was made of—to judge by the taste, I'd guess the chrome bumpers of American automobiles manufactured between 1949 and 1976—but it didn't really matter. I was too taken with this New South.

At the edge of the square stood an Eternal Flame of Freedom, burning in honor of the countless men and women of Jefferson County who served their country in times of war, so that you and I might live in prosperity. As I sat ruminating on all that the fire symbolized, a spry and wiry homeless man clambered onto the base of the monument, turned his face toward the Eternal Flame of Freedom, and—as God is my witness—lit the half-inch cigarette butt that was plugged into his mouth.

His beard damn near ignited like the *Hindenburg*. As I tabulated the many ironies of this tableau, I made a mental note to stop accepting at face value everything I saw in these parts.

Alabama has fewer than half the number of residents of Los Angeles County, yet might be the nation's biggest producer of American sporting giants. Surely it is the densest producer per capita. A population of little more than 4 million people can reasonably claim responsibility for Willie Mays, Hank Aaron, Satchel Paige, Joe Namath, Bear Bryant, Charles Barkley, Bo Jackson, Joe Louis, and Jesse Owens, among many others. Few outside the state realize it, but American sports in the twentieth century have been a veritable Alabamarama.

This phenomenon can be explained in part by the state's unholy appetite for athletes and athletics. Governor Fob James was an All-America halfback at Auburn in the early fifties. Before him, Governor George Wallace was a two-time state Gold Gloves bantamweight boxing champion and captain of the team at Auburn. It is not at all ridiculous that ex-Auburn athlete Barkley is often mentioned, especially by himself, as a future governor of the state. Not when Alabama's most populous city has raised a banner above the main drag into downtown reading, IT'S NICE TO HAVE YOU IN BIRMINGHAM—FOOTBALL CAPITAL OF THE SOUTH.

Anyway, when Wallace's late wife, Lurleen, was governor of Alabama, she signed legislation to build an Alabama Sports Hall of Fame, and its three spectacular stories now rise inside the Birmingham Civic Center. I hastened there after lunch and screened an insightful film: It suggested that an intense desire to avoid a life of Alabama poverty—as a coal miner or red-dirt farmer or, it might have added, a black man before the civil rights era—forged so many sports prodigies among the progeny of this state. The film took as its epigraph the Latin phrase *ad astra per aspera*, meaning "to the stars through adversity."

The artifacts in the hall were unmistakably Alabaman: Take, for instance, the actual paddle—thick as a post and shaped like a cricket bat—that was broken over the ass of Joe Namath upon his induction into the "A" club at 'Bama.

Or the five-foot tusks of an elephant bagged—with breathtaking political incorrectness—by Howard Hill, the rakishly mustachioed big-game hunter who was once the world's greatest archer and a man who did many of the arrow stunts for Hollywood Westerns of the forties and fifties. I don't hunt, but I suspect Freud might have had a field day with some who do. There was a photograph of Hill, for instance, grinning over the dead sloe-eyed elephant, prior to detusking. The caption read like a letter to *Penthouse Forum*. It described the animal as a "10,000-pound renegade bull" felled by a "41-inch arrow" of "tempered hardened gun-barrel steel" which "penetrated 31 1/2 inches" into the elephant, one of two thousand game animals and one thousand fish and reptiles Hill had bagged in his heyday. It all sounded like a boast by Wilt Chamberlain.

Among Hill's fellow enshrinees were men whose first names were Heinie, Wimp, Shug, Runt, Tackhole, Bully, Snitz, Diddy, and Goober. George (Goober) Lindsay—or should I say (George) Goober Lindsay— was not merely a star of *Mayberry, R.F.D.* but the quarterback at Florence (Alabama) State and, for one glorious season, football coach at Hazel Green High School.

But just as one man's Eternal Flame of Freedom is another's Eternal Zippo Lighter of Discarded Cigarette Butts, the Alabama Sports Hall of Fame was also, inescapably, a Hall of Infamy.

Wallace's plaque hung near those honoring Aaron and Mays. "Long known to be a fighter," it read, "perhaps his greatest fight was the fight for his life following an assassination attempt." That, or his fight against integration.

Likewise, the hall's first-ever "Distinguished Alabama Sportsman" was Hall Thompson, who distinguished himself as founder and president of Shoal Creek Golf Club. Shoal Creek had an all-white membership when it was chosen to host the 1990 PGA Championship, though Thompson pointed out that the club *did* allow women, Italians, and even Lebanese to join. "I think we've said that we don't discriminate in every other area except the blacks," he told the Birmingham *Post-Herald* in a '90 interview. (That's 1990.) Black caddies were allowed to play the course on Mondays, Thompson noted, and blacks could theoretically play as guests of members—although Thompson conceded: "That's just not done in Birmingham, Alabama."

Well, what a *fun* place African Americans had been missing out on: In the Alabama Sports Hall of Fame hangs a photograph of Thompson driving a ball on Shoal Creek's first tee—a necktie knotted tightly around his starched collar.

I drove to Selma on the kind of rural roads one sees in a car commercial—winding and hilly and serene, save for a pickup truck riding up my rear like . . . well, like the underwear I'd been wearing for far too long, I'm ashamed to say.

I was tuned to *The Sports Jamboree* on WJOX, "sports with a Southern flavor," and heard a man say, "Ah'm callin' to express mah disgruntledness with the coachin' situation at 'Bama. They got some kinda one-man pony show goin' on up there. . . ." Another said of Birmingham's Canadian Football League team—yes, *Canadian* Football League team—"Y'all said attendance was down last weekend for the Barracudas, but they was competin' with the Kudzu Festival. . . ." Time flew. I found myself in Selma.

Frankly, I was afraid to get out of the car. I wasn't crazy about staying in it, either, given my plates. But I'm not *that* stupid: I stayed inside with the windows sealed and the power locks locked, as if driving through Lion Country Safari.

I made my way down Broad Street, in fastidious compliance with all traffic laws, to the base of the Edmund Pettus Bridge. Beneath it, the Alabama River lay still, smooth and shiny as a polished tabletop. It was thirty years since voting-rights activists marched across that bridge on Bloody Sunday, March 7, 1965, and were met—and gassed and beaten—by police. Two weeks later, Reverend Martin Luther King, Jr., led another march, from Selma to Montgomery, accompanied by federal troops, and a historical marker at the base of the bridge now commemorated those events. I read it. Selma was being made to eat a little (Jim) crow.

It was only a few months after those marches that President Johnson signed the Voting Rights Act, intended to ensure the ability of Southern blacks to cast ballots. And while 60 percent of today's 23,700 Selma residents were black, Joe Smitherman was still the town's mayor, in his ninth term, having first been elected in 1964. An Associated Press article in my possession described him as "a good old boy" who "once referred to King as 'Martin Luther Coon,' a slur he claimed was a slip of the tongue."

Even so, Mayor Smitherprick—*whoops!*—presided over a town whose most bustling store on picturesque Broad Street was called Sneakers, which sold basketball shoes and Starter jackets to a clientele that was entirely black at the time of my visit. I gathered the local pickup hoop scene was also vibrant: Selma High won the state 6-A basketball championship in '94.

Ad astra per aspera.

I stopped at the Benedictine monastery of St. Bernard Abbey in Cullman, Alabama, to see the hillside Ave Maria Grotto: miniature replicas of the world's great wonders, built largely of rubbish, by a Bavarian brother named Joseph Zoettel between 1912 and 1958. It was an oddly moving experience. The domes of St. Peter's in Rome were made of a toilet bowl float, sliced in half like a grapefruit. There was an entire Old City of Jerusalem, a Tower of Babel, the Hanging Gardens of Babylon—I tarried so long in this Lilliput, I had little time left to visit the Jim Nabors shrine in nearby Tauscaugula. Having paid homage to Goober, I wanted to revere Gomer, as well. But it wasn't to be, and I blew off the second half of the Goober–Gomer axis.

Elvis Presley's interest in sports was a neglected area of King scholarship, one that I intended to explore more fully in Mississippi. I hurried there now on Highway 278. But thirty miles from the border, I saw a sign for NATURAL BRIDGE, ALABAMA. The town takes its name from the longest natural bridge east of the Rockies, 148 feet across at its widest span; according to my Mobil guidebook, it has remained largely unchanged since its formation more than 200 million years ago. "Not unlike the racial attitudes of some Alabamans," I chuckled nervously to myself before turning down a heavily wooded road.

Well, I ought to be ashamed of myself. C'MON IN, WE'VE BEEN EXPECTIN' Y'ALL! said a billboard at the turnoff. After I parked and paid a genial man in his late fifties a few dollars' admission to this forest, he asked me where I was from, what I did for a living, and we were off to the races.

Jimmie Denton owned the natural bridge. His wife was from Jasper, Alabama, but he persuaded her to move to his native Edwardsville, Illinois, when they were married thirty years ago. "I always said I rescued her," Jimmie said sardonically. "She always said, 'Don't do me any more favors.'"

In Edwardsville, the Dentons raised nine children. "A whole ball team," said Jimmie, who meant that literally. "On the farm, when the wind was blowin' right, you could hear 'em playin' ball out in the field. Night and day. Momma would go out on the porch and yell, 'Y'all come in for dinner!' And the kids would yell, 'One more out!' It was always 'one more out' at our place."

"One day my boy carried Momma off the porch and said, *"You're* playin' with us," and she was yellin', 'Put me down! Put me down!' You know, pretendin' she was mad. I will never forget the look on her face."

It would seem to be one small moment in a lifetime, but Jimmie was lost in the happy memory of a farmhouse full of children, his eyes going red at the rims.

There were perhaps two other visitors that day at the bridge, which was maybe 300 yards beyond this gatehouse in a sun-eclipsing forest that apparently stretched for miles.

"In 1968," Jimmie went on, "I took my boy to the Art Gaines Baseball Camp west of Hannibal, Missouri." He said this as if reading from a brochure, one I imagine he spent a lot of time studying before splurging on such a trip. "We spent a week there," Jimmie said. "That really *was* the highlight for me." I took him to be referring to his life as a father.

"We had such a wonderful time. In high school, my boy gave up a grand slam to Kenny Oberkfell, who went on to play for the St. Louis Cardinals. My boy said, 'I knew I shouldn't have thrown that ball, Dad. But you got to put it over the plate.' " I didn't know which boy he was talking about—Jimmie tended to refer to his children interchangeably.

But if anyone doubts that sports hold a fastball grip on people's lives, they need only spend an hour with Jimmie Denton. You can find him in Natural Bridge, Alabama, where Jimmie found himself when his wife wanted to return to her roots and a man literally sold him a bridge.

Jimmie's son Dennis was set to take over day-to-day operations of the place, though what that entails for a structure that hasn't changed in 200 million years, I can't say. "He said, 'Momma, I don't want to do this, but I'll do it for you,' " according to Jimmie, who dreamed of building a golf course on the property. "When the soldiers came home from the Big War to East Alton [Illinois], they all learned to play golf," he said, explaining how the 1950s became a peaceful fairway down which Eisenhower drove the nation. "The trouble with most courses is, a man's on vacation, he wants to play golf, but there's nothing for the missus or the children to do." Here, they could visit the natural bridge—which I made sure to dutifully admire after speaking with Jimmie. On my way out, the kind man gave me two out-of-focus postcards of this impossibly lonely place and asked me, wistfully, where I was off to next.

"Tupelo," I told him.

"Elvis" was all he said.

The King's Munsingwear pajamas were lain neatly across the back of his brown Barcalounger. Next to the chair was a table, and arrayed on the table were an ashtray, a lighter, two pipes, a reading lamp, and a pair of reading glasses. The entire display looked like the Eisenhower estate sale. But, in fact, all of these items were recovered from Graceland and moved here—to the Elvis Presley Museum in his hometown of Tupelo, Mississippi. My eyes fell to Presley's favorite book, which lay unopened for all eternity on the armchair. It was *Great Running Backs of the NFL* by Jack Hand. Its cover bore the circular seal of THE NFL PUNT, PASS, & KICK LIBRARY. I recognized this book. I read it when I was eight.

"Oh, Elvis loved his football," said a kindly old woman who caught me admiring this children's book and who had offered to answer any questions when I arrived. "He loved all sports. He played some football in high school, when he moved to Memphis. He warn't too good, mind you, but he always joined in. You know, to be one of the fellas."

I thanked the dear lady for the news, but she wasn't quite through with me. "Now, that bedspread over there," she said, lurching toward another exhibit. "That was made for Lisa Marie when Priscilla was carrying her. The child was lying on it not two hours after she was born. . . ." Several minutes passed in this fashion, the sweet woman leading me around by the elbow as she pointed out the portrait of Mr. F. L. Bobo, who sold Elvis his first guitar, until at last I applied a sleeper hold to the back of her neck and she slumped over in a temporary and harmless blackout. I tiptoed out of Tupelo, passing on the way the Tupelo Hardware Co., where the King of Rock & Roll really *did* buy his first guitar from a Mr. F. L. Bobo, whose name you thought I made up.

From Tupelo, I drove directly to Graceland, 107 miles to the northwest in Memphis. ALL VISITORS MUST WEAR A SHIRT insisted a sign posted at the Graceland visitors' center. Clearly, Elvis would have objected to this draconian dress code, and I registered my protest with a security guard. Then I fell in behind two German matrons and four English soccer hooligans and boarded a bus for the "estate."

Nothing prepares you for the smallness of Graceland, except perhaps the vastness of its gift shop. This is generally a bad sign, portending an inverse relationship. The house itself would be unremarkable in most American suburbs, if not for the avocado shag carpeting on the living room *ceiling* and the fact that several members of the family are buried in the backyard. And even then it might fit in.

Each visitor was issued a Walkman: The house tour was conducted by the disembodied voice of an entertaining and archetypal good ol' boy. "Elvis had three TVs installed when he learned that President Johnson watched all three network news programs at once," said this *Uber-Goober* when the tour reached the King's TV room. "Of course, Elvis preferred to watch three different football games. He also enjoyed situation comedies."

He also famously shot one of his TVs, presumably when football was preempted for breaking news coverage. How regrettable, then, that E. didn't live to see our golden age of 500-channel satellite technology and sophisticated automatic weaponry. Imagine the King with a whole *room*ful of TVs—one for every all-sports network—and a loaded Uzi. He could have lit the room with gunfire whenever Dan Dierdorf opened his mouth on *Monday Night Football* and thus combined what I now knew to be his two great loves as a sportsman: football and target practice. Elvis further fed his firearm passion in a shooting gallery tacked to the back of his estate. To this day, as the tour revealed, the firing range is littered with spent shells.

In 1975, when he was pretty much a spent shell himself, Elvis built a one-court racquetball pavilion in his backyard at the height of the nation's racquetball boom. There is, predictably, a wet bar and piano in the viewing gallery, making the King's primary workout facility look like the racquetball-themed piano bar of a Holiday Inn. This was the penultimate point of interest on the Graceland tour—our last stop before visiting the grave.

Alas, it was also E.'s last stop before visiting same. Or very nearly so. To paraphrase the official tour tape, Elvis had just returned from weeks of touring in August of 1977, the road leaving him tragically out of match shape, when he was seized, in the middle of the night, by an irrepressible impulse to play racquetball. He lasted two wearying matches, then repaired to the piano to play what is poignantly called his "last concert"—*Unchained Melody* and *Blue Eyes Cryin' in the Rain*— before retiring upstairs around dawn, at which time he passed away peacefully on the bathroom floor.

The implication was unmistakable, a revisionist revelation that I wanted desperately to believe. It wasn't drugs or alcohol or his beloved fried-banana sandwiches that killed the King. To the contrary.

Racquetball killed Elvis.

I started my day with the newspaper. The Nashville *Tennesseean* is the
state's second-largest organ (if you will), and the front page of its sports
section carried the bylines of men surnamed Organ and Woody. Fair
enough. But a news brief inside—about a Seattle Mariners pitcher removed from a game due to injury—was headlined JOHNSON PULLED.
And I couldn't help but wonder: Was somebody pulling *my* Johnson?

But it wasn't April Fools' Day. It was the start of Labor Day weekend, and the American Automobile Association estimated that a record
33.7 million vacationers would soon be on the road. Of these, 21 million
were believed to be travel writers rediscovering America. I joined their
number and wound my way out of Memphis.

I didn't get a mile before spotting the Lorraine Motel, its exterior restored to exactly the way it was on April 4, 1968, when King was assassinated on the balcony of Room 306. The room's interior had also been freeze-dried for eternity: the bed rumpled, a room-service tray in disarray beside it. Trees now obscured the rooming-house window from which James Earl Ray fired his shot, but there were still plenty of wackos across the street—protesters evidently opposed to the Lorraine's conversion into the National Civil Rights Museum. Inside, I lingered over one particular photograph: former Selma sheriff Jim Clark beating a hand-cuffed fifty-three-year-old woman on the head.

It was all moving and well done, but I had a plane to meet in Nashville. Greg Kelly, *SI*'s hypochondriacal college hoop editor, was flying in from New York as a kind of *deus ex machina*. He had agreed to join me for a few rounds of golf and to be among the ninety-six-thousand people attending Saturday's University of Tennessee football game in Knoxville. I, in turn, had promised to make tee times at the state's finest golf facilities. But so far, all I had secured was a brochure that advertised: HILLBILLY GOLF! WORLD'S MOST UNUSUAL! HILLBILLY FUN!

Alas, Kelly was unswayed by the remaining text, which promised that "300 feet above Gatlinburg, you will find two eighteen-hole courses with challenging mountaineer hazards." Among the "mountaineer hazards" pictured was a dilapidated outhouse at the edge of a green. But Kelly was having enough difficulty making putts, he insisted, without having to guide them through the missing teeth of a papier-mâché moonshiner. He was, in short, no "hillbilly fun."

So we went instead to the Hermitage Golf Club, a championship course across from the Hermitage, former (and eternal) residence of President Andrew Jackson. I parked next to a Grand Prix with Tennessee plates GONGOFN, and the starter quickly squeezed us in, pairing us with one John Anderson of Peoria, Illinois. Surely, if I were to meet an Everyamerican on this trip, he was it: a man whose name was so common as to seem pseudonymous and a citizen of our nation's bellwether community.

What, you might ask, was on the mind of Everyamerican? Two words: "Ear candles."

I haven't the first clue how he brought them up—I only know that he did so immediately. Ear candles, Anderson enlightened us, are narrow straws inserted in the ear canal to alleviate chronic and epic ear wax buildup. Kelly listened with furrowed brow, always eager to hear about, and thus psychosomatically acquire, a new medical affliction. The straws, evidently, are lit with a match, the ear wax melts, and the ensuing waxalanche is collected in a paper skirt attached to the base of the device. "I can see them becoming big at college parties," said the impish Anderson, who looked exactly like the actor Jerry Van Dyke. " 'Hey, man, let's do some ear candles!' "

To my astonishment, he turned out not to be an ear candle peddler, but a "tinner," or tinsmith, who was driving to North Carolina to visit his son in college. "We're a close family," he volunteered. "The kind that hugs and kisses when someone goes to the grocery store. But my son *cannot* beat me at golf. He gets all flustered when we play." Anderson said this with regret—his son was a better golfer than he—and wondered if there weren't some deeper psychology involved in vanquishing one's old man.

I told him that it took me years to beat my father in one-on-one driveway basketball, despite my eventual six-inch height advantage and *his* abject lack of any ability in the sport whatsoever. But this streak had nothing to do with a reluctance to win on my part and everything to do with my father's forty-pound weight advantage, disregard of all rules, and midgame delusions that he was still a blocking back for Johnny Majors on the University of Tennessee football team, to which my father transferred after two seasons at Purdue.

The current Tennessee star, quarterback Peyton Manning, was struggling to emerge from the shadow of *his* old man, Ole Miss and NFL legend Archie Manning. I was eager to see Manning play in Knoxville the next day, if only to escape Music City.

I use the phrase loosely. Someone in Nashville was surely to blame for a compact disc on the market in which NFL quarterbacks Troy Aikman and Brett Favre, among others, sang duets with country music stars. The very thought of it made me shudder. I mean, have you heard these people *sing?* Country music stars, that is?

No thanks. I put the hammer down, and Nashville receded in the rearview mirror.

In a dreary Mexican restaurant on a desolate Friday night in Crossville, Tennessee, I watched a cockroach crawl out of my nachos. Man, the road can be wearying.

In the morning, we joined Interstate 40 for the seventy-five-mile drive to Knoxville, lading the Pathfinder with McMuffins at the first available drive-through. Kelly passed the time checking his ears for wax buildup and examining his food for live vermin. And occasionally vice versa.

I was preoccupied with my fellow motorists, each of whom had an orange-and-white Tennessee wind sock flying from his antenna and a Volunteers flag fluttering from a window. When the wind swirled, I feared a flag might obscure an entire windshield and a car with vanity plates (UT DORK) would plunge deliriously into the ditch, its horn stuck playing *Rocky Top*, the Vol fight song whose lyrics honestly pay tribute to corn whiskey, hillbilly women, and a happy absence of "telephone bills." Eventually, he would be rescued by a truck whose horn tootled, *FIGHT, VOLS, FIGHT!* and whose plates read UT DORQUE. I have never seen such a festive thoroughfare as I-40 on a Tennessee football Saturday.

The Tennessee River wriggles right past Neyland Stadium, and hundreds of vessels—the Volunteer Navy—likewise clogged that artery, a slow flow of burnt orange. It looked like molten nacho "cheez."

In all, 95,416 people were admitted to a stadium with 91,902 seats. The upper deck of the north end zone was being expanded, so that the following season capacity would exceed six figures. One misstep in those steep cheap seats would send you plummeting to the orange-and-white checkerboard end zone, miles below. No wonder it was called Checkerboard Heaven. Even so, the design put me in mind of the Purina logo.

Kelly and I climbed like Hillary and Tenzing to the press box, arriving just as Northwestern was sealing its televised upset of Notre Dame.

At the final gun, 300 sportswriters cheered. Anyone who thinks the press is objective: (1) has never met a member of the press, or (2) *is* a member of the press.

As for Tennessee—they destroyed East Carolina. The final score resembled the blood-pressure reading of a very unhealthy person. It was something like 240 over 10. Manning threw for a couple of aerial miles, and afterward, in the Tennessee locker room, he was the picture of the 1940s football hero: six-feet-five, in blue blazer, blue button-down Oxford shirt, burgundy tie, khakis, brown loafers, a face like something on a Roman coin. I asked him how he handled the obssessive attention of an entire state, and he actually blushed.

"I try not think about that," he said.

"But it must be difficult to ignore ninety-six thousand customers," I conjectured. "Unless you've had experience working in a post office."

"The first time I ever saw ninety-six thousand people," Manning replied, "I was playing in front of them. I never saw a game here until I was in one. It was my first time in the stadium. I tried, and still try, to pretend it's just a high school crowd."

"What was the largest crowd you played in front of in high school?" I asked.

"Two."

"Two people?"

"Two thousand," he said. "But still, in that kind of crowd, the top row of the stadium can hear the snap count as clearly as your offensive line can. It's a little different in college."

He had already made that point to the nation's best high school quarterback. If Peyton Manning was the next Dan Marino, then the next Peyton Manning was surely Tim Couch, who lived 125 miles to the northeast—in Hyden, Kentucky. Couch had already paid a visit to Tennessee to talk to Manning about possibly becoming his successor. The kid already knew what it was to be the focus of an entire state's attention. Kentuckians, I was told, deified him. I called his dad, Elbert Couch, and arranged a visit down the road.

Of course, I still had custody of Kelly and a whole Sunday to kill. So I took him to Dollywood in Dolly Parton's hometown of Pigeon Forge, Tennessee.

We surrendered our U.S. currency at the door, happily exchanging it for Dolly Dollars. After all, the Dolly Dollar was strong, trading favorably against the yen. And better yet, the bills bore the improbable likeness of Ms. Parton. Her image was everywhere in the park, and at day's end I had a strange but irresistible impulse to have the dual airbags detonated the next time my car was tuned up. I still do not know why. But the road does strange things to a man.

With a light heart, I dumped Kelly at the airport. I was going to Hyden. I was going back to high school.

Elbert Couch parked his white Ford Bronco next to another emblem of American infamy: the Richard M. Nixon Recreation Center in Hyden, Kentucky. "There's two kinds around here," Elbert told me as he got out of the truck. "There's Republicans, and there's Damn Democrats. I'm a Damn Democrat, but we're outnumbered four to one in this county."

This was Leslie County, in the Cumberland Mountains of eastern Kentucky. Forty miles south of here was the Cumberland Gap, and just south of that, the Cumberland Gap for Kids.

As for Nixon, it was here in Hyden in 1978 that he made his first post-exile public appearance, for the dedication of a grand gymnasium that honored his presidency. "Everybody knew us because of Nixon," said Leslie County High School basketball coach Ron Stidham as we stood on the home court inside the Tricky Dick. "But that notoriety aside, Tim Couch has made Hyden—well, if not a household name, exactly, at least people know where we are again."

This was true, for Tim Couch was the best prep basketball player in Kentucky. Elbert's son led the state in scoring the previous season with 36 points per game as a Leslie County High junior. He was the top candidate to become Mr. Basketball of the Bluegrass after his senior season, which was why most Division I basketball coaches wanted very badly to upholster Couch in their school colors.

Trouble was, Couch was also the best prep football player in the nation, perhaps the best high school quarterback ever, one who was expected to break the national records for career passing yardage and touchdown passes this fall.

"Couch is the best quarterback prospect I've seen in seventeen years," drooled Tom Lemming, who published a national recruiting newsletter. "Better than Jeff George, Ron Powlus, and Peyton Manning. He reminds me of John Elway." NFL draft nitwit Mel Kiper, Jr., agreed, ranking the six-foot-five, 210-pound Couch as the second-best pro prospect in the nation, college athletes included. And to think that only two months ago, Couch wasn't even old enough to vote Republican.

I arrived at Leslie High in time to watch practice. An assistant coach lobbed footballs to Couch, who stabbed each from the air with one hand, like a frog's tongue catching flies, and in the same motion threw them tremendous distances downfield, where they landed with cotton-ball softness in the hands of sprinting receivers. He was ridiculously precise, like the robot arm on an automated assembly line.

When practice ended, I introduced myself and told him I was curious: What did it mean to him to have such a prodigious talent, and what did such a prodigy mean to a town of 375 residents?

"Lotta smoke gets blown up his butt," Elbert had warned me, and here I was now, blowing like a smokestack at U.S. Steel.

"Everybody around here is just so happy," Tim said in response to my questions. "They all want to see me go to the NFL and become a big star, and it gives me a lot of pride, the way such a small place has rallied around one person like this."

He was unfailingly polite, with a genuine humility. The Couches were prosperous by local standards: Elbert was a transportation supervisor for the county school system, and his wife, Janice, worked for the county's Department of Human Resources. "Don't call it the Welfare Department," Elbert instructed me.

"Oh, that's all right," Janice assured me. "Everyone calls it that anyway."

On my drive into town, a radio commercial for the Family Market noted, "We gladly accept food stamps." Many of the houses in Hyden were trailers. "Please don't write that we're hillbillies," Elbert asked. "The other day I read in a paper about 'the winding road to Hyden.' " He waved his hand in disgust. "Yeah, we're in the mountains, but give me a break. There aren't three hundred people in Leslie County that make their living off coal anymore."

Indeed, a buddy of Elbert's told me that the "hilljacks," as he called them, were farther up the mountains. "They filmed *Deliverance* up there," he suggested.

Elbert drove me around town in the white Bronco, what he called "the O.J. bus." Leslie County High principal Omus Shepherd said: "Tim's an A–B student. In fact, to see him in school, you wouldn't know he's an athlete. You wouldn't know him from any other student. I don't know of any problems we've ever had out of the boy."

The boy had been excused from class on the second Friday of the football season when Kentucky governor Brereton Jones—Elbert, Omus, Brereton; I was still beneath the Mason–Dixon line—came to Hyden to make Couch an honorary Kentucky colonel. He was the youngest ever recipient of the state's equivalent of knighthood and joined the elite company of men like Colonel Harlan Sanders of Kentucky Fried Chicken fame. "Kentucky," Will Lampton once wrote in *The New York Times*, "where the corn is full of kernels, and the colonels full of corn."

That evening Colonel Couch threw for three touchdowns and ran for two more in a 34–27 win at Woodford County, after which several opponents wanted a piece of the quarterback. "I saw them coming at me and thought we were in a fight," Tim said. Instead, they wanted his autograph.

The next morning Tim drove 124 miles to Lexington to watch the Kentucky–Louisville football game with his folks. En route, they stopped at a small diner. NBA center and ex-Kentucky star Sam Bowie approached Tim's table and told him how much he enjoyed following his career. Emboldened, Adolph Rupp's grandson Chip then told him the same. After the game, the Couches repaired to the Lexington home of NBA guard and ex-Wildcat star Rex Chapman, who simply wanted to meet Tim.

"I told him he was my hero growing up," said Tim. "I told him how I dreamed in the backyard about filling his shoes some day at Kentucky."

"Tim used to shoot baskets outside for hours in the winter until his fingers were bleeding," said his mother. "I always had to make him come in before he got frostbite."

Come summer, he would throw footballs all afternoon with his older brother, Greg. Tim never played baseball. "He told me in eighth grade, 'Dad, I don't want to stand there and let them throw a ball sixty miles an hour at my head,'" recalled Elbert. When Greg became the quarterback at Leslie County High, Tim always attended practice. "In fifth and sixth grade, he was throwing the ball like a rocket," said Eagle football coach Joe Beder, an assistant at the time. "You knew then he would be the quarterback here."

It was then that the boy first realized that he had an exceedingly rare ability, one that came with a responsibility. "The head coach at the time, Mike Whitaker, told me that if I worked hard and progressed, I would be something special," said Tim, who was aware that he is an athletic savant, but talked as if he were merely appointed to that position by his teammates, coaches, and neighbors, whose names he frequently mentioned and spelled for interviewers.

Tim made the high school team as a seventh grader, backed up his brother as an eighth grader, and became the starting quarterback as a freshman when Greg moved on to Eastern Kentucky University. "When Greg went to college, I used to throw at that light pole," Tim said, pointing to a utility pole in the front yard of his comfortable two-story home. "I'd take a five-step drop and try to hit it like it was a receiver on the run." Then he would place two garbage cans next to each other and throw "little fade passes" over the first defending garbage can and into the gaping mouth of the second. "There's not much else to do in Hyden," explained Todd Crawford, a Hydenite, half-apologetically. "So everybody plays and follows sports growing up."

The funeral director in Hyden was Wah-Wah Jones, a Kentucky football All-America of the 1950s. County judge Onzie Sizemore was the Eastern Kentucky quarterback of the early 1970s. (Wah-Wah and Onzie: The beat went on.) "Tim is the best athlete I've ever seen in Kentucky," said the judge, deliberating on Couch down at the county court- and jailhouse. "He is the kind of athlete who comes along once every *several* lifetimes. He is the best thing that ever happened to Hyden. I just hope he doesn't run for county judge-executive, because then I'm out of a job."

They came from everywhere to see him play. On Friday nights, cars backed up for a mile at the toll booth that guards the Hyden exit of the Daniel Boone Parkway. And when the Eagles played an away game, said Rick Hensley, whose son Ricky was the state's leading receiver: "Last one outta town turns out the lights."

There was a sign outside of town that said simply HYDEN: HOME OF OSBORNE BROS. Stars of the Grand Ole Opry, the Osbornes wrote *Rocky Top*, which became the football anthem of the University of Tennessee, whose Volunteers are unanimously reviled in Kentucky. When Tim opened this season with a 44–42 upset of the Fort Thomas Highlands in front of ten thousand fans in Lexington, he returned home to find that benevolent vandals had painted over the sign. HYDEN it read. HOME OF TIM COUCH.

At the time of my visit, Couch had thrown or rushed for all 90 of his team's points, during which time the Eagles had ascended to number two in the Class 3A state rankings. His numbers were preposterous. As a junior, he completed 75.1 percent of his passes, a national record. Against Clark County, he completed twenty-five of twenty-six. He needed 1,000 yards and change to break the career record of 11,700 passing yards set two years earlier by Josh Booty of Evangel Christian High in Shreveport, Louisiana.

Quite simply, the kid had destroyed more records than Hillary Clinton. When Ron Mercer, the high school basketball All-America who went on to Kentucky and the NBA, scored 36 points to set the gym record at the Coaxial National Basketball Classic in Columbus, Ohio, Couch nudged him from the record book in the next game by scoring . . . 60. "The basketball recruiters tell him they're going to put him in the NBA," said Elbert. But Tim had already decided to play football in college.

We drove home from practice on a Thursday in the boy's Mercury Cougar. He waved like a parade marshal to every passing pedestrian, then entered his house and was immediately handed the telephone. "Tennessee," said Janice, and Tim chatted cordially with Volunteer head football coach Phillip Fulmer. Bobby Bowden, Terry Bowden, Lou Holtz, and Joe Paterno—a Mount Rushmore of the current college game—checked in weekly, as well. Tim dutifully logged every call in a notebook.

On August 15, the first day that NCAA rules allow coaches to contact recruits on the phone, Kentucky coach Bill Curry called Tim at 7:30 A.M. Curry was followed that day by two dozen other suitors. Every day Elbert or Janice retrieved thirty letters from their post office box, and Tim had filled a four-drawer filing cabinet in his pin-neat bedroom, which was wallpapered with posters of Larry Bird and Michael Jordan, Drew Bledsoe and Troy Aikman. Trophies and plaques spilled into the foyer. Press clippings were piled like leaves on the carpet. A front-page headline from the Lexington *Herald-Leader* shouted COUCH TO WATCH UK SCRIMMAGE.

Wildcat fans saw a hundred different omens in the gesture; his every word was analyzed out of all proportion. It was like being the Pope, only more so. It was like being Alan Greenspan.

On Friday night, I drove to Tim's game at Johnson Central High School in Paintsville, Kentucky. It was ninety minutes northeast of Hyden and only twenty miles from the West Virginia border. Leslie County road trips could be epic. When the Eagles played Hopkinsville High, they had to travel seven hours by school bus each way.

The route to Paintsville was a roster of east Kentucky heroes: I took the Daniel Boone Parkway to the Carl D. Perkins Parkway to the Loretta Lynn Highway. On the way, I passed a state highway sign—white letters on a green background—that said:

ROWDY

DWARF

TALCUM

Whether this referred to three towns accessible from that exit, as a map later revealed to be the case, or to a curative powder for incorrigible midgets, I couldn't immediately say.

I took my seat among the hundreds in Johnson Central's beautiful stadium, built into a bluff. The woman in front of me—Mikki or Nikki or Vikki—had been a Leslie County cheerleader in 1969, and she chanted along to the cheers: "Clap your hands! Stomp your feet! Leslie Eagles can't be beat!" She asked me where I was staying, and I mentioned the Holiday Inn in Hazard, fifteen miles outside of Hyden.

"Hazard used to be our big rival," she said. "But they stopped coming to Leslie County, 'cause the fans were always getting in fights, getting their tires slashed, their car windows broken. One time some guys picked up the ref's Volkswagen—they were popular then and easy to lift—and set it down in that little creek by the stadium."

There was apparently no such history with Johnson Central, who began now to dominate play. JC had a capable running back named Chris LeMaster, who was the son of former San Francisco Giant shortstop Johnnie LeMaster. Couch's offensive line, meanwhile, was a colander. When he wasn't being sacked, he was throwing interceptions.

And still the game was tied 6–6 with 1:32 left when Leslie took over at the fifty-yard line and the visiting crowd rose to see Couch pull a rabbit from his hat. On the first play, he scrambled, ducked a flabalanche of oncoming linemen, and threw . . . his fourth interception of the game. *This* was the nation's best quarterback?

Johnson County took over at the fifty with 1:09 remaining. It was fourth and four with twenty-seven seconds left when their long snapper snapped too long, over the head of the punter, who had to fall on the ball. Tim would get the ball back at Johnson Central's forty-two with twenty-one seconds to score.

The day before in practice I watched him run a drill for just such a situation, only the numbers were reversed: The ball was on his own twenty, and there were forty seconds on the clock. He won *that* game, but there were no defenders on the practice field.

Leslie's first two plays gained a combined three yards. On third down, Tim rolled right and threw the ball thirty-nine yards. It spun in the air in slow motion, as balls will in bad movies, and fell like wet snow into the hands of wide receiver Ricky Hensley. The scoreboard read 12–6. The clock showed :03.

Even the home crowd went apeshit. Elbert was yelling to me from the sideline, "Put *that* in *Sports Illustrated!*"

Tim emerged from a mob and looked at me as if to apologize for authoring such a hokey moment for my story. "That's why Joe Montana was my hero growing up," he said. "I always dreamed about throwing a last-second pass to win a game."

Tim's mother told me that she once went into Greg's room to get him up for school, and he pouted, "Why'd you wake me up?! I was playing in the Super Bowl!"

Now here was Tim, expected to do just that, one day, in his waking hours. The pressure on him was enormous, particularly the pressure to attend the University of Kentucky. The Cats were on Couch like . . . well, like cats on a couch. Kentucky basketball coach Rick Pitino promised Tim a spot on the basketball team if he signed to play football at UK. Every Omus, Onzie, and Elbert in Kentucky expected Tim to make the Cats an instant football power.

"I may be crazy, but I believe Tim Couch is good enough to get this program back to the Sugar Bowl," wrote columnist Dave Barker in *The Cats' Pause*, a Kentucky sports weekly that Elbert had given me. "Yes, that's right. From 1–10 to 10–1."

"Kyle Macy?" scoffed Elbert's buddy Vic DeSimone, invoking the name of a Kentucky basketball deity. "Lord God, if Tim goes to UK, they'll be namin' babies for him before he plays his first game. Every kid in Kentucky will wear a number two jersey." DeSimone was a candy-bar sales rep and Kentucky sports maniac who drove Elbert and me around Hyden one day when "the O.J. bus" was out of commission. I found myself sitting on a Zagnut bar in the backseat when Vic gave voice to his darkest fear.

"You wouldn't let the boy go to *Tennessee*, would you?" he asked Elbert. "We'd have to break your legs. I mean, the boy can go to Liberty Baptist College and still become a pro, if that's what you're worried about."

"Have to take the Fifth Amendment on that one," said Elbert, who later conceded to me: "If Tim does go out of state, we'll have to move out of state."

Tim was already steeling himself to disappoint a great many people, whatever school he selected. "It's hard for an eighteen-year-old kid to tell a coach who he's grown up adoring that he isn't going to play for him," said Tim, who claimed to be thoroughly undecided at the time of my visit. He expected to make his official visits to Auburn, Florida State, Notre Dame, Penn State, and—*sigh*—Tennessee, in addition to Kentucky.

"The bigger schools all tell me, "You can get national exposure and win the national championship *and* the Heisman Trophy," Tim said at home one evening as the phone appeared to ring literally off the hook, as they do in cartoons. "The smaller schools say, 'You can turn the program around. We'll tailor the offense around you.'"

These expectations were unfair, of course—especially for someone so young—and near the end of my visit, Tim conceded that they troubled him on occasion. "People sometimes think I'm perfect," he said. "But even the best quarterback of all time, Joe Montana, messed up. Still, everybody comes to our games wanting to see something they've never seen before."

And if that weren't burden enough, he could always chew and chew again on his impending choice of a college. "I'm thinking about it all the time," he said the night I left. "Even if I'm just laying in bed, it never leaves my mind."

He had made certain of that. Taped above the lightswitch in his bedroom was a handwritten two-sentence note from a football assistant at Northwestern, pointing out that fans and coaches weren't the only ones he could disappoint. "Your talent is God's gift to you," the note read. "What you do with your talent is your gift back to God."

It was the last thing the boy saw each night when he turned out the lights.

Postscript: Tim chose the University of Kentucky. As a sophomore in 1997, he led the nation in passing yardage, established himself as a Heisman Trophy favorite for '98 and—barring catastrophic injury—a certain first-round draft choice in the National Football League. Elbert, at last report, was driving to every home game, behind the wheel of "the O.J. bus."

14

I have an abiding affection for the people of Kentucky, one that dates back several years to a weekend I spent in a hotel in Florence (the Florence near the Cincinnati airport, not the cradle of the Italian Renaissance). I dialed a room-service operator one evening and said, "I'd like a cheeseburger, please—medium."

And the most pleasant voice on the other end of the line replied with great regret: "I'm *very* sorry, sir, but we only have one size cheeseburger."

Do you not love that? In terms of Americana, Kentucky *is* the cheeseburger, if you ask me. In addition to producing Abraham Lincoln, Kentucky Fried Chicken, and—since 1983—all of the nation's Corvettes, Kentucky has Louisville, which alone gave America the Kentucky Derby, the Louisville Slugger, and Louisville slugger Muhammad Ali. The twin spires of Churchill Downs were framed on every Kentucky license plate, and these hundred-year-old icons held me in hypnotic sway as I drove, drowsily, from Lexington to Louisville.

At a roadside rest stop between the two cities, I parked my car perpendicular to the interstate. Or, rather, just past perpindicular, so that I faced slightly back toward the onrushing traffic. Seated in a driving position, I fell into a fitful sleep.

I awoke at five-minute intervals to find myself strapped to my car seat with semi-trucks hurtling at me and thus came groggily to the conclusion that I had somehow drifted (This is odd) across the median (What the . . . ?) and was now driving (Oh no!) on I-64 (Oh God, no!) in the wrong (Oh shit!) freaking (Oh please God!!!) DIRECTION!!!

As my heart beat a drum solo and my hands floundered for the steering wheel and my knuckle hair sprang to life and I began to spray urine like a Wham-O Water Weenie garden-hose attachment, it occurred to me that I was . . . still parked. At which time I fell back asleep—only to awake five minutes later to the same harrowing illusion. This went on for two hours.

I'll admit it: I was beginning to show signs of wear. My sleep deficit now rivaled the nation's budget deficit. My insides were wound tighter than the cushioned-cork center of a major-league baseball. Perhaps, in some weird reverse anthropomorphism brought on by sports bingeing, I was *becoming* a major-league baseball. I looked in the rearview mirror: My eyeballs were cross-stitched with red seams. My skin was a leathery white.

I slept like a hibernating grizzly at the Louisville Airport Holiday Inn, and as I waited in line to check out the next morning, a front-desk clerk casually asked the fossil in front of me, "How was your stay?"

"How was my stay?" the man replied. He wore a look of intense satisfaction, as if he had been up all night rehearsing a response to that very question. Which indeed he had. "I have six complaints written on this piece of paper," he said, brandishing a sheet of complimentary hotel stationery as if it were a weapon. "I am sending them to management. But first I am going to read them to you, because they ought to be addressed immediately."

Oh for fuck sake. While this Motel Martin Luther posted his six theses ("The room was very warm. . . . I lost a dollar-fifty in the Frito section of the vending machine. . . . You're out of complimentary hotel stationery. . . ." and so forth), I stood behind him, authoring six O. Henry ways for him to die. In my thoughts, this disagreeable geezer:

1. Has his legs ripped from their hip sockets by a ravenous in-room rotating shoe buffer.

2. Is covered head to toe in amenity-kit body lotion, then rolled in the elevator lobby ashtray sand until he resembles a breaded veal cutlet. Is served to Shriners convention in Banquet Room A.

3. Has his hands and feet bound by SANITIZED FOR YOUR PROTECTION ribbons, then is stuffed gangland-style inside a minibar. Suffers heart attack when he sees the price of cashews.

That was as far as I got, for these pleasant visions proved sufficient to cool my thoughts and warm my spirit. I fairly gamboled to the parking lot and drove to nearby Churchill Downs.

I made the Kentucky Derby what it is today. Credit for the race's popularity often goes to a Colonel Matt Winn, for nearly half a century the director of the Derby, but that is only because he (1) subsidized sportswriters to come to Louisville on those early first Saturdays in May, which spread the word to the masses, and (2) defended and promoted the idea of a $2 parimutuel bet for the bourgeoisie. These are the real heroes of the Run for the Roses—freeloading scribes and cheapskate bettors—and I now salute us.

I had never been to Churchill Downs. The track is in a residential neighborhood of southwest Louisville, and I was surprised to see that it carried none of the commercial barnacles that ordinarily affix themselves to such an attraction. There was no Churchill Dunes minigolf, no Go to the Whip strip joint, no Man o' War Manicurist shop blighting the block—only modest houses, nearly all of them white, neatly aligned like numbers in a ledger.

The neighborhood was mimicked on the Churchill Downs grounds, which had a sizable subdevelopment all its own: fifty stables that were home, in peak season, to as many as 1,400 horses. Among the residents of this equine Levittown was a roan named Rapid Gray. He was sixteen years old at the time of my visit—fifty-five in human years—and held the track record for seven furlongs. Alas, the Derby is a ten-furlong race, which may be why Gray finished out of the money in his one Run for the Roses. But the fact remained that Rapid Gray was once at the peak of his profession.

I met the horse after infiltrating a tour group and was immediately struck by how uncannily he resembled a retired sports star of the human race. His massive upper body was borne by creaky old legs. He scratched out an undignified living greeting race fans. They said frank things about him to each other, right in front of his nose, as if he couldn't hear or understand a word of it. Then they came closer and stroked him and whispered sweet nothings in his ear. He was given free shoes for life. He never bought a meal. And women got in line to ride him.

Rapid Gray was expected to spend another nine years growing more gray and less rapid before joining Man o' War and Secretariat in the next life. Indeed, the tour guide was giving an eloquent elegy for those two great champions—"Secretariat's heart was three times the size of the average Thoroughbred's. . . ."—when a hatchet-faced lady in stretch pants piped up: "Is Man o' War stuffed?"

"I beg your pardon?"

"Man o' War. I heard he was stuffed?"

"No, ma'am," said the guide, harnessing every atom of restraint in his body. "Man o' War was not"—he smiled weakly—"*stuffed.*"

The woman curled her lip in a pout, disappointed that famous Thoroughbreds of the bluegrass were not taxidermied for her photo-op edification. Her question elicited some head shaking and eye rolling among the horsey set on the tour, and when I cocked an arched eyebrow of my own at the woman, she blurted defiantly, "Well . . . *Roy Rogers stuffed Trigger!"*

But all in all the day was delightful. I trotted onto the track of sand, silt, and clay and fairly felt the thunder of distant hooves. I weighed myself on a Toledo jockey scale used for sixty-five years in the Churchill Downs jock room and wondered if I was the tallest person ever to do so. I learned in an excellent museum on the grounds that most of the top jockeys—including fourteen of fifteen in the first Kentucky Derby—were black.

How did we commemorate these men? By casting them as lawn jockeys. The proud athletes joined AstroTurf welcome mats and pink flamingos as staples of American exterior decor. I saw several in the neighborhood surrounding Churchill Downs. All were intended as tributes, I am sure.

Before leaving, I drank a mint julep in the Derby Cafe. For some reason, Charles Manson was emblazoned on the stainless-steel cup, and I idly wondered what his connection was to the Sport of Kings. And then it struck me. I was seeing my own reflection. I drove directly to a barber shop.

"You no have an appointment?" the barber said, looking imperiously at an empty calendar.

"No," I said.

"Then I no can cut your hair," he replied, raising his hands helplessly. "You see, I am buked." (Somehow he made "booked" sound like "nuked.")

I must have looked a fright, but I let the man in on a secret. "Um, there is *nobody else in here*," I whispered, sweeping my hand at his empty chairs in the manner of a game-show hostess.

"I tell you I have one o'clock!" he yelled.

This would give him fifteen minutes to cut my hair, a task that only requires five, but I couldn't get the words out before he shrieked: "I am in business to make money, you know!"

I called his attention to the irony of this statement—I would give him money to cut my hair; he wouldn't make a dime otherwise—but instead of thanking me for the lesson in economics, he pulled a shiny metal object from behind a counter and yelled, "Getta the hell outta here!"

His name (PINO) was stitched in script to the breast pocket of his smock, and I idly speculated aloud as to what Pino might be short for. But Pino wasn't listening. "Getta the hell outta here!" he shouted. "I calla the cops on you, you son of bitch. . . ."

He pursued me out the door as I fled to my car, where I paused just long enough to regard my wild-haired reflection in the window. I jumped inside, engaged the power locks, and saw that the instrument of death that this madman was snipping was a . . . thinning shears.

I buried my face in my hands and wondered aloud: "Will the indignities never cease?"

No photographs could be taken inside the Louisville Slugger plant. This had nothing to do with the protection of trade secrets, but rather it was because the batmakers were prone to mug for the cameras, and absentmindedly circular-saw off one or more of their fingers, and send it (or them) sailing through the air into a pile of other off-cuts. "Please," entreatied my guide, a ponytailed young man named Christian. "We have enough of the four-fingered variety."

The Louisville Slugger plant, I discovered with some difficulty, was in another 'ville altogether: Jeffersonville, Indiana. It had been there since 1974. At the time of my visit, Hillerich & Bradsby were building an enormous new plant on the proper side of the Ohio River, but they would not move into it for another year. So I watched the handcrafted bats made (or "turned," in industry parlance) in a suburban warehouse called Slugger Park, which smelled wonderfully of cut wood and sawdust.

The Slugger empire was founded by J. Frederick Hillerich, a German woodcrafter who immigrated to Louisville in the middle 1800s and
set up a shop that specialized in butter churns. His son, Bud, a first-
generation American and thus a baseball fan, watched Louisville Eclipse
star Pete Browning break his bat in a home game one fateful day in 1884
and afterward persuaded "The Gladiator" to visit his father's woodshop.
There, Bud Hillerich turned a bespoke-tailored bat for Browning, who
went three for three the following day and—well, you can take it from
here.

Today, 90 percent of all professional players are under contract to
Hillerich & Bradsby, including 70 percent of all major leaguers. But only
the bats of the big leaguers have been POWERIZED, a word that is branded
around the barrel of the bat, just above the label, and is overscored by a
lightning bolt. The bats for sale to the general public are merely FLAME
TEMPERED, a phrase punctuated on the label by an innocuous lick of fire.

Why was this? I had long been interested in the Powerizing process
and was sure it was somehow related to the one-hour Martinizing system
that dry cleaners were sworn to keep secret. To my small mind, it was
sinister and unfair: I couldn't use a Powerized bat unless I made the big
leagues, but I couldn't make the big leagues with a bat that was
unemPowerized. I could wear a Rawlings glove with an Edge-U-Cated
Heel. I could use a Sher-Wood hockey stick. I could wear a watch with a
Twist-o-Flex band and eat Certs with Retsyn and enjoy the elusive qualities of a million other mystifying American products.

But the only Louisville Slugger I was authorized to swing had been
Flame Tempered. That flamed my temper no end. I considered it outra-
geous and deliberately provocative: As my tour drew ever nearer to the
Powerizing station, I prepared a rant, like the old crank at the Holiday
Inn this morning.

But first, I watched the familiar oval label of the Louisville Slugger
"burn-branded" onto the bat. There was a time when every American
boy knew to hit with the label up, but few, I suspected, knew why. It's
because the label is emblazoned on the weakest part of the wood—at the
top of the grain. By keeping the label up, a batter is more likely to make

contact with the side of the grain, on the ephemeral "sweet spot." Or so Christian explained to me.

And while it was here, at the "burn-branding" station, that the word "Powerized" and the Zeuslike lightning bolt were affixed, this was clearly done out of sequence. The bat had not yet, in fact, *been* Powerized, not yet infused with the breath of life.

I presently watched a man toil at an open blue flame, like a welder's torch. He was Flame Tempering a bat, which drew out the grain of the wood and gave it that beautiful pine-lodge look. (The wood itself was actually fifty-year-old ash harvested in New York and Pennsylvania.) Aside from the obvious aesthetic benefits, the value of Flame Tempering was nil. "It doesn't make the bat any stronger," said Christian, confirming my darkest suspicions. Is it any wonder I never made the majors?

Farther down the line, the bats were "finished" with any number of lacquers, or left with no lacquer at all, depending on a player's personal preference. The most popular look by far among big leaguers was an all-black finish. Some players believed that using black batting gloves on a black bat against a black background—the vast majority of games are played at night—was like swinging an invisible bat. This would indeed put infielders at a disadvantage. But Christian had a more plausible theory for the black bat's popularity: "It just looks cool."

The plant's one shift of craftsmen turned out 1,700 finished bats a day, and these were stacked neatly like cordwood in large shipping containers near the loading-dock doors. This, surely, was where the bats would be Powerized, perhaps by a priest or rabbi.

But I waited and waited and it didn't happen. Christian patiently explained that the bats had already *been* Powerized at the Flame Tempering station. I was confused. "Powerized" and "Flame Tempered," Christian revealed, were two different terms to describe the very same process. Could this *be?* Or was he covering up? I felt my world crashing down around me.

After all, what then accounted for the Power in the Powerized bat? And why would such a force be entrusted to big leaguers alone? "We call the major-league bats 'Powerized,' " Christian answered, "just to make the major leaguers feel special."

Of course. It made perfect sense. I no longer pitied myself, but rather pitied the Powerized big leaguers. For a "Powerized" label did not signify the supernatural qualities of a bat, but instead spoke to the neediness and egomania of the batter.

I left Slugger Park enlightened and slightly ashamed of myself, an Edge-U-Cated Heel.

A further word, if I may, about egomania. In a 1996 survey, NFL rookies were asked to name their favorite athlete. The resounding winner: "Myself," with 28 percent of the vote. Michael Jordan finished a distant second.

I could have saved the NFL the trouble of canvassing its newcomers. Having been in the homes of countless professional athletes, I can tell you those homes are frequently filled with posters, sculptures, and tasteful oversized portraits of the homeowner—usually painted by renowned "sports artist" Leroy Neiman—so that even a utility infielder can sit in his living room and feel like Saddam Hussein surveying downtown Baghdad.

But it was now no longer enough for Deion Sanders to name his daughter Deiondra, or for George Foreman to famously father a George, a George, a George, and a George. No, somewhere along the line, the egomaniacs had to become *megalo*maniacs, as well, intent on global domination. Shaquille O'Neal has a tattoo that reads THE WORLD IS MINE, which is also the name of his clothing line. Shawn Kemp boasts in a Reebok ad, "This is *my* planet." If I had a dollar for every athlete who has said in praise of some teammate's performance, "It's his world; we're just living in it," I would now be Mr. Anna Nicole Smith. All of which strikes me as an affront to God. I refer to point guard God Shammgod— as I write, he is in the NBA, having played his college basketball for (who else?) Providence. And yes, that is his real name.

Athletes are conditioned to think of themselves as Alexanderlike conquerers of the globe. We call league title winners "world champions," even though those leagues are as international as most pancake houses, about as worldly as Carpet World. For three years, the "world champion" Toronto Blue Jays were like the Mordecai Richler character who says, "I'm world-famous all over Canada." But try telling that to a ballplayer. Barry Bonds had portraits of himself sewn into his wristbands, so that he could always gaze upon his own reflection—Narcissus in double knits.

Andy Van Slyke, a former teammate of Bonds with the Pittsburgh Pirates, was once asked, "If you could be anyone else for a day, who would you be?" Van Slyke answered, "My wife, so I could see how wonderful it is to live with me."

And while I know Van Slyke was only joking, I couldn't help but think that these superstar athletes were hinting at a problem I encountered every day in my travels: A great many people, it seemed, resented having to share the planet with me.

Motorists would run my car into a bridge abutment rather than allow me to merge. Waitresses? I could signal them with semaphore flags and still go unacknowledged. Chatting pedestrians walked four abreast down city sidewalks—like paper dolls attached at the elbow, unable to break rank—and scuttled me into the street.

People had become limousines, hiding behind sunglasses, rigged up to personal stereos, wearing T-shirts like the one Jose Canseco modeled in *Sports Illustrated* (as he addressed a throng of reporters), the one that read LEAVE ME ALONE!

"The world is mine," they seemed to say. "This is *my* planet."

Well, I have news for those people: it is Larry Bird's planet. The Earth is a Larry Bird–signature basketball, spinning madly on Larry's disfigured right index finger, which Larry shattered while attempting to catch a softball in the spring before his rookie season with the Celtics, causing that finger to veer grotesquely at the joint, so that when Larry makes the "We're number one" sign, he appears to be saying, "We're number seven."

Larry, who was playing left-center field in that fateful softball game, had long occupied (as you may have already gathered) a disproportionate number of my dwindling brain cells, which I could actually hear popping like bubble wrap with each successive day on the road. And here I was now, down in Birdland, giddily approaching Larry's hometown of French Lick, Indiana. I was delirious, deLarryous, more Birdbrained than ever before. I was rejuvenated—that's the word—from the Latin *juvenis*, which means "youth." I was returned to my adolescence.

Larry had been an obsession since junior high (when I was struggling without success to emulate Dr. J), and he remained a resonant figure throughout high school. I was in the Class of '84, a year forever linked to the eponymous masterwork *1984* (Van Halen's, not Orwell's) and linked, above all, to Larry.

In that *annus mirabilis*, Larry won the first of his three straight MVPs, the Celtics beat the Lakers in seven epic games of the NBA finals, and I left for college in Milwaukee because it was the NBA port nearest to Bloomington, Minnesota.

I graduated from college on May 22, 1988, the day Larry made nine of ten fourth-quarter shots and Boston beat Atlanta 118–116 in Game 7 of the Eastern Conference semifinals, a game Larry and others have called one of the greatest in history. I wouldn't know. I missed the fourth quarter, in which Larry scored 20 points, making baskets serially, compulsively, almost pathologically, unable to throw the ball anywhere but in the hoop. I missed it because my parents insisted that I peel myself from the TV in their room at the Howard Johnson's and pick up my diploma in person. I remember them muttering that "they" had paid $32,000 in tuition, that "they" had driven six miserable hours from Minnesota to see me graduate, that "they" would be damned if "they" let me watch a basketball game. *They, they, they*—it was all about *them.* What about me? I can't recall a single word of the commencement address delivered that day by Supreme Court Justice William Rehnquist, but I cannot forget a moment of the basketball game, which I have since seen dozens of times on tape.

Although—or perhaps *because*—I've never met him, Larry retained a strange fascination for me to this day. He was my Mickey Mantle. Like Larry, I still habitually reached down to rub clean the soles of my Converse (always Converse), as if to strengthen gravity's grip on me. My on-line computer password is L-A-R-R-Y. The access number for my ATM card is BC33 (for number 33 of the Boston Celtics), a fact that even I find a bit embarrassing. And one that I hope you'll forget if you ever find my wallet in a cab.

I was two miles shy of French Lick when a voice on my car radio said, "You're listening to Q-100, French Lick, Larry Bird's hometown and proud of it!" On the outskirts of town, a sign implored me to VISIT DOWNTOWN FRENCH LICK, and it suddenly sounded salacious—"downtown French Lick"—like a hooker's most expensive trick. One performed, perhaps, on Floyds Knobs, another Indiana town along this same Highway 150.

By this stage of my journey, I was finding erotic associations in the Golden Arches at McDonald's. Q-100 played a mournful country song—about a man abandoned by his woman—and its double-entendre title had a terrible poignancy for me: *Thank You, I'm Holding My Own.*

When friends asked if I wasn't powerfully lonely on the road, I now knew what to tell them. "Thank you," I'd say, "I'm holding my own."

But not in French Lick. In French Lick, my solitude would yield to the solicitude of my family. Two of my brothers and my father, all vaguely concerned for my sanity, were driving down from Chicago this morning for a day of golf and Bird-watching. They had booked two rooms at the ancient and grand French Lick Springs Resort, which dominated the downtown silhouette, a giant white wedding cake of an edifice known locally as "The Hotel."

"A lot of townspeople work over there and it's something the town is proud of," Larry noted in his autobiography, *Drive*, my copy of which was dog-eared and battered like an Army chaplain's Bible. "What's funny is that when I grew up, I never did go there." To grow up in French Lick (with its 2,087 people) and not visit the famous Hotel sounded impossible, like living on Liberty Island and never seeing the Statue. But it made perfect sense to me. Larry was simply blinkered by basketball.

He once demanded the final shot in a deadlocked Celtic game on the grounds that he had taken "a million" more jumpers than anyone else. And he had. Of his youth in French Lick, Larry wrote: "Basketball was all I thought about, all I wanted to do. I couldn't wait for school to let out for the summer so I could play ball. I would play at 6 A.M. before school. I would duck into the gym in between classes to get a few shots up and play again after school into the early hours of the next morning, feeling that sleep was a rude intrusion on my practice time."

It was the habit of the French novelist Honoré de Balzac to write all night, take breakfast, write all day, nap in the evening after dinner, then rise at 1 A.M. to write again—sixteen hours a day, seven days a week, a self-described "galley slave to pen and ink." Well, Larry was the basketball Balzac. Larry was Basketbalzac.

He was the only Celtic who ever appeared as distraught or disgusted as I was when Boston lost, perhaps because his world at the time (like mine) really was a basketball spinning madly on his periscopic right index finger. "We're talking about somebody who didn't exactly have a world view," Larry wrote of his young self in *Drive*. And later, "I just didn't have any interest in the outside world." Larry once let slip that he didn't know who Bruce Springsteen was. *Boston Globe* writer Dan Shaughnessy replied helpfully: "Larry, he's the you of rock & roll."

So it's entirely plausible that Larry had been oblivious of The Hotel, though Al Capone and FDR had once walked (or wheeled) its hallways. And what hallways! They echoed and smelled of sulfur and wandered mazily for what seemed to be miles, so that I searched endlessly for my room after check-in. I began to get paranoid, eventually suspecting the front desk of releasing a dragon behind me, convinced that it was now pursuing me through this labyrinth.

But I reached my chamber undevoured and, with time to kill before my family arrived, set out to explore French Lick. There was an eighteen-hole golf course on the expansive grounds of The Hotel, and a driving range, and next to it a disused railroad depot, where dignitaries were presumably disgorged by the carload in the 1920s and 1930s. The depot now served as a visitors' center. I went inside. It was empty save for a Rockwellian old clerk manning a ticket-window-turned-information-booth. He enthusiastically offered me an autumn-in-Vermont blaze of multicolored leaflets extolling the wonders of greater French Lick, both cultural and agricultural. But when I mentioned that I was more interested in the area's, well, more *Larry-related* attractions, his face fell and he abruptly said that there weren't any.

"None?" I asked.

"Nothing on the community," he said, which I took to mean that there were no civic-sponsored tours of historic Larry locales.

I pressed on. "If I want to see his old playground or his boyhood home . . ."

"Nothing on the community," he repeated, somewhat annoyingly.

"I just thought that since this was his hometown . . ."

"Such as it is," the man harrumphed and turned to the musty railroad timetables or shipping registries or whatever it was that suddenly engaged his interest in the back of the booth. He wore the same look most Parisians wear when you ask them an inexplicably offensive question, such as "Where is the nearest Pizza Hut?" or "How long will your poodle be pissing on my leg?"

But on the whole, French Lick was friendly. How do you not love a town called French Lick? Or people called French Lickers? Or the booze emporium on State Road 56 that was *named* French Liquors and was emblazoned with the Rolling Stones' lips-and-tongue logo, boldly infringing on any number of copyrights?

Strolling along 56, I did something I always wanted to do and turned into Larry Bird. Or, rather, into Larry Bird Boulevard. Those words were painted on a striking sign, an enormous basketball, atop a very tall pole, that must have been fifteen feet in diameter—too big to be burgled, or I would have done so. It looked like an enormous lollipop and presided over the town like a Tootsie Pop Tour Eiffel—an appropriate monument, come to think of it, in a place called French Lick.

If you knew anything at all about Larry—and I liked to think of myself as the Roger Tory Peterson of Bird scholarship—it was easy to locate the important touchstones of Larry's life in French Lick. I saw three different playground basketball courts, each of them derelict, their rims missing or mangled, and tried to imagine Larry making the ragged nets of Kimball Park sway like hula skirts with every jump shot.

Kimball Park, I gathered, was named for the same Kimball who founded the Kimball Piano and Organ Company, where Larry's father worked before committing suicide.

Springs Valley High School was shuttered on this summer day, the gym locked tight, and in it the Cinemascope-sized photograph of Larry that looked down on the Eagles' home court "like a chapel Madonna," as the portrait was described in a *Time* cover story of March 18, 1985. I didn't have to go to the library for the date or the quote, as I still have the magazine, along with many other Larry-bearing publications of the eighties. I often overhear people who have just met me say, "He still has a lot of issues from his childhood." And I wonder: How did they know? In any event, the new Sistine Chapel in French Lick was an exterior brick wall at the Village Market. It bore an alfresco mural of a black man sitting on storefront steps, in conversation with a yellow-haired tyke in a

Celtics jersey, number 33, and I stopped to admire it on my walk back to The Hotel.

My family arrived. We happily swapped insults, then left for the windswept French Lick Country Club west of town, where golf cart number 33 was reserved for Larry's exclusive use. While waiting at the first tee, I struck up a conversation with a guy named Carl from Evansville, who described the exterior of Larry's French Lick house, where he still spent time whenever he wearied of his home in Naples, Florida.

"Larry's got a court in the front yard," said Carl. "He was home one spring when the snow melted and found a deflated basketball out there. It was left out all winter, under a basket."

"Probably where it landed when he made his last shot the summer before," I interjected.

"Prob'ly," concurred Carl. "Anyway, the ball was totally flat, like a raisin, and Larry picked it up and looked at it"—Carl regarded with interest an invisible object in his hand—"then threw it the length of the court. BANG! Right through the hoop. Then he walked in the house. Supposedly, it's the most amazing thing he ever did on a basketball court."

Alas, this talk of precision shotmaking had a deleterious effect on the first man at the first tee, trying to coax a 1³/₄-inch ball into a 4¹/₄-inch hole several hundred yards away. Which person was me. My tee shot went boomerang slicing into the ether out of bounds, and my dad sang his comment that is customary for such occasions: "*GOOD*-bye, my Coney Island *baaaaaaayyyy*-beee!" God, that is irritating.

We played our usual *doloroso* round, carving up the course and each other, so that even my little brother, John, couldn't enjoy his 79. He was the only real golfer among us. John was a good athlete, selected by the New York Rangers in the seventh round of the National Hockey League draft as a high school senior, but—how shall I put this?—not the sharpest blade in the skate room.

I once asked him why we play golf when it brings us so much pain, and he said, to my surprise, "I'm a sodomist." I think he meant to say "sadist" (he derived great pleasure from my score of 108), or perhaps "masochist" (which explains why *I* play), but he accidentally combined and dyslexified the two words into a third, wholly unintended one.

Even so, I had a suction cup installed on the end of my putter grip. It allows me to retrieve my ball from the cup without ever bending over.

After golf, we bought a twelve-pack at French Liquors, eschewing the more convenient Larry's Liquors because an unreliable source on the street (possibly an undercover operative from French Liquors) said that Larry's Liquors was unaffiliated with the actual Larry. "Probably another Larry," said this French Licker, "trying to capitalize on Larry's name."

At The Hotel, we drank our beers with an urgency usually associated with pie-eating contests, showered, dressed, and went to dinner in 1948. Which is to say, in the ballroom of the French Lick Springs Resort, where a big band played to hundreds of dining and dancing Midwesterners out for a weekend in what resembled Batista's Havana. It was wonderful. A tuxedoed man made the rounds, gladhanding and giving out business cards inscribed with his grandiloquent name: G. ALAN BARNETT, DIRECTOR OF PUBLICITY, FRENCH LICK SPRINGS RESORT

G. Alan alit at our table and, learning we were Larry pilgrims, suggested that the two best Bird-sighting spots in Indiana were, alas, not in French Lick. They were Larry's restaurant—the Boston Connection in Terre Haute—and his car dealership up in Martinsville. "If you're a really big hitter, he might come up and have his picture taken with you at the dealership," said G. Alan, shooting his cuffs and throwing off charisma like sparks.

"How do I become a big hitter?" I asked, and G. Alan didn't hesitate, responding with seven words that would open the door to Larry's heart:

"Pay full sticker for a Crown Vic," he said.

The evening wore on. We got French-liquored. We drank before dinner. We drank *for* dinner. Then we drank after dinner at a karaoke bar a block off Larry Bird, where I tried unsuccessfully to perform the summer's country smash, *Refried Dreams* by Tim McGraw, the son of former

Phillies pitcher Tug McGraw. I heard the song a dozen times a day on AM radio in rural America, but couldn't recall any words beyond a memorable verse which rhymed "tequila" with "to kill ya."

My dad threatened to sing *Back Home Again in Indiana*—for he was—but burst spontaneously instead into a college drinking song:

> *Oh Purdue, Oh Purdue how you make me quiver*
> *With your old Sweet Shop and your Wabash River*
> *How I love you with my heart and I love you*
> *with my liver*
> *Oh Purdue* [clap clap]
> *By the River* [clap clap]
> *Oh Purdue what a hole by the River.*

Needless to say, we trundled him back to The Hotel at the earliest possible convenience, at which time Tom, John, and I repaired to the nearby K & K Sports Bar (OIL WRESTLING, BIKINI CONTESTS). We bellied up, three dumb men, and ordered shots of Three Wise Men.

"Three Wise Men?" asked the barmaid, regarding the inebriated magi before her. "What's Three Wise Men?"

"Johnnie, Jack, and Jim," Tom said.

The three whiskeys were mixed together into one foul shot, and we each did one in honor of Larry, who loved taking foul shots. Then we did another. The barkeep perked her ears up at the mention of Larry, saying that he had once ducked into this very establishment. Everyone in the joint immediately bought him a beer, she said, so that unopened cans appeared in a line before him on the bar, as in a carnival midway game, waiting to be knocked off one by one. This was more than Larry had bargained for, and he stood up and left, announcing abruptly, "My wife would divorce me and take all my money if she saw this."

I repeat the story not because I want Larry's wife to divorce him and take all his money, but because it made him sound like a swell guy, and French Lick a swell town. The locals still loved Larry long after his retirement. His name elicited none of the eye rolling that, say, some

Minneapolitans give out of towners who ask to see the spot where Mary Richards threw up her hat in the opening credits of *The Mary Tyler Moore Show*.

I was getting queasy. I felt like *I* might throw up a hat. I bummed a Marlboro from a guy next to me at the bar, dragged deeply, and realized that I didn't smoke. Tom was talking to another guy and scribbling something on a cocktail napkin: directions to Larry's house. "He's home," this Deep Throat said. "I saw his wife downtown last week."

We staggered back to The Hotel at two and fell into bed as if dropped by assassins. Four hours later, the alarm clock wailed and my heart started going like Buddy Rich. Tom, John, and Dad, having actual homes and lives to return to, gasped that they needed to be on the road back to Chicago. I reluctantly rose with them.

I had a hangover like you read about—specifically, like you read about in Kingsley Amis's novel *Lucky Jim*, in which Jim wakes to discover that: "His mouth had been used as a latrine by some small creature of the night, and later as its mausoleum." My head felt like one of those Lucite lottery drums when the balls are being agitated. My brothers evidently felt the same way. In the bathroom, Tom was having a kind of anti-Happy Hour—eating a party mix of Tums and Tylenol and swigging Scope straight from the bottle. On the nightstand, I discovered his treasure map: the crumpled napkin describing the route to Larry's house. We were on our way.

I followed my family to the edge of town, a two-car funeral procession. I was sure they made a wrong turn, down a country road full of peeling trailer homes, but then it appeared—Larry's spread, familiar from the film *Blue Chips* and from a memorable Converse commercial that costarred Magic Johnson. The house was white, modest, suburban. Smaller than Graceland. It was thrown in the shade by a five-car garage and Larry's basketball court. We pulled our cars to the shoulder and sat across the road, idling. To the east, a wedge of orange sun was rising in a lavender dawn sky—God tossing up a basketball to tip off the day.

A hundred yards away, Larry slept. Or maybe he lay awake in the dark. After all, following Larry's performance in game seven against the

Hawks—that game I missed on graduation day—Celtic forward Kevin McHale said: "Someday I'll be retired to Minnesota, and Larry will be retired to French Lick, and I'll lay awake at night and think of games like this, and how lucky I was to play with him." I remember thinking at the time that that day would never come. But here it was. And here *I* was, completing a pilgrimage.

I had followed a star to the site of his birth, and now I would pay homage. I opened my door and bowed my head. I could not contain myself. On the shoulder across from his house, I left a gift, one given to me by Three Wise Men.

16

I needed my atlas (and could have used a passport) to cross Illinois, with its small towns of Atlas and Passport—to say nothing of Florence, Naples, Berlin, Hamburg, Glasgow, Brussels, Bogota, Cairo, New Delhi, Palestine, and Paris. Oddly, the immigrants who settled Downstate Illinois turned this Tower of Babel into the most American of all places. Was there anywhere in the United States more normal than Normal, more central than Centralia, a better bellwether than Peoria?

This was my last pass through Middle America, through the Middle West, what weathermen called "our nation's midsection"—the country's symbolic center of gravity. Illinois was in perfect balance topographically, too. If you laid a sufficiently long carpenter's level the length of Highway 50, which ran east–west across the state, you would find it is entirely without gradient. The land was flatter than Tom Brokaw's accent. Illinois license plates ought to read STATE OF EQUILIBRIUM.

In fact, from the moment I crossed the Wabash River via the Red Skelton Bridge and passed from Indiana into Illinois, I thought I could just make out the Gateway Arch in St. Louis, 150 miles due west, on the other side of the state. As it happened, I was a good ten miles from St. Louis when the arch finally did appear, all sixty-three stories of it, enlivening the horizon like a glinting navel ring jutting from a washboard stomach.

The Jefferson National Expansion Memorial—as the arch is officially called—was even more striking when it was still under construction in 1963, two stainless-steel tusks rising out of the earth along the Mississippi riverfront. Workers lowered the last connecting segment into the top center of the arch in 1965, and one can, for any number of reasons, imagine their relief when it fit.

For starters, architect Eero Saarinen's plan generously allowed for a $1/64$th-inch margin of error in connecting the tusks, according to a documentary film that played in the underground museum beneath the arch. For another, thirteen deaths were expected during construction of the monument. Whether this forecast was made for insurance purposes, or for a budget estimate, or was simply the consensus in an office betting pool, the film didn't say. But it's hard to fathom that nobody *did* die, especially when you screen footage of workers strolling along moving beams 600 feet in the air, slapping together sandwiches with one hand and wolf-whistling at women with the other, in that devil-may-care manner of trapeze artists and window washers and construction workers everywhere. How they do this, when I get vertigo drinking Hi-C, is beyond me.

Then again, what better way to commemorate the discovery, settlement, and enduring promise of the American West, and to honor the adventurous spirit of the pioneers, than to erect an edifice so audaciously daring that a baker's dozen lives would be lost in its construction *if all went according to plan?*

I watched the monument's ceremonial completion on film—it had that hypercolor quality of Super 8 home movies—and thought what a heady time that must have been in St. Louis. From the bird's eye view of a sixties construction worker, I could see the concrete bagel of Busch Stadium being built below, and a thrumming grid of gleaming steel cars the size of aircraft carriers, and tiny people dressed in the ultrabright colors of a detergent commercial. The world was bright and shiny—"in living color," as television was saying at the time—and it looked that way again as I emerged from underground and went batting my eyelashes against the St. Louis sunshine.

I walked ceremonially under the arch, passing from east to west. Until Horace Stoneham pulled a Horace Greeley and moved his New York Giants to San Francisco in 1958, St. Louis was the Western terminus of big-time professional sports. Today, the city is but the threshold to the West, which has established a subculture all its own in American sports: a land of late box scores, tofu hot dogs, the Wave (purportedly invented at the University of Washington), that whole come-late-leave-early ethos of the Left Coast. Another world awaited me. I set out to realize my Manifest Destiny.

Between 1851 and 1900, 4.5 million Germans came to the United States, settling in large numbers in New York, Milwaukee, Chicago, and St. Louis, to which they brought their two national passions: beer and bowling.

Following Prohibition, these two primordial elements were happily combined in countless professional bowling teams sponsored by breweries: Falstaff, Pfeiffer's, Meister Brau; Waldorf Red Band, Pabst Blue Ribbon, Falls City Hi-Bru; Schlitz, Blatz, Ballantine. The brand names were strangely poetic, Hi-Bru haiku, and they were pitched to bowlers as naturally as soap operas would be pitched to the housewives who bought soap. Nowhere was this intersection of beer and bowling more prominent than in St. Louis, where the colossal Anheuser-Busch brewery and the fifty-thousand-square-foot Bowling Hall of Fame now stand as towering twin monuments to keggers and keglers, a 7–10 split on the skyline.

It was actually Germany's irrepressible neighbors in Holland who first brought skittles and ninepins to the New World in 1626, and almost immediately, colonists were confused by the game's system of scorekeeping. In 1673, William Penn wrote a letter to a friend: "We were at bowls yestere'en, and though I got more pins at each first roll than my friend, yet so my score was less. . . . They do reckon outrageously, for do I throw the nine pins with one bowl, and hit none at all with the remaining two, still do they account me the more skillful and do bestow a larger account than would fall to me did I strike them all with three bowls."

Before long, the English Quaker got the hang of it, grew to love the game, and even had to stifle giggles when calling at bowling alleys to ask: "Dost thou have sixteen-pound balls?" Or so one might believe after visiting the hall, with its bowl-o-centric view of the universe. One deadpan display announced: "Martin Luther (1483–1546), the German leader of the Protestant Reformation, liked to bowl!"

On the other hand, Henry VIII declared bowling "an evil" in a 1511 edict, writing: "Alleys are in operation in conjunction with saloons or dissolute places, and bowling has ceased to be a sport, and rather a form of vicious gambling." When I considered that both Luther and King Henry left the Catholic Church to found their own enduring denominations—Protestantism and the Church of England, respectively—bowling suddenly became freighted with profound theological implications. I shambled about the bowling hall, contemplating life's imponderables.

Why does God "strike" down some men—as He might have done in raining "bowling-ball-sized hail" on northern Iowa—and "spare" others? Did God create the universe? If not, as the Puritan clergyman and poet Edward Taylor wrote of the heavens:

> *Who spread its canopy?*
> *Or curtains spun?*
> *Who in this bowling alley bowled the sun?*

Should I not take comfort that Proverbs 26, verse 27—"He that rolleth a stone, it will return upon him"—correctly presaged the automatic ball return mechanism two millennia in advance? And who exactly *are* the Holy Rollers, anyway?

I was becoming a pinhead. If there were a Betty Ford Center for the hopelessly sports-addicted, I would have driven myself directly there. And I would have done so in the 1936 Studebaker on display in the bowling hall: Its body was a bowling pin, its Missouri license plate read GO BOWL. Better yet, I could hitch the Oscar Mayer Wienermobile to the back bumper of this bowling pin and pull into detox driving the two things that were driving me: sports and stadium food.

Many sausage scholars credit a St. Louis saloonkeeper named Chris von der Ahe with introducing the hot dog to baseball at the turn of the century. Von der Ahe (speaking of Dutchmen and St. Louis and sports and beer) owned the St. Louis Browns and brought sausages to Sportsman's Park to serve as sop for his popular brand of beer, which he also sold at the ballpark.

A century later, Anheuser-Busch had a bland-beer monopoly at Busch Stadium, the concrete bowl directly across the street from the Bowling Hall of Fame. The Cardinals were evidently in town tonight, because I now watched two young Los Angeles Dodgers get out of a cab in front of Busch. They wore complicated haircuts, gold-rope necklaces as thick as bridge cable, and shiny suits that appeared to be cut from city bus-seat upholstery.

Waiting for their autographs was a gaggle of get-a-lifers, half a dozen acned adults who wore replica uniforms, clutched bricks of base-ball cards, and generally made *Star Trek* conventioneers look well adjusted. The players signed without making eye contact. Or even ear contact. They ignored the deluded, stalkeresque intimacies offered by the autograph hounds: "Say hi to Piazza, he's my favorite player. . . . Take it easy on the Cardinals, fellas. . . . Tell Tommy to lay off the spaghetti. . . ."

"Pathetic," I muttered as I climbed into my car and tossed a post-card of the Bowling Hall of Fame's extensive collection of bowling shirts onto the backseat, where it joined a set of nine "milk bottle caps" emblazoned with portraits of various Boston Red Sox, an ashtray made of the famous photograph of Elvis shaking hands with Richard Nixon, a souvenir replica of the Larry Bird Boulevard street sign, a Field of Dreams corn cob letter opener, a miniature Terry Pendleton-signature Louisville Slugger, a vintage Minnesota Twins cap, a Day-Glo Fort Wayne Wizards Frisbee, and a pack of Topps baseball cards. I thought to myself, Don't these people have anything better to do?

I had bought the baseball cards at a gas station in Illinois and, tingling with anticipation, had torn open the packet on the interstate. What a gyp. Incredibly, there was no rectangle of pink gum, pressed from the same cardboard used in the manufacture of the cards. Or any of the ridiculous old poses—say, pitchers standing ostrichlike on one leg in midwindup in center field in an empty stadium. Baseball cards could make the most graceful player look as wooden as Pinocchio.

But the Topps company's most unforgivable innovation was to do away with the humanizing factoids on the flip side of each card. I recall that the 1973 card of Twins outfielder Bobby Darwin informed me that "Bobby works for a car-towing firm." This was accompanied by a cartoon of a baseball player in full uniform driving a tow truck while leaning out the window to catch a fly ball. The '73 card for Ken McMullen, a Dodger third baseman with eleven big-league seasons behind him, said, "Ken works in a service station in the off-season," and showed the same cartoon player pumping gas in full uniform. "Bill is a salesman during the off-season," said Philadelphia outfielder Bill Robinson's card, which depicted our fully uniformed cartoon friend holding a Fuller brush while ringing a doorbell. As a seven-year-old, I knew that all players worked real jobs in the winter and wore their baseball uniforms when doing so.

Today's cards reflected today's players: They were a humorless grid of statistics and accomplishments that read like a bank statement. It is hard to imagine a current major leaguer putting up with what was on the back of the '73 Rollie Fingers card: "Rollie suffered a fractured jaw when hit by a line drive in 1967," it read, accompanied by a cartoon player's head exploding as a baseball was driven through it. I selected from my pack a '95 card at random: Terry Mathews of the Florida Marlins. "Terry limited right-handed batters to a .205 avg. during the 1994 season," it said, sounding a bit like Cliff Claven, the pedantic postman on *Cheers*.

They don't make players like they used to. Or so I was beginning to think as I cracked open that morning's *St. Louis Post-Dispatch* and found a small story inside the "Metro" section about the "Battling Brocks": Cardinal legend Lou Brock and his ex-wife, Virgie, were involved in an acrimonious divorce settlement that landed them both in contempt of court—and Virgie temporarily in jail. Brock had "refused to make recent maintenance payments because Virgie Brock had withheld some of his personal property," according to the *Post-Dispatch*.

"Specifically, Lou Brock said, his ex-wife had refused to give him his Hall of Fame ring and a painting by Leroy Neiman."

Apart from the Cardinals game, the sporting diversions on offer this evening in St. Louis were a women's collegiate soccer match and a monster-truck showdown between Bigfoot and Grave Digger at the Tri-City Speedway.

Bigfoot was the first and most famous of all monster trucks, the creation of a St. Louisan named Bob Chandler. I once asked Chandler why, in the name of all that is sacred, people would ever attend a monster-truck rally. "People seem to like noise," he said. "They seem to like the sound of metal being crushed." He was absolutely right. Monster trucking—big trucks driving over small cars—reproduce on a grand scale the sound a beer can makes when collapsing against one's forehead. And is there any sound in life more satisfying than that?

"Americans have always had a love affair with cars and trucks," a monster-truck promoter named Charlie Mancuso told me. "By 1989, light trucks accounted for nearly one third of U.S. automotive sales. You see traffic stopped on the interstate at five o'clock, then you see a Ford Explorer with tires six feet tall on it. The average guy thinks, 'Oh, what a feeling it would be to have a monster truck and ride across the top of all these cars in front of me.' Assuming there weren't any *people* in the cars, of course."

Of course. You wouldn't want to kill anybody. Or would you? Monster-truck tires are sixty-six inches tall, their treads forty-three inches wide. Grave Digger driver Dennis Anderson of Kill Devil Hills, North Carolina, recalled pulling into a gridlocked New York City rush hour once with his truck locked inside the trailer behind him. "I tell you what," said Anderson, "I thought about throwin' on the big tires right there and unloadin' that sumbitch in traffic."

Alas, it is illegal to loose six tons of Chevy-powered hell fury on the heathen streets of Gotham, no matter how much Manhattan's cabbies might deserve to shudder beneath the hooves of Digger's 1,500 horses. So drivers stifled any impulses toward vehicular homicide and were instead content to kill each other's *trucks*. Monster-truck shows always prey on the allegiances to various American automakers held by their mostly blue-collar constituents. Bigfoot was a Ford, Bear Foot was a Dodge, Grave Digger was a Chevy. So was the Carolina Crusher, whose bumper—which was seven feet off the ground—asked HAVE YOU DRIVEN OVER A FORD LATELY?

And it all started here in St. Louis, sometime in 1974. An exact birthdate for the first monster truck is difficult to fix, because Chandler's Bigfoot grew gradually, tire and engine dimensions and whatnot escalating portentously over eighteen months or so. And even when that first primitive monster had arisen from the primordial mud, its tires were a now-laughable forty-four inches tall. Chandler was opening an auto-supply store in suburban St. Louis, and what better way to advertise the merchandise than to tool around town in the latest automotive accessories? At no point did he pull a Frankenstein and declare to the heavens that he had created a monster. "But," he told me later, "I have thought exactly that several times since."

Especially when one of those infernal commercials would appear on television late at night: *"SATURDAY! SATURDAY! SATURDAY! SIX MONSTERS SYNONYMOUS WITH DESTRUCTION! THE BAD-DEST, MEANEST, MOST OUTRAGEOUS TRUCKS EVER ASSEM-*

BLED UNDER ONE ROOF!! WE'LL SELL YA THE WHOLE SEAT,
BUT YOU'LL ONLY NEED THE EDGE!!!"

"I hate those commercials," said the soft-spoken Chandler. "Don't
you?"

Yes, I did. And the events themselves were louder than the commercials. Fans attending monster-truck rallies wore the kind of headset-
style ear protectors favored by international-airport runway personnel.
The trucks were always introduced with percussive pyrotechnical displays. I attended one rally in which the PA announced that spectators
wearing pacemakers had best vacate the premises, at which time any
senior citizen with a bad ticker had precisely six seconds to skedaddle to
the parking lot before he or she was hurtled into cardiac arrest.

I decided to go to the women's soccer match.

At one time, St. Louis was "the soccer capital of the United
States," according to page 235 of The Simplest Game by Paul Gardner.
Granted, this is a bit like being called "the entertainment capital of
Switzerland" or "the fashion capital of North Korea." It doesn't take
much. But America really does have its own diehard soccer culture, with
its own soccer fans (defined as people who have made it to page 235 of
The Simplest Game by Paul Gardner). You just have to know where to
look.

St. Louis is a good place to start. Most of the members of the U.S.
team that stunned England, 1–0, in the 1950 World Cup, were from St.
Louis. Throughout the 1960s and 1970s, St. Louis University was the
dominant men's team in college soccer, and they have remained a power
to this day. The dominant women's team, as I understood it, was from
the University of North Carolina, and they happened to be playing Indiana this evening in something called the Collegiate America Cup, at
someplace called Soccer Park, located at 1 Soccer Park Road in suburban
St. Louis. This turned out to be an enormous complex of beautiful green
rectangles. Soccer Park must have looked, from above, like an open-air
poolroom.

I took a seat next to a young man in a North Carolina baseball cap and asked him if he knew anything about the Tar Heel program. A tad bit, as it turned out.

The guy's name was Jim Houghton, and he was a '91 graduate of UNC, and he let me in on a little secret: The Lady Heels were not merely the most dominant team in women's soccer, or the most dominant team in all of soccer, but the most dominant team in all of sports, quite possibly for all time. They had won the last nine national championships, and thirteen of the last fourteen. "They *didn't* win it in '85," Houghton said. "They lost 2–0 to George Mason in Fairfax, Virginia, to finish second."

He could recite these details because Carolina losses were as irregular as Rose Kennedy. Since 1981, the team had won 284 games and lost 6. Ten seniors on the '93 Heels finished their careers undefeated in 72 matches. Nine of the eighteen players on the U.S. team that won the women's World Cup in China in '91 played for North Carolina, whose coach also coached those world champions. He was a tiny action figure of a man named Anson Dorrance. "Born in Ethiopia," Houghton briefed me. "Lived in Kenya, Singapore, Belgium, and Switzerland before coming to the United States."

Unlike any other sport, soccer bred these citizens of the world. Houghton himself had lived in Bologna, Italy, for two years, gorging himself on Italian soccer in Serie A, the best professional league in the world. "I was there when [Marco] Van Basten and [Ruud] Gullit were at [AC] Milan," he said in the shorthand that any fan of football or *futbol* or footie—indeed, any citizen of the world beyond U.S. borders—would recognize without the brackets. "I saw [Diego] Maradona's last game. It was an unbelievable time to be a football fan in Italy."

"Fan" didn't adequately describe Houghton. He grew up in St. Louis, but now lived on Nantucket, where he played for an amateur team called the Elephants in a summer league filled with European expats, including a group of Scotsmen who regularly cut him off at the knees. "Every Wednesday at one o'clock I get *La Gazzetta dello Sport* when it arrives on the newsstands in Massachussetts," he said, referring

to the Italian sports broadsheet. He had flown into St. Louis for tonight's
Carolina match after finding a rock-bottom airfare. Tomorrow, he was
driving 200 miles to Bloomington, Indiana, to watch the St. Louis University men play Indiana. He would then drive back to St. Louis and
catch Carolina in the finals of this tournament on Sunday. Then he was
flying back to Boston.

As he told me this, the Tar Heels were dismantling Indiana. Almost
literally so: They looked like soldiers field-stripping a rifle, so precise and
methodical and efficient were their passes, which were constantly connecting with feet and heads in front of the Hoosier goal. Pele famously
called soccer "The Beautiful Game," and Carolina was playing The
Beautiful Game beautifully. I could see why Houghton had flown in.

It was not unusual for him to do so. He had paid his own way to the
'95 women's World Cup in Sweden and had paid for the trip back by
selling stories to soccer publications. He was now looking for a job as a
writer or publicist in the sport, and God knows he seemed eminently
qualified. What I loved about soccer, I told Houghton, was the international camaraderie it fostered—at least when it wasn't fanning prejudice
and international hatred.

I once attended a Newcastle United match in that industrial city in
the far north of England. I approached an usher outside the stadium and
asked him which gate I was supposed to enter. He was a "Geordie," as
Newcastle residents are known, and he spoke in the heavy accent of that
region which makes the phrase "doing the town" come out "doon the
toon."

"Weddaboots in Minnesoota air yoo froom?" the usher asked me. I
hadn't told him that I *was* from Minnesota, but he guessed from my own
accent, which must have sounded preposterous to him. He introduced
himself as Mike Bell and explained that he had taught school for two
years in suburban Minneapolis. "I was thayre when the Twins woon the
World Sayries in '91," he said. "How's Kent Hairbeck doon? He was my
fayvorite player."

When I told him that Twins first baseman Kent Hrbek and I both grew up in Bloomington and attended John F. Kennedy High School, Bell became my friend for life. He ran me down after the match and introduced me to his wife and daughters, who had come to pick him up. He gave me his telephone number and insisted that I crash at their place the next time I was in England. "I told all of my students in Minnesota to stay at our place when they're in Europe," he said, as if the neighboring continent were one small town. "Sometimes they ring my doorbell and I don't recognize 'em. But their accent sounds right, so I say, 'You're from Minnesota. Come on in.' "

I have nurtured a fondness for English soccer ever since, an appetite for teams like Manchester United and Arsenal that has taken me to English pubs like the Cock 'N' Bull in Santa Monica, California, where Man United matches are televised live via satellite from England at five o'clock every Saturday *morning*. It gets so crowded that owner Tony Moogan, an expatriate Liverpudlian, has to turn people away. Beer sales, alas, cannot legally begin until 6 A.M., at which time the taps start nodding like woodpeckers on speed. Soon the soccer fans are doing likewise.

Houghton was similarly afflicted. After the Carolina match, he took me to meet a couple dozen of his St. Louis friends at an Irish bar called McGurk's. He recalled being in another Irish bar—in Hoboken, New Jersey—waiting to take a bus to the Meadowlands to see Ireland play Italy on the first Saturday of the men's '94 World Cup. The bar was a Jackson Pollock painting of various races and nationalities, but all were singing the traditional soccer-crowd song, which goes:

"OLE—OLE, OLE, OLE—OLE, OLE . . ."

This was the day after the LAPD chased a certain white Bronco up the 405 Freeway, and when footage of that low-speed pursuit replaced soccer on the pub's TV screens, things might have turned ugly. But the crowd instead broke spontaneously into:

"O.J.—O.J., O.J., O.J.—O.J., O.J. . . ."

Ireland deliriously upset Italy, 1–0, that afternoon. But it was that singing in the pub, Houghton and I both agreed, that was soccer's greatest attribute. It didn't matter if you were pulling for Italy or Ireland that day. It isn't about North Carolina or Indiana. The game's greatest spectacle is not AC Milan or Man United.

It's man united.

Near the town of Devils Elbow, 125 miles southwest of St. Louis in the Mark Twain National Forest, I happened upon Fort Leonard Wood, where my dad did his Army basic training, waking each new day to a drill sergeant yelling, "DROP YOUR COCKS AND GRAB YOUR SOCKS!"—just like in the movies.

I had heard about this place, where Dad spent days bent over in a field, picking up dandruff-sized remnants of cigarette butts (which had been torn to confetti and scattered to the wind expressly for this purpose), so that the DI could keep the GIs doubled over for hours, showing nothing but "*ASSHOLES, ELBOWS, AND SHOE* SOLES!"

At Fort Leonard Wood, anyone who mistakenly called his M-1 a "gun" instead of a "rifle" was made to strip naked in front of his company, his rifle in one hand and his dick in the other, and announce repeatedly: "THIS IS MY RIFLE AND THIS IS MY GUN! ONE IS FOR WAR, THE OTHER FOR FUN!"

So I was naturally astonished (*astonished*, I tell you) when, some months after my visit, officials at Fort Leonard Wood came under investigation for the serial sexual harassment of female enlistees. You don't say. The Army found itself in a terrible mess, one that diverted valuable time away from the primary and laudable mission of the United States Armed Forces: namely, the construction and implementation of snappy profane phrases that rhyme.

Having now seen Fort Leonard Wood and Fort Wayne, Indiana, I realized that my father spent his formative years in one fort or another and that this explained quite a lot about him: his Davy Crockett–like fondness for ridiculous headwear, his disdain for firearms and cigarettes, his abject distaste for Louis Gossett, Jr., movies . . .

Mostly, it explained why he always called our house a "fort"—why he looked me in the eye before embarking on any business trip and said, man-to-man, "I'm counting on you to hold down the fort." Though I may have only been eight years old, I would take the charge seriously and was proud that not once—in all the years my father traveled—did Apaches overrun our two-and-a-half-bath Colonial on 96th Street and shoot my mom full of arrows.

I was also proud of the fact that Dad frequently left the security of our fort to brave the wilderness beyond, to sell magnetic tape products around the world for the 3M Company. Those three M's stood for Minnesota Mining and Manufacturing, though Dad preferred to call his employer Mickey Mouse Mining. He could be a real cynic, my dad.

Mercifully, I inherited none of his sardonic ways, but all of his high threshold for endless travel. I drew upon it now, driving south on Highway 63 toward the Ozark Mountains and into Licking, Missouri. BULL LICKING—IT AIN'T FOR THE FAINT advertised a billboard outside of town. There was no hint as to what "bull licking" consisted of, though I feared the words were to be taken literally. The dates, alas, indicated that the bull-licking competition had concluded a fortnight ago. So, denied the opportunity to tongue-bathe a bovine, I did the next most unpleasant thing. I drove into Arkansas.

A mad, skinny dog, his ribs revealed, reeled along the center line of the highway. He looked like a drunk driver failing a sobriety test for a state trooper. The dog was walking toward a freshly dead doe—also on the center of the highway, also skinny and crazed-looking, even in death.

Random items dotted the roadside: a mattress, a rusting Pepsi dispenser, orphaned shoes. Dilapidated shacks buckled beneath the weight of the wet T-shirts and damp socks that drooped from laundry lines strung between houses. Basketball hoops made of wheel rims were nailed to the narrow trunks of leafless trees—the kind of trees in a Dr. Seuss landscape. What was this strange place, I wondered, where even the dogs and the deer were evidently suicidal?

WELCOME TO ARKANSAS replied a sign. HOME OF PRESIDENT CLINTON. It was the only sign spelled correctly for miles. One business was COMMING SOON, another told me YA'ALL COME BACK, a third sold FINE WATCHS, a fourth was called MOUNTAIN PEDDLARS.

The mountains in question were the Ozarks, and all of the signs in these parts had me wondering: Were the surrounding eminences named for former Phillies manager *Danny* Ozark? He was, after all, a leading light of baseball's illiterati, a man who once said, "Even Napoleon had his Watergate." In refusing to allow the front-office types to dictate lineup changes to him, Ozark once told reporters, "I will not be cohorsed."

I once asked Sparky Anderson, when he was managing the Detroit Tigers, why he and other baseball skippers historically had such difficulty with English. Sparky answered candidly, "I truly don't know the language. I wish I could know the difference between a noun and a pronoun and an adverb and a verb, but I *don't* know, and you know, I don't *wanna* know. Why do you have to know English? It's like the word *two:* There's three *twos!* There's tee-oh, there's tee-doubleya-oh, and there's tee-double-oh! Three *twos!* Now, if I put anyone of those down in a letter, you know which one it is I'm talkin' about. It's like *there* and *their.* What's the difference, as long as you know there's a *there* there?''

"Hear hear," I replied.

Gertrude Stein once said of Oakland, "There's no *there* there." Well, I can tell you: There's no *there* here—in northeast Arkansas—either. So I jumped on the interstate.

I was eager to make time, determined to arrive in Dallas, via Louisiana and eastern Texas, to see Sunday's Cowboy game. I wanted to watch America's Team play America's Game in the city that symbolized both the American Dream and the American Nightmare: South Fork Ranch and Dealey Plaza.

I forged south into Little Rock, a spiffy little city whose tallest building bore the letters TCBY, for The Country's Best Yogurt. The Country's Best Yogurt was once known as This Can't Be Yogurt!!, but then the good people at This Can't Be Yogurt!! were sued by a Dallas-based chain called I Can't Believe It's Yogurt!, whose attorneys felt that their company ought to be the only one whose name was an exclamation of yogurt incredulity. All of which is to say: Remember when the tallest building in most cities belonged to a *bank?* My God but there must be money in curdled milk.

I made quick work of downtown Little Rock, then tried to find my way back onto the interstate, which passed above the tattered edge of downtown, yet was maddeningly inaccessible to anyone who wasn't born behind the wheel of a car up there. The city streets that ran beneath the freeway offered no help. I tried every such avenue until I came to an underpass that was fenced off to traffic. There, to my great surprise, were two full basketball courts, both hosting high-spirited games while eight lanes of interstate truck traffic went whooshing overhead.

I joined a dozen other spectating trolls under the highway, parking between a jacked-up white Cadillac whose driver labored to replace a flat front tire and a Buick with its hood up. All the players wore long pants, as if the basketball game had broken out spontaneously during the workday, in the way that dance numbers do in movie musicals.

"Is this a good place to play?" I asked a guy in his twenties who was waiting for the next game. "I mean, under the freeway like this?"

"It's shady," he said. "It's cooler down here." He had a point. Even now, in mid-September, it was eighty-eight degrees in the sunshine in Little Rock, and things really were much more pleasant beneath a canopy of concrete.

"The noise doesn't bother you?" I asked as an endless convoy of eighteen-wheelers stampeded overhead.

"Sounds like a crowd cheering," he replied.

I'll be damned if it didn't. There must have been thirty people down there, and as I retrieved my car from among the other automobiles parked courtside, it began to make sense to me: The long pants, the disabled vehicles . . . surely this basketball game—this entire subarterial world—was populated entirely by motorists who abandoned hope of ever finding the I-30 on-ramp.

I tried once more to find it myself, a disorienting task that sent me racing past the basketball courts again and again. Every time I swept past the hoops, failing to find a way onto the interstate and rapidly losing what remained of my patience, I thought of something that my friend Alex Wolff once wrote. It applied to basketball; it applied to life. "Traveling," wrote Alex, "is a violation."

Later that night, after several hours of driving, I surveyed my seedy motel room in Monroe, Louisiana. There were stains of various provenance on every conceivable surface of the room—carpet, lampshades, ceiling—so that if you were to turn on a black light in that darkened chamber, the place would glow like the Hayden Planetarium.

Needless to say, I dressed for bed in long pants and a long-sleeved undershirt and put on the complimentary shower cap for an added measure of protection. I didn't get hot, because my room was evidently being used as an experiment in cryobiology—the study of the effects of very low temperatures on living organisms. The air conditioner was relentless, an Astrodome-caliber appliance.

I climbed into bed, my eyes alighting on the mottled bedspread, and thought . . .

That Can't Be Yogurt!!

Louisiana license plates read SPORTSMAN'S PARADISE, a boast I began to believe near Columbia, where I passed a Live Bait and Tackle Shop that advertised its LAYAWAY PLAN. Think about that. If you are so obsessed with fishing that you're willing to go into debt to buy bait, perhaps the fish have *you* on the line and not the other way around. I mean, who was hooking *whom* here?

To be fair, many of these people had no choice but to buy crank bait on the installment plan. By all indications, they were subsistence fishermen, selling shrimp and catfish from roadside shacks. The roads themselves were littered with dead dogs. I drove from poor town to poor town, each one more anachronistic than the last: a filling station offered REGULAR LEADED GASOLINE; soft-drink ads announced "new" developments in bottling technology (TWIST A PEPPER!); an old man laconically took a leak alfresco in broad daylight.

And the daylight *was* broad, let me tell you. The sun blazed away with all its fury down here, so that the highway shimmered for miles up ahead. It was like driving on the Reflecting Pool in Washington, D.C.

Washington was on my mind because tomorrow was Election Day in Louisiana. Every yard, storefront, and utility pole trumpeted a candidate for this office or that. NOBLE ELLINGTON FOR SENATOR read one ubiquitous campaign sign. NOT JUST A NAME, WHAT LOUISIANA *MUST* BE.

Noble Ellington! What a great Southern-fried politician kind of name that was. Louisiana had the best names by far of any state I had yet visited—both for people and for towns. D. R. Boney was the pastor of a church outside of Olla. Speedy Long was running for sheriff in Urania. In the town of Bunkie, I was urged to ELECT T-JOE PANICHELLA FOR SHERIFF. Bogalusa. Opelousas. Natchitoches. It was as if a man with a mouthful of gumbo named every municipality in Loozie-Anna.

After several hours of driving, I at long last approached New Or-

leans. Thank goodness. For the last hour, the sun had been sinking behind trees that dripped Spanish moss like funeral crepe, and ominous
insect and amphibian noises began rising out of the bayou, and I generally felt afraid until I had crossed Lake Pontchartrain via the Huey Long
Bridge and was ensconced in the French Quarter. At which time I felt
really afraid.

Ten minutes after parking the car, I saw a man with one leg projec-
tile-vomit into a gutter off Bourbon Street, which would have been unremarkable enough had the man not been wearing a T-shirt that said:

JESUS LOVES YOU

EVERYONE ELSE THINKS YOU'RE AN ASSHOLE

"That second sentence," a friend of mine later explained, "is the
difference between New Orleans and every other city in the world."

There is one other difference. The Big Easy, more than any other
American city, is the site of the Big Game: In 1995 New Orleans hosted
its eighth Super Bowl (more than any other city) *and* college football's
national championship game (the Sugar Bowl) in the span of three
weeks. Both games—to say nothing of numerous Final Fours—were
played in the Superdome, which was celebrating its twentieth year during the month of my visit with a gala anniversary concert by Liza Min-
nelli, which seemed oddly appropriate, as she was every Super Bowl
halftime show rolled into one overwrought performer.

So, on leave in the capital of the Big Game, I went Big-Game
hunting. I ducked into the Aft Deck, a nautically themed bar in the
Monteleone Hotel with great spoked ship-steering wheels overhead and
a TV showing Pittsburgh versus Miami on *Monday Night Football*.
"Lookit Mean Joe Greene," said the guy on the next stool, pointing to
the ex-Steeler lineman who was now the team's defensive coordinator.
"Still the biggest motherfucker on the field."

I nodded my agreement, on the off-chance that he was talking to
me. It was hard to say. The man's eyes were barely visible behind enor-

mous tinted glasses that looked like welding goggles. He appeared to be addressing all of his comments to the TV. When ABC promoed an upcoming Thursday night game, Welding Goggles said, "I got five hundred on that one." When the face of Dolphin receiver Irving Fryar filled the screen, Goggles said evenly, "Irving Fryar beat his wife."

A moment later, Goggles elaborated on the subject, saying, "I don't care *what* she does, you never hit your girlfriend, you know?" When I failed to respond immediately, he turned to regard me full in the face, and I nodded vigorously to the effect that, yes, domestic abuse was a terrible thing.

" 'Cause unless you're a total pussy," he continued, "you're gonna knock her out every time. And where does that get you?"

I was still nodding like a bobble-headed doll at Goggles when I realized that he was a lunatic, and quite possibly dangerous, and that he thought he and I were on the same page, wife-beating-wise.

Super Bowl Sunday is, allegedly, an annual orgy of domestic abuse in living rooms across America, for any number of reasons: Men are drinking heavily, gorging themselves on televised violence, and anxiously risking large sums of money on the game. Goggles was evidently doing all three of these things tonight, *plus* he was in New Orleans, the unofficial home of the Super Bowl. He struck me as a kind of poster child for the National Football League fan, and I left the bar before he just plain struck me or somebody else.

At another bar two blocks away, I fell into conversation with a woman who told me that she carried Mace for protection against the sundry Goggles types who evidently populate the frightening streets of New Orleans. Her friend said that pepper spray was more effective, specifically something called "jalapeño spray," which makes a mugger's eyeballs feel as though they have been plucked from his head and placed in a golf-course ball washer full of red-hot Pace picante sauce, then returned to their respective sockets. I took this as a hint and left the ladies to themselves.

In the morning, I drove west, through Lafayette, Louisiana, home of the Cajun Dome, the Icegators minor-league hockey team, and something called the Players Casino, whose highway billboard declared: BIG-GAME HUNTERS WANTED. I now officially fancied myself Big-Game Hunter and longed for a CB radio with which to broadcast my new handle: "Breaker 1-9, this is Big-Game Hunter. . . ."

I drove on into Texas, hunting big games.

To fully appreciate how ridiculously large Texas is, it is important to realize that you could enter the state at Orange on the eastern border and drive 847 miles to El Paso—roughly the distance from London to Minsk—*without leaving the state*. From Texas's northwest to southeast borders, the distance is even greater—closer to 1,000 miles—and one begins to despair of discovering any unifying theme about such a conti-nent-sized place and instead resigns one's self to collecting a series of postcards from the Lone Star State.

So, Greetings from Beaumont, home of a tiny brick building shaped like a L'Eggs pantyhose package. This was the Mildred (Babe) Didrikson Zaharias Museum, which answered the question "Just how quickly do we forget?"

Didrikson was a three-time All-America basketball player in col-lege, won two gold medals and a silver in track and field at the 1932 Olympics, then took up golf three years later and went on to win twelve major tournaments and seventy minor ones. Bobby Jones called her one of the world's ten best golfers of either gender, and the Associated Press named her the greatest female athlete of the first half of the twentieth century. Is it any wonder? Didrikson was a proficient tennis player, bowler, and roller skater, and she pitched and played third base and shortstop for the House of David baseball team managed by Grover Cleveland Alexander. And yet, the maiden name of this fabulous sports Babe was misspelled "Didriksen" throughout the biographical pamphlet given to museum visitors, who on this day were comprised entirely of one disheveled homeless person reeking of pine-tree air freshener: me.

There were a few tourists *outside* the museum, admiring the nee-dle-nosed F/RF 101 "Voodoo" Air Force fighter jet that was on displa on the grounds, and I half-expected the accompanying historical marker to tell me that "Didriksen" was the first person to break the sound barrier, or that she flew fifty-seven bombing missions in the war, or at the very least that she assembled the F/RF 101 "Voodoo" fighter jet from old golf clubs and spare roller-skate keys. But the plane turned out to be entirely un-Babe-related, and as a result, I drove away somehow disappointed by her stupendous achievements. It's the way you feel after winning $10,000 in the lottery and euphorically telling a friend that he'll never guess how much money you've just come into and having him reply, "A million dollars?"

An hour from Beaumont, I was absorbed into Greater Houston and eventually found myself crawling past the Astrodome, which rose like a fever blister in the suffocating heat of late afternoon. Conceived in the late 1950s and completed in 1965, the Astrodome was now so out of date as to look almost retro-hip—a shiny, metallic, *Jetsons*-like vision of a future that will never be.

It was all the brainchild of Judge Roy Hofheinz, the Houston huckster who, in the words of one contemporary, "made P. T. Barnum look like fourteen miles of bad road." For several years, the judge lived in a famously sybaritic apartment inside the dome, above the right-center field pavilion seats. In 1988, before workers gutted that residence, a Houston Astros publicist named Chuck Pool took the media through for one final tour. The late judge hadn't lived in those chambers for fifteen years, but parts of his crib remained eerily intact, as Pool later recalled to me. Rummaging through the rooms alone, Pool opened one door in the dark, flipped on a light, and was greeted by a disembodied head falling off a shelf: It was the overstuffed noggin of Chester Charge, the Astros' first mascot. Naturally, the experience scared Pool witless. Or something that rhymed with "witless."

Professional sports mascots have always terrified me, too—in the that clowns invariably frighten children. I'm not sure why this But something about mascots—their hydrocephalic faces fro- r—calls to mind those ventriloquists' dummies that always be evil in horror movies. Whatever the reason, I secretly cheered when, a few years ago, a dyspeptic sportswriter punched out the fuzzy green Seattle Supersonic mascot who repeatedly blocked his sight line at a basketball game.

I snapped out of this surreal reverie only to find myself in another one: I had driven into a Houston neighborhood in which all of the shop signs bore Asian characters. The only vaguely English words I saw were on a bar called Soccer+, on a health clinic offering IMMIGRATION PHYSI-CALS, at the Little Saigon supermarket, and in the Washateria Laundromat.

I fetched my fetid suitcase from the back of the Pathfinder and poured its steaming contents into a Washateria washing machine. Seven clean bullet holes whistled at me from the wall behind the machine. Iron bars crosshatched the front door and windows. The greatest danger to Washateria patrons, however, were evidently the Washateria patrons themselves. Several molded plastic chairs in cheddar-cheese orange lined the room, set off by one sturdy white superchair. Surveying the ample-assed washerwomen of Houston, I could easily imagine the atrocity that caused the Vietnamese owners of the Washateria to post the following hand-lettered sign on one wall:

> IF YOU ARE OVER 200 POUNDS, YOU
> NEED TO SIT IN WHITE CHAIR. INSTEAD
> OF ORANGE. WE ARE NOT RESPONSIBLE
> FOR ACCIDENT. (NO INSURANCE.)
> WASH AT OWN RISK.

Throwing caution to the wind, I washed.

And so I arrived freshly laundered in downtown Austin the following morning. The city's Sixth Street, a boulevard of alterna-bars and cyber-cafes, had been closed to traffic to accommodate a three-on-three basketball festival called Hoop It Up. The goateed slackers of Austin—so numerous that the film *Slackers* was shot here—were displaced for the day by three dozen half-court hoop games going on simultaneously.

The game raising the most pierced eyebrows, however, was not a three-on-three contest. It was taking place on the lone full court, where eight men were playing four-on-four with remarkable grace: They seemed to glide effortlessly toward the basket, as if on a moving sidewalk through a crowded airport. They were playing basketball, as it happened, on Rollerblades.

The tallest of these men, I learned from the public-address announcer, stood six-feet-ten—seven-feet-two in his skates. He was Tom LaGarde, former North Carolina Tar Heel, member of the 1976 Olympic basketball team, and six-year NBA journeyman for Denver, Seattle, New Jersey, and Dallas, where he averaged 14 points a game for the expansion Mavericks in 1980–1981. He was, according to the PA, "the inventor of roller basketball," the Edison of in-line hoops. To say that LaGarde looked like a giraffe on roller skates—and he did—is not to imply that he was awkward. On the contrary. It's just that he looked . . . odd: the proverbial fish on a bicycle.

"How did all this start?" LaGarde said afterward, repeating my question while sitting beneath a basket and drinking a beer. *"This* is how it all started." With his right index finger, he traced the S-shaped scars on either knee, the remnants of four separate knee surgeries. "I couldn't play basketball anymore," he continued, "and was looking for a way to not get fat." LaGarde, forty, regarded his minimal spare tire. "I realized I could skate thirty-five miles a day, but couldn't run a single mile. So I put an ad in the papers in New York City, where I live: 'Anyone interested in playing basketball on in-line skates?' That was 1993. I got a few responses and made up the rules as I went along."

He handed me a pamphlet, the rule booklet, which bore both the logo of his National Inline Basketball League and the organization's dubious come-on line: LET'S NIBBL. LaGarde was now touring the country playing NIBBL at street festivals such as this and performing during NBA halftime shows. "I'll be in Phoenix next week," he said.

"Having *played* in the NBA," I asked him, "do you feel any indignity working now as an NBA *halftime* act?"

"I worked on Wall Street as a bond trader for four years," LaGarde said in the same way a man might say he had spent four years in a POW camp. "Finally got out of there. I enjoy this. Little kids grow up on these things now. You should see 'em out there, doing three-sixties."

The sophistication of today's youth was not lost on me. At the corner of Sixth and Brazos, a man at a grill sold me an "Earl Campbell East Texas Sausage Smothered in Special Sauce." The food stand featured a blown-up photograph of the former University of Texas and Houston Oiler fullback wearing blue jeans and a denim shirt—the Western tuxedo—topped off by a black Stetson. In the photo, Campbell stood over an inflammatory grill. A boy who couldn't have been older than ten squinted at the poster and said, "That doesn't look like Earl Campbell."

"Duh!" said his big brother, who I took to be about twelve. "They're trying to project a certain image."

My immediate instinct was to mourn that kids were growing up too fast and too cynically. Until I realized that the older brother's media savvy was a good thing and ought to be encouraged. If only I had known, when *I* was in second grade, that Joe Namath was trying to "project a certain image"—wry, ironic, secure in his manhood—by wearing pantyhose in those TV commercials. I thought he just liked lazing about in women's underwear.

I left Austin at noon and headed north to Dallas, determined to catch the Cowboy game the following afternoon. Along the way I decided to stop at the Texas Sports Hall of Fame in Waco to ponder the wigged-out importance of football to Texans.

In Texas, one can hardly escape the Cowboys—from the moment I had entered the Lone Star State, near Beaumont, and heard a radio DJ call a woman on the phone and say: "Tammi, do you like Troy . . ."

What followed were thirty seconds of Tammi shrieking hysterically before the DJ was allowed to finish the sentence: "Do you like Troy Aikman? Because, Tammi, we're sending you to the Cowboys game on Sunday!"

At this, Tammi began wailing in the manner of Meg Ryan in the deli scene of *When Harry Met Sally*. She followed that with a brief interval of stunned silence, then prolonged weeping, which eventually gave way to a series of soft sobs.

I would have expected nothing less. After all, they publish *high school* football preview magazines in Texas. I once saw Nolan Ryan studying such a tome in the Texas Ranger clubhouse, then look up to ask his teammates: "Who do y'all like in Class 5A this year?"

Indeed, upon arrival in Austin on Friday night, I had snapped on the TV to see high school scores crawling across the bottom of the screen as if they were stock quotations or election returns. And the TV commercials! "I'm Earl Campbell," said the ubiquitous Earl Campbell, now in a purple polo shirt buttoned to the top. "And Chevy Country is *my* Austin car dealer!" The man was still trading on his name in Austin *twenty* years after winning his Heisman Trophy at Texas, which only hints at the grave importance of Longhorn football.

Lyndon Johnson telegrammed UT coach Darrell Royal the week before the Texas–Arkansas game in 1970:

AS A RANCHER, I AM WELL AWARE OF THE HOG AND CATTLE MARKET.
I THINK IT IS SIGNIFICANT THAT STEERS ARE UP AND HOGS ARE DOWN. I HAVE NO DOUBT THIS WILL BE THE CASE SATURDAY AFTERNOON.

Yikes. That Western Union relic hangs in the Texas Sports Hall of Fame, which I found sandwiched between the Chapel Hill Memorial Park and Campground (PERPETUAL CARE UNTIL THE END OF TIME) and the Waco Tourist Information Center. At the latter establishment, I could learn that 6,309 new vehicles were purchased for personal use in Waco in 1994, that the city's total civilian labor force was 100,700, and

that 18.52 percent of the population was aged five to seventeen. I was
told that Dr Pepper was invented downtown at the Old Corner Drugstore in 1886 and that 114 Waco-ites (Wackos?) were killed in a tornado
in 1953. But they could not, under any circumstances, give me directions
to the former site of the Branch Davidian compound leveled by federal
agents on April 19, 1993.

So I made do with the Texas Sports Hall of Fame, with its predict-
able assortment of ludicrously named local legends: Honk Irwin, Boody
Johnson, Putt Powell, Botchey Koch—all were inductees. In preparation
to see the Cowpokes, I venerated Tom Landry's hat and viewed a display on Texas Stadium, the Cowboys' home field, which opened in
1971 with a Billy Graham crusade. The arena's religious beginning—
almost literally a christening—was not accidental. Essentially a dome,
Texas Stadium has a large narrow hole cut in the top, like the coin slot
on a piggy bank. "Texans believe the hole is there," according to the
display at the Texas Sports Hall of Fame, "so that God can watch his
favorite team."

God's home team plays in the Dallas suburb of Irving, so I booked
a room there at the La Quinta Inn—*La Quinta* being Spanish for "next
to Denny's." And still it took more than an hour to get to Texas Stadium, where 64,605 Cowboy fans were attempting to convey themselves through what appeared to be two parking-lot entrances. Eventually, I made my way to remote Lot 17-C—about the same distance from
the stadium as the La Quinta Inn—where I parked next to a silver van
spray-painted on one side with the Noel Cowardesque notation BUDDY
RYAN IS A STUPID FAG! Ryan was the coach of the Arizona Cardinals, the
afternoon's opponent. On the other side of the van were sprayed the
words FUQUE THE NINER'S, a sentence that complied with local public-
decency laws, if not the laws of spelling.

No such decorum inhibited the guy in the FUCK YOU, I'M FROM
TEXAS T-shirt. He enjoyed a pregame barley while leaning on his car,
whose formidable soundcheck-at-Altamont speakers boomed the coun-

try anthem *God Bless Texas*. I heard it throughout my mile-long walk to the stadium: *"Mmmmmmmmm . . . God bless Texas."*

The Cowboys and their fans brilliantly co-opted the themes of God and country: The 'Boys were not merely "God's favorite team," but also, famously, America's Team. During the national anthem, the crowd sang "whose broad stripes and bright *STARS!*", shouting this last word as homage to the Cowboys' logo.

The national anthem was sung by a mononym Latino superstar named Emilo, and the crowd was informed that "Emilo will be appearing after the game in the American Express Corral Tent." Shortly after, another announcement was made: "Free bottles of Pepsi will be handed out as you leave the stadium at the conclusion of the game."

This was the handiwork of Jerry Jones, the Cowboys' owner, who signed exclusive deals with Pepsi, American Express, and Nike in defiance of the NFL's licensing agreements with their competitors. He told the league, in so many words, "Fuck you, I'm from Texas." A three-sided sandwich board bearing Nike logos was suspended by wires above the fifty-yard line at Texas Stadium, and in the first quarter Jones himself materialized in the press box, trailed by a young lady who handed out complimentary Nike coffee mugs to we, the assembled scribes. "If Nike wants to give us something," bitched the grizzled *USA Today* writer next to me, "they should give us shoes." He was eating a free hot dog and drinking a free soda as he said this.

After a moment, Cowboy fans seated directly in front of the press box took notice of Jones and turned around to regard him as if he were a tropical fish in an aquarium. "JERRY! JER-*RY!*" called a guy in a T-shirt that read WENT ON VACATION, LEFT ON PROBATION. In response, Jones pantomimed a pistol shot with his index finger. He looked like Sinatra playing The Sands. A woman shrieked at Jones while pointing at her own chest. She was wearing a shirt with a Cowboy logo on one breast and Pepsi and Nike logos sharing the other. "Oh, that's great!" said Jerry, giving a thumbs-up. "That's beautiful."

The afternoon passed in a silver-and-blue blur: I remember Emmitt Smith running all over Arizona, and Jones pointing and winking and shooting fingers at fans, and a biplane overhead pulling a banner that read RAMSES: ROLL ON ONE, and my Nike mug instructing me to JUST DO IT, and the Dallas Cowboy cheerleaders high-kicking and the woman with corporate logos on her breasts and my heart going like mad and yes I said yes I will Yes. . . .

Sorry. For some reason, I craved a cigarette after the game (a 34–20 Cowboy victory), but, alas, a sign at the end of the tunnel leading from the home locker room to the Texas Stadium turf admonished NO SMOKING ON THE FIELD! Most stadiums have a sign in a similar place that reads PLAY LIKE A CHAMPION TODAY! or some such motivational sentiment. But these were the decadent Dallas Cowboys, who evidently need a weekly reminder that their narcotics are not allowed on the field of play.

The Cowboys' locker room was no less unusual, a place of bizarre postgame rituals. Offensive linemen were thronged by reporters, while quarterback Troy Aikman sat alone at his locker, unbothered. (Aikman, as everybody but me seemed to know, didn't speak after games; he held a formal press conference on the Monday afterward.) Stars Michael Irvin and Deion Sanders *did* speak, addressing reporters while standing atop locker stools, ranting and gesticulating like the lunatics on Speakers' Corner in London.

Offensive lineman Nate Newton also addressed the press, but somewhat more coyly than was his usual custom. Officially listed at (cough, cough) 335 pounds, Newton had become a star through his stomach. "Fat helped me get into this league," he once said in a story I wrote on fat guys in the NFL. "And it gets me attention. It's all you guys write about: fat, fat, fat. Some people think I'm so fat that they have to see it for themselves. So they hire me for a personal appearance and pay me lots of money so they can see how fat I am." (In other words: No gut, no glory.)

"Fat on fat" is how Newton described blocking 335-pound William (The Refrigerator) Perry. "If we rub up against each other the wrong way, we'll start a grease fire."

The man was funny. But as I say, Newton was not his usual glib self on this day. "What are *you* lookin' at?" he asked a radio microphone holder who was staring at Newton's hat. It was a baseball cap with 1-900-RUN NEWT across the crown. "That's my hotline," Newton said. "That's where I give people the real deal on the game. I'm just givin' y'all the jack-around here. You want the good stuff, it's $1.25 for the first minute, $1.61 after that. As soon as I finish the obligations I have to the media as an NFL player, it goes into effect—thirty or forty minutes after the game." Indeed, all of the Cowboys had such capitalist instincts—virtually every one of them had their own local radio or television show. Jerry Jones had taught them well.

Newton agreed that Cowboy games—with Jerry and the cheerleaders and the condom-bearing biplanes—could be occasions for sensory overload. "You go out on that football field," he said, "and two million things are in your head."

But daily life in Dallas for a Cowboy star was occasion for sensory overload, too, was it not? I remarked that things must be sweet indeed in Big D these days for a member of the Cowboys, and Newton replied: "It's good. You can't beat it. People are nice when you're winning. Everyone treats you good. I like it."

Was this just the jack-around, or was this the real deal? I considered calling 1-900-RUN-NEWT, but Newt himself finally conceded that life was more than "good" for a Cowboy star in Dallas. "Life is sweet, man," he said convincingly. "So sweet. I gotta make sure I don't get a cavity."

Life was sweet. My relentless pursuit of leisure had now covered fourteen thousand miles of America, and October was suddenly on me like Nate Newton on a wicker chair. It was my plan to hole up in Minneapolis and hibernate through the winter, then resume my travels in the West come spring. So I now found myself in the even more enviable position of taking a vacation from my vacation. Home was just up the road.

You can drive from Dallas to Minneapolis without so much as using your turn signal, and, alas, many people do. Interstate 35 runs from Laredo on the Tex–Mex border to Duluth, passing through Oklahoma

City, Kansas City, Des Moines, and Minneapolis. I-35 has been called "the nation's spinal cord," and given the road's condition, America has some serious neurological disorders. The road had more rutting than most *National Geographic* documentaries.

DISCOVER THE EXCELLENCE said a sign at the Oklahoma border, and I wondered if this was meant as a challenge, like finding a small item in a scavenger hunt. For as I drove north, taking in Oklahoma's entrepreneurial evangelists (Oral Roberts University) and envangelical entrepreneurs (JESUS SETS CAPTIVES FREE—JOE BOB BAIL BONDS read a billboard near Stillwater) I had yet to find the excellence hidden somewhere in the Sooner State.

That changed in Stillwater, where I had dinner with Professor John Rooney, Jr., head of the Department of Geography at Oklahoma State University. Rooney was a "sports geographer" and coauthor (with Georgia State geographer Richard Pillsbury) of *The Atlas of American Sport*, a scholarly study of the regional fault lines and commonalities among sports fans and participants in America.

Rooney argued that "organization" is what distinguishes American sports from the rest of the world—there are, he noted, 123 boating and sailing associations in the United States—and that our need for organization could be explained in turn by "our overwhelming need to belong." This need, he claimed convincingly, explained why sandlot baseball has all but ceased to exist, replaced by Little League and T-ball teams that put children in smart uniforms as early as age five. Wearing a uniform, in fact, may be the first way in which children begin to emulate professional athletes, which strikes me as a pretty good argument against uniforms.

Rooney sent me packing with a copy of his *Atlas*, from which I gleaned untold oddities: Los Angeles County has the highest concentration of rugby teams in the United States; New Mexico, Arizona, and Utah are home, inexplicably, to the most Ping-Pong players per capita; similarly, Michigan, Wisconsin, Minnesota, North Dakota, South Dakota, and Nebraska make up a kind of Bowling Belt, boasting the densest memberships in the American Bowling Congress, which has some very dense members indeed.

The biggest American sports organization of them all, the National Collegiate Athletic Association, had its headquarters just off I-35 in Overland Park, Kansas. I made my way there via Matfield Green, an I-35 town distinguished by its roadside marker commemorating the events of March 31, 1931, when a plane carrying Knute Rockne crashed THREE MILES NORTHWEST OF THIS SITE IN THE BEAUTIFUL KANSAS FLINT HILLS.

Sure enough, in the distance were the wheat-colored speed bumps that Kansans called "hills," but the stone marker to Rockne's memory was behind a rest-stop Hardee's—with the attendant odors, insects, and Rorschach pavement stains that the area behind a rest-stop Hardee's attracts. It was bad enough, I thought, to have your life abruptly ended on a windswept plain off the Kansas Turnpike. But to have the tragedy serve, forever, to momentarily divert truckers intending only to empty their bladders and gorge themselves on curly fries, well, that seemed downright undignified.

So did the news, which came across my radio as I returned to I-35, that a University of Kentucky football walk-on, burned beyond recognition in a fire, was now being investigated by the NCAA over a possible movie deal for his life story.

The National Collegiate 'Arassment Association was famous for its picayune rules. At 512 pages, the NCAA rule book was larger than your typical Tom Clancy—and only marginally more readable. Article 3, Section 2, Subsection 5, Paragraph 6 of the NCAA Constitution, to give you just a whiff of the writing style, was headed "Reinstatement of Terminated Member" and dealt with . . . what exactly? The surgery performed on John Wayne Bobbitt?

I would have loved to have asked someone in charge, but a spontaneous drop-in on the powers that be at NCAA headquarters—in the tradition of Roger & Me or David Letterman's flower delivery to General Electric executives—proved impossible. The office building, at 6201 College Boulevard in suburban Kansas City, was accessible only by electronic key card. A lobby receptionist said that "visitors" were welcome to "visit the visitors' center" around the corner, but the office floors were, again, off-limits.

Months later, while visiting NCAA headquarters on assignment from *SI*, I learned why: Lunatics popped by frequently. "Somebody once showed up downstairs claiming to be a schizophrenic," said Bill Hancock, the man in charge of the NCAA men's basketball tournament. "He had played four years of college athletics. And he wanted four more years of eligibility. You know, for his other personality."

So I spent my visit visiting the visitors' center. It housed an interactive NCAA museum, the possibilities of which intrigued me: An audioanimatronic Jerry Tarkanian? "Probates of the Caribbean"?

No. It was just another Bataan Death March of a museum, the kind that makes your whole body go limp and fall to the floor with boredom, like you did as a kid while you were waiting in line with your mother at the bank. I was reading a recap of the collegiate lacrosse championships when I suddenly felt myself spinning to the floor with ennui. I stepped outside for some air, saw my car in the lot, sprinted to it, and drove the eight hours to Minneapolis in six. It was time to give sports a bit of a rest. It was time to go home.

Of course, I didn't *have* a home, so I drove to the house I was raised in, where my father still lived, the one that will be called my "boyhood home" if I'm ever elected President. My room was preserved as if in a museum—there ought to have been a velvet rope across the doorway—what with the Minnesota Vikings switch plate still over the light switch and the Reds and Twins pennants on the wall.

Out my old bedroom window I could still see the red neon sign of the Radisson South Hotel. Viking defensive tackle Keith Millard was arrested there in 1986 on a charge (later dropped) of making "terroristic threats." He allegedly told a policeman responding to a disorderly conduct call, "My arms are more powerful than your gun," thus giving new meaning to the phrase "armed and dangerous."

Next door to the Radisson was the Hotel Sofitel, whose French name belied its role in American history. In 1979, in the storied lounge of the Sofitel, then known as Hotel de France, Billy Martin punched out a marshmallow salesman. Cocktail umbrellas there still fly at half-staff for the late Yankee skipper.

Both hotels were on the 494 Strip, a twelve-mile stretch of Interstate 494, which runs a few miles east to where Metropolitan Stadium once stood. During a Twins game at the Met on the evening of August 25, 1970, public-address announcer Bob Casey was informed by police that a bomb threat had been phoned in. Could Casey clear the stadium without creating a panic? He could, he assured the cops. "Ladies and gentlemen," boomed his distinctive voice, "may I have your attention, please. There will be an explosion at nine P.M." (I.e., *run for your lives!*) It was said that my hero, Twins catcher George Mitterwald, fled next door to the Thunderbird Motel, where he sat out the forty-minute delay at the bar, still dressed in full armor, nursing a drink and waiting for a cataclysmic blast that never came.

Or did it? A demolition crew blew the yard to smithereens when the Twins and Vikings moved indoors. And erected in its place was the nation's largest shopping mall, the seventy-eight-acre Mall of America, which will no doubt be the name of our republic one day.

18

Spring came. My last act before embarking for the West was to buy a shiny new hardshell suitcase the size of a steamer trunk, the kind that in other circumstances might look good adorned by odd-shaped stickers reading VENEZIA and HOTEL METROPOLE.

"Are you going on a long trip?" asked the white-haired woman who sold me the case in a suburban shop. When I said yes, she clapped her hands together and held them there, as if in prayer. "How wonderful," she sighed. "How *won*derful."

I slashed across Iowa in a blur, resisting the exits for Van Meter (BOB FELLER'S HOMETOWN), Winterset (JOHN WAYNE'S BIRTHPLACE), and Burchinal (LIKE URINAL, BUT WITH THREE EXTRA LETTERS), arriving at dusk at my sister's apartment in Omaha, where she was a Creighton University medical student.

After a dinner of corn-fed beef, we repaired to a place called Homy's (CHEAP LIQUOR CHEEP flashed its neon sign), regretting that no frowning Frenchmen were there to see us swig champagne dispensed from a CO_2 canister. Throughout the evening, med students told war stories that invariably ended with a male patient telling an emergency room doctor, "I don't *want* you to remove it—just replace the batteries." And I thought: Steak, vulgarity, and "cheap liquor cheep"—I've arrived, at last, in the Old West.

To honor the men and women who settled this frontier, I drove west across Nebraska in the morning to America's original sports bar, a place of legendary and longstanding political incorrectness that went by a variety of names: OLE'S BIG GAME LOUNGE, 200 MOUNTS read one rotting highway billboard; OLE'S BIG GAME LOUNGE & GRILL touted another, slightly newer sign up the road. By the time I arrived in the town of Paxton and parked between Swede's Lounge and the American Legion hall, I saw yet another, grander name on the bar: OLE'S BIG GAME STEAKHOUSE & LOUNGE.

I swallowed hard and entered. A sign above the door said SMOKING IS PERMITTED IN THIS ENTIRE ESTABLISHMENT. *Permitted?* It was evidently compulsory. Just inside the door I glimpsed, through cumulus clouds of Camel smoke, an eleven-foot, 1,500-pound polar bear menacing me from its hind legs. TAKEN BY OLE HERSTEDT, MARCH 12, 1969, ON THE CHUKCHI SEA read a tasteful inscription inside the glass case that housed the angry bear—so that it looked to be attempting an escape from a carnival dunk tank. A nearby black-and-white photograph showed a barrel-chested man with a rifle standing over the fallen bear in Alaska; another showed the same man, now wearing an apron, atop a stepladder in this very bar, pouring champagne into the taxidermied bear's open mouth.

The jovial man in the photographs was Rosser O. (Ole) Herstedt. On August 9, 1933, Ole opened his Big Game Lounge, waiting until

12:01 A.M. to do so—a full minute after Prohibition had ended. The first
beer kegs were carried by Union Pacific railroad to nearby North Platte
and from there conveyed to Ole's in a school bus. Within five years, Ole
had begun to fill his lounge with trophies from his worldwide killing
sprees—a crass menagerie.

So here was a bare-chested Ole, square body and square haircut
squarely framed in a photo, pretending to stab a leopard he had already
shot, while the dead animal was made to look like he was mauling the
hunter.

The head of a 15,000-pound elephant—its trunk raised in full
trumpet, its ears the size of on-deck circles—jutted from the wood paneling above an upright piano. It appeared to be stampeding through the
wall, as in a beer commercial. Its tusks, five feet of ivory, were on either
side of the fireplace.

"Sometimes people complain," bartender Brent Gries said when I
asked what visitors made of the place. "Animal-rights people. Someone
will ask, 'What did the fawn think when her mother was shot?' The one
we get the most complaints about is the American eagle." Above a row
of Bacardi bottles on the back bar soared an American golden eagle that
Ole bagged in 1940. "That's probably the worst," Brent said, thinking
aloud. "We probably shouldn't have that up there." He paused. "We
should put that away," he said again, leaving the eagle right where it
was.

Gries and his friend Tim Holzfaster bought the bar eight years ago
from Ole, who was now ninety-three and living nearby in the evocative
town of Ogallala, uninterviewable and incapacitated by a wrecked hip. A
couple of years ago, two guys who hunt pheasant in Wyoming tried to
buy the Big Game Lounge and transport its contents to Myrtle Beach,
South Carolina, where the mounts would have fit right in on the garish
Grand Strand. "But we thought it'd be a shame to lose our claim to
fame," said Holzfaster.

And famous it was. Knute Rockne was a regular (his handsome
photo hung next to the men's room) and so was Jack Dempsey, whose
autographed autobiography was around here somewhere. USC football

coach John McKay made it to this no-man's-land in the Nebraska panhandle. Dodger great Don Drysdale did, too. Nebraska Senator Bob Ker-
rey tended the bar one night.

That ornate back bar was lifted wholesale from the Frontier Hotel
in Cheyenne, where it served frontiersmen from the 1880s until Ole
took it in lieu of payment for pitching in a semipro baseball game. Ole
was what they used to call a "sportsman," blowing away dik-dik (a tiny
African deer), Barbary and bighorn sheep, bull elk and red fox, warthog
and wildebeest, Grant's gazelle and greater kudu—then rearranging
them in the unnatural habitat of his lounge, so that a jaguar now mauled
a python behind the bar, a scene that looked almost as authentic as its
neighboring tableau: a team of plastic Budweiser Clydesdales slowly rotating around a lamp.

Looking at the 1950 photo of Ole with his Cree guide "on Bitch
Mountain, Yukon," or at the '66 image of him drinking from a shell-like
cup with a wildly Afroed "Somali Bushman" guide in Africa, one real-
izes that Ole didn't care dik-dik if he offended people.

"What one thing most needs to be done in the state or nation?" he
was once asked by the Omaha *World-Herald*.

"Have a hangman's platform and guillotine in front of every county
seat," replied Ole. If he thought criminals executed in the state of Nebraska should then be stuffed and mounted in sports bars, he didn't say.
But there *were* some local mounts in Ole's.

"When someone asks if we have any local mounts," Gries said, "I
always point up there." Above the back bar were six 1940s-era pinups of
naked women.

As he spoke, a man walked in with an old tank-style vacuum
cleaner with hose and sundry attachments. I asked what he was doing.
"Dustin' the mammals," he said.

"We're supposed to vacuum them once a month," said Gries, "but
we don't do it as often as we should."

Most of the money required for animal upkeep had already been
spent on animal downkeep—that is, on killing them in the first place. "If
Ole had a dime, he spent it," Brent said. "He always said he could do all

his hunting on three or four thousand dollars a year, that there was no sense in saving it. He never really had any money. And, of course, he had to pay for the mounting."

I was sitting at the bar. Gries asked if I had ever interviewed any Colorado Rockies. I told him that I had and that I was heading next to Coors Field in Denver to sample their Rocky Mountain oysters, the Western delicacy of deep-fried bull testicles.

Gries said he had some frozen RMOs in back and could fry me up some right here. "They're not bad," he said, "if you don't think about what you're eating. They're not round. They look like chicken fingers." And, of course, people always said they tasted like chicken.

"You know what G. Gordon Liddy said when they asked him what rat tasted like?" I asked Gries. "He said, 'A lot like squirrel.' "

Fifteen minutes later, Gries served me the well-done RMOs. "I've never asked a customer how they wanted these cooked," he said. "Nobody has ever ordered them rare." I sat there drinking beer and eating bull's balls—they tasted, aptly enough, "gamy"—in a room full of big game, feeling very much like the Big-Game Hunter that I fancied myself to be in New Orleans.

"It's exciting," Gries said of tending bar at the Big Game Lounge. "Different people come through every day. I couldn't stand to work in a bar where it was the same people all the time. Yesterday two lesbians were sitting right there in Harley jackets. We got to talking and they just told me they were lesbians."

Imagine that. As I prepared to take my leave of Ole's, Tim Holzfaster suggested I leave a note in "Tom Allan's mailbox." Tom Allan was a longtime sports columnist for the *World-Herald* and frequent chronicler of Ole. His "mailbox" was the preserved head of a baboon resting atop the jukebox. "Ole said he shot the baboon because it reminded him of Tom Allan," Holzfaster said. "Ever since it's been 'Tom Allan's mailbox.' Whenever someone didn't pay a bar tab, Ole would stick the bill under the baboon head and make Tom Allan pay for it the next time he came in."

I signed a business card to Allan and left it under the monkey head.

On my way out the door, I signed the Ole's guest book, too. I leafed
back through page after page, looking for expressions of outrage, but
found none. In fact, most every visitor had written the same sentiment
in the "Comments" column. "Great food," they all scrawled. "I'm
STUFFED!!"

I had planned to eat my first Rocky Mountain oysters in Denver,
where people sometimes called them "swingin' steaks." But now, having
already sampled the indelicate delicacies at Ole's, I saw no need to do so
at Coors Field, where I would actually have to pay for them. (Turn your
head and cough up $5.50.)

The Colorado Rockies also offered their fans a brisket of buffalo
sandwich—don't ask for buffalo chips on the side—though hot dogs
were still the staple of cuisine at Coors Field and every other American
ballpark. Americans eat 20 billion hot dogs a year, which works out to
sixty sausages per citizen. Or so said the National Hot Dog and Sausage
Council, a wiener-advocacy group which projected that 26 million
franks would be consumed this season in the twenty-eight major league
baseball parks alone. Laid end to end, those dogs would stretch from
Baltimore to Los Angeles, a sausage superhighway that now spirited me
into Denver.

On this beautiful spring day, the Broncos managed to dominate the
news. Owner Pat Bowlen wanted a new football stadium, and he wanted
taxpayers to bear most of its $220 million cost, lest he be forced to move
the team—all of which struck one state representative as an act of "ex-
tortion." Nevertheless, the proposal was narrowly approved by the Colorado House of Representatives just yesterday.

Or so I read in the *Rocky Mountain News*, standing with several
other cheap people in Denver's renowned Tattered Cover bookstore,
reading periodicals without paying for them. I put down the *News* and
browsed a copy of *The Independent on Sunday*, a London newspaper
published only forty-eight hours earlier. Above the fold on the front

page of *that* paper was a story on an altogether different way of treating arrogant football team owners.

> Supporters of Brighton & Hove Albion Football Club invaded their own pitch yesterday, wrecked both goals, hurled wooden stakes into the crowd, tried to storm the players' tunnel, and forced the abandonment of the Second Division match with York City.
>
> The fans were protesting at the decision by the clubs' directors to sell the Goldstone Ground, their home for 94 years . . . and share the Fratton Park ground of Portsmouth FC, 40 miles away. Goldstone is being sold to pay off debts of £6 million.
>
> Police had expected trouble. After the club's previous game against Carlisle, 600 fans invaded the pitch, calling for the resignation of David Bellotti, the chief executive. Early yesterday, supporters broke into the ground and painted "Sack the Board" across the pitch and directors' seats.
>
> Mr. Bellotti and his fellow directors were told by police it was in their best interests to stay away from the game, and before play started the 12,000-strong crowd heard an announcement that no directors were present. . . .

Now, I don't mean to suggest for a moment that American fans invade their stadiums and menace team owners with wooden stakes—unless that owner is George Steinbrenner. I'm only saying that, in England, teams seldom move. They do not, near as I can tell, blithely demand £100 million of public money after milking a region for years.

I presume that English owners *are* parasitic bloodsuckers, just as they are in the States. At least that would explain the wooden stakes.

19

New Mexico was on fire when I arrived, eleven thousand acres aflame in the Bandelier National Forest. Terrifying radio reports said that all low-grade plutonium at the Los Alamos nuclear research facility was being trucked away from the inferno in a frantic race against time. And wouldn't *that* be a shame: winning the Cold War, only to have a nuclear holocaust ignite because one German tourist failed to piss on his camp-fire?

Which was, according to news reports, how the latest blaze began. Air tankers buzzed the forest, dropping a red fire-retardant slurry that looked alarmingly like chili powder. Helicopters scooped water from Cochiti Lake and loosed that payload on the fires. *USA Today* said that this was International Scuba Day, and I couldn't help but think of that most excellent urban legend, in which the crispy corpse of a diver—wearing wetsuit, snorkel, and mask—is found in a treetop in a burnt-out forest.

It was an oddly pleasing image—a man swimming peacefully, gazing at colorful fish, suddenly scooped from the water by a helicopter's water basket and dropped, from a great height, on a raging inferno—and it stayed with me all the way to Santa Fe.

Santa Fe was one big adobe-a-go-go. Every building was beige and ice-cube-shaped and made of adobe, or some faux adobe wonder substance. Every adobe storefront bore a sign beseeching me to PLEASE WIPE SHOES BEFORE ENTERING. Sidewalk signs warned NO DOGS, NO SKATEBOARDS, NO BIKES ALLOWED. When my car phone suddenly rang with an electronic sheep bleat, I assumed it was the Santa Fe police, telling me to stop picking my nose.

But it was an editor at *SI*, asking me to cover the Bulls–Knicks NBA playoff game on Sunday. It was now Friday afternoon. I drove straight to the airport in Albuquerque, parked, purchased a ticket, and boarded a plane to Chicago. It was my first flight in months, and I actually missed it: the tray tables, the squawling babies, the inane airspeak of the flight crew.

"How do you take your coffee?" a flight attendant asked.

"Orally," I replied.

It was wonderful to be flying again.

This is what I awoke to on Saturday morning: Dennis Rodman, dressed in a silver lamé evening gown, pink feather boa, and full Tammy Faye Bakker makeup, straddling a Harley-Davidson in front of the Borders bookstore across from my Michigan Avenue hotel. Three dozen policemen, fourteen horses, and 1,500 members of the local literati awaiting a signature on Rodman's new book surrounded the great man. Travel was disorienting enough, I thought, without drawing my drapes open to this.

He was, of course, the unlikeliest athlete to be embraced by Chicago, a hard-consonant city of Ditkas and Butkuses and Mikitas. But embraced he was. A ten-year-old boy sat behind me on Sunday at the United Center, waving a sign that said DENNIS—MY MOM'S BRA FOR YOUR JERSEY.

The Bulls played poorly in the game. Scottie Pippen, Toni Kukoc, and Ron Harper couldn't hit snow if they fell off a chairlift, shooting a combined seven for thirty. Rodman's 12 rebounds showed up on the score sheet, but I missed them on the floor. And yet the Bulls won. By 7. Going away. Without ever trailing. They did this because Michael Jordan simply ate the Knicks alive. With fava beans. And a nice Chianti.

Jordan scored 44 of the Bulls' 91 points, winning the game "almost singlehandedly," in the words of Bulls coach Phil Jackson. This, despite suffering from lower-back spasms that twice forced Jordan to remove himself from the game. ("No," he said when asked afterward if he was ever in pain. "Well . . . *yeah.*") At various times, the Knicks threw three different defenders at him, occasionally all at once. "Harper was tapping my elbow all night," Jordan said of guard Derek Harper. "And the referees weren't looking at it." So he began driving and had his way on the inside for a while. A day that began with even Benny the Bull wearing eyeliner and a feather boa ended with Jordan once again the focus of Chicago.

I felt genuinely lucky to have seen him play—the most renowned athlete of our time in all of his glory—and likewise felt ridiculous to have thought I could take an epic sports road swing in America without contemplating Jordan.

As I stood in the bowels of the United Center, wondering if my possessions were still in my car in the Albuquerque airport parking lot—hell, wondering if the car itself were still there—Jordan approached. He was dressed in a somber black suit and black tie, the world's nattiest Blues Brother, and was flanked by six bodyguards. They fanned out on either side of him, like geese, forming a V that swept me from its path like the cowcatcher on a locomotive.

Six bodyguards? "Four to carry the litter," a New York *Daily News* writer once explained, "and two to scatter the rose petals." In fact, rose petals (or roses, anyway) really *were* scattered at the base of the bronze Jordan statue that seemed to soar outside the United Center.

I stayed an extra night in Chicago, crashing at my little brother's apartment. It was above the kind of bar featured in *Star Wars*, and you actually had to walk through the joint to get to the apartment. The bar's ceiling was my brother's floor, and that floor shook violently all evening from perpetual playings of George Thorogood & The Destroyers on the jukebox downstairs. I felt like one of those little tin players in that old electric football game, in which the men vibrated in twenty-two different directions at the flip of a switch.

I was drifting off to sleep on the sofa bed, soothed by the Magic Fingers of the vibrating floor, when my attention was drawn to the TV. *Late Night* host Conan O'Brien was chatting with Tom Brokaw about that celebrity softball game the two had played in—and I had attended—the previous summer in New Haven, Connecticut. "Michael Bolton had someone carrying a silk bag full of softball bats for him," O'Brien recalled.

"If the bats are like his music," Brokaw replied, "they were somebody else's."

I softly snickered myself to sleep.

G od bless the good people of Albuquerque, who didn't steal my car or anything inside it. I returned their kindness by leaving the state immediately, crossing the continental divide at Continental Divide, joining Route 66 in Gallup, and falling in behind a flatbed bearing stickers reading: I LOVE ANIMALS—THEY'RE DELICIOUS! and FEED THE HUNGRY—SCREW THE HORNY!

Just across the Arizona border, I entered the Painted Desert. My goodness. The sandstone buttes were a surface-of-Mars red—the same color as the fire-retardant slurry falllng from the sky in New Mexico. Viewed in the narrow slot of my rearview, the landscape looked like a letter-boxed movie in Panavision. I had never been out here before, and yet it all looked so familiar: The red rock, the stone-washed sky . . . they were on the cover of the dog-eared guidebook to the U.S.A., published in Britain for Britons, that lay on the seat next to me.

Now I was driving in America, the America familiar from *Route 66* and Roadrunner cartoons. I had a deep and sudden longing to drive a Cadillac convertible with a hood ornament fashioned from steer horns. I have no idea why.

The roadside cacti looked like football referees signaling a made field goal. Or they did to me, anyway. And no wonder. I had been in Arizona twelve weeks earlier, flying into Phoenix for Super Bowl XXX, Dallas versus Pittsburgh. I had to attend the Super Bowl, to witness its orgies of hype and tripe, if I were to adequately cover sports in America. I was not disappointed.

In the most appropriate marketing marriage imaginable, every person attending Super Bowl XXX had received, upon entering Sun Devil Stadium in Tempe, a complimentary pair of Breathe Right nasal strips, designed "to prevent or reduce snoring." The last cure for snoring at the Super Bowl—Joe Namath—had not been available for twenty-seven years. But that was before the Super Bowl came to Phoenix—a city whose very name ended in Roman numerals—and once again received the dignity that such a spectacle deserved.

To be sure, the nasal strips were all that were free in Phoenix. As Deion Sanders said frequently that week, "If it don't make dollars, it don't make sense." After all, what's more American than free enterprise? "On Super Bowl Sunday," *The Arizona Republic* reported two days before the game, "Ron Kaczenski of R. N. Davis Cannabis and Hemp Co. will be selling 'SupherbBowl,' the unofficial marijuana of Super Bowl XXX." The NFL was displeased by this announcement, even though I heard Pittsburgh Steeler coaches talk openly of preparing "nickel-and-dime packages" during practice. Oh, and Sunday's in-stadium postgame concert was by the Doobie Brothers.

Speaking of practices, each one was covered by a single pool reporter assigned by the Professional Football Writers' Association of America, as if this were Desert Storm. One of the dispatches, posted for the more than three thousand correspondents representing 185 nations, was typically incisive and eloquent and vitally important: "Linebacker Chad Brown left practice twice, according to [coach Bill] Cowher, because 'he had the runs.' The nearest rest room was some two hundred yards away. 'Usually we have an outhouse near the practice field,' Cowher said."

Which brings me to Fred Flores of Gilbert, Arizona. On the Friday before the game, Flores won a pair of Super Bowl tickets from a Phoenix radio station. He did so by diving headfirst into a ton of cow shit.

And speaking of a ton of cow shit, that same day I endured Paul Tagliabue's State of the League Address—that's what they called it; I kid you not—in which the NFL commissioner said things like: "Our coaches engage each week in what can only be described as masterful chess matches of strategy." One such grandmaster was Cowboy coach Barry Switzer, who said he refused to let "periphial" matters distract him, who acknowledged "disparagies" between the Steelers and the Cowboys, but who hoped to win the "Orange Bowl" nonetheless. Playing Spassky to this Fischer was coach Cowher, who liked to "slobber and spit," in the words of Steeler linebacker Kevin Greene.

I liked Greene. He was from Anniston, Alabama, and I had seen several of his classic cars on display in the museum at Talladega Raceway. It was Greene who most movingly addressed the press in Phoenix. Sprinkling one press-conference homily with the words "dadgum," "numbnut," and "belly-power"—as in Nate Newton has a lot of "belly-power"—the long-haired Greene told a roomful of sportswriters: "I believe in America, the flag, freedom, and the fact that people have had to die over the years so that we can do what we're doing right now." Which was eating doughnuts in the ballroom of the Doubletree Resort and conducting interviews of epic banality.

Reporter: "Does your beard symbolize the roughness and ruggedness of the Steelers? And is that symbol the key to beating the Cowboys in Super Bowl XXX?"

Steeler offensive tackle Justin Strzelczyk: "I think my beard symbolizes that I don't like to shave."

Many of these *mots justes* were translated into Chinese, Danish, Dutch, Flemish, French, German, Italian, Japanese, Mandarin, Portuguese, Spanish, Swedish, and Navajo Indian, so that people in, say, Beijing would know what Sanders meant whenever he said, "I always give props to my momma."

For some players, this grew wearisome as the week wore on. His visor worn upside down like a papal mitre, Steeler fullback Bam Morris was asked by a Swedish radio reporter to "describe your running game to the people of Scandinavia." Exhibiting few symptoms of the Stockholm syndrome, in which hostages grow to love their captors, Bam confessed: "I'll be happy when I'm finished with y'all."

Not so for Cowboy receiver Michael Irvin, whose press-conference paean to teammate Emmitt Smith earlier in the week fairly demanded to be set off in verse:

> "This man would stand
> Right here in my face
> And say, 'You know I love you.'
> How strong our love is.
> Our love overrides everything.
> It overrides the inferiority complex
> That men have when they say,
> 'I love you.' "

Which brings me to the party that kicked off Super Bowl week. There, in the ballroom of the Hyatt Regency, the actor who said, "I love you, man," in the famous Bud Light commercials led the crowd in chanting that catchphrase. It was unspeakably poignant. Meanwhile, a sluggish and sloe-eyed Budweiser Clydesdale—"That horse looks drugged," insisted a professional wrangler who was present—stood by blinking dolefully as flashbulbs exploded in its face. The horse was reported to have urinated on the very spot in the ballroom from which Tagliabue would later give his State of the League Address.

For once, though, the party that *ended* Super Bowl week was more memorable. It took place outside the victorious Cowboys' locker room, where Irvin made yet another address. "In the last fo' years—I didn't say '*four* years,' I said *fo'* years; I'm layin' some brother on y'all—in the last fo' years, we done won trey rangs," he said.

A man sighed, no doubt having to translate this into Navajo Indian.

"Trey rangs," Irvin said helpfully. "That's 'three rings.' "

Scant weeks afterward, Irvin and Bam Morris were both busted in Texas on unrelated drug charges. You don't say.

20

I drove north on Highway 180 to the Grand Canyon, desperately hoping that I wouldn't fall into it. Loads of people do. Apparently, it's the vertigo-inducing vistas that prompt them to teeter right over the edge, which is the reason why—in movies, anyway—folks who cling to the ledges of tall buildings always tell each other, "Whatever you do, don't look down." So I went to the Grand Canyon and didn't look down. But I'm told it is breathtaking.

When I arrived at the South Rim in late afternoon, hikers were crossing the canyon on Silver Bridge. Mules, a ranger informed me, were obliged to use the Kaibab Suspension Bridge, because it's deck isn't slatted, and thus the beasts cannot look down to see the Colorado River raging below. As a result, they don't freak out and buck, sending you one vertical mile to the canyon floor, where you end your life in what must look from above like a small puff of white smoke, à la Wile E. Coyote. Remaining on the rim of the canyon is scarcely safer. PEOPLE DIE HERE FALLING FROM THE EDGE said a sign posted on the railing from which I awaited the sunset. MOST PEOPLE WHO DIE HAVE GONE BEYOND WALLS OR RAILS. And die they do. On average, one person a month takes a header into the Grand Canyon, leaving behind an equal number of eulogists who struggle to find an ennobling synonym for "imbecile."

And yet I could almost understand how it happens. For the Grand Canyon is not just immense and immensely beautiful, but its depthlessness swallows all sound and moves people to whisper in its presence. The effect is profoundly relaxing, almost hypnotic. When a tour bus lurched up beside me at dusk, air brakes sighing massively, and belched out two dozen elderly Scotsmen and women on a package holiday, I, the lone American among them, couldn't help but feel proud and oddly proprietorial. In thirty minutes, the sky exhibited every shade of eye shadow worn by waitresses in the Southwest—first turquoise, then blaze orange, then a kind of black-eye purple—and twenty-five people looked on wordlessly. When the last of the light disappeared, a wee red-faced man standing near me broke the silence. "Fag's out," sighed the Scotsman, as if the sun were the glowing tip of a cigarette now extinguished.

"Aye," said the man next to him. "Aye. That was a good one, that was."

I spoke by phone to my friend Jay Jennings, an editor at *Tennis* magazine, who told me that I'd find Andre Agassi's hair in a restaurant in Las Vegas.

"In the food?" I asked.

"On the wall," he replied. "His severed ponytail hangs on the wall."

Well, say no more. I drove to Vegas first thing in the morning, stopping only to take a tour of Hoover Dam, where my guide kept saying things like "I'll be your dam guide on your dam tour today, I hope you enjoyed the dam movie on the building of this dam place." Damn, he was annoying.

Anyway, ninety-six people died during the building of Hoover Dam, but none of them is entombed in the concrete, to the obvious disappointment of the tourist who asked that question (who just happened to be me). On the upside, you can, famously, drive across the dam, and walk across it, and even (though it is forbidden) hop up onto its precarious ledge, with its 796-foot drop. Better still, stenciled on that ledge is the message NO PETS ON DAM. You just know there's a good story behind *that*; alas, when I asked the tour guide what it was, he replied, "Dam good question, I wish I knew the dam answer." I soon abandoned any hope of conducting intelligent discourse with this man and—suitably prepared for what was to come—drove the thirty miles into Las Vegas, where plenty of people are buried in concrete.

At the third-largest hotel in the world—the 4,000-room, faux-medieval Excalibur—all staff are required to call guests "M'lord" or "M'lady." Or so said my guidebook. But they didn't call me any such thing when I checked in. Instead, I was greeted with a flier that read:

> HEAR YE! HEAR YE! HIS MAJESTY THE
> KING WOULD LIKE TO WELCOME EACH
> OF YOU TO THE LAND OF EXCALIBUR.
> HE HOPES YOU HAVE A ROYAL STAY
> AND WOULD LIKE TO REMIND YOU:
> LOCAL CALLS AND 800 NUMBERS HAVE
> A FIFTY-CENT CONNECT CHARGE.

Welcome to Vegas.

I ditched my bags in the room—M'lord, but it stunk; it was like living inside a lit cigar—and walked up the Strip to the Mirage, where I purchased twenty $1 tokens. I put the first in a $1 slot and pulled the lever. Nothing. I put in a second token, pulled the lever, and a double bar appeared in the first window, and then the second, and finally the third. There was silence for a beat, and then the machine began spitting coins. It sounded like hail on a tin roof.

A man standing to my left watched the machine paying out, and when I looked up—half-apologetically—I saw that he was Duke basketball coach Mike Krzykewski. I could scarcely believe it. He was shorter than I had pictured and wore the kind of short-sleeved, open-neck print shirt popularized by former Philippines President Ferdinand Marcos. But it *was* him. We made eye contact, and—recognizing that I recognized him—Krzykewski abruptly turned and disappeared among the Marcos-clad masses in the Mirage.

I would have followed, but a small pyramid of silver coins was piling up before me. I took this fortune—$100—and spent a good deal of it in the California Pizza Kitchen inside the casino. All the servers wore nametags identifying them not only by name, but by hometown—a remarkable escalation of waiter/waitee intimacy. My waitress was JEN, from DUNNELL, MINNESOTA. I told her that I was from Minneapolis, and she said that she used to live there. "You know what I miss most about Minneapolis?" Jen said. "Hanging out in bowling alleys. And I don't bowl. But you can do that in Minneapolis—hang out with friends in bowling alleys. You know what I mean?"

I knew exactly what she meant. "All the bowling alleys in Las Vegas are in casinos," she said, and the thought of hanging out in casinos without being paid to do so did not even bear contemplating. Which is why, after a mere five more consecutive hours of slot-jockeying, losing $200 and my mind one quarter at a time, I staggered next door to the shopping mall in Caesars Palace. Near an exact replica of Rome's Trevi Fountain was a shop offering a pair of Mike Tyson's sweat-stained fight trunks—presumably stripped from him as he left the ring—for $1,500. I inquired about Andre Agassi's ponytail and was told that it would hang in the All-Star Cafe, which was not due to open for another month yet.

Sadly, a great many Vegas attractions were yet-to-be-opened or under repair at the time of my visit. This made for some interesting

signs. DRAGON TEMPORARILY OUT OF SERVICE read a notice posted outside the Excalibur. And, at the Mirage: DUE TO REDESIGN, VOLCANO
INACTIVE UNTIL MAY.

I looked in on the sports book at Excalibur, at row upon row of
rumpled, cigar-smoking single men obsessing over baseball games, and
thought: Losers. They probably live in their cars. One man told me to
"always bet against black starting pitchers on the road," which was the
only sure thing in baseball. Racism aside, it was a statistically worthless
observation: There were, at the time of the conversation, five black starting pitchers in the major leagues.

Outside of the frenzied sports books—a daily sports lottery at the
Excalibur takes in $150,000 in thirty minutes—the athletic pursuits on
offer in Las Vegas were limited to trapeze artistry at Circus Circus and
jousting at Excalibur (TWO SHOWS KNIGHTLY). And yet the city was
crawling with college basketball coaches. Outside the Flamingo Hilton, I
spotted Mississippi State coach Richard Williams, who weeks earlier had
taken his Bulldogs to the Final Four. I was acquainted with Williams—
two summers ago, I spent a week touring Finland with him and his
players—and would have liked to have said hello. But he was across the
intersection from me, and crossing against the light on the 3000 block of
Las Vegas Boulevard was tantamount to crossing an active runway at
Heathrow. By the time the light changed, Williams was gone.

Too bad, because I wanted to know what college basketball coaches
found so attractive about Vegas. Or any sports celebrities, for that matter. Tyson lives in Vegas. Greg Maddux lives there, too. Dennis Rodman
practically does. I suppose they could repair there at the end of a pres-
sure-heavy season and fade into anonymity, while still being treated lav-
ishly when that suits them. This yin and yang is the essence of Las Vegas,
which has the most unlisted telephone numbers of any city in America
and is also the world's most conspicuous place to be seen.

It is a dichotomy best expressed on the marquee of the Little White
Chapel, the most famous wedding factory in Las Vegas, which sees a
wedding performed every five minutes, 365 days a year, in one of its
thirty-five chapels. The Little White Chapel's marquee—in addition to

boasting of its 24 HR DRIVE-UP WEDDING WINDOW, which can accommo-
date TAXIS, HANSOM CABS, BICYCLES, SEMIS, RVS, AND BUSES—promises
PRIVACY, while at the same time discreetly hollering: JOAN COLLINS/
MICHAEL JORDAN WAS MARRIED HERE!

As I drove out of Vegas, I couldn't help but wonder: They was?

Across the California border, in the aptly named town of Baker, it
was 103 degrees. Or so read the world's tallest thermometer—about the
height of an air-traffic control tower—which wiggled like a hula dancer
in the heat haze of midafternoon. Baker billed itself as THE GATEWAY TO
DEATH VALLEY, and it occurred to me as I gassed up there that spring
was fading, Death was coming, and the end of the continent was nigh. If
this was to be a journey of self-discovery, it was high time to discover
myself. That's right. Like so many others, I had come to California to
find myself.

Well, I found me. And in Anaheim, of all places. Who knew? At
the Arrowhead Pond hockey arena, I came face-to-face with Steve
Rushin. Or, rather, Steve Rucchin. He was a twenty-four-year-old left
wing for the Anaheim Mighty Ducks. I had been hearing his name—*my*
name—for the better part of a year on sportscasts, and each time I did, it
was as if I were watching my own highlights: "Steve Rucchin with the
game-winner!" I liked the sound of it, even if announcers couldn't seem
to settle on a single pronunciation for the surname.

So I introduced myself after a Ducks game. A native of London,
Ontario, Rucchin was in his first full season in the NHL. He said his
name properly rhymed with "smoochin'," whereas mine rhymed with
"flushin'." However, Rucchin said he was frequently called Rushin, just
as I am often called Rucchin.

Or Rusin. The Miami Heat have issued me a press credential under
the name Scott Rusin. The New York Rangers have accredited me, at
various times, as Steve Rushkin, Steve Ruskin, and—my personal favorite—Steve Puskin. In 1991 the surname on my NBA season media pass
read . . . RUCHIN. What is that—a Chinese transvestite?

"I get those all the time," Rucchin said of the misspellings and mispronunciations. "I get Rushin and Rutchin and Rooshin. Some of the pronunciations are so far out in left field that I can't even tell you what they are. People are always misspelling it with two *u*'s and one *c*. I don't know why. The name isn't that difficult."

But it is. "Dear Mr. Rushin" began a letter I once received from an *SI* subscriber. "Hello my name is Steve Rushin also, and I'm eleven years old. I live in Raleigh, North Carolina. I just thought it was neat to have the same name and SPELLED THE SAME, WOW!! Don't you hate how some people spell RUSHIN (Russian, Rusian, and there's plenty more). I play a lot of sports! I play soccer, baseball, basketball, and hopefully football, but you know moms."

I thought of the letter as I drifted to sleep in the Anaheim Marriott—and listened to the sports anchor on KNBC narrate Duck highlights. Every time Steve Rucchin's name came up, the anchor dutifully called him Steve Rooshin.

About a mile south of Disneyland is Belisle's, the best and most famous diner in all of baseball, where American League umpires meet to eat red meat. I went there for a late breakfast of pancakes the size of garbage-can lids. "You order an eclair there and it weighs, like, seven pounds," patron Roseanne Barr has said. Indeed, the "Texas-Style Breakfast" comes with, among other things, a dozen eggs (any style) and a twenty-six-ounce sirloin steak. It retails for $49.95. "The last time I ordered the meatloaf at Belisle's," California Angel trainer Rick Smith once told me, "my family ate for a week afterward. We had meatloaf burritos, meatloaf chili. I'm serious. The lemon meringue pie is the size of *that*." He pointed to a Gatorade jug in the Angel dugout.

Anaheim Stadium best expresses the blissed-out, vanity-plated ethos of major-league sports in California. I hied over to the Big A for that evening's Angels–Indians game, surveying the players' parking lot on the way in. 3XYROUT read the plates on a gray Dodge Ram van. I TRN 2 declared a blue Toyota Camry. STRIK 3 said a black Porsche. I LOVE DP confessed another car. Of course, if you honk at or wave to the celebrity drivers of these cars on the freeway, they will look annoyed, as if to say, "What a burden it is to be recognized in public."

I once found myself driving away from Candlestick Park in San Francisco, in postgame traffic on the 101 Freeway, as Giants star Barry Bonds puttered along next to me in the right lane at twenty-five miles an hour, an arena-ready car stereo causing his red Ferrari to pulsate like a human heart. He wore something tasteful and inconspicuous, like a canary yellow suit, and the Ferrari's top was down, and he rode about six inches off the ground so that every passing motorist could see into the vehicle, but he never once acknowledged the constant waves and cheers.

Cleveland fans dominated the Anaheim Stadium crowd. Visiting fans always do, given the park's proximity to Disneyland. In fact, actor Tom Hanks was wearing an Indians cap the day he happily snatched and deflated a beach ball that violated his airspace at The Big A, saying: "I've always wanted to do that." Who among us has not had the same impulse?

It was, as ever, a glorious evening in Orange County, and—as ever—the Halos lost. After the game, I sat in the emptied Angels' dugout waiting for a photographer friend of mine to pack up his equipment. There was nothing to do but to stare at the floor, a kaleidoscope of loogies hocked up by twenty-five ballplayers: tobacco chaws, sunflower-seed husks, snot rockets, and Bazooka bubble gum in every conceivable combination. By comparison, movie theater floors are hospital clean. A few young fans congregated at the edges of the dugout—thirteen-year-old girls flirting with batboys and thirteen-year-old boys craning to see inside the dugout. Five feet away, they talked about me as if I weren't there, as fans tend to do around athletes.

"Who's he?" one boy asked another.

"He's nobody," replied the friend.

"Not *exactly*," said the first kid. "If he's in the Angels' dugout, he's not exactly nobody."

To which his buddy replied: *"Whooaaa!* Look at all the goobers!"

When my friend, Angel photographer V. J. Lovero, finally finished packing, we repaired to a nearby sports bar for a late meal. Immediately upon entering, V.J. was waved at by a tall white-haired gentleman dining alone. I looked at the man. My heart leaped, then fell into my stomach, as if through a trapdoor. For it was him, my nemesis, a man I had searched for lo these last six years. The theme music to *The Good, the Bad, and the Ugly* began to play in my head, for I had found him. I had found Jerry Reuss.

Now an Angels broadcaster, Reuss had pitched for the Cardinals, Pirates, and Dodgers (among others) during an extraordinary big-league career that spanned four decades—the 1960s, 1970s, 1980s, and 1990s. The six-foot-five Reuss was nicknamed Q-Tip, for his cotton-swab shock of white hair.

Reuss didn't appear to know me, but he did know V.J. and was eager to talk with him about photography, one of the Q-Tip's avid interests. He insisted that we dine with him, and as I sat down, poker-faced, I told Reuss that we had met before, that I was a writer for *Sports Illustrated*, and that I was now writing a book about my experiences traveling the United States.

"*I've* written a book," he said. It was a guide to finding classic rock 'n' roll hits from the vinyl era on compact disc. I asked him what the highest-charting song still unavailable on CD was and he replied that it was *Mony Mony*, or *Wooly Bully*, or *Louie Louie*. Honestly, I can't remember which, for I was too preoccupied preparing to confront the Q-Tip with details of our previous meeting.

In the middle of dinner, a slightly drunk twenty-one-year-old approached the table and told Reuss that he vividly recalled watching the Tip's 1980 no-hitter for the Dodgers on TV, with his grandmother, who was also a big fan. Reuss mock-winced at the grandma reference, but thanked the guy and autographed a beer coaster to him.

This steered talk to baseball, and the Tip said that Disney—which owned the Angels—was considering renaming the club the Anaheim Almighty Angels, so as to have nominal symmetry (and synergy) with the company-owned Anaheim Mighty Ducks of the NHL. The Angels were rumored to be waiting to unveil their new uniforms in conjunction with the release of a Disney movie, the sequel to *Angels in the Outfield*. As I digested this news, it occurred to me that it was Disney chairman Michael Eisner, and not Anaheim Stadium, which ought to be nick-named The Big A.

As Reuss worked his way through a plate of Wiffle Fries, I began to mention a story I once wrote on the division-winning 1990 Pittsburgh Pirates. "I was on that team," Reuss said.

"I know," I told him. "That September you walked past me in the visitors' clubhouse at Wrigley Field, looked at my press credential, and said, ' "Working press"? That's sorta like "jumbo shrimp." ' "

"Or 'military intelligence,' " Reuss now replied, chewing a sand-wich.

"Or 'baseball scholarship,' " I added. "But that's not strictly the point."

"I said that to you?" Reuss laughed. "Sounds like me. Well, sorry about that." He grinned benignly.

The Tip never actually chloroformed me with his game socks, now that I thought of it, and indeed wasn't menacing me at all on that day in 1990. On the contrary, he was being friendly.

He now wore a WORKING PRESS tag as a member of the Angels broadcast crew. He had written a book and taken up photography. He was, it seemed to me, a hell of a nice guy—a *colleague* even—and he would go so far as to pick up the dinner check, an exceedingly rare act for a current or former professional athlete.

We literally broke bread, the pitcher and me. And though Reuss had been a starter, I felt closure. The referee-shirted waitress came by with a round of drinks on the house, and I had to admit to the Q-Tip: "Working press"—it was a bit like "jumbo shrimp," after all.

21

Los Angeles has baseball's most famous dog-and-kraut combination, if you no longer count Schottzie and Marge in Cincinnati. "Nothing is as famous as the Dodger Dog," noted Lon Rosenberg, general manager of concessions at Dodger Stadium. This is as it should be, for L.A. gave the world the hot-dog-shaped building (see Tail O' the Pup on San Vicente Boulevard) and frankophile movie stars: Marlene Dietrich's favorite meal was hot dogs and champagne, while Humphrey Bogart once said, "A hot dog at the game beats roast beef at the Ritz." You can just hear him, can't you?

One can only imagine what Bogie would have made of today's Dodger Stadium, where vendors hawk Evian water and sushi and where one particular vendor—Roger (The Peanut Man) Owens—collects $2,000 in advance orders from wealthy "season peanut-holders" who then don't have to reach for their wallets every time they call for nuts at the ballpark.

I called for this particular nut at the ballpark—I knew Owens and wanted to inquire as to the status of his unfinished autobiography, *Working for Peanuts!*—but never did spot him. So I set off up the coast, for another town in which a man was working for peanuts—or, rather, in which peanuts were working for him.

Santa Rosa, California—the home of Charles M. Schulz, creator of the comic strip *Peanuts*—was host to the world's best professional nine-ball pool players in the most lucrative pocket-billiards tournament in history. To get there, one drives north from L.A., clinging to the coastline on U.S. Highway 1, retracing the route of an historic 1977 family vacation, and feeling alternately homesick and carsick. For it was here, on the majestic Big Sur, that my little sister became explosively sick in the way-back section of our wood-paneled wagon, in the manner of one of those devices that applies stucco. My dad pulled over at a wayside, wiped up the mess with a pair of boxer shorts pulled from his suitcase, and tossed the entire affair from the cliffside and into the azure Pacific Ocean.

Years later, I like to think, the shorts washed up on the shore of an uncharted Pacific island, where the paisley, size-forty-two underpants of my father still fly as the flag of a proud but troubled nation.

Santa Rosa is the kind of middle-sized American town that isn't supposed to exist anymore, with a bustling independent business district full of bookstores and diners and movie houses and a public indoor skating rink called the Redwood Empire Arena that was built by Charles Schulz in 1969, when the rink that his children had been using closed down. Schulz is, of course, indescribably rich, but he's also a Minnesota native, a member of the U.S. Hockey Hall of Fame, and so he still eats breakfast rinkside most mornings. I didn't see the cartoonist there, but the rink itself made me feel at home, and I could see why Charlie Brown's creator would settle in Santa Rosa. People here, I had no doubt, still said, "Good grief."

So it was oddly appropriate that the city should host three dozen visiting pool sharks, for pool itself was a throwback to an earlier America. The (under)world of pocket billiards was once peopled by stylish legends, cartoonish men like Alvin (Titanic Thompson) Thomas. His eye was so sharp, it was said, that he could pitch a key into a lock from across a room and shoot bullets through washers flung into the sky. When not shooting pool, Rudolph (Minnesota Fats) Wanderone engaged in eating contests. Fats began one contest by swallowing an entire ham and telling his opponent that he wouldn't count it toward his total. That's what they say: Fats spotted the man a ham.

The first story I ever wrote for *Sports Illustrated* was on Willie Mosconi, fifteen-time world straight-pool champion who once ran 526 consecutive balls, calling the ball and pocket before every shot. "I never did miss," Mosconi told me. "I just got tired and quit." I loved these guys. They were the last remnants of that Runyonesque era around Broadway—commemorated *on* Broadway in the musical *Guys and Dolls*. And is it any wonder? The show's composer, Frank Loesser, was Mosconi's Army bunkmate.

Mosconi always wore a pocket square. Say that about the man: He knew how to fill a pocket with style. But when I walked into the Team Player's Billiard Club in Santa Rosa, there were no Runyonesque-looking old guys to be seen—nor anyone in formal wear, for that matter. In fact, that was precisely the problem with professional pool, I was told by today's players. "Pool is a *sport*," asserted five-time nine-ball world champion Allen Hopkins. "And how many sports are played in tuxedos?" That would be none, except for pool, which was always, in my mind, played by fat guys in . . .

"Tuxedos," sighed ESPN producer Bill Fitts, a grizzled patriarch of televised pool, in Santa Rosa to tape the tournament for the cable network. "They had something to do with pool's sinister image. Ever notice how underworld guys always wear a tux when they go out to kill somebody?"

I remarked that I hadn't really thought about it. But Fitts clearly had, and so the monkey suit was banned at this, the World Open Billiards Championship. Even in mufti, however, the pros appeared to be mob hitmen—and hitwomen—snapping open black leather cases and removing their two-piece custom cue sticks. Vivian Villareal of San Antonio, Texas, assembled hers as an assassin assembles a rifle. "It's worth fifteen thousand dollars," she said of her cue. "I take it with me to the bathroom on airplanes."

Chicks with sticks were all over the joint—and for good reason. Sixteen women would compete in nine ball over five days, the survivor to face the winner of the sixteen-strong men's bracket in a first-ever Battle of the Sexes on Saturday night. The champion of that match would pocket $80,000, the runner-up $60,000. These were believed to be the richest prizes in pocket-billiard history, and the thought of making such a bank shot had most of the world's best players holing up at the Day's Inn in downtown Santa Rosa.

CASH IN read the California plates on the Mercedes 230E parked beneath the street light in front of the poolroom, and thirty-two players of both genders had come to do just that. Reigning men's world champion Oliver Ortmann arrived shortly before I did at his own expense from his hometown of Munich, Germany, just to play *Einekleine* nine ball. He joined me for a beer at the poolroom's bar. "Pool is like a drug for me," shrugged the unassuming Ortmann, who manages a ninety-three-table poolroom at home. "I need it all the time."

Equally insatiable was Jeanette Lee, a quasisupermodel who shared the number-one ranking on the Women's Professional Billiard Association tour. Six years ago, the twenty-four-year-old Manhattan native walked into a Chelsea pool hall and saw an old man—"so smooth and graceful," she recalled—picking ball after ball off a green baize table, as if shooting crows on a telephone wire. Mesmerized by the *click* and *drop*, *click* and *drop*, Lee immediately began playing a hundred hours a week, taping her fingers together into a proper grip, or "bridge," before going to bed.

As a result: "She beats me from time to time," said Lee's husband of one week, the number-two men's seed, George Breedlove. George spent the seven years after high school hustling pool out of a motor home—"a '78 GMC Royale," he said regally—with his friend and partner Big John.

"What was Big John's last name?" I asked, taking notes.

"Big John," George said, "is all the name you need to know."

I asked George who taught him to play.

"Nobody taught me nothin' about the game," he said. "At fourteen, I walked into my first poolroom—Mr. and Mrs. Cue on the south side of Indianapolis—and the rest is history." Alas, so was George, eliminated in the first round of this tournament.

Steadily, the other favorites dropped, too, like balls from a table. The tour's top woman, Robin Dodson, fell in the quarterfinals, though hers was still "a story of victory," as she aptly put it herself. Dodson's astonishing recovery from a heroin habit in her twenties—at thirty-nine, she was now happily married and living in Westminster, California—had eight different movie producers waiting to film her life story. "I am a housewife, I have three children, and I love the Lord," said Dodson. "You'd never know I have a pool cue in the trunk of my car."

In fact, Dodson aspired to open a "Christian poolroom" in Orange County, insisting it was not an oxymoron along the lines of "working press." Likewise, George Breedlove had found Jesus and hadn't gambled since. Even the legendary Earl Strickland had gotten his own version of religion. "Ten years ago, I'd have had my hand in your pocket," said the four-time world nine-ball champion after buying me a beer.

"What changed you?" I asked.

"I got morals, for Chrissake."

He also got C. J. Wiley in the men's semifinal draw, which was too bad for Strickland, because all week long Wiley had been clearing tables like a busboy on commission. The owner of C.J.'s Sports Bar and Billiard

Club in Dallas, the thirty-one-year-old Wiley nevertheless said he seldom practices. "I put in all my time years ago, playing ten hours a day
when I was seventeen and eighteen," he said of his misspent youth in
Green City, Missouri (population 629).

A disproportionate number of pool greats came from infinitesimal
towns. Women's world champion Gerde Hoffstatter—who gave up an
Olympic fencing career for pool—came to Cali from Treichen, Austria,
which is "a very small town," she noted. Strickland was from Samson
County, North Carolina. "Me and Michael Jordan were born sixty miles
apart," Earl pointed out. "I got more talent than him, and he's got a
hundred million times more money than me. Figure *that* out."

No one else had the balls to complain about money in Santa Rosa.
"When I began playing pool in Sweden," said Ewa Mataya-Laurence,
the "Striking Viking" who was once featured on the cover of *The New
York Times Sunday Magazine*, "first prize in most tournaments was a
toaster. At one point, my mother had six toasters." The $313,000 prize
pool for this tournament was staked by ESPN, which taped the proceed-
ings and planned to parcel them out over forty hours of programming to
run throughout the coming year. For five straight days in Santa Rosa, the
cameras recorded nine-ball footage from 9 A.M. to midnight. It was like
some Danish porn sweatshop, replete with "Striking Vikings."

But the fact is, an invisible mass of Americans need their televised
pool. Or so the TV producer swore to me was the case. "You can throw
pool up against the Super Bowl and it will do quite well," insisted
ESPN's Fitts. "But the demographics . . ." His shudder led me to con-
clude that *Matlock* skewed younger.

Still, like the game's dress code, that was changing. Increasingly,
pool's biggest draws were young ladies instead of the old men I so admired. "Mosconi and Fats?" spat Lee when I raised those great names.
"That's *over.*" And yet, when I went to take a leak, I noticed that the pay
phones at Team Player's Billiard Club still bore the joint's previous
name: FATS BILLIARDS.

No matter. Each of these pros was a master at imparting spin, and
their spin on every conversation we had was: Professional pool players

are the equal of their counterparts in golf and tennis and ought to be given the same obsequious treatment as the superstars in those respective sports. "People should know me when I walk into a restaurant," said Allen Hopkins, bothered that he was going unbothered in the bar of this billiard hall. "I should be like Jack Nicklaus."

Indeed, Hopkins (who hatched idea for the Battle of the Sexes match) dreamed of a pool "Grand Slam" and spoke of a tour with "four majors," perhaps one in which the winner would wear a green baize blazer. Alas, the only national ink his sport regularly got was in the dictionary, under "miscue" and "dirty pool" and "behind the eight ball." If you ask Earl Strickland—and I did—it was no coincidence that pool produced the phrase "bad break."

"Ain't been nothin' but a struggle for me," the cuestick-skinny Strickland said of his chosen profession. "I'm thirty-four years old and feel like I'm three hundred and four. I've been livin' in dog years. I've been tormented, persecuted, and ridiculed, by my peers and by people who know nothing about the game. I'm in despair all the time. I'm depressed. I'm ill-mannered. *Why?* I'm a talented person. Jesus Christ, I'm a *very* talented person. There are billions of people on this planet, and it's hard to do something better than billions. But nobody cares.

"I've stood on the Great Wall of China, on top of the Eiffel Tower, at the Leaning Tower of Pisa, at the Berlin Wall," Strickland went on. He pulled a formal résumé from the briefcase that he carried and pointed to the list of countries he has visited by way of proof. "I've seen the Eight Wonders of the World," he said.

"I think there are only seven," I interjected, but Earl kept going.

"I've covered every inch of Japan, toured all of China. . . ."

Like a cheap cue tip, Strickland came unglued in the semifinals in Santa Rosa, leaving two less tortured geniuses to compete for the $80,000 top prize. "You have to see the difference between pool and life," stressed Ortmann, one of the men's finalists, referring obliquely to Strickland. "I realize that, away from the table, I am like any other asshole."

His opponent in the men's final was equally equanimitous. C. J.

Wiley told me he had a second-degree black belt in karate. "In true martial arts," he said, "strength comes from the mind and the body working together uniformly." Wiley showed that the same was true in nine ball, defeating Ortmann 7–5 in a "race to 7" format.

In the women's final, Vivian Villareal dispatched an accomplished English snooker player named Allison Fisher, 7–5, to set up what was hyped as "The Texas Tornado [Villareal] Versus the Fastest Gun in the West [Wiley] in a Loser-Leaves-Texas Death Match!" So the pool table was cleaned with a Dirt Devil hand vac—it is, evidently, pool's equivalent of the Zamboni—and Wiley broke the rack. He immediately cleared the table and pretty much did the same in 5 of the next 5 games to take a 6–1 lead in the race to 7.

Villareal managed to "run out" twice before Wiley could again, making her final margin of defeat a respectable 7–3. The thirty-year-old Villareal was not exactly Billie Jean King to Wiley's Bobby Riggs in this Battle of the Sexes, but then she figured to have other chances.

"The men have a twenty-year head start on the women," said Villareal, who first played pool while standing on a box in her *grandmother's* poolroom. "We'll catch up. Pool is not a strength game. It's a mental game. I play the table."

After Wiley had returned his cue to its snakeskin carrying case, he concurred that coed pool may be the game's future. "I own a poolroom and see so many couples come in," he said. "That is definitely where pool's grass roots are. And, professionally, I just like to see the best players in the world play each other competitively."

"Most of the men I talk to think it's a great idea," said newlywed George Breedlove. "And most of the men I talk to think the ladies don't have a chance."

His wife of one week loyally nodded her assent. Sort of. "My mother told me, 'Let the man think he's winning,' " Jeanette Lee said to me in a stage whisper, " 'you'll get along a lot better that way.' "

And then they all packed up and left Santa Rosa, and I did, too. And it occurred to me that I identified with these itinerant people, playing out of their '78 GMC Royales, their cue sticks in car trunks, their mind-numbing world travel. A scant few months after my visit to Santa Rosa, I would find myself in a flight lounge at Changi Airport in Singapore, reading—in *The South China Morning Post*, no less—about Earl Strickland's imminent appearance at something called the "World Nine-Ball Challenge" in Hong Kong.

22

Should some latter-day Gibbon write a *Decline and Fall of the American Sports Empire*, the twelve years just past would fill the first volume, with the passing of the Indianapolis 500, an annual World Series, the Baltimore Colts, the Cleveland Browns, meaningful college bowl games, heavyweight boxing and baseball seasons that opened on Opening Day, rather than the night before, if at all. Each of these was a fixture of the calendar or the culture as recently as 1984. Improbably, that now looked like a Golden Age.

America confers protective landmark status on her historic buildings and officially observes national holidays. She does this because her citizens, left to their own devices, cannot always be entrusted to preserve those institutions worth keeping. Alas, this same force of law does not bind the custodians of American sport. Which is why there will always be a Memorial Day weekend, but not an Indy 500 to mark it.

I drove north toward Portland, Oregon, through holiday weekend traffic, into a perpetual mist. It reminded me of the day that I embarked on this journey nine months earlier, through the same kind of mist in southern Minnesota. Oregon's version made me feel like the straight man in some cosmic comedy: as if God were doing a spit take toward me or spraying my car with a seltzer bottle.

I felt small and insignificant and badly used, and that had much to do with the week's big news: Racing's greatest spectacle, the Indianapolis 500, had been rendered ridiculous. On Sunday, the sport's biggest name—Andretti, Unser, Fittipaldi, et. al.–were performing in the inaugural U.S. 500 in Brooklyn, Michigan, while rookies comprised more than half the field at the Brickyard. And another one bit the dust. In cataloguing the endangered species of sports in America, one could now stamp EXTINCT across Indianapolis.

The Kentucky Derby and the Masters endured, to be sure. George Steinbrenner had not yet acted on his annual extortionist impulse to remove the Yankees from New York. But how many other institutions of stature and long standing remained?

The Super Bowl? Funny, just as the NFL season culminates with the Super Bowl, Indianapolis Motor Speedway president Tony George wanted his 500 to serve as the season-ending capstone to his new Indy Racing League. The Super Bowl analogy was his own. Race in the IRL, George told drivers of the existing CART, or do not race in the Indy 500. So they did not race in the Indy 500. It had come to this: a proud sports tradition wanting to emulate the bad-game, big-revenue, vulgarian Super Bowl. For the want of lucrative Roman numerals, Indy—with its eighty races dating back to 1911—had sacrificed itself. Our Gibbon, I thought while flipping channels in my Portland hotel room, would want to watch the videotape of actor and race fan Paul Newman, who asked with genuine perplexity on ESPN: "Where does all that tradition go?"

Newman was the kind of quaint relic who gave vastly of his time and personal fortune to charity and so he could not be expected to understand what moved today's rainmakers of American sport. "Where does all that tradition go?" It goes where Willie Sutton went: where the money is.

It has ever been so. But when Walter O'Malley moved the Dodgers from Brooklyn, he at least blew smoke about being motivated by something other than naked greed. The move had to do with America's Manifest Destiny in the West, right? Yeah, that was it. Free agency was *nominally* about "freedom," even if what it really meant was that, come 1997, Kevin Garnett would be "free" to reject a $103.5 million contract offer from the Minnesota Timberwolves and hold out for $126 million.

How "free" from any restrictions had our superstar athletes become? As the national news flickered in the dark on my hotel television set, I found it interesting that a group of tax-flouting Freemen, holed up for weeks against the FBI, were doing so in a town on the Great Plains that shared its name with the era's two biggest sport supernovas: The standoff was taking place in . . . Jordan, Montana.

The pretense that money was not the highest good in sports was finally dispensed with when Robert Irsay surreptitiously fled with his Colts, under cover of darkness, from the people who loved and supported them in Baltimore. Since then, owners had been free to wear their true thoughts on their sleeves—sometimes literally so, in the case of Marge Schott's famous Nazi armband.

As a result, franchise free agency, like personal free agency, had further frayed our institutions. When teams change cities as they once changed their managers and players change teams as if changing their uniforms, then only those uniforms remain constant from year to year. It is all that remains to root for. "Basically," Jerry Seinfeld has said, "we're rooting for laundry."

In fact, Seinfeld said that years ago, in that Golden Age when one could still cheer for unchanging laundry. In the week before I arrived in Portland, the Detroit Pistons introduced their new uniforms, logo, and color scheme: a tired teal to match the Florida Marlins, whose left field wall is called the Teal Monster, and the Charlotte Hornets, whose mascot is called the Man of Teal. (These are your new institutions, America.)

Days before the Pistons' announcement, my hometown Timber-wolves unveiled their new uniforms with a meaner Wolf logo. This was in lieu of keeping the *old* unis and putting meaner Wolves *in* them, a concept that would not have addressed the franchise's primary concern during its brief history: that there aren't enough sheep buying Wolves' clothing.

Which was why baseball and basketball teams were now wearing three or four different uniforms each season and why it was only a matter of time before American teams followed the lead of English soccer giants Manchester United—a.k.a. Merchandise United—the sartorial chameleons who, scant weeks before my visit to Portland, changed uniforms at *halftime* of a match.

It could happen on this side of the Arrowhead Pond, too. Our arenas and ballparks were once given ennobling names like Soldier Field, War Memorial, Veterans Stadium, and RFK. Remember? There were Forums and Coliseums that at least made nominal nods to the spectacles for which they were built.

If those arenas seemed archaic now, it was because today's build-ings were erected for corporate tenants, then named for them as well. And now older ballparks were being retrofit with new corporate names. The results ranged from the merely crass—evocative Candlestick Park becoming something called 3COM Park—to the downright Faustian. Of-ficials in my hometown briefly floated the idea of stripping the Hubert H. Humphrey Metrodome of its name and selling it to a high bidder. What the hell, Humphrey was dead.

So was Jack Murphy, a San Diego sportswriter who helped get that city's Jack Murphy Stadium built. It had recently been renamed Qualcomm Stadium. Dead, too, was Joe Robbie, which was why Florida Marlin and Miami Dolphin owner Wayne Huizenga could consider sell-ing the name of Joe Robbie Stadium to American Airlines. Instead, the name was sold to an apparel manufacturer, and Joe Robbie Stadium became Pro Player Stadium. If the numbers crunched right, Huizenga would also peddle the Lincoln Memorial to the folks at Lincoln-Mercury.

Whatever its name, that stadium had recently been named the host of the Federal Express Orange Bowl, which for decades had been played, oddly enough, *in* the Orange Bowl. But the NCAA demanded that the bowl move or be iced out of the lucrative annual rotation to host the national championship game. So, to remain as prestigious as the Tostitos Brand Tortilla Chip Fiesta Bowl, the grand old Orange Bowl abandoned the grand old Orange Bowl. That was one small step backward for Americans, one giant leap forward for American Airlines.

Of course, you may recall that I had flown over the United Center just a couple of weeks earlier and had seen the United Airlines logo covering the arena's vast roof and the bronze statue of Michael Jordan outside the arena. In the two weeks between my visit to Chicago and my arrival in Portland, Jordan had publicly demanded $36 million for his next two NBA seasons because, he said of his employers, "They've made a lot of money here, and it's time to give something back." Jordan's agent characterized the figure as laughably low and said it would take much more than 18 mill a year to sign his client. He would eventually get $35 million a year.

We are familiar with the rare athlete who accepts less than his market value to remain on the team with which he is identified. But in a postmodern variation on that concept, Jordan said he would take less money—as much as $10 million per season less—to play *elsewhere*, should the Bulls not accede to his take-it-or-leave-it demand, which started at one-tenth of the franchise's value. "On principle," Jordan explained.

But he was confused, if you asked me. It wasn't the principle that interested Jordan. It was the interest on the principle in his bank account. If that was what would put him in a Vancouver Grizzly uniform, there was nothing wrong with saying so. It was why the Browns left Cleveland. It was why the Fall Classic no longer happened every fall. It was why Brooklyn was now best known as a town in Michigan, where the best drivers raced on Memorial Day weekend.

They used to do that in Indy. Remember?

I steered north out of Portland, and the rain was relentless.

My plan was to drive into Washington, hang a right in Seattle, and turn east toward Minnesota, across the Great Plains. Seattle would be my last chance to catch a ballgame, so I bought a ticket to watch the Mariners at the Kingdome, a dreary concrete crypt enlivened this evening by a crowd of 44,236 eager to see the visiting Yankees. I settled into my second-deck seat with a hot dog, six inches of sausage entombed in a sarcophagus of bread.

In an unrelated bun-related problem, two former concessions-stand workers at the Kingdome told the Seattle *Times* that they had been instructed to pick flecks of mold off hot dog rolls before serving them (the rolls, not the mold flecks) to the public. The story was credible because the Kingdome's concessions stands had been cited 158 times in the previous three years by the Seattle-King County Department of Public Health for ominous-sounding "red critical" food-safety violations.

I sipped my soda pensively. (The *Times* had also reported that a stand worker at the Kingdome had seen a colleague use an ice shovel to scoop up garbage, then ice for sodas.) For dessert, I made an abortive effort to find one of those ice cream sundaes served in an inverted batting helmet. It occurred to me that fans could satisfy their twin passions for unsanitarily served junk food and baseball memorabilia if concessionaires would only start serving such sundaes in actual game-worn batting helmets.

And then the game began and all other concerns fell away. They fell away because on this night, on my final visit to a stadium in a year of attending contests, the best player in our national pastime had the finest game of his young career—against the most storied franchise in American sports, no less. Ken Griffey, Jr., hit home runs in the second, sixth, and eighth innings, each one off a different Yankee pitcher, each one into the right field bleachers. Griffey stood at the plate after the final dinger, his right arm following through on the swing as if he'd just thrown open a cape, and admired the feat for himself. Junior had also singled and walked to finish four for four with five runs scored and six RBIs. Applause now rained down on him like roses on an opera star.

The M's won, 10–4, and afterward Griffey, who had been in a slump, said of his extraordinary evening: "I can't explain it."

I knew what he meant. I had emerged from my own slump, the personal gloom that overcame me in Portland, and now couldn't quite explain this change in spirits myself. Except that hot dogs and baseball really are a powerful combination, an almost primordial pick-me-up.

"Sports are a primitive ritual of aggression and release—the id hangs out," *Psychology Today* editor Hara Estroff Marano once told *New York Times* food writer Molly O'Neill, whose brother Paul was playing right field for the Yankees tonight. "In such a situation, the primitive part of the brain, 'Me want hot dog,' overrides the restraints of the more rational part of the brain, which would say, 'Am I hungry?' or 'Would I like a hot dog?'"

Tell me that my id hangs out, and I'm likely to check my fly. I only know that food tastes better at the ballpark. It is an association "as strong as the movies and popcorn," according to sports sociologist Bob Brustad of the University of Northern Colorado. But in fact the sports-food bond is stronger. When an ad man tried to encapsulate America for his automaker client, he wrote, "Baseball, hot dogs, apple pie, and Chevrolet," front-loading the jingle with the two most surefire evocations of American culture.

And no, I had decided by now—"American culture" was not an oxymoron. "Of course there is American culture," said Allen Guttmann, a professor of American studies at Amherst. "It includes symphonies as well as jazz, literature as well as comic books." And at its apex are what Bob Dole has called "America's greatest diversions: sports and food."

By the time I left the stadium, the rain had lifted. Reluctant to let the trip end, I took one last lap around the Kingdome in my car—rounding the ballpark and heading for home.

23

If America were an American flag, then all of its stars would belong here, in the upper-left-hand corner of the country. The state of Washington would be a field of blue, and Spokane might aptly be described as "star-spangled": Star-Spangled Spokane.

Three stars of three different sports were raised in this town of 177,000 near the Idaho border. Utah Jazz guard John Stockton, Chicago Cub second baseman Ryne Sandberg, and NFL quarterback Mark Rypien grew up more or less together in Spokane, separated by just four years and five miles.

Sandberg's father, Derwent (Sandy) Sandberg, was a mortician at the Hazen and Jaeger Funeral Home on North Monroe. He used to drink—and watch his son play on WGN—over at Jack and Dan's Tavern, an Irish bar that is still owned by Jack Stockton, John's father. Jack lives 150 yards from the bar's back door in a white house with redbrick accents and a basketball hoop in the driveway. John spends his summers in the house next door. I know this because I had been to Spokane once before, ostensibly to write about its three most famous athletes, in 1992, their year of greatest triumph: Sandberg had just become baseball's highest-paid player, Stockton was playing on the first Olympic Dream Team, and Rypien was four months removed from having been named MVP of Super Bowl XXVI as a member of the Washington Redskins.

And yet as I drove through Spokane half a decade later, near the end of a sports odyssey on a cloudless evening, I thought not about the city's athletes, but about the fathers who raised those athletes. Jack Stockton bought his bar in 1961, the year before the birth of his son, when Bob Cousy was still at the peak of his powers at point guard for the Boston Celtics. Cousy was Jack's favorite player, and when John Stockton was a boy he would dribble all day on the driveway, come visit Dad at the tavern, and then the father would ride the son home on the handlebars of his bicycle. Jack found it preposterous beyond words that his physically unremarkable son had not only made it to the NBA, but had become the league's latter-day Cousy. "The only person in the *world* who thought John would make it to the NBA," Jack said one day at the bar, "was John. And that's the God's honest truth."

I had spoken to Sandberg's mother, Elizabeth, while a piano was being tuned in another room of her home. The discordant thrumming of the strings gave the conversation a mournful cast. When she was nine months pregnant in September of 1959, Mrs. Sandberg recalled, she and her husband could settle only on a name for a girl. But the couple was watching a New York Yankee game on TV one night, and when they heard the announcer roll out the name of the right-handed relief pitcher walking in from the bullpen, "We looked at each other and knew that that would be the name if the baby was a boy." And so the boy was named for Ryne Duren of the Yanks. And why not? Five years earlier, when the Sandbergs lived in Philadelphia, Ryne's big brother Del was named for Phillie slugger Del Ennis.

"My father loved baseball," Sandberg told me across the continent while sitting in a dugout at Shea Stadium in New York, speaking of the dad who died in 1987. "He was a fan of all sports. We never had a lot of money, but he always had enough to buy me a glove and spikes. My dad had a *lot* to do with this."

Finally, I attended a family barbecue at the boyhood home of Mark Rypien, who sat in the backyard telling stories about his father, Bob, an enormous man who proudly wore his potbelly like a prize-fighter's belt.

When Mark was in high school, his father enforced a weekend curfew of midnight. The boy was out late one night, losing track of time at his girlfriend's house, when Bob Rypien pulled the family sedan in front of the girl's picture window, freezing the couple on the couch in his headlights. It was exactly the kind of thing my father might have done if I had ever missed a curfew (or had a date) in high school. Bob Rypien began to sound increasingly familiar to me.

Mark shared a bedroom with his brother Tim, as I did with my brother Tom. Tim, like Tom, was always in by 11:59 on weekends; Mark was often late. "But you have to understand," Rypien said. "Tim would come in with bloodstains all over him, having been in fights with his buddies all night. But he was in by curfew, so no problem. Me, I wouldn't be doing a darn thing but be out till 12:30, and my dad was ready to kick my ass when I walked in the door. The seven worst words I ever heard were 'I'll see you in the morning.' Now I'm supposed to sleep well?"

Like the Rushins, the Rypiens were a Catholic family of five children who remained close as a twin-blade shave and expressed that bond by pummeling and/or insulting each other at every opportunity. I sat outside with the Rypiens for hours that evening, until the sky was drained of all light and the cooler was drained of all light beer.

Bob Rypien died of a heart attack in June of 1988, four months before Mark played his first game in the NFL. But on that night in the Rypien backyard, four months after his Super Bowl victory, Mark suggested that the old man was still around. "He *is* here," he said. "He's right there." He was leaning back in his lawn chair, looking out from under a maple tree in the backyard of his boyhood home, and pointing to a single star in the firmament.

That was the snapshot I still had of Spokane while driving on this cloudless night in western Washington, hurtling toward my own boyhood home. I stopped for gas at the Idaho border, got out of my car, looked to the sky, and thought: Star-Spangled Spokane, indeed.

It isn't true that you can blink and miss Idaho while driving across the state's panhandle, though I strongly recommend that you try. But you *are* very quickly in Montana, where there is no daytime speed limit except that which drivers deem "reasonable and prudent." On this day, Montanans thought 110 seemed about right, which may explain why I counted seventeen white crosses along one stretch of roadway, marking the sites of as many fatal accidents.

Montana was lawless, the bawdy Old West. Just before the border, a theater called the Melodrama offered—*nudge-nudge, wink-wink*—LIVE REVUES. Storefronts were filled with Western Union offices and come-ons from bail bondsmen, twin tokens of desperation that—knock on wood—I hadn't had to redeem thus far in my travels.

A highway sign advertised the ROCK CREEK TESTICLE FESTIVAL—HAVE A BALL! (Alas, it was not for another five months.) Up the road a piece was another civic-sponsored billboard: WELCOME TO DRUMMOND—WORLD FAMOUS BULLSHIPPERS! You don't see these crude punning signs outside most of the world's municipalities (ENTERING GENEVA—KISS OUR ALPS!), and I say that's too bad. The world would be a better place if it were a little more like Montana, for Montanans had the good sense not to take themselves seriously at all. After one 49er Super Bowl victory, an entire town changed its name for a year to Joe: Joe, Montana.

I had half a mind to go there now, to find an apartment where I might live out my days in exile: a grown man, hopelessly obsessed with sports, avoiding adulthood in Joe, Montana.

Instead, I stopped for the night in Bozeman. Only one state—South Dakota—stood between Montana and my dear sweet Minnesota, a fact that didn't hit me until I walked into a national chain bar in Bozeman. The joint was, to my astonishment, decorated entirely in Minnesota Vikings memorabilia, most of it from the 1970s, when the Purple People Eaters were losing a then-record four Super Bowls.

Minnesotans have lost four Super Polls, as well: Harold Stassen, Eugene McCarthy, Hubert Humphrey, and Walter Mondale all ran for President and failed to win, which is just as well, as Minnesotans cannot stand to call attention to themselves. To say that Minnesotans understate things would be to understate things. The Norwest Center in downtown Minneapolis was designed to be a few feet *shorter* than the city's tallest building, the IDS Center. The state has 12,034 lakes—so we rounded the number down to 10,000 for the inscription on our license plates. If Minnesotans had named the Great Lakes, they would be the Good Lakes and Duluth would be on Lake Inferior.

The Vikings did not merely reflect this statewide attitude of one-downsmanship; they created it, pummeling teams all season, every season, before politely rolling over in the Super Bowl. To win, when the whole world was watching, would be unseemly. And so God only knows why this team became my first and truest and most long-lasting obsession in sports—which is to say, in life—and God only knows how that stifles a child's self-esteem and sense of ambition.

But it stays with you. In this Bennigan's in Bozeman, I scanned the jersey numbers on the wall and instantly translated each into a name, in the way that a computer converts binary digits into text. And so there was 10 for Tarkenton, 44 for Foreman, the 81 of Eller . . . but not, sadly, the 88 of Alan Page.

This didn't surprise me. You couldn't buy a number 88 Vikings jersey in Minnesota in 1974. Your parents had to purchase a blank purple shirt and have the numbers ironed on. As far as I know, mine were the only ones who ever did. Before Larry Bird, I—alone among my schoolmates—worshipped Page, the fearsome defensive tackle with a reputation for brooding silence, a reputation that I didn't much care about as an eight-year-old. I cared only that he went to Notre Dame, that he was a genuinely great player (he was the NFL's first defensive player to win the MVP), and that his Afro sometimes resembled Mickey Mouse ears when he took off his helmet. I once watched a prone Page, pancaked by an offensive lineman, reach up and yank the ballcarrier to the ground with one hand, as if pulling the emergency stop cord on a subway train. He was strong and scary and silent, and having him as one's favorite player was a contrarian thing to do. So I did it.

And that is how all of this began.

In the second grade, a classmate of mine invited me to a Saturday night sleepover at the Airport Holiday Inn, which his father managed and where the Vikings—as every Minnesotan knew—bivouacked on the night before each home game. I could actually meet the players as they checked in and—if I asked politely and addressed them as "Mister"— even get their autographs, a prospect that frightened me beyond words. For two weeks leading up to the sleepover, I practiced my pitch over and over in front of the bathroom mirror: "Please, Mr. Page, may I have your autograph?"

I stole both the phrase and my abject delivery of it from the 1967 film version of *Oliver!*, in which the orphan asks, "Please, sir, may I have some more?" Oliver wanted a second helping of gruel from a cruel master and I wanted a signature from Alan Page, but the difference seemed negligible at best.

Saturday came. My mother, bless her, allowed me to leave the house in my 88 jersey, ragged with wear. It was literally in tatters, the kind of shirt worn by men in comic strips who have been marooned on a tiny desert island with one palm tree. The shirt's four iron-on 8's were peeling at the corners, and the letters on the back were hardly more adhesive: My name now read USHIN.

I took my place in the Holiday Inn lobby, a Bic pen in one hand, a spiral notebook in the other, whispering my mantra to myself: "Please, Mr. Page, may I have your autograph? Please, Mr. Page . . ." My friend's father, the innkeeper, cheerily reminded us to be polite and that the players would, in turn, oblige us.

"Except Page," he added offhandedly in the oblivious way of grown-ups. "Don't ask him. He doesn't sign autographs."

Which is how I came to be blinking back tears when the Vikings walked into the Holiday Inn, wearing Stetsons and suede pants and sideburns like shag-carpet samples. Their enormous shirt collars flapped like pterodactyl wings. They were truly terrifying men, none more so than Page, whose entrance—all alone, an overnight bag slung over his shoulder—cleaved a group of bellhops and autograph hounds.

The great man strode purposefully toward the stairwell and I froze as he breezed past, unable to speak, a small and insignificant speck. It was an early lesson in life's manifold disappointments—two weeks of anticipation dashed in as many seconds.

Still, I had never seen Page outside of TV and couldn't quite believe he was incarnate, so I continued to watch him as he paused at the stairs and looked back at the lobby, evidently having forgotten to pick up his room key. But he hadn't forgotten any such thing.

No, Page walked directly toward me, took the Bic from my trembling hand and signed his name, Alan Page, in one grand flourish. He smiled—I remember this vividly—and put his hand on the top of my head, as if palming a basketball. And then he disappeared up the stairs, leaving me to stand there, slack-jawed, forming a small puddle of admiration and urine.

And from that moment forward I was *in*, inextricably, a made member of the sports mob. Alan Page went on to become a judge. His "brooding," it turned out, was actually introspection, a quality too rare and ephemeral to have been appreciated in locker rooms and press boxes at the time. But, heaven knows, he was already showing judicial qualities in '74—steering one child, with the stroke of a pen, toward a productive life's work. Or a career in sportswriting, anyway.

Alan Page is now a justice on the Supreme Court of the State of Minnesota. Whereas I still wait for athletes in hotel lobbies and stadiums, hoping that they'll deign to speak to me. It is nice work if you can get it, and I could hardly do otherwise.

For obsession—"the state of being beset or actuated by the devil or an evil spirt"—is by definition an involuntary act. And, of course, an unhealthy one. An obsession with sports is particularly unhealthy, I have always thought. It is bad enough to avidly follow sports as an adult, but to do so literally—to *follow* sports, around the country and around the world—is especially unbecoming of a grown man, is it not? What kind of job is that—to obey the 1950s television singalong jingle and "follow the bouncing ball"?

But then it struck me. In a bar in Bozeman, Montana, drinking cold beer on a hot night near the end of a long journey, I had looked at a few framed football jerseys and was instantly awash in memories that were as surefire an evocation of my home and my childhood as any that I have. And I began to feel a small nobility about a life spent in sports.

Or as much nobility as a man can feel when he hasn't washed his clothes in six weeks, and his socks smell like blue cheese, and the last four human beings he has spoken to were disembodied voices manning drive-through windows. Perhaps it was time to go home.

I arose before dawn and left skid marks in the motel parking lot, embarking on the eighty-nine-mile drive to Yellowstone National Park. It was there that Dave Emrick of Pittsburgh and his three sons were headed when I encountered them at the Field of Dreams on the first full day of this trip, when Don Lansing said that the appeal of his farm "has a lot to do with fathers and sons."

I had driven more than twenty-two thousand miles since then. "A journey of a thousand miles must begin with a single step," wrote the ancient Chinese philospher Lao-tse, but it was another quote of his that came to mind as southern Montana went by in a blur.

The landscape was a vast emptiness and—cruise control activated, the highway straight as uncooked spaghetti—so was my mind. Everything that I owned was in the glove compartment or in the glorified glove compartment of a Minnesota self-storage facility. Clean socks and old friends and a mountain of mail lay beyond the next state, and my road-weary body was beginning to feel an exhilirating exhaustion, a sensation that might easily pass for peace.

"To be empty," wrote Lao-tse, "is to be full. To be worn out is to be renewed. To have little is to posess."

The odomoter rolled like Old Man River, and I let memories begin to metabolize of this journey now nearing completion. I thought of the guy who owned the natural bridge in Natural Bridge, Alabama: how wistfully he recalled a week with his son at "the Art Gaines Baseball Camp west of Hannibal, Missouri," seven days in 1968 that were the highlight of his existence.

I thought of Tim and Elbert Couch in Hyden, Kentucky. And the families in Cleveland whose Sundays were stolen when the Browns skipped town. And Vernon Presley, whose sports-crazy son gave him a gravestone in Graceland's backyard that was engraved with the words of a sportswriter: WHEN THE ONE GREAT SCORER COMES TO MARK AGAINST YOUR NAME . . .

To judge from my journey, a great many American families were bound together by sports. You might say they serve as a natural bridge: in Natural Bridge or Tupelo, in Jim Thorpe or Joe, Montana.

DO NOT MOLEST ANIMALS read a sign inside Yellowstone National Park, an idea that in all honesty had not occurred to me, even after all these solitary weeks on the road. Yellowstone was unlike anyplace I had ever seen, heard, or smelled before—with its loud belching (of geysers), its sloe-eyed bison (they jammed every roadway), and its unholy and inescapable pong (sulfur fumes, I would discover). On second thought, Yellowstone was a great deal like someplace I had seen, heard, and smelled before. It was an outdoor drive-through version of Ole's Big Game Lounge.

Sure, Yellowstone also had lakes with patent-leather surfaces that reflected scenes of impossible beauty—reflections that looked like picture postcards. Eagles keened. Canyons gaped. My God, they were big. A camper could call out his name at night and have the echo return as a wake-up call the next morning.

I had come to see Old Faithful. It is not as regular as it once was—who among us is?—and now takes anywhere from 45 to 105 minutes to go off, at which time it can spume 8,400 gallons of boiling water 180 feet into the air. But before that can happen, there are a series of sad preliminary ejaculations, each about 3 feet high, with all the force of a Water Pik. At each one of these, five tourists would independently arrive at the same joke: "Well, that was it, kids. We can go home now."

Those last five words were inexpressibly poignant. Old Faithful finally went off like a shaken champagne bottle, and I repaired for the night to the Holiday Inn in Cody, Wyoming. A chambermaid had left behind in my room a generic-looking, industrial-sized aerosol can labeled SMOKE-SCREEN ALL-PURPOSE ODOR COUNTERACTANT (PLEASANT FRAGRANCE, CHEMICALLY NETURALIZES THE SOURCE OF MALODORS, PROVIDES RESIDUAL ODOR CONTROL). It was made by the Zep Manufacturing Company of Atlanta, Georgia, and I shot a tentative mist of the wonder substance into the air: It smelled like every motel room I had occupied on this trip.

Michael Jordan has, famously, "released his own fragrance," something that athletes have been doing gleefully for years, usually in front of a lit match in a locker room. The difference is that MJ released a *designer* fragrance, an *eau de toilette*, and I thought: If I ever market my own signature cologne, it will smell exactly like Smoke-Screen, which smelled of stale towels and yesterday's cigar smoke and the lingering coffee-fuled halitosis of a million long-haul truckers who checked out an hour ago.

My designer fragrance will smell, in short, like the Holiday Inn in Cody, Wyoming. Only more so.

Teddy Roosevelt called the Wapiti Valley east of Yellowstone "the most scenic fifty miles in America," but they are also, surely, among some of the loneliest. Wyoming is the least populous of the continental United States, with 453,000 people in an area the size of the former West Germany, which had 60 *million*. According to my Mobil travel guide, cattle and sheep are five times more numerous than Wyomingites and also have better table manners, so there was really nothing for me to do in the state but to drive and drive and drive across it until I reached the South Dakota border at twilight.

"A big country demanded big art," read the National Park Service brochure distributed at Mount Rushmore, which is, for my money, the best of all American monuments. "Only New York's Statue of Liberty rivals it as a globally recognized symbol of American aspirations and ideals," agreed my British guidebook, but the Statue of Liberty was created by a Frenchman, while Rushmore was the brainchild of a quintessential American, the son of Danish immigrants. Gutzon Borglum invested fourteen years of his life and amassed $200,000 in debts to liberate the craniums of Lincoln, Washington, Jefferson, and Teddy Roosevelt from a shapeless wall of South Dakota granite.

When he saw the mountain, Borglum had a vision. He said, "Let us place there, carved high, as close to heaven as we can, the words of our leaders, their faces, to show posterity what manner of men they were, then breathe a prayer that these records will endure until the wind and the rain alone shall wear them away."

The sculptor died seven months before the monument's dedication, but no matter. Reading his words, one can't help but think of what a great and obsessive man Gutzon Borglum must have been. And how his name sounded exactly like a fart in a bathtub.

Standing breathless before Rushmore, gazing up at Lincoln's mole, itself the size of the Louisiana Superdome, I began to feel better about my own obsessive quest and my feeble attempt to leave a record of that obsession. This book is that record. I had set out to test the Shakespearean assertion that "If all the year were playing holidays, to sport would be as tedious as to work." In doing so, I drove 23,658 miles through all but four of the contiguous United States, skipping Florida (which was being ravaged by hurricanes) and West Virginia, Utah, and North Dakota (on the grounds that they were West Virginia, Utah, and North Dakota, respectively).

For the better part of a year, I had lived a life of epic irresponsibility. I neglected to pay bills, neglected to call friends, neglected to tell the office where I was going to be, in large measure because I seldom knew my destination more than ten minutes before arriving there. I drank too much, slept too little, and ate exclusively those things which cause swift painful deaths in laboratory mice. I watched a fat man in a minor-league ballpark in Colorado Springs spoon chopped onions and pickle relish onto his jumbo frank, then turn to me, a complete stranger, and say, "Vegetables." And scarier still, I shared his pride, for I too had come to view the stadium condiment bar as a veritable vegetable garden.

In short, all my year was a playing holiday. And I could now say, with absolute certainty, that Shakespeare should have been so lucky.

Tomorrow the calendar would turn to June. Beyond the next rise in the road lay Minnesota. I pulled over at the last truck stop in South Dakota and performed a small rite of thanksgiving on my reliable Japanese automobile. Standing in front of the vehicle, I opened a Penguin Classic copy of *The Pathfinder* and recited these words of the otherwise unreadable James Fenimore Cooper: "I thank you from the bottom of my heart, for the service. God will remember it, Pathfinder."

And then I pulled the Pathfinder into Minnesota and lost myself in the small comforts of home: license plates that matched my own, preset radio push buttons that suddenly corresponded to actual stations . . .

Everything in Minnesota was just as I had left it. Except, of course, for me.

It takes ten hours to drive straight through from Rapid City, South Dakota, to my boyhood home in Bloomington, Minnesota, a trip I had made once before, as a six-year-old, in the way-back seat of our wood-paneled wagon. Alas, the only wood paneling that remained in what I

now knew as my father's house was on the walls of the finished basement. Taped to those walls to this day were black-and-white photographs of toothless professional hockey players from the seventies that
my brothers and I had meticulously scissored from the pages of GOAL!
magazine.

It was well after 10 P.M. when I pulled into the driveway and
parked under the basketball hoop, but an amber light still spilled from
the picture window, and I could see my dad's seated silhouette through
the curtains. I had driven directly here on the pretense of picking up my
mail, which the old man had been dutifully collecting, but of course he
insisted that I stay awhile and tell him all about the trip. My brother Tom
arrived shortly. And in the amber glow of the lamplight, feeling the
amber glow of a Grain Belt beer, I told a tale of endless ballgames.

After a pause, my father said somewhat anxiously that the strangest
thing had happened in my absence. Every night of my journey he went
to bed hearing faint voices calling faraway baseball games. He knew how
irrational this sounded and wondered if he wasn't going mad, but insisted
that we go to his bedroom and listen for ourselves.

At first I heard nothing. And then, the barely audible—but unmistakable—sounds of a baseball game. My father was convinced that these
were West Coast radio broadcasts being conducted through his brass
bedpost. I swore that the sound was emanating from the base of the
lamp on his nightstand.

I had no idea if this was possible. I should tell you that neither of us
understands even the most rudimentary technology. Dad once bought a
cheap new telephone, programmed it, then proudly announced to the
family: "Look, instead of dialing 911, all you have to do is push Speed
Dial, then seven, then the asterisk button."

But as the two of us now stood there—my father with his head to
the bedpost, I with my ear to the lamp—we wondered if this wasn't
something larger, a yearlong cosmic connection between a sports-addled
father and his itinerant son.

My brother Tom now joined us in the bedroom, listened with me
to the lamp for a beat, then pressed his ear to the nightstand. Jerking

open the drawer, he pulled out an old battery-powered AM clock radio and said to both of us: "Look, Einsteins, it's the radio alarm. It's going off every night at"—Tom looked at the clock—"11:17."

My father sheepishly raised his head from the bedpost, and I lowered the lamp from my ear, and we sat there like two idiots who had just seen Oz from the other side of the curtain.

My brother and dad turned out the light and returned to the family room. But I stayed behind for a beat and listened to the radio, powerless to the tug of a faraway ballgame being broadcast from the coast. It is possible, I discovered, for a man to feel nostalgic for a trip he concluded only an hour ago.

Seated in the dark on the edge of the bed, I rummaged through my suitcase for the can of Smoke-Screen All-Purpose Odor Counteractant and sprayed a cloudburst of it into the air.

Then I closed my eyes and listened to the game and imagined I was still on the road. I felt perfectly at home.

12/98